BEAUTIFUL
LOSERS

BEAUTIFUL
LOSERS

EVE SEYMOUR

MIDNIGHT INK
WOODBURY, MINNESOTA
MIDNIGHT
INK

FIRST EDITION
First Printing, 2016

Book format by Teresa Pojar
Cover design by Ellen Lawson
Cover images by iStockphoto.com/14223459/©PLAINVIEW
iStockphoto.com/31592066/©VikaValter
Editing by Nicole Nugent

Midnight Ink, an imprint of Llewellyn Worldwide Ltd.

Library of Congress Cataloging-in-Publication Data
Names: Seymour, E. V. (Eve V.), author | Chase, Adam
Title: Beautiful losers : a Kim Slade novel / Eve Seymour.
Other titles: Kim Slade novel
Description: First edition. | Woodbury, Minnesota : Midnight Ink, 2016.
Identifiers: LCCN 2015044400 (print) | LCCN 2016000467 (ebook) | ISBN 9780738746432 | ISBN 9780738747248 ()
Subjects: LCSH: Clinical psychologists--Fiction. | Women psychologists--Fiction. | Male models--Fiction. | Stalkers--Fiction. | GSAFD: Mystery fiction. | Suspense fiction.
Classification: LCC PR6119.E973 B43 2016 (print) | LCC PR6119.E973 (ebook) |
DDC 823/.92--dc23
LC record available at http://lccn.loc.gov/2015044400

Midnight Ink
Llewellyn Worldwide Ltd.
2143 Wooddale Drive
Woodbury, MN 55125-2989
www.midnightinkbooks.com

Printed in the United States of America

To my husband, Ian Seymour,
for his unfailing support and love.

ACKNOWLEDGMENTS

This novel represents a big departure for me. It's the first time I've written with a female main protagonist in eight years and, although I've never been stalked in the criminal sense, I once had cause for concern when I discovered an admirer sleeping in my car outside my house! However, the true inspiration for the story came from a brief stroll through a shopping arcade in Birmingham, where I spotted a painting by Jack Vettriano entitled "Beautiful Losers." Dramatic, sexy, and captivating, the picture grabbed me, and I couldn't help but stare in wonder. It explains why it has a "walk-on" part in the novel.

As ever, big thanks to my agent, Broo Doherty at DHH Literary Agency, who believed in this novel right from the start, and to David Headley for his support. I'm indebted to Terri Bischoff, Nicole Nugent, and Beth Hanson at Midnight Ink for their enthusiasm for the story. Nicole has a sharp eye for editorial glitches and smoothed out my occasional very "English" vocabulary so that US readers would not be bewildered.

Thanks also to Jason Metivier at Triumph, Cheltenham, for his time, patience, and technical know-how on motorbikes. Any mistakes made are mine alone. It must also be said that I couldn't have written the story without reference to *I'll Be Watching You: True Stories of Stalkers and Their Victims* by Richard Gallagher.

Lastly, and importantly, in a society that prizes beauty, it's not easy to write about disfigurement. Indeed, I have been warned that "it isn't very sexy." Undeterred, I am indebted to Changing Faces, a UK based charity that gives support, encouragement, and information to people with disfigurement. Their website is well worth checking out and deserves support.

PROLOGUE

He knew in an instant that something was wrong. He could see it in their faces, the way they looked at him, with pity.

The surgeon, a short man with a bald shiny head who carried too much weight for his size, closed his eyes. The rest of the team watched both of them with haunted expressions, the sense of collective unease palpable.

Someone coughed. A combination of phrases spilled into the room, disjointed, so that he was given the impression of listening to a master of ceremonies with a faulty microphone. *Unfortunately… unable to correct… difficult… given the nature of the injuries.* He blocked them out, ignored the hushed tones and the traded gestures, focused instead on the pale-washed walls, the smell of surgical alcohol, the rotating blades of the fan.

Silence spread through the room like an uncontrollable forest fire.

They huddled together, wary, waiting for him to speak as if he were some oracle. He spoke, all right. He could barely control his anger.

"Things like this don't happen to people like me. Do you know who I am, for Chrissakes? Do you understand the fucking consequences?" His protest tumbled out in a jumbled heap, the slurred words falling from the gap where his mouth should have been. There was no pain. The morphine took care of that.

That's when he began to feel scared.

Perhaps it was the residue of the medication. Post-operative, he was still light-headed, his concentration and coordination impaired. He had a nauseous sensation in his stomach, a hangover from the anaesthetic. Yes, that was it. Once he'd recovered, things would be fine. He couldn't expect miracles at this early stage. He needed time. That was all. They were probably talking to the wrong guy, the bad news meant for some other poor bastard. He voiced as much.

"I'm sorry," the surgeon said, eyes open, his look direct. "There is no mistake."

A plain-looking woman dressed in a white coat that failed to conceal her pregnancy talked about physiotherapy. She had a voice like a cracked plate and kept touching her face with her hands. Her feet, clad in sensible flat shoes, shuffled. Dead giveaways.

He lost all sense of time. People came and went. Meals were brought and removed. Anxious conversations burbled around him. Drugs administered. He was constantly checked, as if on suicide watch.

Finally, he asked to be left alone, insisted upon it. They shambled out, worried about lawsuits, he suspected, as well they should be. Very slowly he got out of bed and tottered towards the only mirror in the room. He'd always loved mirrors, photographs, anything that reflected his powerful good looks. And now…

His heart felt packed with razors of ice. Spots, like tiny tropical fish, darted before his eyes. He wanted to throw up. Oh Christ, he thought, stunned by his reflection. Oh Jesus fucking Christ.

A tight surgical cap clung to his skull. Tubes poked out from behind each ear. He turned slightly to the right, the once-arresting features bloated in a way that was not simply post-operative. He was prepared for the bruising and swelling, but the skin on one side, where it was not discoloured, had the dead appearance of a waxwork. His left eye sloped and would not shut even though the lid drooped. The full lips had lost their shape and form and curved down in a permanent expression of disdain. A persistent ball of spittle hung like a cobweb in the corner of his mouth. He attempted a pose and failed, the message from his brain defeated by the catastrophic trauma to the facial nerve. And only months before he was at the top end of the face business in an industry dominated by colossal egos, fired by vanity and rewarded with obscene amounts of money.

His hands fled over his injured face but there was no sensation. It was of no consolation that only one side was afflicted. In fact it was worse, one half mocking the other. He tried to avert his gaze, but found himself riveted, compelled to look. In his misery he felt powerless to turn away from the monstrous, unforgiving reflection staring back at him. And always the permanent, sad reminder of how he used to be.

Someone once told him that the face was the centre of humanity, every emotion reflected there, in the eyes, the slant of the mouth, the density and colour and texture of the skin. All he saw was terror, a savage fear of being ugly in a society that prized beauty, a dread of being unloved and worthless in a world where youth, or the appearance of it, was king.

They'd told him his injuries could be corrected. They'd said his new look would kick-start his career. After all the allegations, all the bad publicity, it was his chance for a brand-new start. Like a fool, he'd believed them. He'd *trusted* them.

Fury and frustration built inside. He wanted to smash up the room, to shatter his reflection, to tear down the walls. He could do it. He still had a powerful body, beautiful even. But he no longer had a face to match. Tears flooded his eyes. His throat wrenched open with dry sobs. Too late he realised how he'd relied on the eyes of others to define himself. Now he was one of the ugly people, the type of guy who it didn't matter how kind he was, how good a friend, he would never be admired and adored. As the light in the room faded, casting his face into pale luminosity, the rage, which had reached boiling point, cooled, and was replaced by a cold, ruthless anger. It nestled in his gut, stole through his veins, and flooded his poor aching heart. Just as well, he thought, because with born-again certainty, he knew that nobody would love him now.

ONE

"I look hideous."

"In what way exactly?"

"Isn't it obvious?"

"No," I smiled.

The young woman in front of me sighed in exasperation. "Look at my nose, it's huge. Everyone stares at it. My skin's a disaster, pitted and uneven. My eyes, well"—she shrugged—"enough said."

I couldn't see much of my client's face. In spite of the July heat, a woollen hat obscured the brow. Dark glasses concealed her eyes. A hoodie, with the collar zipped up tight, hid most of the lower half of her features. Her GP's referral notes read *anxiety state/depression, abnormal concern with appearance/BDD,* or as it was known by its full name, body dysmorphic disorder, a condition defined as a morbid preoccupation with an imagined defect in appearance. My working day usually revolved around women with anorexia or bulimia nervosa, both disorders highlighted by the patient's disturbed attitude to body image, which was why, even though the young woman sitting opposite suffered from neither illness, she'd wound up at the Bayshill Clinic.

"Would you like to show me, Lisa?"

"You'll be shocked."

"How about you unzip your jacket?" I flicked a lock of blond hair behind my ear, wondering if she'd notice. She didn't.

My client nodded reluctantly. "See," she said, defiantly sticking out her jaw. "I'm grotesque."

I could only see a thick layer of make-up and nothing out of the ordinary about the texture of the skin beneath, apart from it looking a little reddened, either from repeated attempts to cleanse it or because of contact irritation with wool. If hypercritical, I'd say that Lisa's nose was slightly large in comparison to her mouth, but it was an extremely minor flaw by anyone's standards.

"Take your shades off for me?"

Lisa muttered a protest but, persuaded by another warm glance from me, did as she was asked.

Nice eyes, I thought. They were brown and almond-shaped, not dissimilar to my own and I'd always thought my eyes were my best feature.

"Thank you." I smiled encouragement, eager not to trivialise the young woman's beliefs. "How much would you say you think about your appearance?"

"Every nanosecond of the day."

"Do you find you're constantly checking mirrors?"

"Any reflection, really."

I made a note. "How long would you say it takes to put your make-up on? From beginning to end, washing, cleansing, moisturising, right to the last flick of lip-gloss."

"A couple of hours, excluding the time I spend on facial exercises."

"And taking it off?"

"An hour, maybe more."

"So your appearance dominates your life. Would that be a fair description?"

The brown eyes glanced away. "I have no choice."

"Have you always felt like this?"

"Forever."

"Even when you were little?"

"Can't remember feeling differently."

I asked Lisa about her family.

"I've got a younger sister—the good-looking one, according to my parents."

"Do they say that?" I pitched forward a little. I didn't want Lisa to think that I was challenging her account. Nonetheless, she stiffened.

"I just know."

I let it lie and made another note. "Has the way you feel about yourself interfered with other aspects of your life?"

"I can't go out, if that's what you mean."

"So what do you do on your own?"

Guilt stole over her features. She averted her gaze.

"Do you look in the mirror?" I asked tentatively.

"Uh-huh."

"Do you think the mirror lies?"

Lisa looked up and stared at me with hard eyes. "Never."

"You sound very certain."

"It's the truth."

"What else do you do?"

"Take photographs of myself."

I elevated an eyebrow.

"Fuck's sake, isn't it obvious? To work out how I can make myself look perfect."

"Of course," I said, as if I'd only just cottoned on to what she was really saying. "This obviously causes you a great deal of distress."

Lisa's face darkened. "Sometimes I think I'd be better off dead."

"Ever attempted suicide?" I deliberately kept my expression and voice neutral.

The young woman shook her head.

"You never think about it?" I persisted quietly. Outside, I was the professional. Inside, I was treading on finely spun glass.

"Only in an imaginary way. Not for real, I guess."

Another note.

"If you had one wish, what would it be?"

Lisa's face lit up with a broad smile. "Easy."

"Easy?" I beamed back. "Go on, tell me."

"I'd have surgery."

Against every instinct, I maintained the smiley, upbeat manner. "It's a bit radical, isn't it? You're only nineteen."

"Be worth it."

"But it would still be the same you inside the skin."

Lisa blinked. Her eyes lost their lustre and became strangely vacant.

"All right," I said gamely. "Tell me how surgery would make your life better."

She lit right back up. "People wouldn't stare at me any more. They'd like me. I could go back to university, finish my course, get a decent job. I could have friends, a proper relationship."

"Do you reckon that people don't like you based on the way you look?" Without warning, something chimed deep down within me. I cut off the sound before it had a chance to reverberate.

"Get real. It's obvious, isn't it? If you look pretty, people think you're good. If you're ugly, like me, they think you're bad."

"And what do you think?" I inclined my head, allowing the young woman a full view of the left side of my face.

Lisa leant forward then back, the gesture so minute only a sharp-eyed observer would notice. "That's different."

"Is it? Tell me why."

A knock on the door saved Lisa from explanation. Jane, the clinic receptionist, glided in with a mug of coffee and a brown paper parcel. "Apologies for the interruption, Kim. It came by courier for you this morning. Express delivery." She placed the package on my desk. "Thought it might be important."

I squinted at the label, *To Kim Slade*, and pushed the parcel aside. "I wasn't expecting anything." Jane gave a mild shrug and left, quietly closing the door behind her. I sneaked a sip of coffee and returned to my client. "I think what we need to work on, if you're in agreement, is a way of disassociating values of good and bad from what you look like. We need to focus more on you, on who Lisa really is."

"Me?" She looked appalled.

"What are your likes, dislikes, ambitions? What drives you, what turns you on? I want you to focus on all the characteristics of your personality that have nothing to do with how you look, and everything to do with what makes you tick. Think about your favourite colours, food, films and books, music, places you like to visit. Can you do that for me?"

"I can try." She looked dubious.

I spent a couple of minutes outlining my proposals for next time and agreeing the number and frequency of future sessions. Firmly zipping up her hoodie, Lisa reached for her sunglasses with obvious relief and fled.

I put my notes aside, grabbed my bag, and was almost out of the door when I remembered the parcel. Padded, a label in the left-hand corner stating *Fragile*, it sat squat and faintly accusing. Tough, it could wait. But, then again, it might be …

The thought scarpered. It would only take minutes to open, no harm in it. No harm at all. Nothing to worry about, I told myself.

Taking a pair of scissors, I snipped away the tape to discover a thick layer of bubble-wrap. Carefully unravelling the protective covering, I removed the object and stared at it, my own reflection gazing back in puzzlement and, yes, fear.

Oval, set into an attractive stained-glass surround, the mirror reminded me of something similar I'd seen in one of the chi-chi shops in Salcombe, Devon. I checked the wrapping for a note of explanation, or a clue about its source, but there was nothing. Sitting back down heavily, the leather of the chair let out a squeal of protest.

Heat fled across my cheeks. My mouth felt full of mud. A stuttering in my chest told me that my heart rate had suddenly increased. Sweat broke out above my upper lip and underneath my arms. Why a mirror? I tried to hang on to my rational self, the one I used for clients, the one I used for self-preservation.

Irresistibly drawn to the glass, I studied my appearance: dark eyes, full mouth, the way my straw-blond hair fell in layers down to the jawline, the better to conceal the pink puckered skin on the left side of my face. Apart from a couple of memorably humiliating incidents, I didn't generally find my disfigurement a stumbling block.

Okay, so I never got *the look* treatment from passing handsome strangers, which was fine by me but, generally speaking, once I got to know people, men seemed fascinated while women viewed me as less of a threat. I let out a sigh. Who was I kidding?

It was a weird irony that, in spite of the fact that most of my clients were young women, the female of the species had always felt like tricky terrain for me. Sure I had girlfriends, two of whom I counted as pretty close, but somehow I'd always had to make more effort in my every day dealings with the "weaker" sex. Let's say friendship didn't come naturally to me. I had to work hard at it. It wasn't rocket science. Boring textbook stuff, really. As in many things in life, it came down to my unusual upbringing.

"Fuck it," I cursed out loud, slinging open a drawer in my desk, shoving the mirror inside, slamming it shut.

I tore out of the consulting room. Thank God I was meeting Georgia for lunch.

TWO

Georgia's reaction startled me.

"You should take it seriously, in case."

"In case of what?"

"It turns nasty." Georgia crossed her arms underneath her large breasts. She had a no-nonsense look, which I imagined wasn't the one she used in the consulting room.

"Are you serious?"

"For God's sake, Kim, we're in a dodgy business."

"That's a bit overdramatic, isn't it?"

"We rummage through the emotional rubble of people's lives and sometimes those people are frankly..."

"Mad? Is that what you were going to say?" I flashed a mischievous grin.

"I was going to say disturbed."

"Thank God for that."

"Actually, I was going to say mad as a box of frogs," Georgia blustered. "Sorry."

I let out a laugh. Deep down, I hoped it would ease the tension. No chance. I glanced around the bustling bar. A wave of pain rolled across my shoulders.

"Seriously," Georgia said, "you know the dangers."

"We trade in secrets and taboos—both come with a price tag."

"And remember the price tag can be damned expensive."

"You mean transference?" When a client becomes fixated on the therapist was what Georgia meant.

"It happens more often than you think."

"But I'm no longer working in the kind of areas that invite that particular problem. My present clientele consist of terrified young women under the age of twenty-five whose only goal in life is to resist it. They're too self-consumed to pose a threat to me or anyone else, for that matter."

Georgia picked at her salad. "Christ, I hate lettuce," she said morosely. "How come you manage to stay so slim?"

"Genes and nervous energy. At this rate I'll soon be the diameter of a pencil."

Georgia raised a smile and munched thoughtfully. "Do you think it's linked to the mysterious chocolates?"

"Oh those. I'd forgotten."

"You're a terrible liar," Georgia said, her look arch.

I absently ran a finger down the scar tissue on the side of my face and thought about the accompanying message. Made up from assorted pieces of newsprint, the crazy arrangement of letters had set my teeth on edge. It simply said: BEAUTY QUEEN.

"I like chocolates, as you well know." Georgia patted her ample tummy. "But if someone sent me a huge box with an anonymous note attached, it would frigging freak me out." She forked in another mouthful of lettuce. "You kept the note as evidence?"

"I shredded it."

The fork hovered in midair. "You did what?"

"I know. I'm an idiot. Honestly, Georgia, I thought it was a one-off."

Georgia was having none of it. "This speaks of progression, a pattern. First the chocs and now the mirror."

I averted my eyes and took another bite of sandwich in a bid to lighten the atmosphere and distract Georgia, who was homing in on me like a radar device.

"Anything else you'd care to share, Kim?"

"Not especially." I reached for my glass of water, flashed a smile, and asked Georgia about her forthcoming holiday in Italy.

"Is this the technique you usually adopt with clients?"

"I usually use thumbscrews." I grinned. "Stop evading the question."

"Pot, kettle, and black."

"Okay, Miss Marple," I said, with a huge sigh. "For three clear months after Chocciegate, nothing happened. Any unsettling feelings evaporated until ..." I stalled. Stuff like this didn't happen to people like me. I couldn't get my head around it. For fuck's sake, who would want to pay *me* this level of attention? Georgia didn't say a word, didn't fill in the gap, just looked, rapt, all eyes.

I cleared my throat. "Then three weeks ago, there were a number of silent phone calls to the flat."

"Jesus. You never said a word."

"Well ..."

"What did you do?"

"Switched on the answering machine." And poured myself a drink, I remembered.

"Really?"

"Really."

"Did you check the number?"

"Withheld."

"You haven't reported it to the phone company as a nuisance call?"

"I tried. It didn't get me very far." Georgia looked as if she couldn't trust what she was hearing. "I hope you don't stare at your clients like that," I said.

"This is you and me," Georgia flashed back. "I don't normally conduct one-on-ones in a bar." She took a thoughtful bite of chicken. "Are you usually this cool under pressure?"

I forced a smile. This wasn't pressure. Pressure is waking up in the morning and finding the ground from underneath you rent open. Pressure is being trapped in a home life of testosterone, competitiveness, raised voices, and barked commands. Pressure is being teased at school because you're the only kid in the class whose mother doesn't exist. Pressure is being talked about because your face looks funny. This, on the other hand and make no mistake, was abuse of power, a form of control that was potentially criminal. Chest-deep in the past, I almost missed Georgia's next question.

"Does Chris know?"

"Sure."

"And?"

"Obviously he was worried by the calls."

"Worried?"

I let out a giddy laugh. "Will you stop repeating everything I say?"

"Is it any wonder?" Georgia said, not a bit apologetic. "I suppose you blinded him with science."

"If you mean did I tell him that all forms of behaviour, however aberrant, contain a subtext beneath, yeah, I did." I'd blithered on about the ways in which people indulge in inappropriate behaviour to disguise fear and hurt, some more extreme than others. I'd assured him that it was my profound belief that even the nastiest exterior cloaked a good person. What I didn't tell Chris was that making silent phone calls was sometimes the precursor to something far more serious.

"And the caller didn't utter a word?" Georgia pressed.

I shook my head. No threats. No demands. I should have felt relief. I'd felt nothing of the sort. Even then, I knew that it was personal. I dreaded to think what Chris would make of the mirror.

"Want my professional opinion?" Georgia said.

"Nope." I grinned. "But I expect I'm going to get it."

Georgia pushed away her plate, leant slightly forward like a judge summing up a case for the jury. "Slotting the mirror into a clinical context, anorexics and bulimics are as much governed by mirrors as they are scales. When an emaciated anorexic regards herself, she only sees a distorted, overweight version."

"While BDD sufferers stare with the firm hope that their appearance will somehow be acceptable to them, a hope that's always dashed," I chipped in.

"Right," Georgia agreed. "Ergo: the mirror is significant. I reckon it's one of your clients."

I shook my head.

"No?" Georgia had a shrewd gleam in her eye.

"Making silent phone calls isn't a female pursuit. Women are too verbal, too language-orientated."

"There are exceptions," Georgia said. "Whether it's a man or woman, what's the motivation? Is she making a statement about her appearance? Maybe this person is reaching out and saying that she too has been scarred in some way, that she—" Georgia broke off, embarrassed, and splayed the fingers of her right hand as if they would do the talking for her.

"Is like me," I finished off the sentence. Scarred on the outside. Scarred on the inside.

"Sorry," Georgia said, flashing an apologetic smile. "But do you see what I'm driving at?"

Frankly, I'd thought of nothing else. "So this is someone's desperate plea for help?"

"Maybe, but that doesn't mean that she isn't dangerous."

I didn't speak. For all the outward show, an unexpected spurt of anger banged between my ears. How dare this person upset my life. "There is another more obvious motive."

"What's that?"

"He wants to frighten me."

"Why?"

I shrugged. "I can't think of anyone I've pissed off. Confrontation isn't really my thing." Passive aggression, Chris had flung at me once, which I thought was mighty unfair because that was more his line.

"So you've absolutely no idea who it might be?"

"No."

I'd spent oceans of time trying to figure out the personality, attempting to identify an obsessive theme or signs of psychoses, but there was so little to go on and no real indicators. "There's no face on which to focus, no clue to identity, no idea what this individual might be capable of, from which direction he'll come, whether he'll lose interest or step it up."

"He? You're really set on it being a male?"

"Oh yeah, this is a guy, all right." Everything about the situation told me a man was involved. "You know what? I guess, on a professional level, I should be intrigued."

"I hope you're not," Georgia said with disapproval. "This isn't taking place in the safe and cosy confines of the consulting room. He's out there, in your life, in your face. If you admit interest, you'll be entering into the perpetrator's game."

"Maybe that's the object of the exercise."

"Go to the police, Kim."

"With what? It's not as though I've been followed or anything like that."

"Would you know if you had?"

"Of course," I insisted.

"I'm not so certain." Georgia glanced at her watch. "Bugger! I've got to go." She gathered up her belongings and gave me a hug. "Just make sure you keep a note of the calls and detail anything else that happens. Then, for God's sake, Kim, go to the cops."

THREE

I STEPPED OUT INTO the sunshine, tilted my head to a sky the colour of French navy, and told myself that I felt better. Whatever was happening to me was only upsetting if I allowed it. Tonight, I'd drive to Devon; I'd see Chris and all would be well in my little world.

I set off down Montpellier Walk, bars on one side, gardens with bandstand on the other, music from a brass band in full spate competing with the low growls of Ferraris and Aston Martins. The leafy promenade stretched out before me like a wide street in a continental city. Cheltenham at its finest: smiley, glossy, and wealthy.

Cutting across the road at the lights, my mobile rang. A brief glance at the number told me it was Alexa.

"Hi, Alexa," I said, breezy and cheerful.

"Kim, have you got a moment?"

I glanced at my watch and frowned. "I'm heading back to work."

Alexa let out a noise, midway between a groan and a howl.

"What's up, honey?" I headed off past the Town Hall and into Oriel Road where it joined the trendy Bath Road and "Notting Hill" of Cheltenham.

"Brooks wants a divorce."

"Oh God, I'm sorry." Alexa, an old school friend with whom I'd lost touch for the best part of a couple of decades, had tracked me down three years ago. Her marriage seemed fine when we first hooked up. Recently, it had taken a nosedive.

"I thought we'd be able to work it out, but he's adamant," she said, audibly gulping back tears. "He's even gone to a solicitor."

"So he's absolutely serious?"

Alexa's response was a strangled cry.

I waited several beats. "You'd probably be wise to do the same."

"Get a solicitor? But I can't," Alexa wailed.

I kept on walking. Ellerslie Lodge, my destination, rose into view.

"When did all this blow up?" I said.

"Last night." Another torrent of tears broke over the airwaves. I genuinely felt sorry for her.

"You're still in shock, you poor thing. Look, I have to go now, but can I call you tonight when I get back to Devon? We can have a proper talk then."

"Okay," she said, her voice thick with crying.

"Are you at work?" I said as an afterthought.

"Couldn't face it."

"Go and make yourself a cuppa and have a lie down."

"Thanks, Kim. I really appreciate it. Sorry to hold you up."

"You haven't," I said. "It's fine. Speak to you later."

Ellerslie Lodge, a pioneering fifteen-bedded residential home, housed thirteen- to eighteen-year-old anorexic girls. Either they'd recently come out of hospital or were trying the Lodge as a last ditch attempt before it was deemed necessary to remove them to a more clinical setting.

Splitting my time between Bayshill Clinic and Ellerslie, an eight-minute walk away, allowed me a degree of professional latitude. At Bayshill, a white stucco double-fronted house that could easily pass for an insurance firm or design outfit, the atmosphere was serene and calm. Ellerslie was generally messier, the clients higher maintenance, the vibe highly strung. I actually preferred the latter because I believed that I could initiate more change. On a purely practical level, it offered a pragmatic solution to the perennial Cheltenham parking problem. Unlike Bayshill, the Lodge had extensive parking facilities and I parked my silver Celica there every Monday morning and picked it up every Friday after work.

Cathy Whitcombe, the senior nursing sister, greeted my arrival with a friendly smile.

Her kind face and easy-going manner often falsely lulled people into thinking that she was a pushover. "All quiet on the Western front. Ellen's settling in well."

"The girl from Stroud?"

"She seems to have chummed up with Kirsten."

"Brave," I said with a laugh. Argumentative by nature, Kirsten was one of my more challenging clients. "So who am I seeing this afternoon, Cath?"

"Ellen, Carla, and Lauren. Before you do, could you pop into Jim's office? He's got a proposition for you." Cathy wore a wide smile.

"What sort of proposition?"

"More celebrity work."

I groaned inside. I'd already taken part in a television discussion for the BBC in which I'd talked about the work carried out at Ellerslie Lodge. The episode had been the most knicker-wetting experience of my life, and that was saying something. The unscheduled mention of my facial disfigurement by the presenter had felt like random violence. I didn't relish the idea of another stint in front of the camera.

"Is he in his office?"

"Knee-deep in referrals."

"Will I be able to cross the threshold?" Jim's office bore all the hallmarks of a student squat.

"No comment," Cathy laughed.

I crossed a large, comfortably furnished hall that smelt of polish and coffee. A deep-seated sofa ran the length of a wall hung with watercolours of beach scenes. Magazines lay in a lazy heap on a coffee table, and a spectacular arrangement of flowers sat on a pillar near the wide, sweeping staircase, the effect undeniably welcoming.

Jim Copplestone, the resident psychiatrist, looked up from a pile of medical literature. My boss, he oversaw my cases from a medical perspective and took care of the few clients who displayed more complicated and serious disorders requiring drug intervention. Whereas my primary degree was psychology, his was medicine. With his long dark hair, streaked with grey, he had the louche exterior of an out-of-work musician, one of the reasons, I suspected, for his popularity with the girls.

"Just the woman," he beamed.

"I gather you want to twist my arm," I said, returning the smile.

"A finger perhaps, nothing more. It's a phone-in programme, BBC Radio Gloucestershire. They're after a general discussion to highlight the problem of eating disorders. Apparently it's come back into vogue."

I pulled a face.

"Mine is not to reason why," he said, "but anorexia just got sexy again."

"Terrific. I'll make a note to tell my clients."

"Now, now," he chuckled. "Think of it this way, it provides a wonderful opportunity for you to talk about the Lodge."

"How come you're not doing it?"

"They prefer a woman."

"*They* being the same people who think anorexia is sexy?"

"The audience we're trying to reach, darling."

"Cool. I'm fine with that." I recognised when I was snookered. In spite of the rise in the number of boys with the disease, young women were most vulnerable. And young women preferred talking to women. It wasn't scientific; the possible long-term health complications, like infertility and osteoporosis, were particularly gender-specific.

"Good," he said conclusively.

"Not so fast. What's in it for me?" I threw him a playful smile.

He slowly reached up and put his hands behind his head. "You drive a hard bargain, Slade. What would you like?" Leaning back expansively in his chair, the curve of his lips suggested that he was open to offers. You old flirt, I thought. Jim's company and office banter made me feel briefly normal again.

"A couple of bottles of decent wine?"

He flashed me an expression of mock disappointment. At least I thought it was. "You're a terrible woman."

"I know, and none of that cheap two-for-a-tenner muck," I said, determined not to give ground. "When am I expected?"

"Monday, at noon. I've got the name of a contact here, somewhere." Jim plunged his hand helplessly into an overflowing in-tray.

"You'll be there all day. Catch me later." Anxious not to be late for my first appointment, I winked and left him to it.

FOUR

No wonder the girl had gone off the rails.

I closed the door on the last of my clients. For weeks I'd been working with a girl called Lauren: see-through skin, sunken body, fear personified. After careful probing, one event stood out as a major contributory factor to the girl's descent into illness: her mother had abandoned her. And I knew only too well her sense of betrayal.

I updated notes on my laptop, picked up my bag, and walked across the hallway to Jim Copplestone's office. The door was closed, an envelope taped to it with my name scrawled across. I peeled it off, shoving it into my briefcase, and stepped outside. It had gone half past four and most of the girls were in the dining room having tea before they got on with homework before dinner.

The air throbbed with compressed heat, the flickering sun above my head sucking the moisture from anything that moved. Eager to sit in the climate-controlled interior of my car, my feet crunched across the gravelled drive with a quick step, my eyes squinting at the shining streak of metallic silver.

Then my gaze zoomed in on the windscreen of the Celica.

Halted in my tracks, I narrowed and refocused my vision, unsure what to think or do. Nervously, I glanced over my shoulder, briefly comforted by the Lodge's solid Regency architecture. Should I go and grab hold of Jim? Indecision engulfed me. Sweat prickled my palms. My chest tightened as if there was not enough room inside for my racing heart. Although I tried to hang on to my intellect, calm deserted me. I instinctively knew that what I was looking at was part of a warped pattern of behaviour. And if I did go back for Jim, I would have to tell him about the other things. It would blow it into the open. It would be like admitting defeat. It would announce I had a serious problem.

I advanced slowly, eyes scanning the surrounding streets, watching for sharp and sudden movement, anything or anyone that didn't fit, but all I saw were office workers and passersby. Listening for an unexpected noise, the scuffle of footsteps, the only sound was the steady drone of traffic, a chorus of car horns and breaking glass, and the screech of seagulls.

Reaching into my bag, I scrambled about and gathered together a wad of tissue. My jaw set, I leant across the windscreen, recoiling at the glassy eyes, the blood seeping between its open jaws, the tail curled and entangled in the windscreen wiper like a serpent waiting to strike. As I placed my hand over the dead rat, it felt alarmingly warm, soft and fresh to touch.

"Shit," I cursed, repelled as I attempted to get enough purchase to pick it up. Finally, I gripped hold and flung it into a nearby hedge.

"Didn't know you were a litter lout."

I wheeled round. "Christ, Jim, you shouldn't creep up on people. You nearly gave me a heart attack."

"Sorry, I came to check you got my message. What on earth were you doing?"

Cold slithered up my spine in spite of the soaring heat.

"Kim, are you all right? You've gone quite pale."

"It's nothing."

Jim crooked his head. "Problem?"

"Nah." I cracked a smile. "Some idiot mucking about."

He looked at me quizzically. I couldn't fathom out either what he was thinking or what I should say. "I'll see you next week," I finally blurted out, escaping into my car, the clean and welcome smell of leather enveloping me.

Starting the engine, I yanked the seat belt across and looked dead ahead. A tap on the window made my insides twist. I turned, looked up to see Jim madly gesticulating. I pressed a switch in the central console; the glass slid down. He stooped so that his face was level with mine, his breath hot on my skin. "Give my love to Devon and have a good weekend."

I did my absolute best not to react. He'd stopped me simply to say that? "Yeah." I smiled. "You, too."

As I drove out onto the main road I was forced to face one inescapable fact. Someone knew which car I drove.

Someone had targeted me.

FIVE

Packed with screaming kids newly escaped for the holidays, cars littered the motorway. For the first hour my eyes flickered to the rearview mirror. As a precaution, I frequently changed lanes and tried to apply reason to something I felt entirely unreasonable about. All I'd had were a couple of gifts and a few silent phone calls, I doggedly reminded myself as I pulled out into the outside lane. The rat was simply one of those things that happened in urban environments. Could have been one of the girls at the Lodge. Could have been guys out for a night of booze and cheap jokes. Could have been *him*. I clamped down on my jaw, outraged.

Around Bristol, there was the usual inevitable stretch of roadworks. Once past the bottleneck of traffic, the tension began to ease and I slipped an old Red Hot Chili Peppers album into the CD player, smacked my foot on the gas, and felt the gravitational pull that only a fast car can produce. My thoughts eventually turned to Chris, his mane of dark hair, his piercing blue eyes, the way he could floor me with a smile. Originally my lodger, ours was only supposed to be a temporary arrangement. It was no use getting suckered in by his electric blue eyes, his mysterious manner, and the lure of a man of deep complexities.

But I had.

He knew more about me than any other human being. With him, I felt warm, relaxed, and loved. He knew about my late father, about my eldest brother, Luke, who lived in the States. About Guy, my other brother killed in a freak motorbike accident years before. Chris understood that the job in Cheltenham was my way of escaping beaches enshrined in too much history, that my new life upcountry was an escape from my past and my ghosts. In essence, he got me.

And I got him.

I laughed silently inside. Intending to rent my family cottage to Chris and relocate to Cheltenham, to break with Devon and move on, I'd wound up with a foot in two camps. That was almost four years ago.

Traffic clogged the narrow lanes. The sun lay low in a blood-shot sky. I was on the home stretch, intimately familiar territory and, more than ever, I felt relief that I still had a hideaway. The person dogging my footsteps might be able to exert influence in Cheltenham, but not here.

Cormorants Reach overlooked the creek at Goodshelter. My father's last home, it was where we Slades gathered for family get-togethers and, more recently, for funerals. I knew every stone, lintel, cob wall, exposed beam, and dark recess. I knew its secrets. Without warning, the fabric of the building rattled with ancient arguments, slamming doors, bunched fists, and my tears. Startled by the memories, I banished them to the outer reaches of my consciousness.

At the sound of my arrival, the front door was already open, Chris's tall frame captured in a swathe of golden evening sun. Displaying a deep umber tan, he was wearing a brilliant white open-necked shirt tucked into faded denims. His feet were bare. The sight of him made my stomach jitter. I felt hopelessly happy, and the anger and fear that had assailed me disappeared. Seconds later I was enveloped, his lips on mine, his arms holding me with what felt like relief and the thought that he couldn't believe his good fortune in finding me.

"Better unpack the car," I said, drawing away a little.

"Leave it." He hooked me with his eyes and instantly I understood what he wanted, what he needed, what we both craved.

He took my hand and led me up the narrow flight of stairs to the main bedroom. There, he slowly undid the buttons of my shirt, taking his time as though he'd meticulously planned the moment in detail, slipping it off and throwing it across the end of the bed. I hauled his T-shirt up, pulling it off over his shoulders and outstretched arms. Chris's body was sleek and toned, a thin scar on his side the only flaw. Deep in my groin, I flickered with wanton desire, as though we were about to make love for the first time. He kissed the top of my high breasts, my mouth, the base of my throat, tracing the ragged line of scarred skin from the outer edge of my left cheekbone to the hollow of my collarbone.

"You're beautiful," he whispered, releasing the clasp on my bra. And I knew that he meant it, that in his eyes I really was.

I undid the buckle on his belt. He eased out of his jeans and kicked them off along with his boxers while I hastily undressed. Then he scooped me off my feet and carried me to our bed.

He kept his eyes open. He always did. I'd once wondered if it displayed a lack of trust, something with which I was familiar, or was connected to men's endless visual capacity for sexual pleasure. His warm hands slid slowly over me, reacquainting with my body, as if he wanted to explore every inch. I felt dizzy and shameless. We tasted and touched each other, and I told him explicitly what I wanted and what I wanted to do to him. At some stage he let out a low dry laugh, and pulled me on top of him.

Soon I was burning with heat. His hands were on my breasts, his eyes locked onto mine, the expression indecipherable. In that fleeting moment of time, I realised that however long we stayed together I would never truly know him. I sensed that his feeling for me was based more on biological need, on sex and desire, than love. Perhaps this was the way it was meant to be. Perhaps. The thought that you can't be truly intimate with someone you don't really know entered and, as quickly, exited my fevered mind. Too soon I saw his expression change.

Yet still he watched.

Afterwards we lay in bed and ate Thai chicken and basmati rice with torn-off chunks of naan bread. Licking my fingers greedily, I asked what sort of a week he'd had.

"Fairly bloody." He took a gulp from a can of chilled lager. "Usual story: a small hard-core of fourteen-year-olds making life difficult for the rest. In today's enlightened age, there isn't much I can do about it other than dishing out detentions. It's deeply unsatisfying and doesn't really get to the root of the problem."

"Which is?"

"They don't give a fuck. School's an irrelevance."

I whistled between my teeth. My own school days were detestable. I rarely spoke about them because, by comparison to Chris's childhood, I'd led a charmed life.

"Trouble is, I kind of get it," he said.

"That was different," I reminded him. "You were trapped in the care home system. No wonder you were an angry kid."

"Angry and criminal."

"Criminal?" I said, arching an eyebrow. In almost four years, Chris had never told me this before. In fact, he'd revealed little other than the odd highlight.

He flashed a grin. "Don't worry. I wasn't an axe-murderer or anything. A bit of stealing, that's all."

"How much is *a bit*?"

"Food, booze, cigarettes."

"You don't smoke," I said, amazed.

"Everybody smokes at fourteen years of age."

"I didn't."

"That's because you were holed up in a convent."

I let out a giggle. "It wasn't a convent, Chris."

"Might as well have been, from what you've told me."

A bleak vision of metal beds, green walls, and linoleum-covered floors, cold and clammy underfoot, swam before my eyes. I thought back to forced walks in pairs—*in crocodile*, as it was termed—on sheep-shit laden hills, twice-daily assemblies, supervised reading on Sundays, the slow and deadly crushing of identity. Most searing of all, I remembered the feeling of abandonment by those I loved. I jettisoned the thought.

"Anything else I should know about?" I said with a grin.

"I had a penchant for spraying public property with graffiti."

"Quite the hooligan. Were you ever caught?"

"Not once." He sounded immensely proud.

"What brought you to your senses?"

"Mr. H."

I remembered. According to Chris, Mr. Harries, his History teacher, was the first person to really take an interest in him.

"God knows where I'd be now without him," Chris said.

"Well, there you go," I said, poking Chris playfully with a finger, making him laugh. "Stay brilliant and you'll win those little tearaways around to your way of thinking."

Chris swept up the plates and dumped them down on the floor. "And how was your week?" he said.

I told him about the radio programme.

"You're turning into quite a star."

I glanced at him. Had I detected a note of cynicism? "Maybe I could start a whole new breed of psycho-celebrity."

Chris didn't appear to get the joke, didn't react.

"It's good publicity for the Lodge," I continued, "and a great vehicle for highlighting eating disorders," I added, thieving a line from Jim.

"I thought the press did a pretty good job. You can't read anything these days without stumbling across *My Bulimia Nightmare*. The media's full of it."

"The media is also responsible for messages that reinforce the idea that young women can only be happy if they're thin as a blade," I said, unable to dampen the furious passion from my voice, something that had occasionally got me into trouble. Too intense, give it a rest, I'd been told. "If women don't conform, or, worse, are actually overweight, they're perceived as either bad or sick."

"It's okay, darling, you don't have to preach to the converted," Chris said, running his fingers over my bare arm.

I chewed my lip. "Sorry, I didn't mean to be strident. I simply feel so strongly about it."

"I'd never have guessed," he said with a smile.

I flashed an awkward smile in return. What pained me most was that, out of all psychiatric illnesses, anorexia had one of the highest mortality rates. There were young women who were literally taking the slow and agonisingly painful route to death. With all the chat about obesity, somehow anorexia got lost.

"Anyway," I said, eager to wrap it up, "I'm in a better position to talk about eating disorders than some features editor from a magazine."

Chris leaned over and kissed me. "I agree."

I beamed at him and stretched back on the pillows. He wasn't really carping about my brief moment of fame. He was concerned about the unwanted attention it might invite. I couldn't blame him.

Rolling over, I snuggled my arm underneath him so that my cheek lay against his chest. I could hear his heart beating. It made me feel safe. We didn't speak, simply rested in the moment. Then I remembered.

"Oh hell."

"What?"

"I forgot to call Alexa." I sat bolt upright.

"She got hold of you?"

"What, she called here?" I leapt out of bed.

Chris pulled a face. "She left a message."

"When was this?" I said, grabbing my robe.

"About five minutes before you got home this evening."

I let out a groan and galloped downstairs.

SIX

The desperation in Alexa's voice was plain to hear.

"He was my rock, Kim, what am I going to do without him?"

Survive, I thought. That's what we all do. "You'll find a way," I said. "I know it looks bleak at the moment, but you'll come through this."

"Will I?"

"I promise. Take it one step at a time."

"It's just that—" Alexa broke off and broke down. My heart swelled. I knew exactly what she was thinking and where we were going. I waited until her tears subsided enough for me to be heard.

"When bad things happen to us," I began softly, "we tend to think about and dwell on other unhappy events. Sometimes it's difficult to separate them out."

"I know you're right," she gulped.

"But what happened to your friend has nothing to do with Brooks wanting to divorce you."

"First Gaynor," Alexa cried, "and now this."

"It's incredibly tough on you."

"And Brooks was wonderful when ..." Her voice trailed off again.

"I know." I thought about Alexa's missing friend. How can a woman simply disappear?

Another torrent of tears followed. I fell silent and let her cry. When she finally calmed down I said, "What's your folks' reaction?"

"My dad wants to kill him. My mother's more concerned about how I'm going to survive financially. She really liked Brooks." She added bitterly, "She thinks it's all my fault."

"Surely not?"

Alexa gave a dry laugh. "My mother thought he was a good catch."

"Look, I've got some holiday coming up ..."

"No, you've got your own life, Kim."

"Don't be soft. It's fine. I'll come and see you as soon as I'm free. In the meantime, be kind to yourself, and remember what I said, find yourself a decent lawyer."

I returned to the bedroom. Chris looked up, hurriedly switched off his mobile, and put it on the bedside table.

"A late-night call?" I climbed wearily back into bed.

"A text from a supply teacher."

"On a Friday night? Must be conscientious."

He flicked a dismissive smile. "Nothing important. So what did Alexa want?"

I snuggled up to Chris and gave him edited highlights.

"You can't get involved," he said.

"Too late for that."

"You hardly know her."

"C'mon, Chris, that's not quite true."

"If you hadn't allowed yourself to be bullied into a school reunion at that vile institution your father sent you to, your paths would never have crossed."

Chris was right. Secretly, I'd agreed to go because I thought it would bring about some kind of closure for me. It hadn't, but Alexa and I had stayed in touch. Twice we'd hooked up as a foursome for dinner, me and Chris and Alexa and Brooks. Neither occasion had been a success. The first time I'd ended up rabbiting with Alexa about our miserable school days. Brooks, a hedge fund manager, had been more involved with a conversation on his mobile phone than a conversation with Chris. The second time was a disaster.

"I can't turn my back on her," I said evenly.

Chris let out a sigh.

"What?" I said, drawing apart from him a little.

"You don't have to pick up every waif and stray."

"I don't." I flinched at the defensive note in my voice.

Responding to it, Chris suddenly smiled. "I'm not having a go at you."

"Good," I said, softening.

"It's what makes you quite adorable."

"Keep going," I laughed, tucking myself in under his shoulder again, resting my head against his warm naked chest.

"Quite honestly, I'm not that surprised Brooks has decided to head for the hills," Chris said.

"No?"

"You have to admit Alexa is one hell of a high-maintenance woman."

"Highly strung, perhaps, but she's had a rough few years."

"Don't remind me," Chris said. "That last dinner we had with them was a bloody nightmare."

I remembered. Alexa had got drunk and treated us to a full misery memoir. It hadn't felt like dinner, more like a heavy session in the consulting room.

Chris was still talking. "She's needy and self-obsessed. Take that business with her friend."

"What of it?"

"Has it ever occurred to you that Alexa could be making the whole thing up?"

"You can't exactly fake someone's disappearance. The woman's been missing for over a year."

"You can if they never existed in the first place."

I drew away. "She's not a fantasist, Chris. She talked to the police as part of their investigation. Even Brooks confirmed it."

"Okay," Chris conceded, "but she didn't have to lay it on quite so thick. It wasn't as if the police had her down for a suspect. The missing woman wasn't even a close friend. Honestly, Kim, I don't think I've ever met such a drama queen and now she's clinging on to you like a drowning man to flotsam."

"Me, flotsam?" I grinned, trying to lighten the moment.

"I'm serious, Kim. It's positively spooky. She's practically stalking you."

I froze, stayed absolutely still, as if an imaginary line had been crossed. Was it simply an unfortunate arrangement of words, or was Chris inferring that Alexa posed a personal threat to me? His arms felt hard as concrete. Chris was first to break the silence.

"I didn't mean …"

"I know you didn't."

"Any more calls?" He seemed deliberately casual. I glanced up, sensing where the conversation was heading and feeling powerless to prevent it.

"No."

Underneath me, the muscles in his stomach relaxed.

"Chris," I said, running an index finger across his chest. "There have been a couple of developments."

SEVEN

I EXPECTED A SPATE of interruptions, a list of questions, noise. I'd have put money on Chris exploding in anger.

"It's probably harmless. Someone having a laugh." Even to my ears, my voice sounded thin and unconvincing. In spite of what I knew, I didn't want Chris to believe that I was at risk. "There haven't been any threats," I pointed out, catching the too enthusiastic note in my voice.

Chris's continued silence zapped my confidence.

"Okay," I backed down, "the mirror *was* a bit cranky."

"And the rat?"

"Unconnected, I'm sure of it. Okay, okay," I said, caving in under Chris's stare. "A prank in bad taste." I willed us both to believe it.

He finally fell asleep with his back facing me. I wrapped my arms around him, hoping that he didn't fall into the twilight zone of waking nightmares. Sometime in the early hours I found myself on my stomach, Chris lying on his back awake beside me, gazing up at the play of moonlight on the ceiling. I wondered whether he was thinking back to the childhood he never had, the home he never slept in, the mother and father significant only for their absence in his life. Sometimes he came across as detached. Not cold exactly, but as if he wished to keep himself boxed-in from the outside world. It wasn't that unusual. Often people fled to Devon to escape from something. Recently, when he was unaware of me watching him, I'd noticed a haunted look in his expression. Oddly enough, I'd caught it again that evening, when I'd returned from talking to Alexa and he'd put his phone away.

I jacked myself up on one elbow and kissed the corner of his mouth, running my fingers down his flanks, his body weakening as he rolled over on top of me. Whenever I couldn't touch him in other ways, I could always reach him with intimacy.

The next morning I woke feeling good, so good that when "Gimme Shelter" blazed onto the radio as I made early morning tea, I couldn't stop myself from dancing.

"Look at you, Slade," Chris said, shambling into the kitchen, hair sticking up. "What a mover."

I grabbed him by the hand and together we laughed and flailed around, hips twisting, me lip-synching until the track stopped.

"I love the fact you aren't what you seem," he said, as I poured boiling water into two mugs and over a couple of tea bags.

"Who is?" I said.

Later, we decided to have brunch in Salcombe. The sun floated high above, its rays squinting through the trees as we followed the coastal road from Goodshelter creek to the palatial homes that studded the hillside at Mill Bay. A strong smell of seaweed scented the air. Heat-haze settled on the land above the water. There was no breeze though the familiar noise of clanking halyards filled the creek.

By the time we reached where the road split, the top route leading back up towards Holset and Gara Rock, Chris was talking about getting a new car.

"I fancy something more sporty."

"Anything in mind?"

"Alfa Romeo."

"Which one?"

"Something that more than keeps up with yours—the Brera."

"Sports coupe," I smiled appreciatively. "Colour?"

Chris burst out laughing.

"Colour's important," I teased. "At least I showed some interest in the model."

"Black."

"A nightmare to keep clean."

"But very sexy." He gave my arm a delicious squeeze.

We took the narrow lower route to the ferry and could hardly move for people and boats with trailers and yapping dogs. Women with deep tans, discreet tattoos, and expensive hairstyles talked in superior accents and brandished their designer-clad children as though they were Olympic medals. Men brayed into mobile phones. Adolescent girls and boys walked four abreast, yelling beautifully articulated obscenities and screeching with laughter before romping off across the burning sand. It set me thinking. Who were these people? What did they do when they weren't having fun? Where did they live when they abandoned their summer nests? I swallowed hard. The noise and chaos grated on my senses. The beach suddenly felt a very unsafe place to be. Apart from the carcinogenic rays of the sun, the hidden dangers of the water, the lethal mesh of fisherman's lines extending along the shore, it was the perfect spot for abduction. No CCTV. Swathes of open ground. Easy prey. Concealed by the crowd, nobody would notice.

"Are you all right, Kim?" Chris's eyes expressed concern. I flicked a smile. "I thought I'd lost you there for a moment," he said.

"Admiring the view." I grabbed his hand. "Daydreaming."

EIGHT

THE QUEUE FOR THE ferry stretched back almost the length of the jetty. We crossed sand the texture of muscovado sugar and took our turn, me leaning into Chris, basking in the sunshine, desperate to shake off my unexpected fit of nerves.

Ten minutes later, we were sitting in the bleached wood interior of a café, devouring American-style muffins, poached eggs, and cappuccinos. Andy Johnson, Chris's best friend and another teacher at the community college, popped in to join us. He sported a mop of ash-blond curly hair that hung, leonine, over his forehead. With his big, slightly spatula nose and wide mouth, often as not, drawn back in a big grin, he looked like a jolly rugby player. His blue-green eyes reminded me of the ever-changing colours of the creek outside the cottage.

"So how's life in Chelters? You must find us yokels a bit dull by comparison." Never one to resist poking fun, Andy exchanged his Devonian accent for cut-glass Home Counties.

I wiped crumbs from my chin and leant in close to Andy's large happy face. "I'm more Devonian than you are," I grinned, prodding his thick chest with a finger. "You're practically a grockle."

Andy had to laugh at that. His family had moved to Plymouth from Cheshire. Mine were born and bred in the South Hams. Well, kind of, I thought, if I didn't include my enforced incarceration in an all-girls boarding school.

Retreating to a favourite and irritating tack, Andy said, "Must be weird leading separate lives."

"Leave it out," Chris smiled dismissively.

Andy flicked me a cheeky smile. For an unnerving second, something in the gesture reminded me of my brother Guy. I stuck out my tongue. Undeterred, Andy continued, "I don't understand why you two don't get on, do the decent thing and tie the knot."

"We're perfectly happy as we are, thanks." I laughed, but in truth I felt a bit defensive. "I get to do my thing. Chris gets to do his. And we have a fantastic time together. It's perfect."

"Must be a stressor getting your stories straight," Andy joked, taking a deep slurp of coffee. A layer of foam coated his upper lip.

"Fuck off, Andy." Chris's accompanying smile lacked warmth, I thought.

"It's about trust," I said, catching the prim note in my voice and hating it, not least because trust remained my weak spot. When you're nine years old and your dad pops you on his knee and warns you never to trust anyone in case they hurt you, it has an effect—even when your adult brain tells you it's bollocks.

I glanced warily at Chris. The thought of him playing away had never crossed my mind, for which, I supposed, I was a tad naive. A good-looking guy, working in an environment with a number of attractive women, he must get tempted. Devon was no different to any other place except that its peculiar geography and social structure provided a particularly rich playground for inappropriate liaisons.

"Anyway, how's your love life these days?" I asked Andy, trying to shift the spotlight.

"Sweet, as it happens."

"Go on. What's her name?"

"Jen." Enthusiasm lighted his features. "She's a sports instructor at Totnes Leisure Centre."

"And?" Chris said. "What's she like?"

A dreamy look stole over Andy's face. "She's got a lovely arse."

I burst out laughing.

"What kind of a statement is that?" Chris said.

"A bloke's," I said with a dry smile. The backdrop to conversation at home during the blissfully long school holidays was football, cars, and women—especially women.

Andy looked at both of us with a wolfish grin. "Her hair's kind of light brown—"

"He always goes for light brown," Chris interjected, taking a drink.

"You're right," I said, remembering a number of Andy's old flames. He picked up and dumped girls with the same alacrity public officials awarded themselves fat pensions.

"And brownish eyes," Andy continued.

"When do we get to meet her?" I said.

"Give the poor girl a chance. I don't want you two lovebirds frightening her off."

The discussion descended into general gossip, something for which Andy had a natural talent, and chat about films, Chris's big passion.

"They've got a rare late-night showing of *Red Cliff* at the local cinema next week," Chris said. "I'm hoping to catch it."

Andy looked quizzical. "Never heard of it."

"Chinese epic big-budget movie costing around forty million pounds to make."

"Bloody hell," Andy said. "Is it subtitled?"

I maintained a straight face. "Didn't you know Chris is fluent in Mandarin?"

"What?" Andy's mouth gaped open.

"Gotcha," I said, letting out a gale of laughter. "Of course it's subtitled, you fool."

"Ha-bloody-ha." Andy punched the top of my arm. "So what's it about, Chris?"

"The last days of the Han dynasty and the struggle for power. Basically, it's a war film."

"Right up my alley," I said.

"You're just fucking weird, Slade," Andy snorted. "Women aren't supposed to like all that action-adventure, blood, and guts stuff."

Chris and I exchanged a conspiratorial smile. "You need to get out more, mate." He grinned.

At Andy's suggestion, we agreed to continue the conversation at the Fortescue, a pub popular with locals and yachties alike.

"You two go on ahead," I said. "I want to pick up goodies for tonight."

"Tonight?" Chris said.

"Claire and Charlie's. Dinner, remember?"

His face briefly clouded. "Of course," he said, thumping his forehead with the palm of his hand. "Stupid of me." He forced a smile.

"You okay with it?" I flashed with anxiety. I couldn't possibly change the arrangement now.

"Sure," he said bullishly. "No problem."

I sauntered slowly in the direction of Island Street, nodding and smiling to people I knew, stopping briefly to talk to a local musician. Devon, or to be more specific the South Hams, had not only become a refuge for ordinary people, but a chosen sanctuary for the cool and trendy. Pop stars, actors, and the new breed of celebrity had moved and set up camp in droves. It often didn't take them long to move back.

After buying chocolate truffles and cheese from a local deli, I went to the pub. Packed and sweaty, the bar enveloped in a boozy glow, there was no sign of Andy or Chris, so I ordered a tonic water with lots of ice, swiped a spare newspaper from the bar, and sat down near a window. Chris appeared a few minutes later.

"Where's Andy?" I asked.

"Had to go."

"Where?"

"Aveton Gifford. Jen phoned. Not sure what the problem is."

"Must be keen if he can pass on a pint of beer. Is he bringing her here?"

"Didn't say."

"Think she's a keeper?"

"God, Kim, that's jumping the gun. Let's hope she lasts longer than the last one. Are you all right for a drink?"

I lifted my glass, gesturing that it was full. Chris pushed his way to the bar, ordered a pint of Directors Best Bitter, and settled himself back down.

"What time are we expected tonight?" he said.

"Seven thirty or eight."

"Know who else is going?" He viewed me over the rim of his pint. It was asked as a casual aside, but I knew that the question carried hidden meaning. Chris was not what you'd describe as a social animal. Ever the shrink, I put it down to his fractured upbringing.

"Haven't a clue."

He didn't say anything. I leant forward, squeezed his knee. "Relax, it will be fine."

He flashed a smile, as if grateful for the reassurance, and taking out his phone, checked it.

"Are you expecting a message?" I said.

He slipped it back into his pocket. "No."

"Right," I said, perplexed.

It wasn't long before he became lost in thought, hunched over his beer, unreachable. A gloomy look had taken up residence. "What are you going to do, Kim?"

So we were back to that again. For a few moments in time I'd blissfully forgotten. I took a sip of my drink to give me time to think. "I don't know who's responsible," I said, at last, meeting Chris's brooding expression. "It's not as if I've been assaulted. I haven't even been spoken to."

"And the phone calls?"

I didn't answer.

"He left a fucking dead rat on your car."

I flinched, caught the startled expressions of a couple at the next table, and flashed an apologetic smile.

"I don't like it," Chris muttered. "It feels all wrong. It feels dangerous."

"At least the focus appears to be in Cheltenham, not here."

"Because whoever's doing it thinks that's where your world is," Chris said. "Could it be someone connected to work?"

I felt a pinch of alarm, my mind immediately fixing on Jim Copplestone. He *was* a flirt. He'd half frightened me out of my wits the way he'd crept up on me. But wasn't it too obvious? And in any case, I really couldn't believe it. Jim would never take such a risk. His reputation was at stake. He had too much to lose.

"Perhaps it's someone who's seen you," Chris said, "a client maybe, or a parent of a client. Someone who knows what you do."

"Is that why you're opposed to the radio phone-in?"

"I'm not against it, but you have to admit it puts you in the spotlight. Maybe that's how this creep hooked onto you in the first place."

"The TV thing?"

He nodded. "Honestly, I think you should go to the police. They take that kind of thing seriously now. The new laws mean much heavier penalties."

"No." My fervour took me by surprise. "What I mean," I added with a tentative smile, "is that they don't have enough to work with."

"So you're going to wait until they do?" Chris's voice had reached a higher pitch.

My mind turned to quicksand. "I don't..."

He reached across and covered my hand with his. "You can give them records of times and dates."

"Funny, that's what Georgia said."

"You spoke to Georgia?"

"Well, yeah."

Chris stroked his chin, meditative.

"Is that a problem?"

"You should be careful who you discuss this with."

"Oh come on. We trained together. We go back years. She's a good friend."

"I know," he said, "but the fewer people in the loop, the better."

I wasn't sure about his logic and let it go. He glanced away. With the sun streaming through the window, his skin looked bleached of colour. He tapped a finger on the table. "It's vital you find out who it is."

I downed my drink and made a silent vow. My face, my life. I have to stop him.

NINE

"I've no idea what to wear." Dressed only in my bra and knickers, I pressed my fallback little black dress against me. "What do you think, Chris?"

"Looks great for Cheltenham, but too formal for Devon."

"Claire mentioned one of the guests is a lawyer."

"Doesn't mean he'll be wearing a wig and gown."

"Very funny," I said, inexplicably miffed.

"Everyone will probably be wearing jeans."

"Do you think so?"

"How about your long white skirt with your new top?"

"I suppose." I returned the dress to the wardrobe and picked out other clothes.

"Much better," Chris said admiringly as I slipped them on. "It makes you look softer, no hard edges."

I gawped at him. Sudden tears filled my eyes.

"Sweetheart," Chris said, cupping my face in his hands.

I couldn't tell him what I was thinking. It sounded too pathetic.

"Whatever has brought this on? I meant it as a compliment."

"I know what you meant," I said, my bottom lip trembling. "People smell my distrust of them at fifty paces. I, somehow, give off the wrong vibe." By *people*, I meant women. Masters at picking up on nonverbal communications, they easily spotted my weakness. I'd lost count of the times I'd been accused of being spiky, standoffish, aloof, and variations of all three. It was why I was so emotionally reliant on the tight circle of female friends I had managed to cultivate.

"Kim, honestly, please don't get upset. Here," he said, pulling me close. Maddeningly, it only made me worse. Suddenly I wanted to bawl my eyes out.

"I wish I hadn't said anything. Me and my big mouth."

"It's not your fault," I said, my voice thick. "It's mine."

He held me away from him, looked into my eyes, and shook his head. "For a confident woman you can be so insecure."

The problem with being a shrink is that I knew myself only too well. Strangely, at times like this, rationality didn't come into it. Deeper, more primal emotions insisted on leaking through. Chris understood this better than anyone. It's probably why we clicked.

I grabbed a tissue, dabbed my eyes, and prayed that my unexpected burst of emotion hadn't screwed up the carefully applied make-up that concealed my scars.

"Here," Chris said, patting the bed. "Sit down for a moment."

I did as he asked. He put his arm around my shoulder, held me tight. "You are a lovely, lovely woman. I have absolutely no idea why folk sometimes get the wrong idea about you. It doesn't make any kind of sense to me at all. Maybe it's because you're passionate about what you believe. Maybe it's because they're jealous."

I cracked a smile, grateful for Chris's attempt to make me sound noble. The dark truth was so much simpler.

My mind flicked back to a vagabond home life, to housekeepers who came and went, some only lasting a couple of days, a mother who wouldn't stay, random women who fancied their chances with my father to the extent that I never knew when I came home for the holidays who would be in the house. I remembered arguments fuelled by heat and passion and hard drinking, of me shouting loud to be heard above the clamour of men. I thought about my parallel existences, the buttoned-up schoolgirl and the wayward daughter, rules and routines versus domestic mayhem. I recalled having to behave like a man at home to survive; behave like a good little girl at school. Frequently, I got it mixed up, got it all wrong. As a grown-up, I'd adapted, done everything to shake off the traces of my past. Professionally, I pulled it off. Personally, I sometimes failed.

When I spoke my voice felt dull and leaden. "I'm fine. I was being silly. Let's go."

TEN

"More pudding?" Claire smiled, spoon poised.

Claire Lidstone was the kindest, sweetest human being I knew. We'd been firm friends since primary school and had continued our friendship despite me being sent away to school.

I passed my plate. "Just a small helping."

"I can see your work doesn't interfere with your appetite." Gavin Chadwick's laugh was light. His expression seemed to say *Yes, the story behind your face is intriguing but I'm too polite and sophisticated to ask or stare.* He had receding hair, which he swept back from time to time, and a face that exuded arrogant intellect. He wore a crumpled linen suit, the collarless shirt beneath oozing shabby chic. Throughout the evening I'd caught myself watching the criminal defence lawyer with a professional eye. Deferential to his hosts, he gave every appearance of clear interest in his fellow guests, but the sense that he was commanding the situation was definite and apparent. Maybe my observation was unfair. Maybe I was tired and a bit strung out. And what did it matter a damn? Whatever I thought, the Chadwicks were clearly enthralled by their new lives in Devon.

"It's such a slow pace of life." Lottie Chadwick smiled. "Everyone has time to chat. There's no pressure. It's like going back to the Britain of my parents' generation."

Careful not to puncture her illusions, my flat smile disguised the fact that my own observations were tempered by time, detachment, and experience. I could have informed Lottie about the crippling unemployment, the high cost of living, the stresses of residing in a holiday area where supermarkets are routinely plundered and roads blocked. I could have enlightened her about the merciless level of gossip, the *them and us* mentality that springs from moneyed people moving into an area where wages were well below the national average. "It's certainly a delightful place for children to grow up," I admitted.

"I couldn't agree with you more," Lottie enthused. "Ours have only recently broken up from school so it's all rather new to them. Milton's at Winchester. Serena's at prep school."

I caught Claire's protective expression. She was one of the few people to witness my profound misery at being parked in a boarding school.

Claire's husband Charlie topped up everyone's glass and plumped back down next to me, his large frame, clad in a check shirt, solid and dependable. More used to seeing him in mud-spattered jeans and Wellington boots, I couldn't ever remember seeing Charlie make such an effort to look smart.

"I think it's wonderful what you do," Lottie said, leaning tipsily towards me with a lopsided smile. She had large brown downturned eyes that made her look vulnerable.

"She's not a neurosurgeon," Gavin said, as though apologising for his wife's gushing manner.

I spotted the flex in Chris's jaw and caught the tail end of Claire's anxious frown. Gavin settled himself in his chair as though preparing for an entertaining debate. "How do you regard the current trend for counselling, Kim?"

This felt like the conversational equivalent of a light starter. Sooner or later, he'd be dishing up the main course. "Depends what you mean."

"Do-gooders."

Oh God, is that how you view me, I thought with a shudder. Heavens, I was too knackered for this. Time to go for the line of least resistance. "Naturally I'm not too impressed with enthusiastic life coaches who take a six-week course and then start mucking about with people's psyches," I said with a laugh.

"Did you know that when top-flight footballers leave and go to another club, the Football Association has counsellors on hand for bereft fans?" Charlie said, eager from the look in his eye to put the conversation onto a neutral footing.

"That's my point," Gavin said, handing him an appreciative smile. "We live in a society where everyone expects to use a counsellor, whatever the situation. I'm beginning to wonder whether we've bred a nation of feeble-minded wimps and losers."

I smiled, said nothing, believing that my silence should move things along to the next topic.

Gavin, apparently, wasn't done. "My difficulty with any form of therapy is that it's too unquantifiable. There are no facts by which you can measure it."

"There speaks the lawyer," Claire said good-naturedly, heading off Chris's mutinous look. I lowered my gaze and plunged my spoon into a wildly elaborate chocolate confection and pushed in a mouthful. But Gavin was not easily deflected.

"In a largely secular society, therapy, the talking cure, whatever you want to call it, has almost taken on the role of religion."

"For God's sake, Gavin." Lottie gave an embarrassed laugh and looked apologetically around the table. "You're not addressing the witness stand now."

"All I'm saying," Gavin opined, "is that, unlike other sciences, it's largely open to interpretation."

I glanced at Chris and saw the dangerous crease in his brow. He had a face like a man being told his lottery ticket is one number short. I understood. He was feeling protective of me.

"What do you think, Kim?" Gavin pressed.

"Me?" I spluttered. Dabbing at my lips with a paper serviette, I met his crafty expression with a straight look. "You're surely not asking me to rubbish my own profession?" Please don't ask me to enter the witness box, I thought. Please don't tempt me to bang on about the things I most care about and, consequently, make a fool of myself.

"I'm asking you to defend it."

Why? I felt like slinking off home, running a hot bath and, snug and warm, heading off to bed with Chris. Judging by the expressions of my friends around the table, *sock it to him* seemed the prevalent mood. I couldn't tell exactly what Chris was thinking. He refused to meet my eye.

Forcing a game smile, I decided to turn the tables. "Never mind me. I've always wanted to understand how lawyers make the moral leap to defend a guilty client."

"Atta girl," Charlie muttered under his breath.

Gavin's smile exposed small, pointy teeth. A sudden image of the dead rat flashed through my brain. "Everyone's entitled to a defence, guilty or otherwise," he said.

"But surely when a client has committed a serious crime ..."

"Like murder or ..."

"Stalking," I said, eyes level with his so that I couldn't see Chris's expression. I have no idea why I said it. The words simply fell out of my mouth without thought or consideration.

"Where the evidence is irrefutable?" Gavin added helpfully.

I nodded. "How does the lawyer square it with his sense of morality?"

"He doesn't. Morals are irrelevant. In fact, it could be argued they're dangerous."

"How do you work that out?" Claire interjected.

"If a lawyer takes a moral stance, he's in effect making a judgement. That would be fatal. He's not there to judge."

"But surely if he *knows* his client is guilty ..."

"Then he'll advise him to plead guilty. Simple as that," Gavin said. "The lawyer's duty is to uphold the law, to work within its constraints, to see that it's correctly applied."

"To exploit technicalities," I said.

"To argue points of law," Gavin insisted, humour in his eyes now that I'd foolishly waded back into the conversation. "To assert the burden of proof," he continued.

"What about miscarriages of justice?" Chris said.

"It happens," Gavin conceded, raising his glass to his lips, "but that's not usually our fault."

Chris let out an exasperated laugh. "Whose fault is it then?"

He shrugged. "Miscarriages usually happen because of problems with chains of evidence."

"You mean the police are to blame?"

"More often than you'd think."

"No wonder cops have such a low opinion of lawyers." We all looked at Chris, the growl in his tone loud enough to be heard in the next county.

"On occasion the feeling is mutual." Gavin smiled thinly. "A police officer doesn't have the onerous responsibility of representing a client."

"For which the lawyer is paid handsomely," I pointed out.

"A little simplistic, if I might say," Gavin said as though he thought it uncommonly naïve of me. "Have you ever seen anyone appear in court unrepresented?"

I said that I had not.

"Defendants don't have the faintest idea how to put forward the evidence," Gavin said. "They wander off the point. They waste everyone's time. They're cannon fodder for the prosecution. Believe me, there's nothing fair or just about that."

I scraped up the remnants of my pudding, wishing I'd asked for a bigger portion. I was in no doubt that the meddlesome lawyer was warming up for a second round. I was also terribly aware that we'd all had too much to drink. Licking my spoon, I watched him watching me. He had that predatory smile on his face again. It made me feel peculiarly self-conscious.

"Cheese and biscuits, anyone?" Claire piped up with a tight, anxious smile.

To my relief, the conversation swerved off in a different direction. It didn't take Gavin long to do the verbal equivalent of stalking me again. Swift in his conversational moves, I hardly had time to see it coming, let alone prepare. We were back onto the subject of my work.

"Surely, these girls you treat make self-obsession a luxury?"

I countered with a dry smile. "Nothing glamorous about starving yourself to death."

"Attention-seeking then?"

I took a sip of wine to cloak my creeping irritation and fiddled with an earring, the sign to Chris that is was time we went, but he wasn't looking my way. He was surveying Gavin with dark, murderous eyes.

"You don't accept that eating disorders are symptomatic of a greater underlying conflict?" Chris said.

"Conflict is an inescapable fact of life, my friend."

"I'm not your friend."

The room fell silent. I braced. Here we go. I wondered why the hell Claire and Charlie had invited the ghastly Gavin and his wife in the first place. It wasn't as if they appeared to have anything in common.

The lawyer gave a strained smile. "I meant no harm, nothing more than a turn of phrase. I apologise if I've caused offence."

"None taken," Chris said, eyes like stone.

"The point I was trying to make," Gavin said, spearing me with a look, "is that therapy and the mental ailments that supposedly afflict us are a uniquely Western problem. In the Third World people are too busy surviving and finding enough to eat to indulge in psychological nonsense."

I arranged my expression into one of neutrality. He really was quite the most odious man I'd met in a long time. God save me from ever needing a criminal lawyer. Feeling cornered, I put down my glass, smiled, and focused my gaze.

"Whether you live in the Third World or here in the Western world, there's a hell of a common denominator," I said.

Gavin took a deep drink from his glass. "What's that then?"

I waited a beat. "We're all terrified."

Had I suddenly spoken in Farsi, he couldn't have looked more perplexed. "Not sure I follow you."

"Our paranoid fear of growing old, losing our youth and looks, our monetary potential, something that Westerners are consumed by, and the inevitability of death frightens the hell out of most people."

Gavin shook his head. "And you really believe that shit?"

First profanity of the argument meant he was on slippery ground. I noticed Chris accept more wine from Charlie, who was flashing him a *What the hell is going on here?* look.

Gavin fixed me with an elastic smile. "Most of us would get better without having to shell out huge sums of money to people who play on our neuroses."

"Isn't that what lawyers do?" Chris said, raising a ribald murmur of agreement around the table.

"I'm not being personal, you understand." Gavin's expression assured his guests that it was simply a lively discussion between intelligent people. "You get where I'm coming from, don't you, Kim?"

That was the point. I didn't. Here I was, supposedly having supper with friends, and this man had singled me out. In the same way, and in spite of quietly minding my own business, a stranger had also selected me for special unwanted and unwarranted attention. What had I done to deserve it this time?

Pressing down hard on my nerves, I treated Gavin to my warmest, most confident smile. "Let's take an example from your line of business. A guy comes to you asking you to defend him. To do that, you need to gather all the facts."

"Absolutely."

"He needs to communicate with you. Communication is the key."

Gavin agreed with his eyes.

"And we like to think we live in an age of communication, right?"

"Yes," he said, "Voicemail, email, mobile phones, text services ..."

"Exactly. We can talk to each other at the push of a button. We can tweet and Facebook ourselves into oblivion, but there's no real human interaction. In fact new technology provides us with a cloak for avoiding contact."

"You can spend days talking to recorded messages," Claire chipped in.

I nodded. "In reality, at some strange subconscious level, people are more keen than ever to shy away from personal contact."

Gavin frowned. "I'm not sure I quite understand."

Everyone's eyes fell on mine. It felt as if all sound had been sucked out of the room. My heart stuttered in my chest. *Maybe it's because you're passionate about what you believe.* Reckless and unable to help myself, I explained, "Family ties are not as strong as they once were. Our marriages are failing. Friendships are often among the people with whom we're employed and are therefore transitory, or we may have tons of imaginary friends, faceless people we meet on the Internet through social networks. We work long hours. For some, there's no division between work and pleasure. Even the gym, where lots of us meet, has a competitive component."

"Nothing wrong in that," Gavin cut in, bullish.

"Nothing at all," I agreed, "but sometimes activity becomes an excuse for not spending time with friends and loved ones. Then we feel lonely, isolated in our technologically advanced little bubbles, our own private worlds. We lose the art of communication and with it our sense of being so we seek out TV talk shows with their cod-psychology, baying audiences, and hounded victims. We regard soap operas as a means to connect with others vicariously. More dangerous than this, because of our failure to genuinely communicate, we blunt our instinctive nose for danger. We don't spot it when it's staring us in the face." I swallowed, the truth of what I'd said hitting home like a stray bullet. "When we're really having problems and life chucks its worst at us, we need someone *real* to talk to, someone we can sit in a room with, whose face will express a reaction to what we say, someone who will listen, but won't judge. And that's where people like me come in. It's my job to inhabit the silences, join up the dots, fill in the spaces, make sense out of what seems very real chaos in my clients' lives. I might be an overpaid listener in your book, but to some very damaged people I'm a lifeline."

"Hear, hear!" Charlie stood up and raised his glass. "I'll drink to that."

Claire flashed me a look of triumph. Chris caught my eye and winked. Lottie gawped, rapt at the feet of Mother Kim. Me? I was rosy-cheeked with stress. Perspiration gathered in my armpits. Had I been too intense?

"Perhaps you missed your calling," Gavin conceded with a reluctant smile. "You'd make a worthy adversary in court."

"Coffee?" Claire beamed.

I pushed back my chair. "I'll give you a hand." As I got to my feet, my knees clanked together.

"Jesus," Claire fretted, kicking the door shut behind us, and leaning hard against it. "All I can do is apologise."

"Don't be soft," I said, my accompanying laugh tinny. "Was I bit, you know, over the top?"

"Not at all, he really seemed to have it in for you."

A sharp peculiar tang of misgiving assailed me. "Do you think so? He just likes the sound of his own voice."

"I thought Chris was going to hit him."

"Thank God he didn't. Our lawyer friend would have had him in court quicker than you can say Gav."

"That depends on whether the witnesses were prepared to give evidence," Claire said with a cutting smile. "I, for one, would have denied all knowledge."

I smiled, tried to lighten my mood. It really was only a lively exchange of views, I told myself. A bit of sparring. Nothing to it.

"Where did you find them—under a rock on the beach?"

Claire groaned. "Charlie's idea. They met at the amateur dramatic society."

"I didn't know Charlie was still into all that."

"Frankly, it's a pain. There's enough to be done on the farm without him disappearing for rehearsals, but you know Charlie."

I did. Charlie the unstoppable.

"I wouldn't have had Chadwick down as a wannabe actor."

"Oh no," Claire said. "He's helping with set design."

I couldn't help but give a wicked grin. "You mean carrying props?"

"Probably," Claire giggled.

"Lottie seems all right, bless her."

"I feel sorry for the woman. Fancy being married to that tosser?"

"How long have they lived here?"

"Four months, or so. They live out at Harbertonford. He commutes, though I gather he's got time off at the moment."

"Lucky sod." It shot out a little too quickly.

"Problems at work?"

"No more difficult than usual," I bluffed. Claire eyed me in a way that suggested I wasn't entirely believed. "How on earth did you make that fabulous-looking pudding?" I said, changing the subject.

"Impressive, wasn't it?"

"A masterpiece."

Claire's eyes sparkled. She looked exceptionally pleased.

"Don't tell me. You bought it."

Claire nodded, a distinctly naughty expression on her face. "I invested half the weekly housekeeping in a cookery delivery service called Posh Nosh."

"Brilliant. Does Charlie know?"

Claire's eyes rolled in amusement. "What do you think?"

I let out a laugh. "Is this payback for his rehearsals?"

"Nothing malicious about it."

The word *malicious* made the smile freeze on my face.

"Hey, things all right?" Claire touched my arm, the fun of the last few moments smashed in bits, sprawled across the floor.

"Sure," I tensed, forcing a reply. "Good. Everything's good."

ELEVEN

SUNDAY PASSED IN A boozy blur. We got up late and ate bacon sandwiches.

"Fancy a ride out?" Chris said.

This was code for a spin on the motorbike, a Triumph Tiger Explorer. It had taken Chris a couple of years to persuade me to ride pillion. After what had happened to my brother Guy, I hadn't been keen, but eventually he'd won me round. The first time I'd stepped on board I'd found it exhilarating and quickly became a convert. Taking instruction from Chris, I'd even ridden it illegally myself when we'd ventured out to Dartmoor on the more lonely roads, where motorists were rare and I couldn't get into trouble.

It was too hot to bother with leathers so we grabbed our helmets and set off, Chris's muscular body upfront, me in the perfect sightseeing position with a warm wind against my face. Journeying into Kingsbridge, we looped round to Modbury, finally finishing back at the creek where we took off our boots and ambled barefoot, skimming pebbles, a bright sun perforating an ocean of blue sky.

A bleep from Chris's phone signalled a text message. He checked the caller and returned the phone to his pocket.

"Aren't you going to read it?" I said.

"I did."

"Who was it?"

"Someone trying to sell me loft insulation."

We walked some more. Sixth sense told me that Chris was gearing up to something. I was right.

"Why did you mention stalking?"

"What?"

"When you argued with that jumped-up creep last night, you mentioned stalking."

The sudden note of accusation attacked me like a random blow from behind. "Did I?"

"Who the hell did he think he was, going after you like that?"

"He wasn't that bad." I wanted to blot out the episode. No offence meant and none taken.

"Yes, he bloody was. What got me, the fact he's the outsider. We've all known each other for ages—you and Claire go back almost thirty years."

"Makes me sound ancient."

"Then Mr. Prick, the lawyer, turns up and starts mixing it."

"Probably in his genes." I really wanted to play it down, forget about it. It was Sunday, for God's sake. One more day before I had to drive back.

"You mean there's a genetic code for arrogant prat?"

I glanced across, caught his eye, and felt a nervous ripple of mirth bubble up from inside.

"What?" His face cracked into a smile.

"You." I shook with laughter. "I love you when you're mad."

"Mad angry, or mad deranged?" He melted into a broad grin and pulled me towards him.

"Angry, you fool."

———

Afterwards things got strained. The phone rang. Chris tore into the sitting room and snatched it up. I barely paid attention to his response at first, too busy preparing vegetables in the kitchen. With my forthcoming birthday, it was also possible that Chris was planning a surprise, but something caught my ear—the tone, or slight catch in Chris's voice. Against my better nature, I found myself eavesdropping.

"It's rather awkward to talk." Chris's voice sounded unnaturally quiet. "I appreciate how you feel about it … yes, of course … I realise that … yes, but I don't want her hurt. It's not worth it, you understand. Look, I have to go … What? The usual routine, I guess … Yes, now I really have to go. It's not a good time. See you on Monday. Cheers."

Chris walked back into the kitchen. I issued a breezy smile. "Andy," he said.

"What did he want?"

"Checking up on dates for parent-teacher evenings. He seems to have lost his sheet."

"Funny, I thought he'd have it all recorded on his laptop."

"You know Andy."

I thought Chris's accompanying smile was lame. I didn't buy it.

Later, while Chris sat at the kitchen table marking essays, I opened a crisp white sauvignon and drank while I cooked. The cottage was as quiet as air. I welcomed it.

On impulse, pushing a saucepan away from the gas, I went over to Chris and slid my arms around his neck. He carried on marking, his handwriting reminding me of my father's, stylish but impossible to read. My mouth nibbled the top of his ear.

"I have to get these done," he said pointedly.

"Not now." I laughed, tousling his hair.

"Don't." He pulled away. Something deep inside froze. A memory of rejection, long buried, threatened to push through into the present. I smothered it. He touched my arm. "Sorry, Kim, the heat is making me crabby."

I drew up a chair and forced a sympathetic smile to prove that I wasn't really hurt or alarmed. "Are you okay?" It sounded ridiculous—*of course* he wasn't. Neither was I, if I were honest.

He rubbed his eyes and fixed on the papers in front of him.

A rush of irritation coursed through me. Whoever was playing with my life was having a destructive impact on both of us. "What if I tried to get a job closer to home?"

Chris started. "Doing what?" We both knew that Bristol, almost a hundred and twenty miles away, was about the nearest I could get for my particular line of work. He put his pen down. "Is this because of what's happened, or because that's what you really want?"

My stomach creased with disappointment. I'd wanted him to be ecstatic. I longed for him to be too delighted to challenge it. Shit, I thought, is this my way of asking him to commit, the thing that most women seemed to need from the man in their lives? I backtracked quicker than a politician exposed in a fierce debate. "It was only an idea. I haven't thought it through. Silly of me."

He leant over and crooked a knuckle under my chin. His eyes were level with mine. Blood and heat surged through my temple. The rest of me was cold.

"I don't want you to rush into changing everything for the wrong reason," he said.

"I understand."

He nodded. His eyes seemed more grey than blue.

"I expect he'll eventually lose interest and go away." I didn't believe a word of what I said. Whoever it was had latched on. I was rapidly becoming the centre of his universe. Even if he stepped things up and I involved the police and they had a word with him, it wouldn't alter his behaviour.

The knuckle tightened. A tense expression entered Chris's face, but it was gone so quickly I thought I'd imagined it.

"Think about any decision carefully, yeah?"

I inclined towards him, my heart dancing in my chest, and lightly kissed his mouth. "I will."

TWELVE

AND I DID. ALL the way in the car early the next morning, I thought of nothing else. I told myself that Chris was protective of me. He didn't want me to make any decisions based on a knee-jerk reaction. I'd grown up under the guardianship of men, so this type of response was normal to me. In a more sober frame of mind, I was also taken aback by my off-the-wall suggestion. It wasn't like me to be impulsive.

I arrived back in Cheltenham shortly before eight in the morning. Home there was a second-floor apartment in Lansdown, a short hop from Montpellier. Built in a Regency style, including large, airy rooms and an ornate wrought-iron balcony, it was indistinguishable from originals that populated the town. I loved it for its grandeur and style even if parking was a nightmare. Instead of leaving the car at the Lodge as usual, I parked it on a meter nearby so that I could drive the short eight-mile journey to Gloucester for the phone-in later.

As I went inside the stucco-columned entrance, I bowled into Lizzie, my downstairs neighbour, on her way out to work.

"Hiya! Any luck with the sale?"

Lizzie smiled and tossed her butter-coloured hair over her shoulder. She had small feline features and a worryingly slight build. "We had a couple round at the weekend but I'm not sure if they were that interested. The fact that it's a ground floor flat put them off. People worry about security. We've got more viewers lined up this week, so fingers crossed."

"As long as they're nice quiet types," I teased.

Lizzie shot a smile. "We'll do our best to vet them."

I dashed upstairs, bubbly inside. I convinced myself that it was due to natural apprehension about the radio show. Deep inside, I knew that nerves underpinned my fear of entering the flat. Had there been any silent phone calls, any messages, any notes shoved under the door? Listening hard for the telltale beep of the answering machine, I let myself in; relief seeped out of me on seeing everything the way I'd last left it. To be really sure, I reclaimed my territory: through the narrow hall with its large gilt-framed mirror, into the sitting room and dining area with golden-coloured walls, silk drapes at the windows, elegant cream leather sofa.

Sitting down, I glanced up at the limited edition print cresting the feature marble fireplace. Entitled *Beautiful Losers*, the work portrayed a tense drama played out between two men and a woman. Heavily atmospheric and sinister, it was a fine example of Jack Vettriano's style. I often sat and mused upon the relationship between the man standing and the man who sat with a weary expression smoking a cigarette. And what was the exact nature of the relationship between the woman and the two men? Had they been lovers? What was going through their minds? And what type of man had left a dead animal pinned to my windscreen? What kind of person was vying in the most bizarre fashion for my attention?

I ran a bath and chose what to wear. I often dressed casually for work and wore jeans. Pure psychology. With a young clientele, I didn't want to "get down with the kids," yet neither did I wish to come across as too far removed from them. But today I could dress in full authoritative mode even though unseen by the listening public. I decided on a peacock-blue sleeveless dress and high heels.

On the point of sinking into a foamy layer of bubbles, the phone rang. My watch told me that it was before nine. Probably Chris checking that I'd arrived back safely. Stepping out, I grabbed my robe and padded through to the sitting room, leaving a trail of damp, soapy footprints. The answering machine kicked in as I reached out for the receiver, hand hovering, unsure whether to pick up. "Come on, Chris," I muttered. Oh damn it, I thought, snatching up the phone.

There was no familiar voice, nothing other than the faint noise of someone breathing. Instantly, my pulse rate stammered as though I'd popped amphetamines. My legs trembled and I felt mildly sick. In spite of an instinct to slam down the phone, I gathered up every bit of courage and forced my mouth open. The voice that emerged didn't sound like mine.

"Look, whoever you are, this isn't going anywhere. I don't know why you're doing it, but it's not welcomed. Go and talk to your GP or, if you're embarrassed, you can phone a mental health line and a member of staff will find someone in your area to counsel you. Please don't contact me again. Ever."

I hung up and wondered whether I'd done the right thing. I should have ignored it. I shouldn't have engaged. If only I hadn't been so rash. And then the cold thought entered my mind that the caller had waited for my return, seen my arrival, knew that I was there. Christ, I thought. *He's watching me.* Livid, I crossed the room, briefly scanned the street, wrenched the curtains closed, then returned to the bathroom and locked the door after me.

As I sank beneath the surface of the water, a question plagued me. Could it be Phil, my ex-husband?

I hadn't given him a thought in years, but this was exactly the brand of obsessive behaviour he'd indulged in. He'd almost broken me with it. But that relationship was years ago, when I was young and gauche and inexperienced. It couldn't have any bearing on the present, could it? Why would he crawl out of the pit to intimidate me now, after all this time? More likely, he was exercising his jealous streak on another poor woman. Still, I was forced to consider as I reached for the soap, was it possible? And if so, what could I do about it? The last I'd heard he was in Canada.

Twenty minutes later, my scars itching, I carefully applied camouflage cream, eternally grateful that the titanium dioxide, acting as a high-density primer, managed to mask most of the discolouration. Lightly dusting my skin with finishing powder to make it waterproof, I applied make-up to the rest of my face, leaving my lipstick until after I'd eaten breakfast—not that I felt much like eating—then clipped on a pair of gold earrings. Halfway through a miserable slice of toast, the phone rang again. Leave it, I thought, taking an insistent bite. It kept ringing. Ignore it. Still it rang. *Mustn't* touch it. The messaging machine kicked in and the caller rang off.

The toast hovered in midair. Rooted, I regarded the phone as if it were primed to detonate. Can't breathe in. Can't breathe out. Willed the thing to stay silent, to shut up, to fuck off. He knows I'm sitting here like this. He knows that I'm waiting. The phone started up again, this time it blared, deafened, screamed. So insistent. So intrusive. Oh God, anything to shut off the bloody noise…

"Piss off!"

The smooth reply sounded faintly amused. "I'd no idea you swore with such vigour, Kim."

"Jim," I spluttered. "I'm terribly sorry. I thought you were someone else."

"They must have upset you a great deal to elicit such a florid response so early in the morning."

"It's a private matter," I said, silently cursing. Jim was smart. He'd piece it together with the "litter" incident. "Nothing I can't handle."

"Glad to hear it," came the disbelieving response.

My stomach squirmed. My professional persona had slipped and I hated looking out of control, especially in front of Jim Copplestone. How had things spiralled so quickly? Why hadn't I simply let the answering service collect the call?

"About this morning," he said. "All set?"

"Looking forward to it."

"Good, thought I'd give you a ring to wish you luck."

"Thanks." As I signed off I wondered if Jim Copplestone was featuring too heavily in my life.

THIRTEEN

"As already stated, eating disorders are not about food."

"But isn't that a contradiction?" Imogen Kulp, an American presenter, had a businesslike manner and machine-gun delivery. "If you're a sufferer the whole focus is on food, surely?"

"Only in so far as it's symptomatic of the disorder," I explained. "The weight loss is what catches our eye. To an outsider or a loved one who's in the agonising position of watching a young woman starve herself, the food issue appears to be the root cause."

"So anorexia's not a slimming disease?" Kulp said.

"Too blunt a description. It's what's going on in the sufferer's mind that's the crux of the problem. The restriction of food is a genuine expression of chaos."

Kulp addressed the listeners, "We will, of course, be giving out a list of contact numbers for those seeking help, or you can visit our website for information after the programme. Right, we have another caller on the line. Kyle Stannard wishes to pick up on the issue of body image. What's your question, Kyle?"

"How does your expert feel about the use of plastic surgery to correct conditions like body dysmorphic disorder?"

Kulp pulled a face. "I fear this is going outside our sphere of discussion." She looked meaningfully at me. I spread both my hands, deferring to her greater experience. In return Kulp raised one eyebrow and smiled. I touched my mouth, gesturing that I was prepared to take the call. Kulp nodded for me to go ahead, a silent moment of conspiracy between us that made me fleetingly wonder why I had such a ridiculous, closely-guarded hang-up about "the sisterhood."

"BDD, as it's known, has certain similarities with eating disorders but exists within a field of its own. For the listener, I should explain that sufferers have an obsessive preoccupation with an imagined defect in appearance, most usually on the face. It's very distressing and the condition can persist for years. Patients literally feel repulsive."

"And surgery?" the caller said.

"Preliminary clinical reports suggest that surgery does not benefit patients. Either the patient remains focused on the perceived defect or they simply move on to another physical feature. So, no, I'm not in favour of it."

"Not in any circumstances?"

Kulp drew a finger underneath her throat. I raised both eyebrows in a *Let me just wrap this up* gesture. "It's true that plastic surgeons can significantly improve the lives of those injured in road accidents or suffering from serious burns, but—"

"Are you speaking from a personal perspective?"

I mentally skidded to a halt. He might as well have pressed needles into my eyes.

"You've had plastic surgery, haven't you?" the caller persisted.

Kulp registered surprise, shut down the fader, and cut the caller off. She pushed a glass of water in my direction. "Maybe plastic surgery would be an interesting area for discussion on another occasion, Kyle," she said, her voice as smooth as warm caramel. "Just to remind you, folks, we have Kim Slade, a clinical psychologist specialising in eating disorders, on the line. We're standing by, ready and waiting to take your calls."

The rest of the phone-in took place in a haze. I went onto autopilot, reeling off facts and statistics, promoting Ellerslie Lodge, recommending forms of treatment and various organisations and associations. The whole time my brain snagged on the sole male caller: Kyle Stannard. He'd talked for such a short interval, yet I remembered every nuance of his voice. Low in timbre, precise, educated, without distinguishing accent. I estimated he was in his thirties. He didn't sound weird. On the contrary, he seemed lucid and rational, but his remark about my face set off alarm bells. *Was it him? My stalker? Was Kyle Stannard his real name?*

Kulp wrapped up the programme. "That's all we have time for. Our thanks to Kim Slade for joining us this morning. It's twenty-nine minutes past midday." The programme faded out to the sound of Roy Orbison's "Pretty Woman."

"That went well. Pity about the bozo. We're usually a little better at screening them out, but you did good. You okay?" She shuffled some papers.

"Fine," I said, distinctly unsteady.

"Say," Kulp said, looking straight at me, ghoulish fascination in her eyes, "how *did* you get that scar on your face?"

FOURTEEN

On the short journey from Gloucester to Cheltenham, I stuck my foot down, the gears meshing as the car powered along a nice straight stretch, making the muscles in the small of my back vibrate.

People were rarely so direct. Of those bold enough to ask, I'd witnessed every type of reaction, from shock to repulsion. Special camouflaging make-up had improved dramatically, but it was never entirely successful. Sometimes people came straight out with it, as Imogen Kulp had done. Sometimes I found myself taking the initiative by getting the subject of my scars out of the way so that I could move on. I'd largely come to terms with the fact that people were curious, and I'd discovered that, by adopting a dismissive tone, the questioner felt less awkward. If I made out that my injury was no big deal, they tended to do the same. But if pressed, as sometimes happened, I always gave the same answer: An accident when I was little.

I overtook three cars at warp speed. However much I tried to lose myself, I couldn't shake off the growing sensation of rage. I felt infected by it. Attempting to grab a slice of perspective, I persuaded myself that it was only human to focus on stuff that goes bump in the night, to meet imaginary terror coming from the opposite direction, but no amount of psychological trickery helped. Despite my determination not to be fazed, I found myself checking the rearview mirror, wary of any vehicle following too closely, flinching as a black-clad motorbike rider roared past. Every lucid argument I could come up with turned to fine sand in my hands. I felt hunted.

Driving into Cheltenham's one-way system, my mind clamped onto Kyle Stannard. Whoever he was, he had a certain amount of knowledge about what I did and who I was.

Time to find out about him.

FIFTEEN

Kyle Stannard, one of the highest paid international male models, critically injured in street brawl.

Male model for Quartz Agency rushed to London hospital with serious facial injuries.

Was Kyle Stannard singled out for his good looks? Police are looking into…

I stared at the straplines and the photographs of him in his prime and felt something inside wither. With a cold and outwardly calm voice, I pressed the intercom, signalling my readiness for the next client.

That evening, I went out to friends for dinner. The Flemings lived in what had once been a tumbled-down house in leafy Pittville, the place previously split into flats and let to students. The day Molly had dragged me along to view, it was a mess of crumbling plaster, nicotine-coloured walls, rusted ironwork, damp, mould, and woodworm. Anyone else would have been deterred. Not Molly.

She kissed me exuberantly on both cheeks. Dark and flashing, with a temperament to match, she had the held-together stance of a Flamenco dancer. We stood in an elegant hallway, the floor Harlequin patterned in black and white. Sunshine from a declining sun bounced off a single chandelier. The staircase, which was wide and thickly carpeted, seemed to stretch up to the heavens. I handed Molly a bottle of wine.

"Thought we'd eat in the courtyard," she said, "go on through. Simon's already out there fixing the drinks."

I walked into an extravagantly bohemian-styled sitting room where a pair of bronze African figurines flanked the marbled Victorian fireplace. French windows opened out onto stone steps that led down to a tiny, enclosed courtyard where hanging figs adorned one wall. Simon, his back to me, was engaged in easing a cork from a bottle. On hearing my tread, he turned and flashed a brilliant smile of greeting. As blond as his wife was dark, he had deep smoky-blue eyes, good looks and, a former paratrooper and fitness fan, a strong and athletic body.

Following a satisfying pop, he filled three glasses and handed one to me.

"So how's life in Civvy Street?" The bubbles prickled my nose. I stifled a sneeze.

"Plenty of cut and thrust," he joked, a mesh of lines crinkling the corners of his eyes.

Simon's career had been chequered since leaving the armed forces. He'd recently joined a firm of up-market estate agents.

"Molly will be pleased," I said. She'd always worried about the inherent dangers of army life.

"Yeah," Simon said with little enthusiasm.

"Still finding it difficult to adjust?" Once, in an intoxicated moment, he'd described himself as a killing machine. Not much scope in civilian life for people like him, he'd told me. I'd thought little of it at the time. Now…

"So-so," he said with a grin. "What about you? How's things?"

"I'm fine—all good."

"And Chris?" Simon was polite, the tone casual, but the way in which his eyes fixed on mine, the way his hand gripped his glass suggested that he felt anything but indifference. He and Molly had met Chris twice on one of Chris's rare forays to Cheltenham. They'd got on superficially, though I sensed that there had been no great meeting of minds. I had to admit that Chris wasn't especially easygoing. His complexity was one of the things that attracted me.

"He's well, thanks."

There was a pause, a few beats too long. I opened my mouth to plug the gap. Simon was already ahead of me. "Kim, are you sure you're all right?"

Was it that obvious? Was I going to spend the rest of the evening lying to two of my oldest friends? Cornered, I took the plunge. "There's something I want to talk to you about."

Simon fixed his full magnetic gaze upon me. I cleared my throat. "I suppose," I said, with cool, "I've got a problem."

"How tantalising," Molly exclaimed, scooping up a glass and joining us.

"Do tell."

So I did.

"Basically, you're being stalked."

We'd eaten silvery-skinned sardines with oregano followed by luscious lemon chicken cooked with sherry and fat bulbs of garlic served on a bed of fragrant saffron rice. Simon's cold observation elicited a protest from Molly.

"A bit strong, isn't it? I mean, in some ways, it's rather flattering."

We both looked at Molly as though she'd offered to take all her clothes off and run down the Promenade singing "Rule Britannia."

"Well, I'd find it exciting to have an unknown admirer." Molly's lips curved into a generous smile and she ran the tip of a painted fingernail along her husband's arm.

"A heavy breather, a guy who doesn't have the balls to make anything other than anonymous contact? A dead rat?" I said.

"The rat is probably some kid's idea of a prank," she flashed.

I quelled a response. Hadn't I used the same duff explanation to Jim and Chris?

"C'mon, Molly, you know better than that," Simon said. "Going back to the radio phone-in, Kim. Do you think it was him?"

"I wasn't certain this morning. After checking out Stannard, I'm prepared to suspend disbelief." A picture of him blazed in front of my eyes. He bucked the current trend for androgynous heroin-chic; there was nothing skeletal and offset about his features. With film-star good looks, he was the kind of man who, whether eighteen or eighty, would remain handsome. "The fact he was injured explains the connection," I said.

"It doesn't mean he and the stalker are one and the same," Molly pointed out.

"Agreed, but, clinically speaking, he ticks the right boxes."

"Why didn't Stannard cloak himself in anonymity then?"

I couldn't answer. Simon stroked his chin. "What does Chris think?"

He didn't know about the latest development, but I didn't tell Molly and Simon this. "That I should go to the police."

"He's right."

"Georgia said the same."

"Then get on and do it," Simon said.

"What else does Chris say?" Molly glanced at Simon in a way that made me suddenly defensive. "I mean how does he *feel* about it?" she added.

"Upset, annoyed, concerned." I didn't say he was edgy, that it was starting to turn our relationship upside-down.

Molly touched me lightly on the back. "Couldn't he come up and stay with you, sweetie?"

"He has a job, Molly."

Molly arched an eyebrow. "What about those fantastically long holidays he gets?"

"They're not that long," I said, chippy. I didn't add that it was almost impossible to winkle him out of Devon. In almost four years, he'd stayed at the Cheltenham flat no more than a dozen times. "Anyway, I go back every weekend and, in a couple of weeks, I'm taking a break."

Nobody spoke for a moment. Molly got up to change the CD.

"It's important you report it, Kim," Simon said. "I don't understand why you are so reluctant."

Because it's like saying: Hey, you've got me. I'm afraid. You win. Any adversity in my life, I'd overcome in my own way, on my own terms. And what would the police do about it? In spite of legal changes, it took time for law to filter through and translate into action. It would more likely be a case of take a statement, make enquiries, and see you later. There was also a more obvious reason.

"Stalkers are pretty resistant to changing behaviour," I said. "It may make matters worse."

"How?"

"It will wind him up," Molly said as though Simon were being dim.

I agreed. "Engagement and recognition runs the risk of giving him the attention he craves." I have to find another way, I thought darkly. I have to slide into his slipstream and channel him away; to somewhere he can't hurt me.

Simon was adamant. "That's no reason to hold back."

"I'm with Kim," Molly said. "If you think this bloke's a really serious proposition, then I say leave well alone."

"It's not as if I'm a celebrity or a politician, or anyone in the public eye, for God's sake," I said, appealing to the line of least resistance, which, in this case, was Molly.

Simon rested a hand on mine. His felt warm and clammy. "You don't have to be. I'm sure your bosses will understand, if that's what's bothering you." He gave me a sympathetic smile.

It wasn't. Well, not much it wasn't. "If I bring this out in the open, I'm playing into the guy's hands. I'll be feeding his sense of self-importance."

"Treat him like a two-year-old throwing a tantrum," Molly said, heading off a furious look from Simon. I couldn't tell whether it was because Simon disagreed, or because she'd touched on a raw subject. The likelihood of the Flemings ever having children of their own was a rare possibility.

"Ignore him?" Simon flashed, his jaw set.

Caught in domestic crossfire, I topped up everyone's glass. Molly, who'd fallen silent, looked pensive. "You don't think it's Phil, do you?"

"He had crossed my mind," I confessed, "but why pop up now, out of the blue?"

"Ex-husbands are usually top of the list." There was a cold edge to Simon's voice. "Do you want me to talk to him?"

"Are you still in contact?" I was astonished. It had never occurred to me that Simon might still be in touch.

"On and off." He looked suddenly sheepish. "The odd telephone call, nothing more."

"What's he up to these days?" I wanted it to sound casual. It sounded anything but.

"IT Consultancy and stuff," he added vaguely.

"Last thing I heard, he was working in Canada."

"He's back in the UK."

I did my best to hide my shock. "Do you know where he lives?"

"Not exactly, but I can track him down." Simon's eyes had turned a pale and dangerous shade of cobalt. I instantly saw what Simon meant about him being a killing machine.

"I don't know," I said, part of me uncomfortable with the prospect of Simon pulling strings on my behalf, the other part bewildered.

"Think about it." Simon raised his glass, took a drink. "In the meantime, keep everything this guy sends, dead animals included. He hasn't sent you shit or dirty needles?"

"Simon!" Molly burst out.

"Has he?" Simon persisted, ignoring his wife.

"No," I replied.

"Good. Anything you receive, bag it. Keep a note of times when you think you're being followed, drive-bys, anything out of the ordinary. Let your phone pick up all your calls and get a new unlisted number for anyone else to make contact. Has he called you on your mobile?"

"No."

"When he does, change it."

"*When?*"

"Keep a phone with you at all times, especially at night, and make sure you use your entry phone. Does the flat have an alarm system?"

I shook my head.

"Have one installed or get a big dog."

"Don't be daft, Simon. I—"

"And get a personal alarm for yourself. They make a hell of a racket and can buy valuable time in a tricky situation. If you think you're being followed in the car, drive to your nearest police station. Whatever you do, don't drive home or to a friend's house."

My head felt full of clay. Simon's advice made absolute sense, but I couldn't help think a bit of him was getting off on it. "This sounds so extreme."

"They're basic precautions. If he gives up and goes away, that's great, but you can't afford to take that gamble. In the meantime you have to reclaim control by taking steps to protect yourself. Do you understand?"

I nodded. Control was good. Control equalled survival.

Molly threw me a solicitous look. Turning to her husband, she said, "What if that fails?"

Simon smiled with a salute of his glass. "I hear Devon's a jolly nice place to live."

Later, Simon accompanied me home. We walked companionably, arm-in-arm, the route lit by streetlight and the glow of distant shop fronts.

He was in his element. "You need to be on the alert for anything different, anything out of place, something that doesn't feel right."

"How will I know?" Drink had loosened my defences.

"You're the psychologist." Simon laughed lightly. "You're paid to pick up on things."

It wasn't the same. I was accustomed to working in a controlled environment. My clients, whether they admitted it or not, welcomed, or at least were open to help. It was a partnership, psychologist and client working together. By contrast, my stalker knew a great deal about me. He knew where I lived, what I did for a living, where I worked. So how was that for one-sided? This freak had entered my life and latched on with the tenacity of an incurable disease.

But that was going to change.

We rounded a corner and crossed the road. Regency buildings towered impressively in the moonlight; ironically, the large police station was only a stone's throw away.

"I'll be all right now," I said, meaning it, my fiercely independent and maverick streak coming to the fore.

Lizzie's place was suffused in a comforting glow and the main entrance lit up with spotlight, but Simon insisted on seeing me to my door. "Another tip," he said as we went inside the communal hallway. "Always opt for the stairs. Wherever you are, you don't want to get stuck in a lift with Mr. Creepy."

Mr. Creepy. I snuffed out the soubriquet as I snapped on the bedroom light. Staying alert was second nature to Simon; soon it would be second nature to me. I realised that I had to wise up and wise up quickly.

Drawing the curtains, I plumped down on the bed, kicked off my shoes, and went into the kitchen, bare feet slapping against the cool tiled floor. I filled a glass of water and took a deep drink. Perhaps I'd call Chris. I'd tried to phone him before going out that evening, but he hadn't picked up and I'd left a brief message to the effect that I was all right, my only reference to the radio phone-in that it was *interesting*.

A glance at my watch revealed that it was well past midnight. However much I wanted to hear his voice, it was probably not a good idea. Once, I wouldn't have hesitated. Once, we would have been on the phone for hours. Only a day apart and we'd be telling each other how much we missed being together. Once, Chris would have signed off with "I love you." I hugged the memory tight, felt it wriggle in my grasp and steal away.

Drained, I walked over to the sitting room window and kinked back the curtain. Daylight always gave a clear view of the road where it funnelled into Montpellier with its stylish shops, bars, and beauty salons. At night, the buildings lost definition, the roar of traffic dropping to a low burble, the road melting into the blackness except for scattered illumination from street or house. Without warning, I caught a faint outline, a sudden movement. I craned forward, strained my eyes. Nothing.

Apart from the reddish glow of a cigarette.

I stood perfectly still, mesmerised. I squinted, trying to make out a face, but it was swathed in a spooky haloed glow from the streetlight. Was it him? Could he see that I was watching him watching me? Something buckled inside. Was this the ultimate connection?

Silence roiled around me. Shaken, I retreated behind the drapes, rested my head against the wall, and closed my eyes. My heart clattered in my chest. My skin crawled with goosebumps. Make notes, Simon said. Log times and locations. Think, I ordered myself. Use your mind. *He* wants you to see him because it's critical to the game.

I clenched both fists, willing myself to confront the fear writhing inside me. Whatever happened now, I would not walk away. I would not let it go. I would not be beaten.

I snatched back the curtain. The light from outside splashed across my face and arms. Whoever it was had vanished.

SIXTEEN

Kirsten Matherson was plucked from obscurity at the age of twelve to begin a fledgling career in modelling. So far so inoffensive, I thought, reviewing the girl's notes. Then came the hitch: the agency in question didn't like the naturally occurring changes in the girl's body shape as she reached puberty. By the time she was fifteen, Kirsten had resorted to a combination of starvation and amphetamines to fulfil the skeletal proportions required by her employer. Three years later, her physiology screwed up, anorexia nervosa had ravaged her. Thin, wispy, close-cropped blond hair clung to her skull for dear life. Luminous dark eyes dominated her face. Transparent skin stretched over bones as tight as a drum. In spite of the heat, she wore a loose-fitting sweater that swallowed her up, and when she hitched up the sleeve to scratch her arm, a fine covering of downy hair lay like animal pelt, the body's response to low body mass. She sat perched on the edge of the seat, hands resting in her shallow lap.

"So how are you feeling today?" I asked.

"All right."

"Cathy says you're doing well, eating more, and I gather Jim's cut down your drug treatment."

"Yeah."

I scanned the notes. "You've put on a couple of pounds. Does that bother you?"

"No."

"Not frightened?"

"Not especially."

"That's good. What about the exercise regime?"

"Nothing more than a walk in the grounds."

I smiled approval. "And the lists?"

Kirsten had arrived with a thick wad of notebooks in which every item of food and drink consumed during the previous three years was noted. At the suggestion that they might be taken away, she'd screamed and yelled for almost an hour.

"I've cut down."

"Terrific." I beamed, genuinely pleased. "Last time we talked about what you wanted to do when you leave here. We discussed the possibility of you going on to further education, remember?"

The girl shifted her weight, listless, her focus on a far away point beyond the room or even the building. I attempted to coax her.

"You said you were interested in textiles, fashion design."

"I wouldn't be good enough."

"Why not?"

"Haven't got the right qualifications."

"Then get them."

"I *said* I'm not clever enough." There was sudden rage in her voice. Perfectionism was a hallmark of the condition so I wasn't surprised, but I was taken aback by what she said next.

"I'm not a good person." Her mouth pinched into a thin, brittle line.

"Who says?"

"I *know*."

"Is this about not wanting to take risks, about a fear of failing?"

She eyed me with sullen dislike.

"Kirsten, who are you letting down exactly?"

The door suddenly flew open. "Sorry to interrupt," Jim burst in, unusually brisk, "but I need you to come with me."

"Why?" I suppressed a streak of irritation.

"There's something you need to see."

"Can't whatever it is wait?"

"Frankly, no."

I stifled a huge sigh. "Excuse me a moment, Kirsten."

Spotting an opportunity to escape, the girl got to her feet and began to shamble out of the room. Jim raised the flat of his hand. "Sorry, can you stay here please?"

"Fuck's sake."

"Don't you *fuck's sake* me," Jim snarled.

I stared. Whatever the provocation, Jim never swore at clients. Kirsten plumped back down.

"What's this all about?" I hissed, following at speed. He didn't reply, simply stalked in the direction of the common room. At his approach a gaggle of girls scattered. Clocking me, they burst into laughter, hands smothering their mouths. I knew instantly that I was the figure of fun. My face flamed with historic hurts.

"That's enough," Cathy said, crossing the hall out of nowhere and shooing them into the garden. I tried to catch her eye, but Cathy refused to meet my gaze.

Jim entered the common room, shut the door behind us, and pointed in the direction of the computer screen. I approached and, winded, stopped. It was hard not to fasten on the image of a semi-naked woman wearing a black suspender belt and stockings, back arched, nipples erect, one hand cupping a breast, legs apart revealing a wide open vagina.

"Christ!"

"Pretty graphic, isn't it?"

"I don't understand," I spluttered in confusion. "How? Who?"

"Emailed from an anonymous source."

"What?"

"Apparently, it's perfectly possible."

"But, but," I protested, half winded. "It's not me."

"It looks like you. I mean …"

"It's my face," I snapped. "Some crank has done this." Before Jim could protest, I launched forward, hit delete, emptied the trash, and yanked the plug and cable out of the back of the computer.

"That wasn't very smart," he muttered.

"But very fucking satisfying." I sat down with a thud.

Jim grabbed the back of another chair, scraping its legs across the floor and, twisting the seat around in front of me, sat astride as though riding a horse. "A manipulated computerised image?"

"Of course it's a manipulated image."

"It's okay, Kim," Jim said softly. "What you do in your downtime isn't an issue here."

I gaped at him as though he were suddenly speaking in tongues. "I didn't do it. It's not me." Hot tears of shame and anger sprang down my cheeks. Jim gallantly pulled out a clean handkerchief. I took it, blew my nose vigorously, and let out a wail. "Oh God, how many girls saw it?"

"That doesn't matter now."

"*Doesn't matter*?" More unsettling, I wanted to waste the person responsible. Unfamiliar with such extremes of emotion in myself, I felt as if my mind had split in two. Had I reverted to type under pressure? Had I been so conditioned by the masculine concept of venting rage, striking first and talking later? I shook my head. My current response had no connection to my past. Mine was simply a classic reaction: shock, fear, followed by anger. It's how we all behaved, I assured myself, feeling shaky.

"I have a first-class honours degree in damage limitation," he said, clearly trying to calm me down. I didn't want to be calm. I wanted to shout, scream and yell. I wanted it to stop. "Sometimes stuff happens, Kim."

"Not to me," I said through clenched teeth. On the emotional spectrum, I was probably hitting around nine out of ten.

"Clearly, there are sexual overtones."

"I'll say." I was heartbroken. How could someone do this to me at my place of work? How could some sick bastard undermine me in this way? I'd worked so hard to succeed and build a professional reputation, to be good at my job. When everything else was going to rat shit, work had always provided a solid ballast to my life. I enjoyed my work at the Lodge and at Bayshill. I liked the people and the clients. And now this? Suddenly, every obstacle I'd overcome, every relationship forged, every achievement won felt worthless. The stranger with malice in mind was threatening to rip away everything. I would not let him.

Jim continued to talk. "And that's a tad worrying. Could it be an old lover, perhaps? Someone scorned?"

Immediately, a light went on in my head. What had Simon said? *IT.*

"Yeah?" Jim said, spotting recognition in my eyes.

"Leave it with me. I'll check it out," I said, determined and feeling a sudden surge of energy.

"Because if it's a creature from your past, we'll prosecute."

"Prosecute?" I said, aghast. "I'd have to go to court."

"And we'll back you all the way."

"I don't know, Jim. What about the publicity?" Then another possibility grabbed me, an easier possibility, a possibility that didn't pack an emotional punch; one that made sense, and one that did not require legal or criminal intervention, or a jury staring at a grotesque replica of myself. I shuddered at the thought of some techie police officer mining the computer and retrieving what I prayed to God was irretrievable.

I looked Jim in the eye. "It could be one of the girls. You know how highly strung they can be, that they don't always appreciate support." I failed to curb the expectant note in my voice. "Obviously, if that's the case, I wouldn't dream of…"

Jim shook his head and held my gaze. Horribly weary, as though someone had injected me with anaesthetic, I crumpled. The thought of disclosing all to Jim and, by default, Cathy did not appeal. None of this was my fault, yet I felt inexplicable shame. Another textbook psychological response to what was going on around me, I recognised. Not that it helped. How could I treat my clients in the future knowing what they'd seen?

"I'm not technologically adept," Jim said, "so I don't know how easy or difficult it is to post an image. I'm pretty certain the police have dedicated officers who—"

"No," I burst out, alarmed that Jim had given voice to my most immediate fear. "Absolutely no way."

"Kim, I appreciate—"

"You don't. You have no idea. I feel violated."

"But it's not you," Jim said, grabbing hold of me by the shoulders. "You said so. It's just a picture."

"If it's *just* a picture," I said, "why are we sitting here having this conversation? It's got my head on it, my face, my…" I struggled to get it out, "… scars."

Jim let out a slow breath and dropped his hands. "All right, I respect your wishes, but if anything else happens, we're going to revisit it."

"Deal?" I felt like I was driving a trade-off with Mephistopheles.

"On one condition."

I inclined my head.

"You tell me everything."

"There is nothing to—"

"Everything," he said through tight lips.

SEVENTEEN

I EMERGED AN HOUR later, the afternoon sessions postponed, the day wrecked. My confidence and status at work undermined, I shot out of the building as though rabid wolves snapped at my heels. Was this a warm-up, a preliminary to violence? Was he plotting something truly awful? I nibbled thoughtfully on a nail. Assailed by a paralysis of confused feelings, and recognising every damned one of them, I settled into a slow trudge. Familiar streets that usually brought a smile to my face seemed somehow blighted. Buskers along the way sang out of tune. When Connor, a homeless old guy and permanent fixture near the smarter shops, called a hello to me, I almost passed him by.

"Sorry," I garbled.

"You all right, Kim?" Connor looked up at me from his pole position on the pavement. I'd slipped him the odd sandwich and hot drink on previous occasions and we'd struck up a rough kind of friendship. He'd hit hard times two decades before when his business failed, his wife left, and he'd been done for assault. After a short spell in prison he'd wound up on the street. What was supposed to be a temporary event had turned into a lifestyle.

"Yeah, lost in thought, nothing more." I pulled out a couple of quid from my bag and pressed the coins into his hand. His skin was the colour and texture of bark. The tang of unwashed clothes and skin hit my nostrils full force.

"God bless you," Connor said. Chris's "waif and strays" remark hammered through my brain. Part of me wanted to call him, to tell him what had happened at the Lodge. The other feared his reaction.

Crossing the road to the apartment block, Lizzie was up ahead. She spun around, a mass of smiles. "We've got someone lined up for the weekend. Cash buyer. Apparently the area's perfect and there's no problem with the flat being ground floor. Looks promising."

"Good for you." At least something was going right for somebody. "Have you found anywhere?"

"We don't dare. You know what it's like. You're afraid to get excited because you know it could all fall through in an instant. It's such a stressful experience."

"I'll be sorry to see you go, but I hope it all works out."

Remembering Simon's advice, I checked for shadows that didn't exist, eyes swivelling to all corners of the sunshine-filled staircase. Bunch of keys digging into my palm and at the ready, poised, I heard the phone beeping as soon as I stepped inside.

Catching sight of my reflection in the hall mirror, I saw that, in the space of twenty-four hours, I'd developed lines. My skin looked waxy. My eyelids drooped. Fear, I thought. What the hell had happened to my determination to nail my stalker? How come he'd so easily knocked the fight out of me and damaged my resolve?

I slumped down on the sofa, eyeing the phone. I didn't know how long I stayed like that, watching the flashing light, listening to my own shallow breathing and the insistent cheep of the messaging service. In the end, I got up, crossed the floor and went for it.

The phone revealed two messages. The first from Chris: "Away for a couple of days escorting a grubby group of eight years to Huckham for a *team-building* exercise." This raised a smile. Sceptical of using corporate terms for school activities, Chris particularly disliked the trend to upgrade the title of secondary schools, designed for eleven- to eighteen-year-olds, to university status, eighteen plus, and to exchange art or technology blocks for *campuses*. "If you can't get hold of me, it's because communications out there in the wilds are pretty poor. Best if I give you a call as soon as I get back. Lots of love." I felt a sick pang of disappointment at not being able to talk to him. Fed up, I listened to the next message and brightened. "Hi, Kim, it's Simon. Sleuthing on your behalf has paid off. Phil is working in London. Do you want to talk?"

You bet. As soon as Simon picked up, I came straight out with it. "Give me Phil's number."

"Has something happened?"

I hesitated, foolishly revealing the lie, and made a mental note to get better at deception. "No, I simply need to rule him out."

"Is this a good idea?"

"Yes."

"Only then he'll know that I've given you his number."

"Is there a problem with that?"

"Tell you what. I'll phone him and explain."

"Explain what exactly?"

"Look, Kim. I'm in the middle of something right now. Give me five minutes, and I'll call you back."

"With Phil's number."

"Yes," he said, defeated. "All right."

"You promise?"

"You have my word."

I headed to the fridge, took out a bottle, and poured a glass of wine. Taking it over to the window seat, I sat down and stared outside. Rather than dropping away, the air had reached new levels of humidity. It looked like a whiteout, the trees and shrubbery shrivelled in the nuclear heat. You'd have to be suicidal to venture out there for pleasure, I thought.

Twenty-five minutes passed. I drained the glass and poured another. My stomach jittered at the thought of speaking to Phil after all this time. I reminded myself that I was intelligent, a shrink, for God's sake, impossible to be pushed around, let alone manipulated, and yet my marriage had once reached a point where I felt that I couldn't breathe without permission. Chill tiptoed along my spine. Was there something about me that invited that kind of attention? Was it my fault, a defect in my personality? Was it happening all over again, only this time with someone I didn't even know? Even if Phil were guilty, he wouldn't admit it, not on a telephone, not ever.

The phone rang shrill. I picked up. "Hi, Si."

"Kim Slade?"

I frowned and tried to connect the voice to a face. The caller had a precise and controlled way of speaking. "Who is this?"

"We haven't met."

I reached for a connection: male, low pitch, cultured tone. Then it walloped me.

"You," I gasped. "Kyle Stannard."

"I contacted the phone-in."

"You also concocted that vile computer image."

He didn't speak for a beat. "What image?"

I couldn't work out whether it was confusion or deception. "The pornographic one, you liar."

"Are you mad?"

My responding laugh was hollow.

"Why would someone do something like that?" he said.

"That's my next question."

"Kind of embarrassing, I guess."

"Not for someone like you, *I guess*. Isn't that the sort of thing you get up to on photo-shoots? Drugs and sex and rock and roll?"

"Your information is out of date." Stannard's voice was as cold as chilled water. "I left the game some time ago."

"So what *game* are you playing now?"

"I haven't a cl—"

"You admit you sent it?"

"I already told you, no."

"Why are you following me, standing outside my flat, sending me ..." I faltered. "... things?"

"Kim, I'm not."

"Don't you fucking use my name."

"Why not? That's what you're called."

Smart mouth. "What do you want Mr. Stannard?"

"Your professional help."

"I only treat women with anorexia." Which wasn't true, but hey.

"I saw you on that television programme."

So that's how this all started.

"I really admire your style and courage."

Flattery will get you nowhere.

"We're two of a kind, you see. I thought we might meet informally for a drink unless, of course, that might upset your boyfriend."

"I don't do drinks with clients." I sidestepped the issue of boyfriends.

"Well, I'm not strictly a client, am I?"

No, you're a stalker.

"There's a terrific little cocktail bar off Cambray Place."

"Which bit of my answer don't you understand? I only work in a limited sphere. You need a different sort of professional." Someone who can cure your delusion. "I can give you names."

"Won't you make an exception for me?" It sounded more threat than plea.

"No."

"You're supposed to help people, aren't you?" The tone rattled with accusation. "Why won't you help me?"

Cut the call. Now. Hang up. Just do it.

"People generally do as I say. I've waited a long time to find the right person."

"I'm not the right—"

"And I always get what I want."

My vision snarled up. The walls slurred and blurred. "Then I'm sorry to be the first to disappoint you."

"I don't do disappointment, Kim. Not in my vocabulary." He hung up.

EIGHTEEN

ALEXA PHONED TEN MINUTES before my working day got going. She raced straight to the point with no gear changes in between.

"Brooks has organised an entire media campaign against me."

I blinked for two reasons. One, I had my own shit to deal with. Two, it didn't seem very likely. Brooks surely had better things to do with his time and, even on a cursory acquaintance, he didn't strike me as a vindictive sort.

She continued, "People are saying the most horrible things about me on Facebook and Twitter."

"Then don't read them."

"But these are supposed to be my friends."

Adept at lowering the emotional temperature of my mostly teenage clients, I struggled with Alexa. "Anyone who stoops to such levels isn't your friend. Ignore them. Better still, delete them."

"Does he hate me so much?" It came out like a wail. I had an image of ululating women in foreign climes.

"I'm sure he doesn't," I said.

"But…"

"Alexa, I'm so sorry, but I have to go. I'm at work."

"You'll call me when you get a chance?"

"Of course," I said. No sooner than I'd cut the call, I received another.

"You must be in trouble."

My stomach flipped. What had Simon told Phil? "Hi. Thanks for calling me."

"I haven't heard from you or your lawyer in ten years," Phil said.

I tried to laugh. It came out mangled. "Are you well?"

"What is it, Kim? I'm a busy guy, stuff going on." His tone implied that he was doing fine until he heard I needed to speak to him. After the call from Stannard the previous night, the conversation with Phil seemed like a pointless waste of everyone's time, but now he'd phoned I thought I might as well cover all the bases. "Have you visited Cheltenham lately, or attempted to look me up?"

"Are you cracked? Why would I do that?"

"It doesn't matter, a long-shot."

He let out a chill laugh. "You must be really in trouble."

I privately agreed, said good-bye, and instructed the Bayshill receptionist to hold off all calls from anyone she didn't immediately recognise without first checking with me. I made the same arrangement with Cathy Whitcombe at Ellerslie Lodge.

During the morning I saw three clients. The hours passed with the same gait as a dying snail.

At lunchtime, Chris called. Giddy with relief, I told him about the phone-in. I told him about Kyle Stannard. I didn't tell him about the pornographic image.

"He's clearly kinked. Go to the police. They can do him for harassment."

"He denies everything."

"He threatened you."

"But it will be my word against his. It's not as if I recorded the phone call."

"Do it, Kim. It will frighten him off."

"Will it?" Somehow I didn't think so.

"This is ludicrous," he burst out. "If you do nothing it will continue. Now he's got his hooks into you, he's not going to go away." Chris was silent for a moment. "Is anything else wrong?" There was a peculiar catch in his voice as if he expected trouble.

"Not really."

"Something's up," he said, wary.

"I've already messed up once this morning." Twice, actually, but I wasn't going to mention Alexa's *cri de coeur.*

"Oh?"

"I got Phil to phone me."

"Okay." He took it a lot better than I'd expected. "Why?" Chris said.

I pulled a face. I could hardly tell Chris about the IT connection. "Because he's nasty enough to pop back out of the woodwork."

"Got you."

"Anyway, it's not him," I said briskly.

He thought for a moment. "Why not get Simon to find out about Stannard?"

"Like what?"

"Where he lives, what he's doing with his life."

"I'm not sure that's a good idea."

His momentary silence gave the impression that he was cross with me for not agreeing to his suggestion.

"You're interested in him, aren't you?"

"Interested?" I said, bewildered.

"In Stannard."

"That's rubbish. I don't give a damn about him."

"But he intrigues you."

"Don't tell me what I feel." And don't suggest that I feel sorry for him. "Look, I have to go. I'll be late."

Chris wasn't easily dismissed. "What are your movements for the rest of the day?"

"Why do you want to know?"

"Keeping tabs."

"I'm at work, Chris."

Unsettled, I left the Bayshill Clinic and stepped outside onto a cement drive. It felt hotter than ever. The air tasted of diesel and petrol fumes. En route to the Lodge, I called Simon, told him I'd got nowhere with Phil and, reluctantly complying with Chris's suggestion, asked if he could put his soldierly skills to good use.

"You want me to check out Kyle Stannard?"

"I can hardly check him out myself. It would show unhealthy interest."

"Damn right. Leave it with me. I'll do my best."

I crossed the road, each step marred by my last conversation with Chris and the trepidation that something else was about to happen. What if my stalker had stuck something even more unspeakable on the windscreen?

I skirted the entrance to the Lodge and walked around the back to the parking bays, keen to get out of the burning sun. Jim's Morgan, highly polished in racing green, glinted in the strong sunlight. The Celica should have been next to it. Except there was no car; only empty space. I raced up and down, checking, running through events in my mind. Yes, I'd driven the car there after the phone-in. Yes, I'd parked it here, right here. But it was gone. Fear flared and expanded into anger.

I tore back inside and spoke to Cathy.

"Are you sure?" she said.

"You can't mislay several grand's worth of vehicle by accident."

"True."

"Cath, I'd be grateful if you didn't tell Jim. At least, not yet."

She cast me a sympathetic look, paused a few moments to think, and then took charge. "You give the police a ring. I'll take a walk outside." To be honest, I could have kissed her.

It took me five minutes to get through and explain my predicament. I was told I could expect someone to be with me later.

"How much later?"

"Can't really say, madam."

"Will it be today?"

"Possibly not. I'm sorry, but we're dealing with a major incident. Could you give me a number we can call you on?" I gave my mobile number. Feeling frustrated enough to kick something, I sat down hard and rested my head in my hands. Stannard had taken a step too far. He had in effect committed a criminal act. I brightened. Hello, I thought, that was a good thing. Whereas before I had nothing really concrete to go on, now I could hand the police a solid piece of evidence and press charges.

The door to my office swished open and Cathy appeared. "Found it."

"What? Where?"

"Good news: it's tucked under the shade of a plane tree. Bad news: it's parked on double yellow lines in Vittoria Walk and you've picked up a parking ticket."

I gawped, mystified. "Is it all right?"

"No dents, no scratches, good as new." Cathy looked at me uncertainly. "Are you sure you didn't leave it there? You've got a lot going on right now."

I covered my true feelings by flashing a smile. "You're right. My mistake. What an idiot. Thanks, Cathy, you're a star. Would you like to ask Ellen to pop in?"

NINETEEN

THE CAR WAS EXACTLY where Cathy said it was. No marks. No signs of abuse. Wondering madly if the vehicle might be booby-trapped, I crouched down and peered underneath, except I had no idea what I was looking for. Using the remote, I opened the driver door. Gingerly, I climbed inside, the soft lining of my stomach catching at the thought of Stannard sitting in my seat, his body on the pale grey leather, his hands on the steering wheel where mine rested. I examined the ashtray and glove compartment, searched for notes and gifts, but there was nothing. Even the air smelt undisturbed. There was no telltale scent of aftershave or cologne. How had he got hold of a key?

I drove back to the Lodge, re-parked the car, tore off the penalty notice, and returned to Montpellier on foot. The insane heat had died down. People were sitting in outdoor cafés and wine bars for early drinks. The streets felt relaxed. Adopting a siege mentality, I popped into a delicatessen and bought salami, Parma ham, a slab of waxy Gran Padano cheese, purple-skinned olives, sun-dried tomatoes, and artichokes marinated in olive oil, plus two bottles of Barolo and two bottles of creamy-dry sparkling white Prosecco. Minutes later, I was toeing open the door to the apartment, arms aching, chin resting protectively on the wine, my first thought to get the Prosecco chilled as quickly as possible. It wasn't until I'd stashed the food, and was coming out of the kitchen that I noticed the single typed A4-sized brown envelope on the floor poking out from underneath the door to the apartment. I stood anchored to the carpet. Had he descended while I was unloading shopping, or had it been there all along and I'd failed to spot it? From that distance I could make out that there was no stamp, no postal markings, only my name typed on the envelope in capitals. I didn't need to be an Einstein to work out that someone had delivered it by hand. And I had more than a rough idea who.

Wary, I picked it up and ripped it open. Inside was a single sheet of white paper.

> THANKS FOR THE LOAN OF YOUR GORGEOUS HEAP OF METAL. (I WAS TEMPTED TO SPEND THE NIGHT IN IT—ONLY JOKING!!) NO, REALLY IT WAS VERY GOOD OF YOU TO LET ME BORROW IT AND I JUST WANTED YOU TO KNOW THAT YOUR KINDNESS IS APPRECIATED. WHY ELSE WOULD I SEND YOU CHOCS—SORRY ABOUT ROLAND—MY IDEA OF A JOKE. TALKING OF WHICH, IS THERE ANYTHING ELSE YOU'D LIKE, SOMETHING MAYBE TO TURN YOU ON? YOU LOOK SO GOOD NAKED. HAVE A THINK BECAUSE I'M NOT ENTIRELY SURE WHAT YOUR TASTES ARE IN THAT DIRECTION. I HAVE MY OWN IDEAS, OF COURSE, BUT I DON'T WANT TO SPOIL OUR RELATIONSHIP BY OFFENDING YOU. DON'T WORRY ABOUT LETTING ME KNOW. I'M

NEVER FAR AWAY AND, ALTHOUGH I'M NO SHRINK, I CAN READ YOUR MIND.

Throwing the printed sheet of paper onto the coffee table, I scooped my keys back up and raced out of the flat. Taking the stairs two at a time, I tore off towards a small garage and lock-up in Lansdown, heart lifting at the sound of heavy rock signifying that they hadn't yet packed up for the day.

I stood for what seemed an age as a mechanic finished working on a battered-looking Vauxhall Cavalier, feet sticking out from underneath. Another young guy, an apprentice maybe, poked about in the innards of an Escort. Patches of oil spread over the ground, rainbow-coloured in the late afternoon sun.

My focus fell on scrap metal and tyres, monkey wrenches and jacks. Nobody paid me attention. Finally in frustration, I approached the mechanic buried underneath the Cavalier and tapped the sole of his heavy boot with one foot. The heels moved forward and a lined face popped out.

The guy rolled to one side then scrabbled to his feet, wiping oily hands on dark blue overalls. The top three buttons were undone, exposing an expanse of ghostly white skin. His head was shaved, pouched eyes narrowed to slits. Drink problem, I guessed.

Staring hard at me, he addressed the young guy. "You going to be there long, Mark?"

"Nah, almost done."

"The bloke wants to collect in twenty minutes." He looked me up and down and pulled out a packet of cigarettes. "Now what can I do you for?"

"I wondered if you could help me," I started hesitantly.

"Maybe, maybe not."

This wasn't quite the response I was after. I suppose showing up out of nowhere seemed strange. I cleared my throat, and began again. "My name's Kim Slade. I live over there," I said, waving my hand in the general direction of home. No idea why I'd done that. He couldn't have looked more disinterested if he'd tried. "I'd like to pick your brains," I said, getting to the point.

He let out a short earthy laugh. "Sounds nasty." His hands shook when he lit up.

"The thing is, you see," I burbled awkwardly, "someone moved my car."

"Vehicle theft is pretty hot around here."

"It wasn't stolen."

"A joyrider?"

"Maybe," I said, evasive. Admitting to it being taken and left a couple of streets from where I worked would sound plain weird.

"Out of interest, what sort of motor?"

"A Celica."

"Nice. Do much damage?"

"That's the point. There's not a scratch on it, so how would a stranger get in, do you think?"

He blew out a big cloud of smoke, some of it gusting my way. "Was it alarmed?"

"Yes."

"So he couldn't have run a wire inside and disconnected the central locking?"

"Not without creating a racket."

"Then there's only one possibility."

"What's that?" My voice quickened.

"He got in the same way as everyone else, darlin'. He had a set of keys."

"But that's impossible."

"You sure you didn't leave them in the ignition?"

"Of course not."

"Amazing how many people do," he snickered. "Isn't that right, Mark?" He looked across at the young apprentice.

"Yeah, too right."

"Is there any way he could get a key cut?" I said to the older man.

"A skilled locksmith can rustle up a set of keys in less than an hour, but they generally need the car in place."

"So the car has to be stolen first?"

"Uh-huh."

He eyed me in a way I couldn't quite fathom, took a drag of his cigarette, narrowed his eyes against the smoke, and scuffed the ground with his boot. "Have you reported it?"

"Nothing to report." I met his eye.

Two thin streams of smoke drifted out of his nostrils. "Villains in the old days would break into a car, hot-wire it, take it to a dodgy motor repair shop, and get the locksmith to pull out the ignition and check the serial number against the make and numbers listed in the car's manual. Once it's matched, he can work out the key specification. Now it's all more technological. Not half so easy."

"And there's really no other way?"

He looked down, kicked the ground again, jettisoning a cloud of dust.

"No," he said slow-eyed, "not that I can think of."

TWENTY

Sparkling white wine seemed the most inappropriate drink—this was hardly a celebration—but I opened a bottle anyway and poured a glass. Someone had stolen my keys. Only one person held another set: Chris.

Glugging steadily, I picked up the letter and flopped down with it on the sofa. Unlike the pasted-together note attached to the chocolates, the script was more specific, the thrust personal, sexual and delusional, the language familiar. A stranger reading it could be forgiven for thinking that there was a preexisting relationship.

Shit.

There must be some kind of mistake. Chris wouldn't do something like that. Didn't stack up with the Chris I knew. But what about the one I didn't? I suddenly recalled an evening not long after he'd moved in. We'd both had far too much to drink.

"So what happened?" I said.

"I was taken into care when I was five."

"Do you remember your parents?"

"I remember my dad. He beat the hell out of me." Chris spoke in cool tones. I recognised the device—his way of distancing himself from the violence. Accustomed to muting my own responses, I still struggled to conceal my dismay.

"And what about your mum?"

"Drunk, or incapable, or frightened—take your pick."

Jesus, I thought. "Horrible for you," I said.

He took another drink. "I was lucky. I got farmed out to foster parents. They were nice people."

I flooded with warm relief for him. "That's good."

"Yeah," he said almost dreamy before a dark cloud appeared to cross his field of vision.

"And?" I pressed.

"I fucked up."

I frowned.

Chris looked me square in the eye. "I had a temper, like my dad. They couldn't cope. Five years later, I was back in the system."

I ran my fingers through my hair. So that explained the petty vandalism. Such a familiar story; such a sad waste.

"In common with most youngsters, I got ejected when I was eighteen," Chris continued. "Told to go and stand on my own two feet."

"But by then you'd already been taken under Mr. H.'s wing, right?"

"Yeah," Chris smiled. "My guardian angel, a bit like you, in fact."

So that's when Chris's return to the land of the living began. Plenty of youngsters went off the rails and became well-adjusted adults, I reminded myself, which meant that Chris was innocent and had taken no part in moving my car. Deliberate, a classic piece of manipulation, Stannard had to be behind the Houdini trick. How he'd got hold of my keys I hadn't yet worked out.

I finished my drink, helped myself to another even though I knew it wasn't a great idea, sat back down, and took a deep swallow. Immediately, my mobile phone blared. Fired up with booze, I picked it up, spoiling for a fight.

"Hello, is that Kim Slade?"

"Yes," I snapped, "and before you utter another word—"

"It's Police Constable Cunningham. I understand you reported a missing vehicle this morning."

I sat up straight. Making a conscious effort to formulate the words in my brain before they poured out of my mouth, I said, "It's been found."

"Oh good," he said, in a way that suggested he was keen to cut the call and avoid a mountain of paperwork.

"Thing is," I said, "I'm being stalked."

TWENTY-ONE

TELLING THE POLICE WAS every bit as bad as I'd expected. It was like climbing a mountain with a Steinway grand piano strapped to my back.

PC Paul Cunningham had an open and trusting face, like a cherub. The accompanying officer was an altogether different proposition: older, short hair the colour of mercury fillings, his face and manner worldly. He had a firm handshake and introduced himself as PC David Grant.

I invited them to sit down. They sat opposite me. Grant took out a notebook. Cunningham told me to take my time. It was the sort of thing I might say to a client. It felt strange to be on the receiving end. Having exchanged the wine for water, I took a sip and began to speak. I believed that once I got going, it would be easy. It wasn't. At the mention of the pornographic image, a host of questions ensued. I couldn't imagine what it must be like to be a rape victim.

Cunningham sucked the end of his pen and addressed Grant. "Posted from a site, do you reckon?"

"Then dumped."

"Dumped?" I said.

"Taken down. Technology now means that someone can send anonymous emails that self-destruct in twenty-four hours. Gives us no time to trace the source, let alone the person behind an obscene image. Have you received any personally abusive emails?"

I shook my head.

They fired more questions. When I'd finished, the cops did a recap.

"You're a psychologist," Grant said, scribbling a note.

"I know what you're thinking, but I've never met this guy professionally or in any other capacity."

"Stannard?"

"Yes."

Grant looked perplexed. "Then how come you're sure it's him?"

I looked from one to the other. "Of course it's him. He's the guy who called the phone-in. He pestered me at home. He was very clear about not taking no for an answer."

"But he denied sending the image," Grant stressed.

"Because he's lying."

Both men exchanged glances.

"Look, I'm not trying to stitch the evidence together." I flicked a nervous smile. "However you look at it, Stannard's the only rogue element. My life was going along nice and smoothly until this random stranger crossed my path. What are you suggesting, that it's someone I know?" I stared at them incredulously. Out of nowhere, a voice inside whispered Chris's name.

"We're not suggesting anything," Grant said. "We're simply asking questions."

I did my level best not to visibly bristle. I didn't quite pull it off.

"You'll know that to take and move someone's car without damaging it is no mean feat," Grant pushed back. "How did this man you allege you've never met get hold of the keys?"

"Maybe he has contacts, a friendly locksmith, I don't know." I felt as if I had a wet mattress where my brain should be. I knew I wasn't making sense and yet felt incapable of clarity. All at once I felt about eight years old, trying to stand my ground against my father.

"Any sign of break-in here?" Cunningham glanced around the room.

I shook my head.

"And Stannard hasn't made direct contact with you since you told him you wouldn't meet?"

"No."

"And that was yesterday?"

"Last night, yes."

His expression suggested it wasn't much to go on. Heat spread up my neck and marched across my scalp.

"Can I see the letter again?" Grant asked.

I showed it to him, watching his face for a response. He gave a brief nod and looked at Cunningham. Excluded, I found it impossible to read either of their expressions.

"Unsigned," Cunningham said.

"Does it make a difference? He's hardly going to sign it 'yours truly', is he?" I said with a forced bright smile. "It's Stannard, I'm sure of it."

Cunningham's face bore the mark of diplomacy. "He looks a fair possibility from what you've told us."

Hurrah.

"Have you shown the note to anyone else?" Grant asked.

"No."

"We could try to lift prints off it." Cunningham said to his colleague. He appeared to float the idea in an abstract way.

"Wouldn't hold your breath. If he's smart, he'll have worn gloves."

"Run tests on the car?"

Grant pulled a face. "Techs have got a lot on and he's unlikely to be on our database."

My dismay turned to frustration. "Can you be sure of that?"

Grant shrugged. "Could put in a call, I guess," he said as if to appease me, "but can't promise anything. Means your car will be out of commission."

I smiled again. I really wanted to get them onside. "Is there a way you can track where the paper came from?"

Cunningham shook his head slowly. "It's bog-standard photocopier paper. It could have come from any number of computers."

I ran my fingers absently through my hair. "Might you get someone to profile the text?"

"'Fraid not. We don't have the resources on site," Grant said. "Cuts to funding, and suchlike," he added with a withering look. He waited a beat, his look thoughtful. "The letter suggests you already have a relationship."

"That's what he wants you to think." Come on, guys. Funding has nothing to do with brain function, does it? I looked at them imploringly. "How about you track Stannard down and pay him a visit?"

Neither looked convinced. Grant spoke, "If he lives outside Gloucestershire, we'll have to alert another constabulary."

"Oh," I said, taken aback.

"The image you received at work, can you print it out?"

"I deleted it. Emptied the trash too," I murmured, aware that my own brain function could seem compromised.

Grant held my gaze in a vise. "Chocolates?"

I chewed my lip. "I threw them away, and the note with it, but I've still got the mirror," I added, triumphant. "It's in my desk at the clinic."

"Not much to go on."

"No," I said, spirits momentarily crushed. Did they think I was making it all up? For a brief, insane moment, I wondered if I were delusional.

Cunningham waved the letter. "Can we keep this?"

I consented with an eager nod.

"You say you split your time between Devon and Cheltenham?"

"I work here but drive down every weekend."

"And nothing's happened there?"

"No."

"Interesting." Grant interjected. I smiled. *Interesting* was good. "Do you have a boyfriend or partner, Miss Slade?"

"He lives in Devon."

"Name?"

I told him.

"What's he do for a living?"

"Chris is a teacher." I wondered what they were thinking, how they were slotting the disparate pieces together. Would they try to force Chris into the jigsaw? Should *I* be forcing Chris into the picture?

"And how long have you been together?"

"Over three years, nearly four."

"No previous relationships that might be tied to what's happening now?" Grant's look was steady. They definitely weren't buying the Stannard theory.

"I was married and divorced ten years ago. My ex-husband, who I never see, is not part of this."

"Are you sure?"

"I've already spoken to him."

"Better have his name," Cunningham said breezily.

"Is it strictly necessary?"

"To be on the safe side."

I gave it.

"Do you use social networking sites, Twitter, Facebook, and so on?"

I shook my head. I recognised the dangers. Besides, the eternal pursuit of *moi* didn't do it for me.

"Anything else you've missed?" Grant said.

"Nothing I can think of. But there's something I wanted to ask you."

"Fire away."

"Can you stop it?"

Cunningham looked to Grant, who let out a breath.

"It depends on how fixated he is, doesn't it?" I said, grim.

"Worse case scenario, it can go on for years."

"I see." I should have felt undone. Couldn't afford to let that happen.

"If we have enough evidence, we can put him in prison for a substantial period of time, which gives you a reprieve, but it won't necessarily stop him in the long term," Grant said.

"I appreciate your honesty. And what are the chances of him turning nasty?"

Cunningham again looked to Grant. I waited expectantly.

"Most stalkers are not physically abusive. There's an increased tendency towards extreme violence in cases where celebrities are involved..."

"Mark Chapman and John Hinkley," I cut in.

"And stalkers who've had a previous sexual relationship with their victims, ex-boyfriends and husbands, for instance."

"So the chance of me being open to attack is small?"

"If it's a stranger," Grant said, "though there are exceptions." Again, the straight look. "It's a pity you didn't save the pornographic image."

There was a note of censure in his voice. Again, I considered whether they could take the computer and let loose a high-tech team on it, but as nobody suggested it, I wasn't keen to press the point. To be charitable, given the little they had to go on, I understood their caution.

"We take this sort of thing very seriously," Cunningham said, sensitive to my frustration, "and rest assured that your complaint will be fully investigated." He ran through the same list of precautions as Simon, adding that I should alert neighbours, friends, and people I worked with to what was going on if only to act as witnesses should something happen. "The more detail the better. Any more email messages, print out a hard copy and do not delete the original. Keep notes of anything you see or hear and try to alter your daily routines where possible."

"That's going to be difficult."

"Under no circumstances should you meet Stannard, or anyone else you suspect," Cunningham emphasised. "Don't pick up the phone—ever—before checking the caller number. Get a male to leave a recorded message on your main line along the lines that you can't come to the phone at the moment."

"Don't say you're not at home, as that might leave you vulnerable," Grant added. "If by accident you pick up and it's him, keep calm. Don't engage. If you come face to face with your stalker, don't confront him, but walk away, preferably to the nearest crowded area. If you're in fear of immediate threat, call us."

He said that they would give me a log number to quote so that, if I needed to alert them to any fresh developments, my call would come straight through. "We'll take a quick look round the flat, check your security, if you don't mind."

"Not at all."

I watched as they examined the windows and doors, paying particular attention to the wrought-iron balcony.

"It looks pretty secure," Cunningham said. "But you could do with a proper alarm system."

Mirroring Simon's advice, I remembered.

"How long have you lived here?" Grant said.

"Six years."

He looked around admiringly and turned his attention to the painting. "I see you're a fan of Vettriano."

"I like the drama, the suggestion of tangled relationships, the thought that you're not quite sure what's going on beneath the surface."

"Art imitating life."

"Yes," I agreed, uneasily meeting the unwavering expression in his eyes. I walked with them to the door. "Is this a common problem?"

Grant answered. "Stalking is one of the fastest-growing crimes."

"Any particular reason?"

"Access, opportunity, and the explosion in communication technology and social networking," he said. "Whether it's press and the power of the telephoto lens, or a public eager to know the latest, we all think we can have a slice of other people's lives. We regard it as our right. I'm afraid you're in good company. There are a lot of victims out there."

I flinched. "I'm no victim."

Grant looked at me with a cool grey stare. "I'm afraid you are, Miss Slade. You'd better learn to accept it. It might save your life."

TWENTY-TWO

I WATCHED THE SKY change from gold to pink to indigo. I'd finished off one bottle and opened another and felt stone cold sober. *Victim*, the most hideous word in the dictionary. I'd looked it up once. *Living creature sacrificed to a deity; person or thing injured or destroyed in seeking to attain an object.* Well, I wasn't destroyed way back then and I wasn't going to be destroyed now. Not by life. Not by him.

I tried to process what the police said. There were so many don'ts and must do's, so many rules in a game alien to me, a contest where the goals were not clear. It felt as if my life had suddenly changed and that made me sad. I realised how much I'd taken normal freedoms for granted.

Pouring the fresh glass of wine back into the bottle, I made coffee. Part of my job was to remember what was said in front of me even if it made little sense at the time. Grant's observation about Devon stuck in my mind. He'd described the lack of incidents there as *interesting*. I assumed he meant that Stannard hadn't yet worked out where I disappeared to at weekends. Perhaps it was only a matter of time. Or was Grant inferring something else? Was it possible that my two worlds were not as compartmentalised as I believed?

I took a shower, washed my hair vigorously, lavished my skin with lotions, and painted my toenails a defiant scarlet. I didn't phone Chris. After the spat that morning I decided to leave it. Dutifully, I returned Alexa's call and was relieved when it went straight to voice-mail. I left a pleasant message hoping that she was feeling better. The call from Simon came through on the landline as I was climbing into bed. I picked it up as soon as I heard his voice and told him about the car and the subsequent visit from the police.

"What were the cops like?"

"Like cops."

"Were they sympathetic?"

"As much as they could be, if that's what you mean. Told me all the same stuff, gave me the third degree, offered good advice."

"They're taking it seriously?"

"Sort of, although they don't appear to think Stannard a contender."

Simon said nothing, which I thought strange. "Why the call?" I said.

"I've found out about our man."

"That was quick."

"Easier than you'd believe; Stannard is in my current line of work."

"He's an estate agent?"

"Property developer. By all accounts, he's quite a sharp operator. Must be doing all right as he drives around in a Maserati. He specialises in old houses, does them up, full architectural spec, and sells them for a profit. He's got offices in Imperial Square, all very respectable."

I let out a breath. "That's close. Where does he live?"

"Wellington Square."

One of the most expensive areas in town, I notched.

Simon cleared his throat. "There's something else you should know." I sensed he was leading up to the punch line.

"Go on."

"There's no easy way to put this. The fight Stannard got himself involved in."

"What about it?"

"It resulted in a serious facial defect."

A sour taste bubbled up from the back of my throat and spread into my mouth. I didn't speak. I couldn't.

"Are you still there, Kim?"

"How serious?" I murmured.

"Right side of his face is fine."

"Left side?" I absently touched my skin, feeling the jagged ridge of scar tissue.

"The surgeon apparently cocked up during reconstructive surgery. He cut through a facial nerve. Stannard successfully sued the arse off him."

I didn't know what to say that wasn't blindingly obvious.

"Are you all right?"

"I'm swell," I snorted.

"Shall I come round?"

"There's no need. Looks like Mr. Creepy really has a deal with me."

"Sorry to be the bearer of bad tidings. Try and get some sleep. Anything else I can do, let me know."

There were three occasions that I could remember when I'd been advised to get some sleep. After Guy's fatal road accident, the night my father died, and the time I'd tracked down my mother and received a miserable audience. Each had been moments of high emotional drama. Sleep had evaded me then as it did now.

As I'd feared, my disfigurement was the connection.

I touched my face, felt the smooth, uninjured skin, then traced the line of raised scar tissue, the secret area where my hair refused to grow but was cleverly concealed by an excellent haircut. I ran a finger along where the lobe of my left ear should have been, hidden by day with a large clip-on earring. The physical trauma—the nightmare of changed dressings and skin grafts—remained deep in the past, buried. The emotional scars had closed over in a way I didn't quite understand. Friends suggested my father's sturdy influence. Others said that the character-building attributes of boarding school had stood me in good stead. I agreed with neither because only I could know that certain wounds never heal, that, by nature, I would always be drawn to the dark side.

I did my best. I played a part. I managed to fool myself in the same way that I fooled others. Sometimes, I even forgot my losses and my perpetual mourning for a life not of my choosing. I was the first to admit that nobody likes a person who wears grief like a second skin. It's wearing and boring and tedious. Smiley is best so smiley is what I did. Mostly it worked. My only certainty was that, in a society where a disproportionate value was weighted upon looks, I'd managed to overcome prejudice and find my own niche. Stannard wasn't so lucky.

In spite of what Stannard was doing, part of me felt pity. What had happened to him was catastrophic. I could understand his need to reach out, but he didn't want my help. He wanted a connection. He saw me as a soul mate. It all made perfect sense. And yet…

I leant back on the white fluffy pillows. It didn't entirely gel. The Stannard of my imagination was a social misfit, a loner and sad inadequate, not some intelligent clever-dick property magnate with oodles of money. And another thing—how in his busy schedule did he find time for his stalking activities?

The flat seemed a mass of noise in the silence. Pipes creaked. Air vents opened and closed. Fridges and machinery on standby hummed. I craned for the sound of incursion—the scrape of a key in a lock, the spring of shoes on carpet, the bump against an unfamiliar piece of furniture. At seven in the morning, a dog outside yapped, the boiler inside roared into life, charging up the hot water system. I twisted and turned. Some time later I must have dozed off, Grant's last words preying on my mind: *victim*.

TWENTY-THREE

Heather Foley had been trying to sell her house for months. She realised it might not be that easy. A six-bedroom pile in need of considerable refurbishment was not to everyone's taste, but she hoped that someone with vision would come along and snap it up. It would make a fine family home, or charming bed-and-breakfast, and the location was superb, an eager-faced estate agent told her one dark day in January.

Recently, there had been vague mutterings of another possible price reduction, the thought terrifying her almost as much as the prospect of spending another winter there. The leaky expanse of roof needed replacing, the fuel bills were astronomical, and mushrooms were taking root in one of the damp bedrooms. She'd tried to keep on top of the garden but, in spite of her best intentions, the lawns resembled savannah and the beds choked with weeds. She'd watched a plethora of property programmes and picked up that the secret of successful selling was to depersonalise one's home, get rid of the clutter and every vestige of personality. She'd given it a go. Apart from doing nothing to improve her prospects, she felt peculiar showing viewers around rooms with only the odd chair propped against the wall. She'd stripped the house to such an extent it felt like a museum without exhibits. To make up for the absence of home comforts, she found herself talking too freely, explaining her life story, desperation seeping through her every pore. She was sure prospective buyers had taken flight because of her mad ramblings and every month that passed without even a sniff of a reasonable offer represented another chunk of money down the drain. Her money. Her reward for years of servitude to a man who'd left her for a woman a year younger than their daughter.

She looked at her tired, puffy-eyed reflection in the dressing room mirror and wondered how and when age had crept up on her and distorted her looks. The trim figure had lost the plot from the waist down. Her thighs were of particular disgust to her. Mottled with cellulite, they made a chafing noise when she walked. Her hair was still quite good thanks to regular haircuts and tasteful tints, but her face, oh my God, she thought. Too many foreign holidays had scored indelible lines upon her skin and coarsened the texture. Worse, her features simply did not look as though they were in the right place any more. Most had migrated south. Her chin had lengthened while her lips had thinned. And where was the fine bone structure, the taut jawline? The shadows underneath her eyes made her look as if she had a kidney complaint.

She put the flat of her hands to her temple, yanking the skin up to where it used to be. Much, much better, she thought. She even felt like her old self again, a woman who was fun and dependable and confident. So that was the solution. Her face needed fixing. To her mind, it was no different to having a cap put on a wonky tooth, or taking antidepressants in a crisis. With the sale of the house, she'd have plenty of money to splash out on her new image. The technology was there so why shouldn't she avail herself of it? She'd read about the wonders of Botox, dermabrasion, laser treatment, fat injection, and acid peels, but apart from thinking she needed something more radical, she didn't want to go through excruciating pain if it wasn't going to yield first-class results. It was no use tinkering. Only a full face-lift could give her back her youth.

Forced to put her programme of rejuvenation on the back burner, her hopes for the future mired by the lack of interest in the only bit of capital she had, she hadn't bothered to sound out her friends. Anyway, she lacked courage. A ghoulish fascination for scalpel slaves and the latest procedures might take up hours of animated discussion over a cup of morning coffee, but it wasn't the sort of thing women talked about from a personal perspective. It wasn't smart. They'd much rather explain their looks in terms of good genes, the latest craze for Pilates, or vitamins. And there was the other barrier to cross. Should she have the bravado to reveal her secret desire, she'd be given the *You look fine as you are* line because, when it came to the crunch, no woman wanted a friend to look in better shape than she.

She reached for an advertisement she'd clipped from a magazine and read it again.

EMPOWER YOURSELF BY LOOKING YOUNGER

Thinking about cosmetic surgery? Then be reassured by one of our highly qualified representatives in the comfort of your own home free of charge. At The Parks clinic we have accredited plastic surgeons to carry out a wide range of cosmetic procedures to the highest standard. Beauty is only a phone call away. For an initial appointment…

(Financing available)

Her face creased into a smile. Her heart quivered with the small luxury of excitement.

At last she was in with a chance. She'd received the most interesting phone call that morning from Damian Fairweather, her estate agent. Mr. Stannard, a local property developer, wanted to view her house the following morning. He'd already done a drive-by, Fairweather said, and had fallen in love with it, but there was a slight difficulty.

"I appreciate that it's short notice but no-one from the firm is free to accompany the viewing."

Heather assured him it wasn't a problem.

Fairweather cleared his throat. "I feel that I should warn you that Mr. Stannard was in an accident some years ago. He has a slightly unusual appearance."

So what, she thought? She didn't care if he looked like Quasimodo as long as he bought the house. "It's not a problem, Mr. Fairweather."

"Good, good," he said with open relief. "I simply thought it fair to give you a heads-up. We regularly do business with him and I'm sure his interest is genuine."

For the first time in a while Heather Foley's heart surged with hope.

TWENTY-FOUR

"What's your favourite film?" Chris said.

"*Godfather II*," I replied.

"Why?"

"Because Michael Corleone's story . . ."

"The tale of a good guy corrupted by his family . . ."

"Could happen to any one of us," I smiled. "And yours?"

"1950s French movie *Les Diabolique*. Don't bother with the remake, which was grim."

I'd nodded at the time, feigning knowledge in a pathetic bid to impress him. Truth was, I was mesmerised by Chris. Later, I'd checked out the film. It was a nasty little tale of a vicious man, his wife, and a mistress. Essentially, the mistress and wife conspire against him, except there is a sting—the wife is secretly in league with her husband—and together, they frighten the mistress, who has a heart defect, to death. A trio of unhinged people, I'd concluded.

"Kim, are you up to speed?" Jim said.

I blinked. "Absolutely," I said, squashing the memory.

Having arrived bog-eyed for work, I'd spent the first hour slumped gratefully in a staff meeting while Jim held forth about schedules, treatments, and budgets. As soon as he'd finished I made a silent exit. Jim had other ideas. He marched straight into my office without knocking.

"About yesterday."

Fuck. "Cathy told you?"

"The police."

I attempted a smile but couldn't manage it. It all came out in a jumble. Stannard the stalker; Stannard not the stalker.

"The poor guy had botched surgery." As soon as the words left my mouth, I realised that Stannard had manipulated my emotions.

"Poor guy?" Jim sneered. "He's not the Elephant Man."

This time, I did smile. Jim's frankness cheered me. I felt nothing but affection for him.

"Don't you see, whatever the man's agenda, guilty or innocent, he's playing on your sympathies, manipulating your good intentions?"

I looked at him squarely. "His surgeon botched his reconstruction." I'd had an excellent plastic surgeon. My father had seen to that.

Jim didn't say anything for a moment. I could almost hear the electrical activity whirring behind his forehead.

"Setting aside Mr. S., I'll see what I can dig up about . . ." He hesitated, choosing his words with care. "The sort of person we're dealing with, from a psychological perspective."

"A loner, obsessive, delusional," I said. "Anything else you can bring to the trauma table, let me know."

Jim arched an amused eyebrow, opened his mouth to speak, and clearly thought better of it.

“I’ve let Cathy know my schedules at Bayshill and vice versa,” I said, businesslike.

“Good. We’ll do our best to screen things from this end. Whatever else, for God’s sake, Kim, try not to dwell on it. If you need my help in any way, or if you’re finding work difficult, let me know. You’ve got a holiday due soon, haven’t you?”

“Three weeks in Devon, starting a week on Saturday.” With Chris. The Chris who I snuggle up to on the sofa, the Chris who likes Led Zeppelin and U2, the Chris who can talk to me for hours about Shakespeare’s characters and make them sound like fun. *The Chris who likes strange films with dark story lines.*

“Best make the most of it,” Jim said.

My last patient was a bulimic forty-year-old woman with a long history of the disease and, consequently, terrible discoloured teeth. Afterwards, I fled from the Lodge with an unshakeable determination to concentrate on the weekend ahead. And that meant food.

Charlie and Claire were coming to dinner. I’d already devised a menu, the finale a sumptuous confection of Cornish cream and raspberries glazed with a thick layer of sugar—an excuse at last for the purchase of a professional blowtorch. Maybe I’d go the whole hog and buy a couple of other items on my wish list. I suddenly felt the pull of serious culinary retail therapy. A sucker for cooking gizmos, I browsed kitchen shops in the way most blokes walked around massive auto centres. Besides, I was glad to be *doing*. If I kept active and my brain busy, I didn’t have to dwell on the other stuff.

With the sun bright overhead, I could feel the tension draining away as I walked along the street. It made me feel like a schoolchild on the last day of term.

After a brief dalliance with a four-slice glacier-blue retro-style toaster, I homed in on a fabulous set of kitchen knives with rock-hard titanium blades. They weren't on my shopping list, and I already had a decent number of knives in both homes, but I found the temptation irresistible. There was something about blades, which I supposed was a bit kinky. I liked the weight and feel of the handles. I admired their versatility. Sleek and unyielding, knives required skill and dexterity. With a knife in your hand, you were invincible. To fully persuade myself of the wisdom of an entirely unnecessary purchase, I imagined the ease with which I'd be able to bone out a piece of meat, slice and pare an over-ripe fruit, fillet a sea bass ... *defend yourself*, a small voice in my brain interposed.

You could never have too many, I concluded, doggedly hefting the block and taking it to the counter. Next, I turned my attention to a chrome-plated blowtorch. According to the blurb on the box, it skinned, seared, toasted, and glazed—a sexy and serious piece of kit. With a flame temperature of 1500 degrees C, it was potentially lethal. It would require a degree of nerve. I'd have to be super careful. Still, it was a steal.

Laden with two heavy carrier bags, I trudged steadily back towards the Promenade, pausing now and then to window shop. Almost past Cavendish House department store and about to cruise down the classy row of designer shops, I felt as if something inside had tightened like a screw. I stopped, caught sight of my own suspicious mirror image, and spun around.

There were hundreds of shoppers in a myriad of colours, attitudes, and moods. But was Stannard among them? Screwing my eyes tight against the sun, I scanned faces—black, white, Asian—my instincts on full alert. Young couples walked hand in hand. A tanned businessman carrying a briefcase brayed loudly into a mobile phone. "Close the deal, for Chrissakes, or we're fucked ..." Mothers chastised children. Adolescents cheeked parents. One small girl lay flat on her back in the middle of the pavement, drumming her tiny heels and screaming. Small boys with streetwise faces and pierced ears careered in and out of the crowds on skateboards. An old woman dressed in an oversized man's jacket shouted obscenities at the sky. The place crawled with humanity in all its weird complexity and Stannard was out there somewhere. I *sensed* it.

Alarmed, I crossed over to the other side of the square, picked up pace. A small crowd of Japanese tourists, hanging around outside Waterstones, made it almost impossible to pass. I squirreled my way into their party and, on impulse, hitched a glance over my shoulder, above their heads, and cast a long look back. The place seethed and, among the sea of people, one man stood out from the crowd. Wearing dark glasses, his face was canted permanently to the left. The newspaper he held in his hand, as if to protect his face from the harsh rays of the sun, gave him a slightly lopsided appearance. As he drew close with a purposeful stride, I could see that he was tall, probably over six feet, his body spare and toned. Every inch a businessman, he wore black tailored trousers with sharp creases, a short-sleeved ice-blue linen shirt, and dark silk tie. *Was it him*? I angled my head to get a better view. My palms stuck to the plastic bags as I dumped them and pulled out my phone, my police case number taped on the back in case of emergency.

I held up the mobile to check the signal, which was good. He came closer still. I could make out a fine head of hair—dark, thick, and straight. In spite of the sunglasses, the side of his face on display was lightly tanned. He had a strong jawline.

Now, he was only a dozen or so shop fronts away. Tourists scattered. Still he kept moving. As if breaking out of a trance, I glanced anxiously around, getting my bearings. Stay in a public place, the police said. Don't confront him. Walk away. Phone.

He was looking straight at me. That's when he took off his sunglasses and let the newspaper slide.

I caught my breath. Terror slipped its chains.

One eye, including the brow on the left side of his face, sloped disastrously so that the region around his long slim nose was overcrowded. The mouth, which was wide and generous, curved down in a perpetual expression of displeasure, as if he were the victim of a serious stroke. Perversely, the skin was smooth—too smooth, for it looked inert, plastic. There was no evident scarring or puckering, no signs of fire, only blotchiness along the hairline like you see in skin that has been surgically treated. The area below the cheekbone caved in. From his fixed expression, I guessed that all involuntary movement was severely restricted. It was like looking at a death mask except the eyes were too bright. Almost a deep shade of topaz, they burned with an amazing intensity, lighting up his skull.

Twenty paces away and counting, I knew I should turn and run but couldn't. I stood rapt and rooted, like the princess in Sleeping Beauty, knowing the spindle was to be avoided at all costs, that it was dangerous, but unable to prevent disaster. With this man, I felt that same inexplicable fascination. More than that, I shared a strange affinity with him.

"Kim." There was desperation in his eye.

The spell broke. I plunged my phone into my pocket, gathered up my bags, and took two steps backwards.

"Stay away from me."

"I simply want..."

"Piss off." I looked round, tried to catch the eye of a well-dressed woman walking past. The woman shook her head minutely and carried on as if I were trying to sign her up for a donation. I turned my gaze to two barefooted young men with dreadlocks. Same response. I was in a public place but nobody wanted to know. Nobody wanted to get involved.

Stannard spread out his hands inches away from me. I registered the plea, yet my heart was like stone, and I turned on my heel. At the sound of my name, I shoved the bag from my right hand into my left, pulled my phone from my pocket, and made a big gesture of putting it to my ear. Smart footsteps behind, I speeded up, the shopping like lead weights, making me list to one side. A blare of car horn and a burst of obscenities, a car speeded past and almost knocked me over. I didn't care. Stealing a feverish glance over my shoulder, I saw Stannard left behind.

Unappeased, I broke into a trot, ran past the imitation of the Trevi fountain, crossing the road at the lights, and let myself be swallowed up by a crowd moving in the opposite direction. Weaving and zigzagging across the pavement, I did my best to break up my outline so that I'd be less obvious to him, and thanked God for shade as I passed a row of parked cars beneath a canopy of trees. The operator picked up my call as The Queens Hotel reared into view. I rattled off the log number and explained the situation. Asked if he was still in pursuit, I looked back. By now I was level with Montpellier Gardens, where people spread out among the flowerbeds, eating sandwiches and sunbathing. I thought my heart would give out at the sight of Stannard only a short distance away, no break in step, no increase in pace, simply a dogged determination to get to me.

"He's still after me," I bellowed above the sound of a jazz collective playing a seductive version of "Summertime."

"Where are you exactly?" the operator said.

I gave the location. "I'm heading for the Bayshill Clinic."

"Can you make it to your destination?"

"I think so. I don't know."

"We'll send a patrol car. It may take a few minutes."

Breathlessly, I gabbled a brief description of what I was wearing. I broke into a jog, felt the pull on my muscles. My shopping weighed a ton and I could taste car exhaust and benzene. Sweat bubbled out of me. My chest heaved. A group of youngsters shambled towards me, threatening to slow me down. I cannoned through them, prayed for the police to hurry. Risking another glance back, I stopped short.

He wasn't there.

Rooted, lungs bursting, muscles screaming, heart pounding, I combed the street again, scoping the other side, narrowing my eyes against the fierce glare of afternoon sunshine. He could be in any of a dozen doorways. My breath erupted in short and painful bursts.

I had no time to consider. A patrol car pulled up.

PC Grant stuck his head out of the window. "Want a lift?"

TWENTY-FIVE

I DESCRIBED WHAT HAPPENED. Grant drove back into town and made a quick fruitless search of side streets, then took me to the Bayshill Clinic.

"I think it's time we had a chat with Mr. Stannard," Grant said before dropping me off. "We'll make it plain that his interest is not appreciated."

I couldn't ignore the warm thrill of righteous vindication. At last I was being taken seriously; someone was listening.

Triumphant, I phoned Chris. It was supposed to be easy. A quick call to tell him what happened; say it was being dealt with, that I was fine.

"Christ, I could kill the little shit for this."

"But it's all right now."

"It isn't, is it?"

Disappointment descended like smog. "It's a whole lot better than it was."

"What are you doing?"

I flinched, immediately and inexplicably guarded.

"Are you going back to the flat, coming home, or what?"

"I can't jump ship. I've got clients. I'll go back to the flat, have a shower, get changed. Thank God it's Friday." I managed a smile.

"You'll return a little later than usual then?"

"Yes."

"You'll come straight back?"

"Is there a problem?" *Why do you want to know?* was what I really meant.

"No, of course not."

"And Chris?"

"Yeah?"

"Don't tell anyone I was rattled."

"Kim, it doesn't mat—"

"I don't want anyone to know. I don't want that bastard ever to find out I was terrified."

Kirsten Matherson's parents were waiting for me. They seemed brittle. I wasn't sure whether there had been a difficult journey, a private argument, or it was my fault for being late. I apologised unreservedly.

"Accepted," Marie Matherson said, clipped. Tall and graceful, she had straight blond hair, cut short. She wore a dress of palest green that fitted her lithe figure perfectly. By contrast, her husband was thickset, barrel-chested, and his suit looked like it was a size too small.

They sat down and I brought them up to speed on Kirsten's progress. Marie seemed relieved by the improvement in her daughter's condition. Frank Matherson merely grunted. Hard to say whether it meant approval. It occurred to me that he'd been strong-armed into making an appearance.

Striking a neutral tone, I looked at Marie Matherson and said, "I gather she's interested in fashion design."

"I've tried to encourage her, but she undervalues her abilities."

"That's extremely common in anorexics," I assured her. "There's a tendency to focus on negatives. It's connected to a general problem of low self-esteem."

"Are you saying it's our fault?" Matherson burst out. His neck flushed red.

"Not in the least," I said, taken aback.

"I hold that damned modelling agency responsible for this," Matherson roared.

"Please, Frank," Marie warned.

"You should never have got her involved."

He blames his wife, I thought, watching the minor domestic drama unfold, family dynamics endlessly fascinating—and revealing. I tried to change the mood.

"I see you have two sons."

"What's that got to do with you?" Matherson snarled.

"I'm trying to help, Mr. Matherson," I said, issuing a straight look.

"They're quite a bit older than Kirst," Marie said, clearly trying to head off the possibility of further confrontation.

"How have they reacted to Kirsten's condition?"

"They're concerned," Marie said. "They're working abroad at the moment so they're shielded from the problem."

"That might be a good thing. Having an anorexic in the family can make siblings feel helpless. It stirs up all types of diffuse emotions of anger and uselessness, which can make them feel guilty."

"Guilty? I've never heard such crap in all my life," Matherson raged. "Come on, Marie," he said jumping to his feet. "I've had enough."

Marie looked at me in apology and stretched out a hand to her husband. He snatched at it. I noticed her gentle squeeze. A contrived picture of unity, and for whose benefit, I wondered?

Before he ploughed out of the consulting room, Matherson turned to me. "The only people who should be feeling guilty," he said, his spit flying onto my face, "are those bastards responsible for our daughter's illness."

I was almost out of the door when the police called.

"We picked up Stannard," Grant said. "He was hanging around outside your apartment block. Came up with some cock-and-bull story about viewing the flat below."

My stomach gave a sickening lurch. I put a hand out to the wall to steady myself. Lizzie's flat, I realised, the creep. "What was his defence for this morning's episode then?"

"He got clever, said he was unaware of a law preventing two people from having a conversation. He maintained you'd made the first move."

"He said what?"

"According to Stannard, you were waiting to speak to him outside Waterstones. He said you looked deliberately in his direction and that you waved to him."

"That's ridiculous."

"Were you looking for him?" The serious note in Grant's voice made me suddenly feel as if I were the problem.

"I thought he was following me."

"So you admit you looked."

"I admit nothing."

"Calm down, Miss Slade," he said in a way guaranteed to agitate me. "I'm trying to get a handle on what actually took place."

Giving myself the equivalent of a mental shake, I repeated slowly, "Stannard followed me. Does he deny the other things?"

"Yes."

I throbbed with irritation. He'd done a good job selling his side of the story. A brief silence signalled stalemate.

"Whatever the ins and outs, Stannard knows we've got his number," Grant assured me. "He says he intends you no harm. I believe he's genuine in that regard. I think he really believed because of your, how can I put it … er … shared difficulty …"

"My face is not a difficulty," I said. Hell, what happened to the change in public opinion following the Paralympics? What happened to the new attitude towards disability?

Grant coughed as though he had a hairball in his throat. "I only meant that he's a victim. He must have been a good-looking man before his accident."

I thought I was going to choke with frustration. For a man to make such a comment about another man displayed the extent of Stannard's manipulative ability to engender pity. He would always have the drop on me. "I was forgetting," I said with a cynical laugh, Gavin Chadwick's words clanging in my ears. "We're all victims nowadays. We're all flaming losers."

"There's no need to adopt that tone."

My cheeks burnt red. I tried to strike a more conciliatory note. "So that's the end of the matter, is it?"

"I'd say so," Grant said crisply. "It's really unlikely he'll bother you again. I think in his own way he's sorry."

TWENTY-SIX

HEATHER FOLEY WELCOMED KYLE Stannard into her home with a frozen smile. My God, she thought, experiencing a tang of fear. The afflicted side of his face looked, well . . . terrible. She supposed it could have been due to some sort of illness, a form of palsy, perhaps, but a dent in the lower half of one cheek together with the general sloping appearance of his features, suggested something far more invasive. Poor man, she thought, and how brave. Fed on a diet of cheap romantic novels, she felt sure that he must have done something heroic to sustain such dreadful injuries. Best not to look. Best to make every effort to avert her eyes when she spoke. The pity was that his good side was indescribably beautiful. She thought he had the face of a fallen angel.

"Thanks for seeing me at such short notice," Stannard said, shaking her hand. "I really appreciate it."

He had a nice voice too, she thought, especially bearing in mind the damage to the left side of his mouth. And he dressed well. She'd already noticed the car. The more expensive the mode of transport, her husband once told her, the more serious the buyer. She reckoned Mr. Stannard could afford to pay top dollar for her home.

"I see it was built in the mid-nineteenth century," Stannard said, alluding to the plaque attached to the northern side of the building.

She hoped he was not going to ask too many questions about its history. That had always been her husband's department. "Would you like coffee before we start, or afterwards?"

"The house first, if you don't mind."

"Good," she said cheerily. She'd devised a plan based on biblical principles. Like the wedding at Cana, she was going to save the best until last.

She started off with the dismal mausoleum of a kitchen, its only advantage size. Cheap cupboards and Formica-topped units clung precariously to walls that were pockmarked and cracked. The worn linoleum-covered floor had farmyard appeal—it looked dirty no matter how hard it was cleaned. A trellis of exposed and rusting pipework poked out from a recess housing a decrepit-looking Aga; hard to remember that it was an iconic range of cooker. The whole room needed knocking down and rebuilding. Stannard looked around and gestured for them to move on. She quickly led him through to what she called a utility room but in reality was storage. Remembering a snatch of history, she informed him that it used to be the maids' quarters. Stannard gave it a cursory glance, walked to the back door and opened it. It looked out onto a courtyard.

"Would you like to go outside?"

"Later," he said decisively.

She walked him back through the long dark hall to a cluster of rooms. The sitting room was comfortable enough for her needs. Florally decorated, it had sash-windows and a wood-burning stove. Then there was the study, a darkly masculine chamber, the lair from which she presumed her husband had discussed and organised his sordid assignations. It still pained her to walk inside. Stannard's observations were brief and he spoke little. Either he was feigning disinterest as a means to drive down the price, or he was genuinely unimpressed; neither was to her advantage.

Time to play her ace. She led Stannard to the other side of the large polished wooden-floored hall and threw open the door, a cascade of brilliant sunshine casting Stannard into the light. Like a vampire after sunup, he shot a hand to his face, automatically shielding his bad side with the set of details he carried. Acutely embarrassed, she pretended not to notice. She twittered something about the glorious weather they were enjoying and walked in ahead of him in a poor effort to protect him from the blatant sunshine. In the middle of the floor, a shiny grand piano sat like a large black carrion crow.

Stannard's eyes followed the line of ornate coving and came to rest on it. "Do you play?"

She grimaced. "It belonged to my ex."

"Would you be prepared to sell it to me?"

His eyes were an extraordinary colour, she thought, pale brown, almost orange like a tiger's. At that moment they were full of guile.

She smiled graciously. "That depends."

He nodded. They had a deal. She rippled with excitement. While things were going unexpectedly well, she took Stannard back along the corridor. Square and dark, with York flags and dado rail, the dining room had an air of unrealised grandeur. There was no dining table and the walls were painted a flat deadly green.

"Not my idea," she explained. "With a little imagination, it wouldn't be difficult to return it to its former glory." He agreed.

At her suggestion they walked up the long sweeping staircase, Stannard on her left, his good aspect giving every impression that he had once been a fine-looking man. They were so close she could smell his seductive aftershave. Vaguely unsettled, she thought it best to show him the mushroom room first and get it out of the way. She started to rattle an explanation but he cut across her.

"Once the roof's fixed it won't be a problem. The details suggest you have a cellar."

She assured him she did. "You can access it from both the hall and the garden."

The tour of the bedrooms and bathrooms took longer than anticipated. Stannard admired the large main bedroom with dressing room and en suite, and its views over the lawns.

"I'd like to have another walk around the house on my own before we venture into the garden. Is that all right?"

Eager to please, she smiled approval. "I'll make coffee."

Ten minutes later, they were sitting in the drawing room. Stannard had put on a pair of sunglasses, making him look more normal, she thought.

"You have a lovely home, Mrs. Foley. Thank you for sharing it with me." Charming manners, she glowed. "It must be quite a wrench to leave."

"One has to move on."

He raised the cup to his mouth. She averted her gaze. There was a brief embarrassed silence, punctuated by the clatter of fine china.

When he finally spoke, his voice assumed a hawkish tone. "You realise that neither of us are going to be happy with the deal."

She gave him a sharp look. He turned the good side of his face towards her and attempted a smile. "We are both grown-ups. What I mean is that when I buy a property I want to pay the lowest price I can, and you, as the vendor, want the highest you can get. Somehow we have to meet in the middle so neither of us comes away disappointed."

"Or feeling short-changed," she added.

"I find the opening up of honest dialogue to be key to successful negotiation," he continued. "If there's something you're not happy with when we come to crossing i's and dotting t's, you must let me know. I'll do the same."

"I can't argue with that." She found herself nodding, mesmerised by the prospect of a deal. This was it, the moment she'd be waiting for. A face-lift was within grasp. Her life would be changed. The future suddenly trilled with giddy promise. "Top-up?" she beamed.

Afterwards they went out into the garden and followed the paved path that led from the front door right around the enclosed walled patio to the small stream and bridge. Overgrown, the basic form of the original flowerbeds remained. Stannard traced the line of the boundary and Heather directed him down three steps from the terrace to a white wooden garden door that led to the cellar. They went inside. It was dark and smelt of earth. In spite of the maze of struts and supports, the area was large enough to turn into another room.

"We'd thought of turning it into a games space."

Stannard nodded politely.

"Or maybe a wine cellar."

Stannard said nothing.

Heather gave a nervy laugh. "You probably have your own ideas."

He didn't comment.

Confounded by the silence, she twitched a smile, and made for the opposite side of the room, up the stone steps, out through the door and into the hall. Back in the main body of the house, she felt a dizzy sense of relief. Stannard emerged a minute later and followed her down the hall to the front door.

"Right," Stannard said decisively. "I'll get my people to contact your people." He stretched out his hand. She took it, felt the cool skin. When she thanked him she tried not to look too closely at his face.

TWENTY-SEVEN

"And you believe him?"

We were in the kitchen. Music oozed through the speakers. Crowded House was singing a depressing song about tears and slow turning pain.

I spread my hands. With the pressure off, and from the safety of my Devon nest, I endeavoured to view things through a less narrow perspective. I could afford to be magnanimous. I could feel sympathy for Stannard. A bit.

Voice raised, arms crossed, Chris remained resistant. "The cops are useless. We both know he won't give up that easily."

"We *don't* know anything." Chris's ire might have been overwhelming had I not been schooled in wrath. He'd been edgy and moody from the time I'd stepped through the door the previous evening. I'd tried to jolly him out of it and failed. This was the unattractive side of his personality that pissed off our friends. I felt at a loss how to help, particularly as he appeared to be glued to his mobile. It was as if there were three of us in the room, not two. Chris was not even sufficiently cheered by his purchase of a sleek black Alfa Romeo Brera.

"Look," I said, making one last attempt to get through to him. "I'm dazed. I want to believe it's all over. I need to believe, do you see? It's the best I can hope for. From your point of view it's not so easy."

"Not easy?"

"You haven't had time to catch up with the shift in events," I pushed on. "I appreciate that. In a way I've got the advantage."

Chris fixed on me, an unyielding expression in his eyes. To deflect him, I did what I'd learnt to do a long time ago: I smiled. Then I explained, "Because I've experienced all this first-hand." I also believed, but didn't say, that men were less able to process risk-assessment when it came to their nearest and dearest. Either they were in hackles-up, full-on defence mode, or they were shooting the breeze, oblivious. As a child, I'd experienced fierce overprotectiveness and spine-tingling neglect.

"Have you forgotten yesterday?"

I clenched my jaw, felt a vein pulse in my neck. Seeing Stannard's face had given me an unwelcome insight into how others might view me. I shook my head.

"I can't get the sound of your fear out of my mind. You seemed so crushed, so very frightened. I've never heard you like it before."

"Did I? I don't think..."

"Have you any idea how crap that makes me feel, how powerless I am to protect you? He could come along at any moment, when he chooses, and I can't do a damn thing about it." Weary, he drew up a chair at the kitchen table and sat down. "Maybe you're right. I just..." His voice tailed off. Sleeves rolled up, he clawed at a bare arm. I caught his despondency and, for reasons I couldn't pin down, I didn't think it was remotely connected to me.

"What?" I reached over, stayed his hand.

He hooked me with his haunted eyes. "This is changing both of us. We mustn't let it. We have to get our lives back."

"And we can." I tried not to show fear. When bad things happen to couples or families, it doesn't always unite. Sometimes it shatters. I knew this for a fact. Dad had sought solace with other women; some who wanted me to call them mother. My brothers, that much older, had concentrated on exams and work and, in Luke's case, carving a career. I could see how, rather than bonding us, Stannard had split Chris and me into different camps.

I gave his hand a gentle, hopeful squeeze.

His face relaxed into a smile. "We will be all right, won't we?"

"Of course." My voice tentative and faltering, I said, "Maybe now is the time to make changes. Good changes, I mean." I couldn't discern whether Chris was still looking at me with apprehension or expectation. "Perhaps," I gabbled, "we've both got a bit too comfortable in our own spaces. Maybe we've become selfish and set in our ways, complacent even. I mean," I said, searching for the right words when all I could find were the wrong ones, "are we always destined to live apart?"

The silence screamed in my face. His expression was unfathomable. I didn't dare move. Then, as if remembering that he was supposed to respond, his face softened. He gave my hand a gentle tug. I got up and edged my way around the table, let him pull me down onto his lap. He wrapped his arms around me, buried his head into my neck.

Yet he didn't utter a single word.

TWENTY-EIGHT

"Crikey," Charlie exploded.

Claire looked stunned. "And it's all over?"

"Yes." It better be.

We were sitting in the shade on the small terrace outside the kitchen, overlooking the creek. Blades of sunshine played off the water. Iridescent-looking insects hovered above the glassy-green surface. I'd opened champagne in a feeble attempt at celebration, my conversation with Chris, or rather the lack of it, seriously undermining my confidence. I couldn't rule out the niggling fear that he didn't want me to move to Devon on a permanent basis. Perhaps my regular absences were part of the appeal of the relationship and that, I realised, meant that Chris was the one with the power. I'd heard a theory that whoever declared their love first was always at a disadvantage thereafter. I couldn't remember who said what and when at the beginning of our love affair. I'd never considered it before, but now it needled me. Stannard had turned things upside-down, infiltrating both our lives in a way never anticipated.

We ate a light mousse of freshly caught Salcombe crab followed by crisply glazed duck breasts seared by my new culinary toy. I'd spent the afternoon getting the hang of using the blowtorch, sealing meat, skinning tomatoes and peppers, caramelising sugar and fruit and anything else that moved. My childhood accident ensured an almost phobic fear of fire and heat, but it wasn't so bad as long as I could control it—gas flames on a hob were okay, likewise irons and fires in grates as long as there was a guard in front—but I wouldn't venture near bonfires, and the thought of burning buildings almost induced a panic attack. That afternoon, in the sanctity of my own kitchen, it took nerves of steel to conquer my intrinsic fear. But I did. From an early age, it was what had always been expected of me. Get a Grip should have been my surname.

Over coffee, Charlie and Chris discussed the merits of various cars, talking torque, electro-hydraulics, and cylinders. It took a lot of effort on my part not to feel drawn in.

"Why didn't you tell me about him, Kim?"

I looked at Claire. "Stannard?"

"Yes."

I saw hurt in her eyes and Claire was the last person I'd ever wish to offend. "If I talked about it, I risked giving it oxygen. It would make it all too real."

"As though he'd won already?"

"Something like that."

She let out a sigh.

"What?"

"Nothing."

Nothing meant something. I attempted to force the issue, but Claire simply said, "I only wished you'd told me."

"I'm sorry."

"I knew something was up the night of the dinner party."

"Yes, but it's over now, thank God."

After a brief uncomfortable silence, Claire asked if I'd seen anything of Molly and Simon.

"I went round for dinner recently." It felt like a confession. After all, I'd discussed Stannard with them at some length before I'd even mentioned him to Claire. I decided to change the subject and asked after the Chadwicks.

"I received a thank-you phone call from Lottie and an invite to a drinks party next month. I think we were asked out of a sense of guilt," Claire confided with a laugh.

"Are you going?"

"You must be kidding. I'd rather walk barefoot through nettles. Anyway, I don't think I'll be feeling much in the mood." I observed the accompanying shy smile. There was something familiar in her expression. I'd witnessed it three times before.

"You're not..."

"Four months gone," Claire beamed.

"Oh, Claire," I said, reaching over and kissing her on the cheek.

"She's been suffering badly with morning sickness this time, so we're hoping it might be a girl," Charlie said, breaking off from his conversation with Chris.

"Bound to be, they're always the source of trouble," Chris laughed, slapping Charlie on the top of his arm. "You're building up quite a brood."

Claire wrinkled her nose in delight and looked lovingly at her husband. "We always wanted a big family, didn't we?"

I watched my friends with a stab of envy. They looked so content in that rare way when two people are clearly meant for each other. Looking at Claire's face, soft and serene in the candlelight, I longed for what she had: a lasting relationship that was solid and stable. It didn't diminish how I felt about work, which *was* important to me, but I needed more. With a rush of self-knowledge, I realised Chris and I were living a make-believe existence. It was as if we'd never progressed past that first early mad stage of falling in lust, the enforced absences prolonging the mystique and conveniently concealing the flaws. I glanced over to Chris and smiled. He met my eye, held my gaze, then looked down. I creased with disappointment, felt the sparkle fade from my eyes, the sensation cruelly familiar to me. Too often, I'd experienced losing.

The phone rang as soon as Claire and Charlie departed. Chris raced to get it. I slipped off my jacket and watched his face. His monosyllabic response indicated that he was unimpressed by the late-night intrusion. Perplexed by his constant dalliance with the phone, I stood as if spot-welded.

He held the receiver away. "For you." *Alexa*, he mouthed silently.

Feeling guilty for harbouring suspicion, I stifled a moan and took the phone. "Hi."

"Is Chris all right? He seemed a bit short."

"We've just cleared up after dinner and it is quite late."

"Is it?"

I glanced at my watch. "It's nearly one o'clock in the morning."

"Uh-huh." She sounded distracted, as though she didn't know where she was.

"Alexa, has something happened? Are you all right?"

"Brooks has been seeing someone else, has done for some time."

I plumped down on the nearest chair and signalled to Chris to leave me to it. Despite the hour, I could tell this was going to be a long phone call and I didn't have the heart to blow Alexa off. I was starting to think that she phoned me only because she'd alienated everyone else. We weren't even close friends, after all.

An hour later, I put the phone down, yawned, and stretched. Chris was already asleep by the time I showered and climbed into bed. I lay awake listening to his steady breathing, my mind returning to Stannard and the extraordinary effect of seeing him in the flesh—his twisted looks, the way his eyes shone like burning flames in his skull. I'd been afraid, almost to the point of paralysis and, yes, for a strand of time, I'd fallen under his spell. He must have been magnificent. I wondered about the tragic hand of cards he'd been dealt, and the details of the story behind them.

Stories. Every person had one. Not the once-upon-a-time variety, or tales of the daily round, but *this is what happened that changed me* story. It might include a single event, tragic or otherwise, or an important influence, a parent or lover or mentor. Every day I listened to my client's life histories, replayed them, interpreted, reworked, and retold them. Stories of loss and loneliness, of jealousy and false expectations, of crippling fear and rage. But I hadn't listened to Stannard's story. I'd refused. I'd done what was expected of me. I'd done as I was told. Don't talk to him, they said. Don't engage. Walk away. And I had. But really I'd fled for my own reasons, because when I looked at Stannard's face, I recognised a piece of my own narrative.

And I saw a cruel reflection of my past.

TWENTY-NINE

HEAT CRUSHED ME. THROUGH the crack in the curtain, I glimpsed the sun floating high. I heard the splash of water, the low burr of unfamiliar voices, then the sound of an engine spluttering into life and the nasal whine as a boat sped off along the creek.

Aroused by his touch, I'd responded sleepily like I'd done many times before when we'd enjoyed slow, languid sex. But this time was different. This time there was desperation and recklessness. He pinned me down as if he needed to break flesh and bone. There was determination; no violence, but Chris fenced and parried my every move. Not like this, but like that. I felt as if I'd had an affair and been forgiven, and this was his way of repossessing me. Events blurred. Teeth clashed, limbs collided, nails tore, skin on sweaty skin. Stubble rasped against my chin. My lips itched and swelled and bruised. I didn't dare shut my eyes. I moved into another zone where words didn't count or matter, only acts.

He caught hold of me and forced me in front of a long antique mirror that had belonged to my father. Kicking my legs apart, I feasted my eyes on him as he went down on me. My legs trembled as he bent me over and fucked me from behind. Dazzled by the undulating contours of our bodies, I felt revered and dirty, like an actress in my own porn movie. The computerised image flashed into my mind. I snuffed it out. Afterwards I lay there spent, letting the silence seep in.

"Like a drink?" Chris said.

Vodka, I thought. "Fruit juice," I said.

He pulled on a robe and went downstairs. At that moment I felt a million miles away from Stannard. No longer a nameless, unknowable, frightening entity, he was simply a disfigured man who, for a short period of my life, had shouted for my attention. Sex that morning had reset the boundaries. Like it always did.

I rolled over onto my stomach, one arm outside the bed, the tips of my fingers trailing the polished wooden floor, and heard the sound of voices accompanied by a sudden torrent of laughter. Mystifyingly, I caught a silvery female tone. I rolled out, pulled on a pair of knickers, threw on Chris's shirt, and went downstairs.

Andy sat in the kitchen. A wide smile split his face. Self-conscious, I rolled up the collar, did up another button, and briefly wondered what they'd been laughing at, what I'd interrupted. Two men, one woman, I shivered, remembering the painting in my flat.

"I told him his timing was crap," Chris said in mock despair.

I exchanged a glance. "I didn't hear you arrive, Andy. No camper van?" Andy's mode of transport was a running a gag between us.

"We cycled here."

"We?" I looked around the kitchen as though someone was about to pop out of a cupboard.

"Jen and me. She's in the loo."

"Must be mad," Chris said, handing me a tumbler of juice. "Haven't you got anything better to do at half past ten on a Sunday morning? Newspapers to read, a car to clean, a woman to screw?"

"Leave Jen out of it, and how do you know what we were up to first thing?" Andy grinned.

"Leave Jen out of what?"

I followed the voice. Jen was exactly as Andy described and more: big eyes, big lips, big breasts. Andy carried out the introductions. I apologised for my state of undress.

"Don't worry about it, maid." Jen pulled up a chair close to Andy. "We're not bothered, are we, babe?" she said, squeezing Andy's meaty thigh.

"Coffee?" Tight at the intrusion, I smiled in a vain effort to conceal it.

Andy nodded.

"Shall I be mother?" Jen said, making to get up.

"No," I started, swiping the kettle and filling it with water. "Wouldn't dream of it," I added, forcing a smile. Wasn't Jen's fault she used an expression I couldn't actually stand. My father had once had a fleeting relationship with a big-breasted woman fond of the phrase. She was fond of him too and hadn't lasted five minutes.

Jen made herself at home. "Mine's black, two sugars."

"To what do we owe the pleasure?" Chris leant back and linked his hands behind his head.

"We're having a drinks thing in the garden next Saturday," Andy said.

"You haven't got a garden."

Jen let out a screech of laughter. "He's right, And."

"Yard then," Andy continued, unabashed. "We'd like you both to come."

I prayed Chris hadn't forgotten.

"Sorry, mate. We can't. It's Kim's birthday."

"Shit, I forgot, stupid of me."

"But that's brilliant," Jen said, eyes popping. "Come to ours on Saturday and we can make it a real party."

I turned away to mask the expression of frozen horror marching across my features. Andy's bashes were surreal affairs—loads of alcohol and desperate people with nothing discernible in common. Above the clatter of mugs, I heard Chris say four magic words.

"Made other plans, mate."

I glowed inside. What and where? "What a shame," I smiled, stamping four mugs of coffee on the table, like bullet points on a PowerPoint presentation.

"Spoilsport." Jen pouted pink lips. I didn't know her well enough to spot whether it was mock disappointment or the genuine article. "We should go out for a girls' night."

"I'll check my diary," I said, with what I hoped was a convincing smile.

"Like the new motor," Andy said to Chris. "Any chance of a spin?"

"I'll give you a ride on Friday to celebrate six weeks of unfettered freedom."

Andy grinned and made a passable stab at the chorus of Alice Cooper's "School's Out For Summer."

Jen gave his arm a playful slap. "You're such a laugh," she shrieked.

I did my best to turn down the volume. "Andy said you teach at Totnes Leisure Centre, Jen."

"S'right, keeps me in shape."

"Certainly does that." Andy cast her a lascivious grin.

"You should try it, Kim," Jen said, her gaze locking on to my neck. "It's a good little confidence booster."

"Not something she needs," Chris said, smiling at me with an intimacy that made me thrill. Feeling impossibly grateful, I questioned what on earth I was doing standing in my own kitchen in such a state of undress. Fortunately, with curvy Jen in such close proximity, Andy seemed blissfully oblivious. He took a slurp of coffee and asked if I'd got any holiday planned.

"Three weeks," I said.

"Bloody Norah, and there's you going on about us teachers. What are you two going to get up to?"

"That's the beauty of it," Chris said with another warm smile.

"Nothing at all," I agreed, catching his vibe. Yes, things were going to be fine.

"Us girls should get together," Jen said, returning to a favourite theme.

Maintain the smile, I thought. "Well, I ..."

"Better still, we can make it a foursome."

"Fabulous," I lied.

THIRTY

Chris pulled me into the shower. He kissed my mouth and held me as rivulets of water sprayed our faces. He ran his fingers over my breasts, touched my belly, reached down, and touched the soft flesh of my inner thigh, making me pulse with desire. He flattened me against the cool-tiled walls and, as he entered me, I felt Stannard's spell to be truly broken.

After we dressed, he suggested we pack up a picnic. "I'll organise it."

I raised an eyebrow in amused surprise.

"I thought we'd have doorstep sandwiches and bottles of pop," he teased. "You're not the only foodie round here, you know. Move over *Masterchef*."

Inevitably, the conversation led back to Andy's latest squeeze. "What did you think of Jen?"

Chris let out a groan. "She was gruesome. Why on earth did you agree to a foursome?"

"I'd already batted her off twice. It was starting to look rude. I don't know how he manages to pick them. And that laugh." I shivered.

"Don't you see, she's exactly Andy's type: no brains, big tits."

"Sex without commitment."

"Classic Andy," Chris said. "I guess, from a purely physical point of view, she goes in and out in all the right places."

"Should I be jealous?" I teased.

"Don't be silly." His laugh was shaky, almost shy, and I laughed too.

We headed for Mill Bay on the Triumph, sea air in my face, the roar of the arrow sports exhaust in my ears. Predictably, the beach bustled with febrile activity. Despite this, something had shifted. I couldn't put my finger on it but my spirits soared. For the first time in a while, I was determined to hope.

"You okay?" Chris said, putting a protective arm around me.

I peered from underneath the brim of my sun hat. "I'm blissfully and deliriously happy. Let's head back to the coastal path. There's that rocky outcrop round the corner. It will be quieter."

The rocks were black and shiny like overlapping mussel shells. The waves caught against them and sent up a fine saltspray. I could taste it on my skin. We inched along close to where cormorants perched and the land fell away to the sea below. I paddled my bare feet in a small natural pool edged with a thick, crusty layer of seaweed while Chris laid out the towels side by side. Stretching out, a hard layer of shale resting against the small of my back, I tipped my hat over my face, determined to extinguish all thought of the drive back to Cheltenham the following morning. I wanted to rest in the moment, be still and snuggled in our private world. Later, we ate. In spite of the heat, I was insanely hungry.

"God knows what Andy must have thought this morning." I bit into a roll filled with lettuce and salami.

"Don't worry about him. He's almost part of the furniture."

"I'm sure he'd be very flattered by that description."

"Well, you know what I mean," Chris grinned, chucking me a packet of crisps. "Andy is ..."

"Andy," I giggled.

An hour or so passed. Half asleep, euphoria dissipated, I felt perfectly serene and sorted.

When Chris announced he wanted to take a photograph of me I barely stirred.

"You know I hate having my picture taken," I murmured lazily.

"Go on. I've only got one pic of you."

"The one where I look wasted." I'd been trying to avoid the flash. "You said you'd rip it up."

"No, *you* said." He laughed and playfully poked me in the ribs. "Go on, it won't take a moment. Look behind you and then turn back. That way it will look natural."

I moved slowly, got up, pretending to do him a huge favour. "If you must."

When he finished and we'd both stretched back out again, he said, "You never told me about your phone call with Alexa."

"I didn't think you'd want to know."

"If someone phones at that time, it has to be important."

"Only to her."

Chris crooked himself up on an elbow. "And?"

"Brooks has met someone else."

"Oh."

"Is that it?"

"What else can I say? Shit happens." He lay back down.

I guess you're right, I thought, suddenly tense.

THIRTY-ONE

Olivia Mallory kissed her son full on the mouth. Her hands rested on his shoulders and she held him away a little with concern. "You look tired, darling."

Wearing his trademark sunglasses, Kyle Stannard tipped his head to one side. "I'm fine, mother. You worry too much."

She let her hands drop, linked her arm through his, and walked him through to the sitting room where Gerald was waiting. The men exchanged restrained greetings. Gerald offered Kyle a glass of white wine. "Chilean sauvignon," he said, as if it were something unusual.

At his mother's insistence, Kyle sat down in Gerald's favourite wingback chair. If Gerald was jealous, he didn't say so. He asked his stepson about business. Olivia excused herself to check on the meat's progress. As soon as the door closed, Gerald pushed himself forward in the chair, any pretence of civility gone.

"So what was it you wished to talk to me about?"

Kyle's mouth twitched. "There's this woman," he began, pausing to remove a fruit fly from his glass, flicking its sodden body away between thumb and finger. "She's of interest to me. I don't really know her but, what I've seen, I respect … greatly." He noted a tick pulse in Gerald's neck. No matter. "She's got a good mind," he continued, "she could help me."

Gerald frowned. "Help you? How?"

"I need to talk to her. We share certain things in common."

"Like what?"

"Scars."

The pulse increased. Kyle watched with detached amusement.

"Is she married?" Gerald said.

His mind went blank. The thought had never occurred to him. "I don't think so."

"Then what's the problem?"

"She alleges I've been calling her and sending her stuff. She even accused me of following her in the street."

"Kyle, for God's sake, are you stalking her?"

He gave a short incredulous laugh. "Don't be ridiculous."

Gerald opened his mouth, as if to speak, and closed it. He took a long swallow of wine.

"Anyway, I went to view this flat for sale in Montpellier," Kyle continued. "Ground floor and smartly appointed. Before I knew what was happening, some copper picked me up and carted me off to the police station."

"Jesus." A spit of wine dropped onto Gerald's beautifully pressed shirt. He rubbed a hand over his jaw and inched forward in his chair. "Let me get this straight. What were the police doing there?"

Kyle hiked one shoulder. "Haven't a clue. They said she lived in the block."

"She?"

"Keep up. The woman I told you about."

"In the flat for sale?"

"No." He frowned in irritation. "She lives in the one above."

"And you didn't know?" Gerald's eyes narrowed with suspicion. "It's too much of a coincidence."

"Coincidences, like accidents, happen." Kyle thrust him a crooked smile and took a drink.

"You really expect me to believe that?"

"Believe what you like." He threw his stepfather a challenging look.

Gerald swallowed and drummed his fingers against the glass. "What did the police do?"

"Read me the riot act."

"You denied it?"

"Of course I denied it," he flashed with anger.

Gerald held his gaze. "They haven't charged you with anything?"

"No."

"No caution?"

"No."

Stony silence.

"I won't have your mother upset," Gerald said eventually.

"That's why I'm talking to *you* and not *her*. The thing is, I don't know why this woman is saying these things. We happened to chance upon each other in the street the other day. She waved, beckoned to me." His voice grew hard and malevolent. "I thought we could talk, and then she does something like that. It's as if she's playing games."

"Then don't play."

"It's not that simple. She can help me, and she's drawn to me. I *know* it."

"In this country we have a Protection from Harassment Act and it has recently got more robust. However innocent your motive," Gerald said, giving Kyle a bloodless stare, "you must forget about her. Forget about the flat, too. You stay away. Do I make myself plain? You've already been in trouble with the law."

"I don't need reminding."

"It seems to me you do," Gerald said. "Whatever this woman's problem with you, it won't look good. You've got history."

Kyle swept off his sunglasses, his eyes flat and cold. He knew that his stepfather could never bear to see the full extent of his disfigurement. "There was no evidence. The allegations were dropped."

"No smoke without fire."

Gerald drained his glass. Olivia appeared at the door. "Lunch is ready." She beamed radiantly at both the men in her life and stretched out a hand to Kyle as if he were her boy-toy lover. Kyle got up and took it.

"You two seem to be getting on famously." She gave Kyle's arm a tender squeeze. "Have I missed anything?"

THIRTY-TWO

AT ABOUT FOUR O'CLOCK, we walked back home and took another shower. This time I initiated sex. Full on. Blistering. Afterwards Chris insisted on cooking spaghetti. I watched as he chucked in butter, oil, and wine.

"Are you trying to give me a coronary?"

He turned and grinned. "I don't remember any complaints about the picnic, Miss Slade. Sit there, shut up, sip your drink, and look decorative. This is going to be fabulous, trust me."

And it was. After we'd finished off a bottle of plum-ripe Merlot, we watched a film, an action-adventure with a high body count, guns blazing, tons of blood, and an implausible plot line, but hey, what did I care? It was the perfect distraction; I loved it.

We went to bed early and I fell asleep and dreamt about the dead. Guy was outside in the darkness, his face half lit in the green glow of a bonfire, boasting like a latter-day Abednego that he could walk through it and not be hurt. I tried to stop him, but he laughed and touched the flames with his hand.

I woke up with a jolt, perspiration exploding across my brow, sheets drenched, mind whirring with thoughts of my imminent return to Cheltenham. It took me an age to go back to sleep and, when I finally awoke, I'd overslept.

Darting out of bed, I hurriedly washed and dressed, and crept over to Chris to wish him a silent good-bye.

Standing in the early-morning light, watching an amber sun splay its first tentative rays across Chris's face, I bent down and kissed his mouth. He stirred and reached up, sliding a hand across the back of my head, his other moving my hair, exposing the scar tissue, tracing the ridge with a finger. His eyes were quite open now, studying me. It felt peculiar, as if he were viewing me for the last time, charting every line and contour, mapping me, recording every detail like a phrenologist, and committing me to memory. I tried to twist away—I was running hellishly late—but he held me fast. In other circumstances, his grasp would have felt deeply inappropriate. Something in his eyes, like an apology, troubled me.

"I have to go," I said, awkward.

When he said good-bye it felt as if it were final.

THIRTY-THREE

I PULLED INTO THE nearest gateway and cursed. Already late, I'd got stuck behind a tractor for three tortuous miles and then, pulling out of Loddiswell, and taking the twisty and slow-travelling lane that led to the A38, the car started handling badly. I knew immediately what was wrong: a puncture.

I scrambled out, feet hitting the dry, dusty earth, the hem of my skirt snagging on brambles. Cursing more, I examined the rear of the car and extent of the damage. The nearside tyre was blown. It was nothing short of a miracle that I'd managed to manoeuvre it successfully off the road. I guessed providence was looking after me, but now what? I hadn't changed a wheel in an age and didn't relish the prospect of broken nails, and dirt and oil on my clothes.

Changing a tyre was the first lesson my father taught me in a bad-tempered exchange after I'd passed my driving test; I'd only ever practiced once. I ran through the motions in my mind. Shove on the hazard lights. Put the car in first gear. Get out wheel nut spanner and lever off jacking point cover. Position jack. Turn the jackscrew clockwise to raise it. I once did this in forty minutes, but if the wheel nuts were too tightly fixed, or I had trouble unlocking them, it would take longer. I pulled out my phone and called Cathy.

"Sorry, I'm going to be late."

Heather's head throbbed. It was all moving too swiftly and common sense dictated that it was not a good idea to have work done on her body at the same time as her face. The sleek-looking beauty representative parked in her sitting room begged to differ.

Heather noted the smooth and unlined skin, the plump cheeks, sculpted jawline and platinum-blond hair swept back in a style that would have challenged a younger woman. Only the neck and hands gave the game away, she thought, observing the creased skin.

After being shown a collection of before and after photographs, the conversation moved at a giddy pace.

"I'd advise a composite lift," the woman said. "It means that all areas of the face—fat, muscles, and skin—are moved at the same time."

Moved where, Heather quaked inside. Before she could comment, she was thrown another question.

"Do you have a date in mind?"

A date? Was it really that simple? Shouldn't they be discussing her medical history first? "Well ..."

"Only we have an exclusive offer at the moment. What with people away on holidays, it's rather a dead time for us."

"I see," Heather said, cringing at such an unfortunate expression. "When do I get a chance to speak to the surgeon?"

This was met with a persuasive smile. "Mr. Self has a cancellation tomorrow morning."

Heather fretted. If the surgeon was that good, surely he'd have a waiting list, or was this stroke of luck simply meant to be? She calculated how soon Stannard would take to complete the transaction. Somewhat to her surprise, she'd received a lovely card from him that morning in which he'd expressed delight with the house. News of an official offer was firmly promised, but when exactly?

"I'd like a little more time to consider," Heather said, ignoring the audible click of the woman's tongue. "Is there any chance of an appointment at the end of the month?"

"I'll have to check with Mr. Self," came back the tight-lipped reply. Heather couldn't help noticing that the woman's expression remained neutral no matter the emotion, which, according to her voice, shrieked irritation.

The woman gathered up the photographs. "If money's a problem, we could arrange financing."

"That won't be necessary."

She gave Heather a shrewd look. "It's common not to receive support from your nearest and dearest. Husbands and partners can be remarkably resistant to change in their wives and girlfriends. I've seen the same intransigence when women lose weight." She lowered her voice to a confidential level. "It brings out the green-eyed monster. Husbands are frightened their wives are going to be attractive to other men."

Heather broke into a hopeful smile.

I stared, absolutely floored. Chris was right and Grant was wrong. After the puncture on the way to work, this was turning into a really crap day.

The card had slipped through the net because Cathy thought it a birthday greeting. Coffin-shaped, black, there was no inscription. The design said it all. Looked like my stalker was in for the long haul. He'd rather destroy me than let go.

Telling myself to stop emoting and use my brain, I picked up the envelope and attempted to decipher the sorting office. Unfortunately, the postmark was blurred. All I knew was it was sent on Saturday, the day after Grant had spoken to Stannard.

Even with my professional experience, it wasn't always easy to predict human behaviour. But I'd so wanted to believe that Stannard would disappear from my life. Now what? Go back to the cops and complain? And what would they do? Stannard would only deny sending it. So I decided that if I could keep silent, stay safe, last out until Friday, I'd be all right. I could forget about my urban stalker and walk away for three whole weeks. If he tracked me down in Devon, he'd have both of us to deal with. The idea appealed. In the meantime, maybe I *would* think seriously about changing my job, changing the trajectory of my career. Even my existence? God, I thought, Kyle Stannard is doing his best to evict me from my life. Not a damn chance.

Jim stuck his head around the door. I stuffed the card away in a drawer and explained that the police had spoken to Stannard.

"That's a relief."

I flicked a smile, muttered about punctures and running late. Undaunted, Jim loped in and perched on the edge of the desk. "I've come across numerous fascinating details."

"Really? Look, Jim, I've got a number of…"

"Apparently most stalkers have a history of failed relationships. Stalking is their way of taking back control, their chief motivation one of anger. I'd always assumed sex to be the dominant theme," he said, as if amazed by his lack of perspicacity. "Another interesting snippet is that it's not unusual for them to start late in life. You know the old adage, life begins at forty? Well, quite often so does stalking."

I'd already worked out Stannard's age—thirty-eight, or thereabouts. "Quite often, you say?"

"Well, not exclusively, of course. There's always the exception to the rule when it comes to the human psyche."

I resisted the urge to tell Jim that he was stating the bleeding obvious.

"And," Jim said, working up to the finale, "stalkers will often rope in family members to defend their cause."

I hoisted an eyebrow. Jim spotted the heightened interest. From the spellbound look on his face, he was revving up for another pronouncement. "From the little you told me, Stannard's not your stereotypical oddball. He's a guy who saw you as a potential confidante and, when you weren't interested, got uppity, his feelings of rejection a little extreme, I appreciate," he said in answer to my exasperated expression. "I'm glad the police have sorted it so quickly. Apparently we're not that clever at curing the problem. Riveting stuff." He smiled. "So, you're all right then?"

"Never better. Thank you," I added, the pitch forced, a little too bright, a tad too upbeat. My smile made my face muscles hurt. I looked pointedly at my watch.

"God, is that the time?" he said, loping back out of the room.

THIRTY-FOUR

Peeking into shop windows, looking out for Stannard's mirrored reflection. I took a less than obvious route to the flat. When a bloke shambled across the street and accidentally bumped me, unforgivably, I tore into him.

"For Chrissakes, watch where you're going."

"Sorry, love," he muttered in a twenty-fags-a-day voice.

Horrified that I felt so up for a confrontation, I moved off, my fight-or-flight response seemingly jammed on alert, attack first and ask questions later. Walking quickly, mindful of being ambushed, I threw myself into the flat. Shutting the door fast, I dragged the chain across.

Everything looked comfortingly normal. No sign of break-in. No notes. No calls. Relieved, I prepared dinner and lost myself in the rhythmic slicing and dicing of vegetables, the slow preparation of a smooth, creamy white wine sauce to which I added pink fleshy prawns and flakes of honey-roast salmon, the final touch a bowl of glossy green tagliatelle. I made a point of sitting at the small kitchen table with a solitary glass of claret, a novel propped open against a vase of tightly budded scented yellow roses. Against a background of classical music, a favourite piano piece by Debussy, I nibbled and drank and read, and created an immense sense of calm within. Only four days and four nights to go and I'd be in Devon to regroup and refresh among my closest friends. Then the doorbell rang.

My pulse jittered and gathered speed. The doorbell rang again, more insistently. I stood up and spoke into the entry phone. No answer. I crossed the floor and looked out the window. No one. Creeping up to the spy-hole, I peered onto the empty corridor. Drawing away, waiting a few moments, I did the same again. Nobody.

Stomach flooded with acid, appetite abandoned, I reached for the phone and called Chris. The messaging service clicked in. Assuming he was monitoring his calls, I asked him to pick up. He didn't. I called his mobile—switched off. I wondered what he might be doing and decided he'd probably gone for a drink with Andy, or perhaps was engrossed in a film, either at home or at the local cinema. Downhearted, I replaced the receiver and toyed with calling Luke in the States. He'd be at work and, knowing me so well, would pick up that something was bugging me. He was bound to have a view, something I didn't welcome. For all my growing-up years I'd been surrounded by older and, by inference, wiser siblings. It didn't matter if I was thirty or seventy, the dynamics would never change. I would always be the kid sister, not so bright, not quite cutting it. At least I'd elevated myself from being, as my dad once memorably told me, "no bloody good" to "not bad." At a loss, I called Molly. Simon picked up. Two sentences later, he insisted on coming round. I backed off.

"It's all right. I only want a chat." I hated being the centre point of drama.

"I'll be round in ten."

Seven minutes later he was sitting on my sofa. Wearing shorts and vest and running shoes, Simon smelt strongly of sweat. His legs were brown, smooth, and hairless, at odds with his hunky build. His lashes looked unusually dark. It was like having a drag queen in my sitting room.

"Just got back from a jog when you called," he explained.

I told Simon about the latest twist in what I feared was becoming a miserably boring saga, and braced for a lecture. Simon would surely urge me to go back to the police. To my surprise, he didn't. He asked about Chris.

"It's difficult—for both of us. It's put quite a strain on the relationship but I think, or I thought, we were over the worst. I don't want to load him with any more."

"So he doesn't know about the card or the mystery visitor?"

I shrugged my shoulders. That wasn't all he didn't know. "Probably someone buzzing the wrong flat." Now that Simon was with me, I had a clearer perspective. "I called Chris a few minutes ago but he wasn't in."

Simon issued a straight look. "How often have you tried to contact him and got no answer?"

"I'm not sure I understand what you're getting at." I did, but I wasn't travelling down that rutted path with Simon.

Simon's expression didn't alter. His gaze didn't shift. "Have you been noting times and locations when you think you've been followed?"

"I can show you." I sprang to my feet, glad of a chance to leave the room, and went into the bedroom and rummaged in a drawer. Phone directory, address book, useless leaflets with worthless information, oh yes, stalking diary, I thought irreverently. Retrieving the notebook, I handed it to Simon. Flicking through the mostly empty pages, he looked like someone calculating formulae—never a strong point with me. He put it down and gave me a hard look.

"How long have you known me?"

"Got to be ten years," I replied, wary.

"We're good mates?" His expression was intense.

"I think so." I attempted a smile. "And Molly, too," I added hastily. Something made me look at the door. How long would it take to yank it open and flee outside?

"So you trust that whatever I say, whatever Molly and I think, I'm only telling you because you're our friend."

I nodded vacantly. I didn't like the way this was shaping. He was going to say something horrible, I knew it. People got away with the most atrocious things when they used the friend line: *I don't mean to be nasty but, as a mate, your breath smells; because you're my friend, I thought you should know that your husband is in grave debt, is having an affair, is gay, enjoys the company of prostitutes, and/or hustlers.*

"Stalkers rely on one thing to carry out their activities," Simon pronounced.

"A victim," I said merrily.

Simon remained straight-faced. "Time. It's like a job to them. They need to be either in part-time work or an occupation that allows them the freedom to move around."

I stifled a sudden surge of anger. Why was it everyone but me seemed eager to discount the obvious? I looked straight at Simon. "I've no doubt that Kyle Stannard is stalking me. From what you've said, he's also in a position to manage his time to suit his nasty purposes. The perfect candidate, in fact."

Simon leaned towards me, his expression uncompromising. "If Stannard was that intent, he'd have tracked you to Devon."

"What are you trying to say, Simon, that it isn't Stannard?" Heat fled across my cheeks. The scars on my neck felt scratchy. I wished that Simon would go away. Because if it wasn't Stannard then …

Simon continued, unchecked. "Maybe Stannard is harmless. Perhaps his intention to talk is born out of genuine interest."

"Have you forgotten the way he followed me, his threats, the way he tried to scare me witless?"

"Did he? Are you absolutely certain?"

"Please don't tell me I'm imagining it." My heart caught in my ribs. Was I having some kind of mental breakdown? Was I delusional? Was I gripped by paranoia? I gulped. Shouldn't I *know*?

"Of course I'm not, but sometimes things can get out of hand and be misinterpreted."

Shame on me, but at that precise moment I wished Simon would drop dead.

"He's an ambitious man," Simon said, "unhappy with taking no for an answer."

I threw back my head and laughed. It sounded staccato. "The hallmark of the stalker."

Undeterred, Simon said, "He's got a reputation to uphold. Stannard wouldn't be so stupid."

"Stupidity doesn't figure. This is about obsession."

Simon shook his head. "A significant number of stalkers know their victims. They're often ex-partners …"

"So we're back to Phil again," I very nearly snapped with frustration.

"Hear me out, Kim. How well do you actually know Chris? You said yourself he's hardly ever at home."

Did I? I tried to get a handle on the one or two specific times I'd called Chris and found that he was out. I tried to remember his timetable. He taught solidly every day. But then there had been that two-day visit to Huckham. No, silly, I thought. It didn't tie in, didn't make sense. Stannard was already in the mix by then.

"Does he have the key to your flat here in Cheltenham?"

"Yes."

"The key to your car?"

"It's on his key-ring as a precaut—"

"There rests my case."

I felt as if he'd hit me over the head with something heavy and then applied chloroform to my mouth and nose. Entertaining something in your mind was one thing; somebody else breathing life into the thought was quite another. Taken aback, I couldn't formulate the words, couldn't speak. I thought of the weekend, Chris's mood, the heightened sex and new accord. I hadn't fully processed it. Part of me felt like a woman in jeopardy. The other …

"He doesn't seem committed to you," Simon said more gently.

"For God's sake, we're not tied to each other at the hip. We both have careers." And I was prepared to give up mine for Chris, but he wasn't so enthusiastic. There was that whole criminal thing loitering in his background. And he was acting strangely, his moods as unpredictable as riptides. I'd put it down to Stannard, but what if …

"You don't know him," I said hotly.

Simon gave a deep sigh. "Too right. He rarely ventures out of Devon. In four years, we've met him three times. He never wants to see your friends and he hardly ever stays with you in Cheltenham even when he has his wonderfully long holidays. He's a loner. He's solitary. He's—"

"Stop," I said, my voice unpleasantly shrill.

Simon didn't understand what living in Devon did to people. Seduced by the scenery and the illusion of the good life, people became extraordinarily insular. It took either ambition or boredom to effect a change. And it didn't matter whether you were born there or were chasing a dream. Once cuddled up under the large, fluffy, sleep-inducing duvet of Devon, it was easy to be deceived. People found it difficult to escape. But sometimes they had to. Sometimes the illusion was revealed. Sometimes they got scorched living there. But Chris, with his history of broken homes and foster care, could be forgiven for digging in.

"It doesn't make him my stalker," I gasped, tears in my eyes.

THIRTY-FIVE

How well do I know Chris? Answer: Not very.

I edged myself into the day. I'd had one glass of wine the previous night but my mouth was dry and my eyes felt pickled, a clear case of psychology influencing physiology. I gobbled down a couple of painkillers and arranged for a guy to come and fit an alarm system at the flat, something I should have done sooner.

Next, I phoned Chris. No reply. I ordered myself not to jump to the wrong conclusion and, in an immensely calm and what I hoped was an unemotional voice, left a message for him to call.

Walking to work, I felt less contained. Consumed by questions, Simon's seed of doubt took root, bloomed, and spread like creeping ivy. Where was Chris? Why hadn't he called? Could he be my stalker? Could Stannard be a misfit with appalling timing?

With a tight throat, I checked in with Cathy, who treated me as if I were returning after a spell of compassionate leave, and gathered with a dozen other staff in the common room for a meeting to *touch base*, as Jim fashionably termed it. I couldn't help but study faces, picking out the men and combing suspiciously through their personal details as if they were case histories.

With Jim glancing a bit too often in my direction, I itched to get back to my room so that I could phone Chris's school. Waiting for what seemed an interminable amount of time, I finally broke free and spoke to one of the secretaries who confounded me with one sentence: "He's not in this week."

"Are you sure?"

"That's what it says here."

"Does it say why?"

"Personal reasons."

Feeling like a betrayed wife, I explained who I was. "Do you know who took the call?"

A muffled discussion took place between two female voices. "Sorry. Would you like me to find out?"

"Please, and could you ask Andy Johnson to give me a ring when he's free?"

I waited and waited, saw the last of the girls on my list for the morning session and, under the guise of entering up notes, pretended to work. I sharpened a pencil, poured a cold drink, and spent a long time checking emails and Internet news.

Personal reasons. So personal, it didn't include me? Was Chris having a breakdown? Blinded by my own problems, had I failed to spot the signs?

I went to the loo, looked at my face in the mirror, tipped my chin to the light, watching it play on my less than perfect skin. Faces held stories. Every line and groove, every fixed expression clues to the emotional history of the wearer. I thought of the girls I treated, some with faces wizened by self-inflicted progeria, those born with facial defects, victims of Cherubism, a rare condition resulting in bulging eyes and lengthened jaws, those who'd been disfigured through injury, or disease, or plain malice. Without warning, Stannard's weird, beautiful and crazy face loomed in front of my eyes.

"Fuck you," I swore aloud and strode back to the office.

The phone rang as I tipped cheese into a risotto. Believing it was Chris I snatched it up.

"Kim."

One word. My name. Blood-freezing.

"Why did you tell the police a pack of lies?"

My jaw dropped with indignation.

"In the absence of an answer or an apology, I propose we start over again." No plea. An order.

God, he was good. Most blokes would have backed off, but not him. Stannard was coming on with a vengeance. I flashed with temper. "There's nothing to start. If you don't leave me alone, I'll go back to the police."

"Are you sure about that?"

"Is that a threat?"

"For a shrink you're remarkably quick to take offence."

"You're stalking me."

His response was cool and superior. "Do you actually know what it means?"

"Of course, I damn well ..."

"According to the Concise Oxford English Dictionary, it means to steal up to game under cover. I don't consider you as prey and all my actions have been quite open. Incidentally, if I was really stalking you, you could get the cops to slap a restraining order on me, not that it's always a good move. I understand from some of the legal circles I move in that it can sometimes inflame a situation."

Legal circles, I registered with a jolt. "You send me spooky cards. You take my car. You send a pornographic image to where I work. You hog my phone line. You pester me in person, *and it isn't what I think it is*?"

"Sounds like you have a heavy-duty problem."

"I do: you."

"You know perfectly well it's not me." The tone was patronising.

"You're lying."

"Bullshit. Incidentally, I've got a perfectly good car of my own."

That much was true, according to Simon's information, but no way did it let Stannard off the hook. I would not allow this utter shit to beat me.

A telephone distance apart, he could be right outside the flat. I peeped out of the window. No sign of him. Screw the rules. Time to turn the tables.

"Do you have family?" I said.

"Do you?"

"I asked first."

This seemed to amuse him. "Yes."

"You're in regular contact with them?"

"I visit my mother often."

Stalkers will often rope in family members to defend their cause. "Where did you grow up?"

"Kent. What about you?"

"Never you mind. Are you on medication?"

He issued a laugh. "A moderate amount of wine each day helps me sleep."

"You have a problem sleeping?"

"I'm an insomniac. I have bad dreams, day and night."

"By day?" I silently cursed my failure to conceal my professional interest.

"I imagine I'm in the middle of a crowd. There are literally hundreds of people cheering, the cream of society. They're all beautiful, gorgeously dressed—McQueen, Marc Jacobs, Armani, Chanel." His voice had taken on a strange intonation. "I can smell them."

Smell. One word and my alarm bells sounded. It hinted at an imaginary world more thrilling than reality, indicating that he was perpetually in mourning for the life he'd lost. My lungs felt seared with acid. I knew what he meant. I *knew*…

Stannard sliced and diced my thoughts. "Are you superstitious?"

"What?"

"Cracks in the pavement, touching wood, magpies? One for sorrow, two for joy. Best thing to do is run over the bastards."

Christ, he was sprinting away with the conversation. I snatched it back. "Where did you go to school?"

"The local comprehensive."

"That's not where, that's type."

"Clever," he purred. Maddeningly, I felt flattered. "I went to school in Kent. What you're really trying to find out is where I live."

"Wellington Square." I bit my lip.

"Well, well. Who's stalking whom?"

"I like to know where the enemy is coming from."

"Tsk, Kim. I'm not your enemy."

Snookered, I adopted a less combative approach. "Do you live with anyone?"

"Mind your own business. Your technique to extract information lacks finesse, if you don't mind my saying."

I did mind. "Why don't you talk to her, or maybe it's a him?"

"Neat try. Points for that." He issued a smug laugh.

"So?" I said, persistent.

"I'm straight and I live alone—like you." His voice slipped into a low, seductive tone. "How do I make you do what I want?"

"You can't browbeat people."

"Learned behaviour, darling. Sometimes it's the only way to get things done."

"I'm not your darling and I don't respond to being railroaded."

"Don't be haughty, Kim. It doesn't suit you."

Exhausted, I fell silent. The quiet stretched for at least thirty seconds, maybe more.

"Hello?" he said. "Cat got your tongue?"

Temporarily refusing to engage, I said nothing. I needed to gather my mental resources.

"Are you still there?"

"I am."

"Good. I'll pay twice the going rate."

"Look, I understand your difficulties and I'm sorry but—"

"I only want to talk to you, for God's sake. Where's the harm?"

"Kyle, I can't." Damn, should never have used his Christian name.

"What do you want me to do, beg?"

"I don't want you to do anything." I was weary of him, of his games, of everything. "I simply want you to leave me alone."

"Is that your final word?" He sounded as though he was giving me one last chance to change my mind and redeem myself.

"It is."

Silence stretched out like an empty road in the desert.

"Secrets and guilt." He articulated the words slowly.

"Pardon?"

"It's what you trade in. And I have to share mine with you."

Have to. "Why me?"

"Because you shimmer with sadness."

The hairs on the back of my neck awoke from a long, faraway sleep and stood erect. "Like I said," I repeated, thick-tongued, "my expertise is in an entirely different field."

"Did you know that the only attributes a convincing liar needs are nerve and front? Swear to a story often enough, people swallow it."

"I don't know what you mean." I rubbed at my eyes. "I don't understand how this is relevant."

"You could treat me, if you wanted to. You could help me."

"I can't. I'm the wrong person."

"You're exactly the right person. It's why you became a shrink, isn't it? The mind becomes so much more interesting when one's looks are compromised."

"Fuck off."

He let out a laugh. "I like that about you—no shit, straight to the point. It's quite a muscular trait, unusual in a woman."

"That's—"

"Let me finish. It's rude to interrupt." It had been some time since I'd been told to shut up. *Children should be seen and not heard.* It hurt as much now as it did then. "I haven't yet got past the point of feeling bitter," Stannard continued. "Naturally, it's not as bad as it used to be, thank God. At least I can function. It's a kind of trick, isn't it?"

"That's self-pitying rubbish. I wouldn't know."

"I think you do. I think you understand only too well. Were you burnt a long time ago, Kim? Was it a tragic accident?"

I slammed down the phone.

I was seven years old and bubbling with excitement because it was Guy Fawkes Night. For a month gales had whipped from the north, crossing sea and land, smearing it with a thick blanket of yellow sea fog, confining fishermen to port. Then the rain stopped, replaced by a bitter winter chill.

Stepping outside, the breath punched out of me. My tiny feet felt numb. Ears tingling, they turned itchy and were probably bright red. My gloveless hands were raw. Daddy forgot things like that. Jackets, too. I only started to clean my teeth and wash properly later on when I was sent away to school. My brothers teased me about it. They taunted me about lots of things—grace before meals, deportment, elocution lessons, the la-di-dah accent that replaced my slow drawl Devon roots, and what they called my new airs and graces. They viewed my going away to school as our dad's attempt to turn me into a little lady, and took every opportunity to rib me about it. I felt like a cuckoo, not quite fitting into either world. One alien environment with strict and incomprehensible rules, the other where there were no rules at all. And therein lay the tragedy.

My adolescent brothers had spent days hauling bits of dead tree and wood to build a bonfire. It stretched up to the sky as solid as a fortified castle.

We ransacked Daddy's wardrobe and found one of his old jackets. It was checked and dung-coloured and stained. Then we found an old pair of trousers and a funny Russian hat, lined with fur, that he'd bought long before I was born. Luke persuaded the gardener, who came in once a week, or maybe it was the girl groom, couldn't remember now, to sew the clothes together. I don't know why but I thought Daddy would get cross and threatened to tell. The boys didn't like that and accused me of being a scaredy-cat. When I screamed blue murder, they gave me sweets and crisps and pop to shut me up. Afterwards, they filled the guy with straw kept for the ponies and threw him up onto the waiting bonfire and waited for darkness to fall.

We all trooped outside. Daddy cooked hot dogs. We ate them with fried onions and gloopy ketchup. I drank loads more pop and my tummy hurt.

Daddy lit the bonfire first. I thought it would go off with a terrific whoosh but it didn't. It crackled and spat and went out. "Too much damp," Daddy said. The boys suggested putting petrol on it and got well and truly told off. Daddy chucked on dry wood and lit it again, and this time the twigs crackled and spat. At last, tiny yellow flames flickered into life, creeping slowly, igniting branch and leaf, spreading a relentless flow of fire. I gazed mesmerised, feeling the power and heat, watching the light play in my brothers' eyes, seeing it ignite the blackened sky. I took a step forward and squealed as Daddy grabbed hold and dragged me back. He gave me a stern talking to, warning of the dangers of getting too close. Out of the corner of my eye I saw Guy smirk.

We started off with sparklers. I held one in each hand, circling them, making patterns. Daddy had made a firework trail and scurried across the grass, a taper in hand, lighting first one and then another. I didn't like the shouty Jumping Jacks and bangers and clamped my hands over my ears and screwed my eyes up tight. I liked pretty Roman candles and Catherine Wheels best. Holding Daddy's hand, watching the blaze of colour, I felt cosy inside. For once, I'd forgotten about my mummy.

Then the phone rang. It blared across the garden. Daddy didn't look anxious. He looked pleased and excited. I think he was expecting a call from a lady friend. He lit a firework and called to Luke to look after me while he ran across the frosted grass and shot inside.

Luke's hand was hot and sticky in mine. We glanced back but Daddy was gone and so we fixed our eyes on the firework. It was a big rocket, yellow and red stripes, with a finned tail like a shark's. It stuck, argumentative, into the ground. A teasing tendril of smoke curled from its base. We waited and stamped our feet on the frozen earth, but nothing happened.

"It needs relighting," Guy said, patting his pockets. "Got any matches?"

"We should leave it," Luke pointed out. "You know what Dad said. Never go up to a firework that hasn't ignited."

"Yeah, but this one's gone out." His voice sounded like a cracked plate. Half boy, half man.

"You don't know that."

"Duh, stupid, yes I do."

“Just leave it.”

“You’re scared.” Guy’s thin face, all edges and angles, looked mean in the moonlight.

Luke jutted out his chin and squared up to my other brother. “Not.”

“You are so.”

Luke let go of my hand and took a swing. Guy, quicker and more agile, punched him in the face.

I screamed and told them to stop. Blood pouring from his nose, Luke launched himself at Guy and brought him down. Dismayed, I watched the tangle of bodies, a seething mass of kicks, grunts, and shouts. I tried to haul them off each other but I wasn’t strong enough. A stray fist glanced off the side of my head and knocked me flying. Sprawled on the frozen ground, drumming my feet, how I cried, but the boys didn’t notice. And it seemed to me then like nobody ever did. I was Little Miss Invisible.

Luke had Guy pinned down. His hand raised, his fist balled, I sensed, little as I was, that one of them was about to be badly hurt.

“I’m not scared,” I yelled, scrabbling to my feet. “Look, you two, it’s easy.” I ran towards the rocket as fast as my stout legs would carry me. The rest was jumbled. A whoosh. Flames. A shrill scream. A killing sensation of hot and indescribable pain. Yelling.

Drum roll of boys running.

More shouts.

A sour smell of burnt flesh, burnt clothing.

Panting.

Stop the pain.

Nerve endings stripped and minced.

Someone picked me up and rolled me in the frozen grass. A man’s voice, loud and unnatural. My small hands peeled from my face. Searing, screaming, shattering, breath-stopping pain. There was black stuff and blood in my hands—my molten skin, my flesh and blood.

THIRTY-SIX

I DIDN'T BELIEVE STANNARD's patter about *simply* wanting to talk. A talk would lead to more conversation. One meeting followed by another. Before I knew where I was, Stannard would think he was in a full-blown relationship with me. He'd be planning visits home to his mummy and wedding bells. Given time, he believed that his feelings would be returned. This was the make-up of Stannard's interior world. Delusional.

Over a second cup of tea, I continued to pool information. What was he really planning to talk to me about? His self-pity, his inability to come to terms with his disfigurement? His lack of courage? Something he didn't appear to be short of from where I stood. I scowled. It was no use trying to view him as I would a client. Stannard was driven by another agenda. Me.

My mobile rang. I snatched it up. Knowing that I was in no fit state to help anyone, I took the call anyway. It was Alexa with a litany of "he said that" and "I said this." At one point I almost cackled with hysteria. Twenty minutes later, I extricated myself with platitudes and a promise to talk again soon.

I showered and dressed, phoned Chris, and left another message. As Andy had still not returned my call, I caught him at home. He answered after three rings and sounded half asleep. Irrationally, it made me testy.

"Didn't you get my message?"

"What message?"

"The message I left at school for you to ring me."

I heard him yawn. "Must have disappeared in the general swamp of administration."

I stifled a curse. "Never mind, have you seen Chris?"

"I've been working my bollocks off putting the finishing touches to a programme for a local company. Had a bit of a time frame." Andy's moonlighting was a lucrative, if time-consuming, sideline. He made no secret of it and often talked about chucking in teaching and going into it full-time.

"When was the last time you saw him?"

"Last time I saw you—Sunday morning."

"You know he hasn't been at school this week."

"Uh-huh."

"Do you have any idea where he is?"

Uncomfortable silence.

"Andy, is there something you're not telling me, something I should know?"

"No." He sounded flat.

"I can't get a reply. I'm worried something's happened."

"Like what?"

"I don't know," I bluffed. "It's so odd that he hasn't returned my calls. Could you go over to the cottage? Give me a ring back?"

"Sure, but it's probably nothing."

I replaced the receiver and wondered why the sense of dread was so compelling. What was Chris trying to tell me that very last time? I visualised the scene, re-visualised the look of apology in his eyes. Was it connected to those damn messages on his phone? Impulsively, I dialled Claire's number but cut the call before it connected; she'd be knee-deep in children and the school-run. There was nothing else to be done, I told myself and, if I didn't leave soon, I'd be late for work.

On the way out, Lizzie popped out of her flat, a look of simmering excitement on her face. "Ta-dah! We've had an offer."

"And you've accepted?"

"You bet. We couldn't refuse."

Grant's words whistled through my brain: *Came up with some cock-and-bull story about viewing the flat below.*

"Time to crack open the champagne," Lizzie hugged me.

I threw her a bright, congratulatory smile. "So what are my new neighbours like?"

"*Neighbour.* Single guy. I didn't get to meet him. Pete showed him around. Actually, he felt a bit sorry for him. Apparently the guy has some sort of facial disability, but he seems pleasant enough." The excitement fizzled out of her voice in response to my crumpled expression.

Suddenly light-headed, I clapped a hand over my mouth. Breakfast worked its way up from my stomach to the back of my throat. I tried to swallow.

"What is it?" Lizzie asked in consternation.

Devastated, I tore outside and threw up on the steps. Lizzie followed me. "What's the matter? I didn't mean …"

I rummaged for a tissue, wiped my mouth. Vomit spattered my shoes. "Kyle Stannard's going to buy your flat, isn't he?" My voice came out thinner and squeakier than I'd intended.

"You know him?" Lizzie's body stiffened.

"He's stalking me," I blurted out. I must have looked stricken. Lizzie grabbed hold of my arm as if to steady me and led me into her flat, sat me down, and gave me a glass of water. Five rambling minutes later, I watched Lizzie's expression change from shock to disbelief to anxiety.

"Are you asking us not to sell?" Lizzie's face was tight and uncompromising.

"I don't know what I'm asking."

"Oh God, Kim, we've waited so long to get out of here." Lizzie ran her fingers distractedly through her hair.

"I know."

"Are you sure? Pete's a good judge of character. He said he was charming and polite."

What was the point in arguing? Lizzie and Pete wanted to move. This wasn't their problem, and it wasn't in their interests to take my side; I'd only complicated the issue.

Lizzie stood up and looked at her watch. "Leave it with me. I'll have a word with Pete." Her expression lightened. "There is an alternative."

I arched an eyebrow, weak and hopeful.

"You could always move instead."

Slow-burning chaos. My world was in anarchy.

I arrived late for work. Feeling third-rate and empty of insight, I winged it by sheer luck. At the first opportunity I phoned Claire, who knew nothing about Chris's movements. Sounding exhausted, Claire sweetly offered to go and check up on him.

"Andy's already taking care of it."

"Oh good," Claire said with obvious relief.

"It's out of character for him not to contact me," I said, unable to play down my grating unease.

"I'm sure there's a simple reason. Maybe he's not well." It was good to hear the calm in Claire's voice. I so wanted to believe that everything would be fine, nothing more than a case of over-reaction on my part. When under pressure it's the simplest thing in the world to see sinister intent behind innocent actions. That's the way humans ticked. With shame, I recalled my anger towards Simon. Claire was still talking.

"Although we didn't think he seemed quite himself last weekend."

"Didn't you?" Simon's accusation did a double flip in my brain and landed with an awkward bump, like a gymnast fluffing a routine.

"Probably the strain of that bloke bothering you."

I agreed but wondered if I was wrong about the reason. In the past twelve hours, I felt as if all my judgements were flawed.

"Everything else all right?"

"Yes," I said hastily, not wishing to add to Claire's fatigue. "I'll see you at the weekend." With a distinct lack of enthusiasm, I remembered my thirty-sixth birthday.

I spent the lunch hour poring over books, trying to make a stab at what type of personality disorder Stannard suffered from. The more I read, the more questions arose. Was he fuelled by a desire to be loved, or was rejection the key to his behaviour? Was he driven by envy, viewing me as someone who had more than her fair share of happiness, or fury, or something entirely other? Had he done it before and, in spite of his modest claim to drink only in moderation, did he use drugs to crank himself up? Was his mother a sound influence or a colluding, cloying partnership? Without talking to him, I'd never be able to discover the answers and yet contact was out of the question. I'd already strayed across the boundaries and done the verbal equivalent of throwing a Jumping Jack in his face. Ironic.

At almost two in the afternoon, I stumbled across a fact that chilled. When it came to stalking, the victim wasn't the only person in danger. Those closest were also in peril. Partners and relatives ranked top of the list. My God, Chris, I realised. My instinct was to drive straight to Devon. Fortunately, Jim was easily persuaded.

"We can handle your workload for the rest of the day, and the week, if you like."

"I hope that won't be necessary."

"Of course, but the offer is there. Kim," he said as I gathered up my things, "before you leave, phone the police. Tell them what's happened."

I blanched. "I don't know if anything's happened."

Jim flicked a tense smile. "Keep them in the loop is all I'm suggesting."

THIRTY-SEVEN

I DIDN'T. I DROVE at lunatic speed. Angered by the volume of traffic, I wove in and out and switched lanes with naked aggression. Chris was the one barrier to Stannard's ambition and, if what I'd read contained a grain of truth, he was in real and imminent danger.

I was off the motorway and travelling along the A38 towards Kingsbridge when my mobile phone rang. Breaking the law, I picked up.

"He's not there," Andy said.

"Are you sure?"

"Well, I guess he could be hiding under the bed."

"This isn't funny."

"Sorry, you're right."

"What about the car?"

"Gone."

"Bike?"

"Still there."

"Right," I said, mouth drying. I didn't know if that made things better or worse. "Andy?"

"What?"

"Is Chris seeing someone?"

I heard a noise, the scuffling of dozens of pairs of feet, scraping of chair legs, chatter.

"I've got year ten pouring in," he shouted above the din. "I'll have to go. Catch you later, yeah?"

I slowed down. I crashed gear-changes and misjudged distances. I didn't remember any part of the journey to the cottage.

Cormorants Reach emerged swathed in sunshine, its thick, squat chimney poking up into an expanse of cloudless sky. It seemed exactly the same—cared for, attractive, and welcoming. A lie.

On the mat were several envelopes, greetings cards, I supposed, to celebrate my forthcoming birthday. I scooped them up and scanned each one, relieved to match the handwriting to the sender, then entered the living room with its low ceiling and the chair near the window in which my father used to sit. A long-forgotten image of me in my short white socks assailed me. I sat next to my dad, my shoes not touching the floor. We had plates of congealed food on our laps, loneliness in our hearts.

In the early days, not long after my mother left us, a cleaner used to cook our meals at lunchtime and leave them on the boiler for when my dad finished work and picked me up from school. I hated those dinners. My adult aversion to gravy was a direct legacy of terrible meals eaten in silence.

Stifling the memory, I called out Chris's name, heard the shake in my voice, the sound sucked into empty space. Elsewhere, the room was neat and orderly, as Chris liked it. No mugs on the coffee table. No newspapers on the floor. The hearth cleared. Aggressively clean. I peered into the study, my private lair dark and womblike; papers on the desk where I'd left them days before. Everywhere an eerie silence blunted my senses.

I walked down the two steps to the kitchen with its honey-coloured tiled floor, Belfast sink, the cross-paned windows that looked out over the terrace and creek below. My heart briefly lifted at the sight of the spare keys to the motorbike hanging up where they should be. Worktops and the cherry wood kitchen table with its four chairs neatly arranged, fastidiously uncluttered. Only the phone in the corner, the messaging light winking at me, disturbed the picture of calm. Against the beat of my heart, I heard the slow tick of the kitchen clock, the gentle purr of the freezer. Then I saw the envelope propped against the kettle, my name written on it, Chris's unmistakable handwriting. Proof that he was safe, my heart gave a small lift of relief. Short-lived. The bunch of house keys next to it winded me.

I touched the envelope, which was white and narrow, and picked it up between thumb and forefinger. The flap had been folded inside and, as I pulled it out with trembling fingers, the paper felt cheap and flimsy.

I drew up a chair, sat down, and read. A concession to his illegible handwriting, it was typed.

Dear Kim,

I know this will come as a shock but I'm leaving. I wanted to do this some time ago but then with the other business I didn't feel it right to abandon you when you so clearly needed me. The truth is there's someone else in my life and has been for a while. We've decided to go away together and start a new life. I wish you well, Kim. I hope, with time, you can forgive me. What we had together was good and special. I will always remember you.

Chris

THIRTY-EIGHT

That was it: a few lines to say good-bye to four years.

The paper slipped from my fingers and onto the floor. My throat swelled and dry sobs scraped against the roof of my mouth. Can't be true, I gasped, my sense of denial compelling.

Not again.

I bent down, snatched up the note, reread it, studying the flourish of his handwritten signature, digesting every word, looking for hidden meanings, searching for hope when there was none to be had, hating myself for feeling this desperate. I wanted to howl but was too blindsided. I'd so wanted a letter as evidence that Stannard's mind games were taking their toll, a plea for space, perhaps, a desire for thinking time. Not a sorry and good-bye. Not an ending. Not like this.

In a bid to hold the wounded remains of myself together, I cursed his cowardice, swore at him for his weakness, criticised the note for being full of the stuff people trot out when they've made up their minds and already have a firm foot outside the door. Who was this bloody woman who had taken him? And how could I have been so stupid? With astringent clarity, I understood his sudden desire for sex, a weird form of apology, one last service he could do for me. Either that, or he was making a last territorial attempt to stamp his identity on my body, preprogrammed to ensure he, as the dumper, felt better about ending the relationship with me, the dumpee. Even the photograph was nothing more than a trophy, a badge of fucking honour. I felt like such a clown. The moods, the irritation, the dominating sex, the obsession with messages on his mobile, were nothing more than symptoms of his conflicted desires, his damned affair.

I rushed upstairs to our tiny bedroom. Symbolic of our ending, the bed was stripped bare. I threw open the specially designed wardrobe that had been built into the eaves, pulled out the drawers. What few clothes Chris possessed were gone—shoes, possessions, the lot. The tiny en suite bathroom told the same story. Shaving accoutrements, toothbrush, aftershave, and after-sun all vanished. So it was true. I sat down hard on the floor, my spine digging into the wall, drew up my knees to my heaving chest, and buried my face in my hands. A wave of tears engulfed me, déjà vu in its entire vile and vivid colour.

I didn't know for how long I sat there on the cool bathroom floor yowling like a tethered, beaten animal. Grief slid into self-pity as I descended into meltdown. Memories clamoured like angry ghosts: the difficulties of growing up in a household where public displays of emotions were rare and tears disapproved of, the day I'd started a period at home and didn't know how to get rid of the soiled sanitary towels, the energy devoted to being the best I could despite my best never being good enough.

Much later, I forced myself to return downstairs and opened the doors to the terrace to clear the musty air. I read the letter once more, my lover's rejection like dirty rain on new sidewalk. Then, crushing it between my fingers, I took the envelope, sped outside, and threw both into the water.

Pressing a fist to my mouth, I watched the paper curl and sink. Concern for him, worry about the impact of Stannard upon his life and, all the time, Chris had been seeing, loving, having sex with another woman. Maybe even in *our* cottage. And, like a fool, I'd made it easy. I'd not been around to witness an increase in the number of showers he took, the greater attention paid to his appearance, the new clothes, old lies, those lengthy furtive phone conversations, all the hallmarks of infidelity. I felt a dull, compelling thud of jealousy but far greater was my intense sense of abandonment and the obliterating realisation that we fear most the things that have already happened to us.

I had only few strong memories of my mother. I remembered the smell of her scent, her enchanting smile, what I would now describe as her vivacity. There was nothing to suggest a heartless streak. That came later. I remembered her leaving only in the sense of feeling discarded. My father had taken care of my daily needs in a rough and ready fashion. I was stoutly ignored if I asked when Mummy was coming back, discussion of the subject firmly discouraged. All he would say was that she'd gone away. One day I overheard him speaking to my older brothers. They were now a triumvirate, he said portentously. It sounded grand and important except I found out later that it was a Roman phrase of office meaning three, not four. The move to boarding school only served to confirm my feelings of rejection. There were two girls in my year whose mothers were dead. I envied them. There was something dramatic and sad and noble about their loss. And it was final. How could I explain that my mother had left me, didn't want me, was alive but unavailable?

So I retreated into a different world, a world in which my mother was good and beautiful and loved me. Sometimes I thought she'd return. I wished it, willed it, prayed for it. But it never happened.

I was fifteen when, unknown to my father, I decided to hunt my mother down. Guy, then twenty-two, supplied the information and arranged a clandestine meeting at a café in Exeter. I travelled for nearly two hours on a stuffy bus to get there, my heart bursting with excitement and trepidation. The café, or more accurately a tearoom, was around the corner from the cathedral. White starched table-cloths graced the tables. Waitresses wearing bleached white aprons with black high-collared shirts, skirts and stockings and flat shoes served with unnerving civility. My mother sat in a corner near a window. She looked a great deal younger than my dad, pretty, maybe a little careworn. I felt thrown, not because she didn't square with the person of my dreams but because I saw how much I resembled her, similar eyes and nose. I didn't know it then, but afterwards I realised that when my father rebuked me, he was really rebuking her.

There was an embarrassed exchange in which we awkwardly hugged. Did I imagine that she clung to me for a fraction of time? Without much preamble, she remarked upon my face, offering condolences as if someone had died and, as if because of it, my life was forever blighted. I tried to ask the questions that had been dogging me for years, but she had a habit of deflecting them with platitudes and excuses while looking frequently out of the window. Perhaps she was nervous. Perhaps she felt guilty. I didn't know, but I knew she didn't really want to be there, that she couldn't wait to escape. In answer to the big question, the reason she left, she said:

"You're too young to understand, Kim. You'll probably never comprehend. Here," she said, pressing a ten-pound note into my hand. "I have to leave. I have a train to catch. Good luck."

I surged out of the café on a tidal wave of anger. It sustained and supported me, and gave me that brand of courage so highly spoken of and prized by others. Afterwards, I dedicated myself to a job requiring the compassion I'd missed out on.

Blinking away the memory, I remembered little of the next couple of hours. At some stage, I wandered across the drive to the garage. Neither of us parked our cars inside, but the Triumph was exactly where we last left it, like a strange parting gift. Perhaps it didn't fit into his new life with his new woman, I thought, half crazed.

Back in the cottage, I listened to my own increasingly desperate phone messages to Chris, moved stuff into the spare bedroom, and set up camp there in a weak attempt to embrace a single life again. Had I been at the Cheltenham flat, I'd have found it easier to kid myself. The cottage had once represented unity. Walk into any room, and I'd remember something he said. Sit in this chair or that and I'd recall a certain expression on his face. It was as if he'd died. Everywhere seemed inhabited by his ghost and the spooks that had fled before him.

Now I was really on my own, with nobody to hold or protect me, nobody who, in turn, I could love. My life had come full circle.

And Stannard was still out there.

On my third glass of wine, it occurred to me that Andy had known all along. I swore, feeling the acuity of double betrayal. I wondered how many others knew, or how long it would take for the drums to beat and the whole community to hear. With big-busted Jen on the scene, it would be all over the South Hams in moments.

Claire had hinted at something in their last conversation. Had she been about to reveal all, but backed down? Could one of them be persuaded or coerced into telling me about the other woman? Did I really want to know, and what good would it do?

With tired resignation, I conceded that my friends were right, and I was wrong. Obviously, I had a tendency to form unsuitable relationships out of the shattered and grisly remains of life-changing events. Not only was I a hopeless chooser of men, which seemed odd given that I'd been brought up almost exclusively in their company, but I was also on a crusade for love, a quest that led me into all the wrong places. So what was stopping me from leaving this time? Why not give up the bolthole in Devon, sell the flat, and start over somewhere different … somewhere Kyle Stannard would never find me?

For the next hour, my overloaded mind grappled with what had happened. Some time later, clarity returned and I picked up the phone to Luke and got through to him half past four in the afternoon US time. I told him I was putting the cottage on the market, that I was perfectly fine, work was good, and that there was nothing wrong.

THIRTY-NINE

Heather Foley didn't drink at lunchtime but she needed something to stiffen her spirit. She'd heard from Damian Fairweather that morning. The longed-for offer had been made and it was a good wedge lower than expected. Forty thousand, to be precise. Stannard, she thought angrily, the ugly little freak.

Visions of being trapped in a home she couldn't afford, her life stuck in a hideous time warp, held no appeal. Until the house was sold there was no way out. The dismal truth was she was no good on her own. Without a partner, she felt as if she was living a half life. She didn't belong anywhere and it was killing her. And she was very, very angry at the world. Her friends thought her ludicrous. They simply didn't understand.

She poured herself another sherry. It wasn't right that Stannard had taken advantage of her situation. She'd no idea that he was buttering her up with his neat speech, his crooked expression of sincerity, in order to fleece her. Gentleman, indeed? Bastard, more like.

At the end of the day, to quote Fairweather's knackered old expression, she concluded that she had no realistic choice. An offer accepted was better than none at all, and it would only take a little of the money to provide the longed-for enhancement of her appearance. It would return the confidence she so badly lacked. It would facilitate an escape route. Anything would be possible afterwards. Before she lost her nerve, she phoned Fairweather and accepted.

"But there is to be no dispute following the survey." No reduction in price for the leaky conservatory, the decrepit boiler, was what she meant.

"I understand the position, Mrs. Foley, but I have a duty to tell you that, if you accept Mr. Stannard's offer, you cannot show anyone else around the property."

"Why not?"

"It isn't fair."

Fair on whom, she wondered? "Until a place is sold, anything can happen. Are you telling me that someone else is interested?"

"We had an enquiry this morning but, unfortunately, the gentleman can't view until next week."

"The more the merrier." The tide was turning in her favour. "Book him in."

"No can-do."

"Excuse me?"

"Mrs. Foley," Fairweather said, "we do a lot of business with Mr. Stannard. He's an extremely good client. You'd be well advised to accept his offer."

"Oh," was all that she could think to say. It was blatantly obvious that she was being steamrollered, but she didn't know what to do, or with whom to discuss it. "You really think it would be in my best interests?"

"You won't get a better offer in the current climate. If the house were in mint condition, then we'd be speaking a different language."

"All right," she said, defeated.

"Well done, I'll get on to Mr. Stannard right away."

She could almost hear Fairweather clap his hands in delight.

FORTY

MID-CALL, I'D CAVED IN and blurted out that Chris had left me. Luke advised me to do nothing. "Wait until the dust's settled. You're too upset to make an informed decision. It's what Dad would have said."

I grunted agreement and went into Kingsbridge the following morning, spoke to two estate agents, then drove round and parked the car in Salcombe, visited another, and made appointments for a valuation with all three.

Ambling back past the boat-builders and on towards Whitestrand and the main street, I felt coldly vengeful. A thirst for retribution was common in my clientele, usually when they were on the mend. I always counselled against it. Unproductive, I'd say. False judgement. People usually do the best they can even if they let you down. In the majority of cases, most bad actions are mistaken, not malign. I tried hard to take my own advice and failed. I mused how easy it would be to pin the blame for the breakdown of my relationship with Chris on Stannard. Unfortunately, I was forced to accept that, had it not been for Stannard, Chris would have long since departed. I felt no gratitude. Stannard was the bogeyman, the embodiment of everything bad. All had been well until he parachuted and crashed landed into my life uninvited.

I called in at a café awash with red-skinned holidaymakers and crying children, and ordered a cold drink. Melting into the crowd, I watched out for an offset face, glad not to find one. Afterwards, I walked outside and parked my rear on a castellated section of wall that overlooked the bay. I loved the sea and would miss it, but there were other seas to sail, other places to settle. Where exactly was anyone's guess. Blitzed by possibilities, I ruled nothing out and nothing in. Overnight, the cottage had ceased to be an intimate part of my history. It had never really belonged to me, in any case. It was, and always would be, my father's home. I was an impostor. Claire and Charlie and Andy, and all those people and faces I'd known and recognised since I was little would be dearly missed. To some, I'd promise to keep in touch, even visit, and yet I knew that, in time-honoured fashion, absence would extinguish every relationship apart from the closest.

Resolve hardened, I drove back up the steep, narrow road from Salcombe, through Kingsbridge and Frogmore, over the creek and wended my way towards Holset, finally making the steep descent to Goodshelter. Drawing near to the cottage, I scanned the gravel, looking for footprints or tyre marks, raking the surrounding countryside, but there was nobody and nothing to see.

Inside there were no signs of disturbance, simply the silence and emptiness. I showered and changed and wandered about the house hating the bleakness of my surroundings. A sudden memory of Luke crying darted through my brain. Haunted and half insane with grief, I fled.

Along the tidal road, the car's wheels splashing in the shallows, I took the higher route up the winding hill to the church where my father and brother were buried. The next six miles were a blur of disjointed thoughts: Chris with another woman. Chris when I kissed him good-bye. Smiling Chris on the beach. Chris recoiling from my touch. *Don't.*

Every view, every building held a memory. I passed my old primary school in West Charleton, the cricket and rugby grounds in Kingsbridge where I'd cheered on the sidelines and watched the boys I fancied and who often didn't fancy me.

I remembered illicit beach parties and barbeques. The odd-one-out, I was the girl who didn't quite belong because I was not one of them, because my face, in every sense, didn't fit. Apart from Claire, the other local kids made it clear that I could never be part of their set, not with my posh accent and snotty-nosed alien expressions.

With a shiver, I passed the stretch of road where Guy had careened off on his motorbike and hit a tree, no other car involved. Not especially morbid, I hadn't thought like this in years and it rocked me. Well adjusted, psychologically stable—I'd had the assessments to prove it—I was a walking good news story and yet, abandoned for a second time, I saw how much it was a lie.

I was a classic textbook screw-up.

I was a fraud.

Stannard was in my hair, on my skin, in my blood, all conscious and unconscious thought manipulated by him. He was out to get me.

I had to get him first.

FORTY-ONE

"Don't you think Crozes-Hermitage smells of horse piss?" I thought it screechingly funny. Everything seemed hilarious. Even Chris bunking off with the games teacher amused me. It seemed so commonplace and predictable. I'd met the bitch once. Carolla Dennison. Unusual name. Great figure. Pretty face. No scars.

We'd drunk Andy's peace offering in record time and were three-quarters through our second bottle. The flowers were for my birthday, he explained. The party had been postponed—too many people away or unable to make it. Jen had opted for a girls' night, instead.

"How long had it been going on?" We sprawled on the terrace in deck chairs, a couple of straw hats planted on our heads. Andy wore his lightly tipped over his face at a rakish angle.

His mouth screwed into a frown. "Is it helpful to have a post-mortem?"

"Probably not but, as a shrink, I specialise in them."

He gave in with a smile. "I found out about six months ago. I think it had been going on for two or three months before."

"Oh God. That's long enough to have a baby!" The length of time for which he'd deceived me sobered me up. Had I really been so dumb? How come I hadn't picked up on it? Because I wasn't there, I thought. Like an idiot, I'd handed the possibility of an affair to him on a plate. No wonder he didn't fancy me moving back. And that's why he'd bought a smart new motor, a means to impress his new love. In my inebriated state it all made perfect sense.

Andy was contrite. "I should have told you."

I shook my head. "It might have burnt itself out and I'd have been none the wiser." Who was I trying to hoodwink?

"In spite of all the arsing about, I really believed you two were meant for each other. You seemed so good together." There was real regret in his voice.

I thought so too, believed we were made for each other. I took a large gulp of wine to drown out the sentiment. "Who else knows?" You couldn't do anything in Devon on the quiet. Relationships broke down and moved around as erratically as musical chairs. Adulterous liaisons were something of a spectator sport.

"It was kept pretty schtum. I expect the Head put two and two together. To be honest, I was shocked to hell. Chris was my friend. A dark horse, I know, but I never expected this."

Tell me about it, I thought, grim. "Do you know where they've gone?"

Andy averted his eyes. "He wouldn't say."

I struggled to sit up and abandoned the attempt. "Because he knew you'd tell me?"

He looked straight at me. "I tried to talk him out of it, Kim, honest."

I looked into Andy's wide, open face and saw the concern in his eyes. "Thanks." I rolled across and kissed his cheek.

He flashed a smile, lowered his voice as if letting me in on a great secret. "They were planning to go to the States. Carolla's mother lives there. Michigan or Massachusetts."

"Hell, Andy, there's a bit of a difference."

"Sorry, geography's not my strong point."

"Great admission for a teacher."

"Only if you're teaching geography," he countered, making me shriek. I drained my glass unsteadily. A drop of wine dribbled down my chin and plopped onto my shirt. Normally, I'd be embarrassed. I didn't give a fuck and wiped it away, poured out more, and stared at the empty bottle. I wasn't drunk enough, not by a long way. "Perhaps we should drink a toast to the happy couple," I said, tipsily raising my glass.

Andy started, as though I'd poked pins in his eyes.

"Well, I've got to be grown-up about this," I said airily. "It's why I've decided to move away, go back to civilisation." Grow up, straighten my head out, and get on with my life. Fresh start.

Andy sat up. He had a half smile on his face. "You can't be serious?"

"Deadly," I sniggered. "I've visited three estate agents and they're all going to give me the benefit of their expert opinion."

"You don't hang around." He looked genuinely shocked.

"That's my point. I've hung around for too long." And obsessed for too long. I was starting to sound like one of my own clients with an extra dash of paranoia for good measure. Not good. Not good at all.

I lurched to my feet and tottered towards the kitchen, bouncing off a wall as I negotiated may way to the wine rack.

"Bugger, things are getting serious. We're down to the last bottle." I opened it with a tremendous flourish and, brain and feet muddled, headed back to the terrace.

"Don' look at me like that."

"Like what?"

"As though my knickers are caught in my skirt."

"I'm not." He grinned, eyeing up the fresh bottle. "But do you think that's a good idea?"

"Absolu ... absolu ..." For the life of me I couldn't think how the word finished. "Yeah," I said, merrily splashing fresh wine into our glasses. "Pity Jen's not here to share in the celebrations. You did well there, Andy. Looks like we'll have to put the foursome on hold."

He gave me an old-fashioned look.

"Did Chris tell you I've got a fan club? Very select. Jus' one member." I lunged towards him with a giggle and pressed a finger to my lips. "Shhh. Don' tell anyone, but I've got my very own personal stalker."

Andy gaped.

"You didn't know?"

He shook his head, astounded.

"'Course not. Dark horse. Chris tol' me not to tell anyone."

"You mean someone's following you," he said in shocked disbelief.

"Not here." I gestured, waggling my thumb. "There."

"Cheltenham?"

"Yeah. Police have sorted him, 'cept he won' go way. Keeps on coming. Got to stop him, the bastard. Sen' me stuff, borrowed my motor, porn."

"You're not making too much sense, Kim."

I agreed with a smile. Things were getting a bit blurry. There were now two Andys in the room and the sound of helicopter blades whirling above my head. Somewhere in my brain I registered that I was displaying a disgusting lack of self-control. What the hell?

"This guy following you," Andy said slowly.

"What about him?"

"Have you actually seen him?"

A cruel laugh sounded out of nowhere. It took me a while to work out that it was coming from me. "Can't miss him. Got a face like mine. Well, bit of an exaggeration. One side's irresistible, the other, yuk."

"And you're sure it's him."

"Positive."

Andy leant towards me, a determined expression in his eyes. "I could sort him out for you."

"You're lovely." I patted his knee and did my level best to focus. "My knight in shining armour."

"God, you're pissed as a fart."

"I know."

Serious again, he said, "I mean it, Kim. If this guy bothers you, you let me know."

"No need. All taken care of. You're a sweetie, Andy, but you don' understand. Mr. S. is in for the biggest shock of his life."

FORTY-TWO

I'd been sick.

Eyes pickled, tongue glued to the roof of my mouth, brain in a tumble-dryer, I reached for the painkillers. *Happy birthday, Kim.*

I didn't recall what time Andy left. I had a dim memory of rambling about my dad giving me my first taste of alcohol when I was ten, a crème de menthe frappe, and instructing me never to eat spaghetti on a first date. Andy had coaxed me to eat a cheese sandwich and drink a pint of milk in a belated attempt to line my stomach and sober me up, not that it had done much good. The grease lay on top of the booze like an oil slick.

The conversation floated back in fragments. Chris. Games teacher. Stalker. Unlike on the previous evening, the idea of Chris falling in love with Carolla Dennison didn't seem the least bit funny. I felt humiliated. There was only one thing worse than losing the love of your life: the realisation that he'd never loved you at all.

Trying to stem another tide of rising nausea, I showered gingerly, letting the cool water mingle with and wash away a fresh surge of tears. Then I dressed in a loose-fitting shirt and jeans and went downstairs.

I picked up the collection of envelopes, sat down at the kitchen table, and opened them, smiling weakly at the particularly daft card from Luke. Halfway through a cup of heart-starting coffee, the doorbell rang. I put a hand to my pounding head and squinted painfully through the window. Claire stood on the doorstep. Beyond, I spotted Claire's SUV parked in the drive, Charlie and the boys inside. When I opened the door I was immediately enveloped in a hug.

"Andy told us. I'm so sorry, Kim. Happy birthday anyway." Claire wore a sleeveless dress, the child she carried conspicuous by the roundedness of her belly beneath. Our two situations in life couldn't be more polarised.

"Do you want to come in?" I glanced at the car. The suspension bounced furiously, Charlie shouting at the boys in an effort to retain order.

Claire broke into a smile. "We want you to come out."

"Oh no, I don't think . . ."

"Birthday surprise." Serene and calm, Claire slipped her arm firmly through mine.

"I can't. I've got things . . ."

"It's no use," Claire said with a laugh, giving my arm a gentle tug.

"But I feel absolutely dreadful," I protested, ethanol seeping out of every sweaty pore. My body felt as if my blood had reached boiling point. A sudden lurch in my stomach signalled an urge to vomit again.

"I know," Claire said, her expression one of maternal reproof. "You've looked better, I have to say."

"Had a bit of night of it with Andy."

"Fresh air is what you need and a change of scene."

The decision was already made; I'd be rude to refuse. "All right, let me pop to the loo first, splash my face with water, and get my bag."

"Wicked!" Tommy gave an ear-piercing shriek as he emerged from the death slide, button-brown eyes gleaming with raw excitement. I was feeling at that stage in my hangover where it could go either way. Food would be the deciding factor.

"Are you having a go, Auntie Kim?"

Auntie Kim felt more like chucking up again. "Don't think so, darling. I'm not sure my tummy would cope. You go again, if you want to."

We'd been on the water chute, the assault course, and the nature trail. Super-dark sunglasses in place, I dragged along with the others, hot and shaky, wishing that I didn't feel quite so horrific. The aftermath of heavy drinking left me weepy. Anything set me off. Claire's stupendous efforts to give me a nice birthday, my favourite chocolates from the boys, a shiny hardback glossily illustrated cookery book on Italian cuisine from my friends, and all the time there was the desolation that was my personal life.

Claire spread out a red and white checked tablecloth. On it were plates of sandwiches, quiches, cold meats, savouries, and salads.

"Hair of the dog, birthday girl?" With a sadistic grin, Charlie held aloft a bottle of chilled champagne.

I let out a long sigh and smiled weakly.

They toasted my birthday. Awkward yet loved, I let the burn of alcohol course down my throat. After an unfeasibly short time, my head magically cleared and I felt surprisingly better. I watched in wonderment as the boys fell upon the food, fat little hands darting like rogue hamsters, Claire and Charlie batting them off for taking too much in one go.

Slightly cooler by the river, I settled back in the shade of a willow tree and watched the picnic with benign detachment. I'd forgotten how good it felt to be part of a family, to have that sense of belonging. Temporarily, it made me feel safe, wanted, and valued. Why leave the place and the people who matter most, I thought drowsily? Why the desperate need to challenge and confront my fears, to play out my blistering anger in the blind belief that I could change the past?

And then I saw him.

He walked down the path, head held high, sunglasses in place, newspaper in hand.

He looked oddly dressed—charcoal grey pinstripe business suit. I wanted to say something to Claire and Charlie, but they were lost in domestic chatter, and the words refused to budge from my mouth. I slid down, flattening my back into the hard ground, hoping he wouldn't see me. Maybe if I kept very still he'd walk on by. Then little Harry got up and pointed to him. "Look, Dad. See the horrible man. What's wrong with his face?"

I held my breath, watched the hopeless look in Stannard's eyes, saw him turn and move towards me. He was calling now, shouting my name, yelling, steel in his voice…

"Kim, Kim!"

I sat bolt upright. Charlie had his hands tight on my shoulders. Claire was kneeling at my side. I looked around, feverishly scanning the woodland. No sign of Stannard. "Has he gone?" I felt extremely frightened.

"You fell asleep," Claire said soothingly. "You were dreaming, Kim."

"Was I?" I wanted so much to believe her.

"Honest." Charlie's brow chiselled with lines. He offered me a drink of water.

Taking a sip, I tried to make a joke of it. "Delirium tremens," I said, rubbing the tops of my arms. Heat spent, I felt icy inside.

Claire exchanged worried looks with Charlie. "The boys are in the playground," she said, pointing to an enclosed area nearby.

I felt cagey. Was this code for *We're going to talk*? I reached for a Scotch egg, nibbled at it.

"If it makes you feel any better," Charlie began, biting into a sandwich, "I never liked him."

"Who?" I said, bewildered.

"Chris."

"We went along with it," Claire said, "for your sake."

I looked at the pair of them, not really knowing what to say. "I'm sorry then," I said, numb. "I'd no idea." Like a wife who is the last to discover that her husband has been unfaithful, part of me closed down inside. These were my best friends and for four years they'd humoured me. Claire cast me an anxious look.

"He was secretive," Charlie said, as if defending his corner, "something not direct and honest about him. You never knew what he was thinking. Of course, now we know the reason why. Two-faced bastard."

Catching the mean expression in his eye, I wanted to get up and run.

"Ask him anything and he'd speak to you like he was some person you'd flagged down in the street for directions to the local cinema. Routine. Set of facts. No emotion. Then, without warning, he'd get bolshie and defensive, as if about to lose it." Charlie narrowed his eyes in a way that spooked me. "Inconsistent, if you ask me, volatile, something missing."

I knew all this, and yes, Chris had betrayed me. He'd abandoned and hurt me deeply but, whatever I felt about Chris's behaviour, I found the way Charlie talked disturbing. The corpse of my relationship was still warm. If anyone should be slagging Chris off, it should be me. Nobody else had the right. Not now. Not ever.

"We'd suspected for some time," Claire said.

Hurt, I rounded on her. "You're my friend. Why didn't you tell me?"

Claire started and pinched the skirt of her dress. "Because it wouldn't have made a difference."

"It might have made a difference to me." My voice, against every intention, was raised.

"We didn't know who the woman was for certain," Charlie said, clearly trying to take the heat out of the situation.

The afternoon suddenly spoilt, Claire called the boys back for birthday cake. I watched their shiny laughing faces as six token candles flittered in the sunlight. Out of steam, I blew them out after two attempts.

"Where's Chris?" Tommy said with a sly grin. Claire and Charlie exchanged uneasy glances.

"He's gone away," I stammered, thinking how much I sounded like my father talking about my mother.

"Andy says you're selling up," Charlie said, once the boys were out of earshot again.

"I've got nothing to stay for." It sounded like a challenge. I supposed it was.

His pale blue eyes fastened on me. "You've got us."

Afterwards we packed up the picnic and wandered back to watch a creepy middle-aged clown. The kids ate ice cream. I passed on watching a young fire-eater and went back to the car to wait. Hopelessly adrift, I felt that my brief foray into family life was over.

Politely declining an invitation to go back to the farm, Charlie took me home after we'd first dropped off the boys and Claire en route. Conversation became stilted.

"I meant what I said, Kim."

"I know."

He looked across at me. "About you staying in Devon."

I looked straight ahead. I knew I was being an awkward cuss, but couldn't find it in my heart to behave in any other way.

"If you're worried, I could always keep an eye on the place while you're away."

"Thanks, but it's not necessary."

"Or, if you need any jobs done in the house ..."

"Charlie," I pleaded, "please, let's just leave it."

He drove the rest of the way in silence. Pulling into Cormorants Reach, he asked when I was taking time off.

"Why?"

"Curious, that's all. Maybe we could all get together."

All didn't quite have the same resonance any more.

"I'm back in Cheltenham tomorrow evening and for the rest of the week. After that marks the start of my break."

"What are you going to do?"

I lied without difficulty. "No idea."

I said good-bye, clambered out, and walked briskly inside. In spite of everything, I looked for signs of Chris's return. Were the cushions on the sofa a little bit squashed? Slightly out of place?

Imagination, I thought, nervously running my fingers along the cushions, checking to see if they were warm. They weren't. I was definitely letting my mind run away with me.

Food holding no interest, I poured myself a forbidden glass of white wine, clasped it in my hands as if it were a crystal ball, and took it out onto the patio, where the heat felt more dissipated. Like a maggot in my brain, Stannard burrowed in and refused to shift. His face swam before my eyes. Good side. Bad side. The memory of his voice was strangely seductive to my ear, hypnotic even.

How to get rid of it?

FORTY-THREE

SLEEP WAS SO TOTAL, so without dreams that, when I awoke early on Monday morning and reality kicked in, the realisation that Chris had left cut through me like a ragged blade through raw flesh.

When I swung my legs out of bed my stomach growled, my legs wobbled, and my throat felt sore and dry from too much booze. Light-headed, I tottered downstairs, stood in the kitchen, munched a slice of bread and butter with disinterest, and washed it down with fruit juice. Everything I did and everywhere I looked blared that I was single again.

Dressed in a pair of jeans and T-shirt, I collected several old removal boxes from the garage and started on the study. Books and papers not specific to my current work, long-dead flowers, all were whisked away. Moving on to the kitchen, I chucked out a couple of shrivelled apples from the fruit bowl. Opening a cupboard, I was shocked by the amount of gadgetry acquired. Milk frothers, slicing implements for every vegetable and fruit known to man, graters and separators, culinary machines, all came under close inspection. I mentally split things into three piles: stuff to be junked, nonessentials to be packed away, items to leave where they were. More ruthless than I thought possible, it occurred to me that to do my job required a modicum of toughness. Hard to confront, there were times when my efforts failed, and young women died.

When Alexa rang at around ten thirty, I was less than my sparkling self. She made no pretence of pleasantries but launched straight in. I had to hand it to Chris, he was right about her obsessive nature.

"I can't see me ever having children."

"With Brooks gone, you think there won't be time to meet someone else, is that what you mean?"

"Yes." Her voice was small.

Join the club, I thought. "You can't know what the future holds."

"It's unlikely, though, isn't it?"

"Women are leaving motherhood until much later these days."

"Just my luck to miss the biological boat."

"You could always adopt."

"As a single parent?" The tone of her voice suggested that I had serious mental health issues. She was possibly right.

"Maybe that's not such a good idea." I picked up a broken whisk and flung it into the junk pile. It landed with a satisfying crash.

"Not that Brooks need worry; he can have children whenever he wants."

I burbled something neutral.

"There's something else," she said. I waited for the punch line. In my experience, clients and people in general always saved the most significant points until last.

"What's that?"

"I feel haunted."

"Is this connected to Gaynor?"

"How could she disappear into thin air?"

"Unfortunately, people do." Against my will, I thought of Chris.

"Something bad must have happened to her."

"The police never found a body, Alexa."

"That's true, but I sense it."

"Not everyone who goes missing dies." I grimaced. I'd been through this with her many times. It was a circular argument that never went anywhere. Maybe it couldn't. "She might have walked out of her life to start another." My heart skipped a beat. Isn't this what Chris had done—just like my mother?

"No," Alexa said. "She's dead. I know it."

A few minutes later, she signed off. Shaken, I went back to sorting. After an hour and a half of clatter and bang, I lost interest. In another fifteen minutes, the first of the estate agents were due to arrive. Scouring my address book, I picked up the phone and called a number I hadn't used in years.

"Professor Fallon?"

"Kim? What a lovely surprise."

"I wondered if I could pay a visit?"

"We'd be delighted," he said, unabashed by my sudden desire for contact. "Any particular time in mind?"

"I'm free from next weekend."

"Pity, we're flying to Seville next Saturday for a fortnight's holiday. How are you fixed lunchtime?"

"Today, are you sure?"

"Of course I'm sure. I'll tell Iris straight away."

Forewarned is forearmed, I thought.

FORTY-FOUR

Bastard, Heather thought, throwing the missive from Stannard's lawyers, passed on via her solicitors, onto the kitchen table. Apart from disliking the tone of the legalese, she felt fury at the number of points they wished to have clarification on, including the confirmation that the site be cleared of rubbish and gardening residue. She had a ton of the stuff and it would take several skips to remove it. Bearing in mind that Stannard was going to gut the place, it seemed a petty thing to request. Why couldn't it be lumped in with his debris? But the real stinger was the area directly outside the rear, where she occasionally parked the car. News to her, it belonged to the Highways Agency. Stannard and his legal dogs wanted her to sort it out to "save all possible future aggravation about boundaries and rights." Quite what she was supposed to do about it, she hadn't a clue. Land Registry clearly stated that the parking area belonged to the property. According to Stannard's solicitors, it could be used by anyone. The letter seemed to imply that she, as the vendor, should come up with a deal with the Highways Agency—as if.

The simple alternative, as they put it, a reduction in price.

Outrage didn't cover her emotions. As for Fairweather, suspicion turned to conviction. He'd deliberately entrapped her. What was in it for him, she considered shrewdly, a backhander, perhaps? Picking up the phone, she contacted Damian Fairweather and explained the latest development.

"The problem, as I see it," Fairweather said, "is that if you don't comply, Stannard will drop out."

Good, she thought. "But you said there was another interested party."

"You agreed, if you remember, to accept Stannard's offer."

"That was before he started playing fast and loose," she said. "It's not as if I've ever encountered a problem parking. We've always assumed that it was our right to use it exclusively. There are no yellow lines. And it's not as if it's the only parking space. There's plenty of room around the side of the house."

"It's a question of privacy."

How much privacy does he actually need, she thought. "He's got six bedrooms' worth of privacy to roll around in."

"If Stannard changes his mind, anyone else interested in the house may also insist on a price reduction. I recognise you're incurring an additional loss of funds, but it might be worth your while to investigate."

"Perhaps Mr. Stannard would like me to put a swimming pool in the garden," she said tartly, "or maybe he would prefer a Victorian facade instead of the original Regency. The details are quite clear, Mr. Fairweather. The house already has a perfectly adequate form of parking. I've had no problems with boundaries, rights, or anything else in the past and…"

"I *do* appreciate where you're coming from," Fairweather broke in, "I'm simply trying to get you into a situation of going forwards."

God save me from meaningless lingo, she thought, crazed with frustration. All she wanted to do was sell the house, have her face-lift, and get on with her life. And there were all these bloody men standing in her way like checkpoint guards.

"Won't you at least consider the proposition?" Fairweather's voice was nothing short of wheedling.

"I'll look at it," she said, her jaw stiff with indignation, "but I promise nothing."

FORTY-FIVE

GRAND LOCATION, MISS SLADE.

Three separate firms of estate agents with different profiles, but responses and tone the same: gushing and gung-ho. Who to choose, I wondered.

As a young lone female, I felt at a distinct disadvantage, talked at rather than talked to about anything from buoyant markets and profit margins to government policy. There was little consensus about the value of the property; the differential between the lowest and highest figure was in the region of fifty thousand pounds. Out of the three, I decided to select the Salcombe agency because they had more flair, seemed to have better contacts outside the West Country, with a particular handle on the London market. The clincher was an open sense of humour—not particularly sound business principles but good psychology.

Shortly after eleven, I was on the road. Traffic on the motorway was light though lanes on the opposite side of the carriageway, running into the West Country, were a mess of five-mile tailbacks. I drove without listening to either radio or CD and achieved a rare moment of stillness and calm.

Within spitting distance of Cheltenham, I came off the motorway early at Gloucester and doubled almost back on myself to the second capital of the Cotswolds, Cirencester.

Passing through a semi-rural hinterland of houses and light industry, the countryside became more undulating as I approached the pretty market town. A heat-haze of phantom mists, like forgotten Roman soldiers, shrouded the hills.

Parking in the main car park in the new part of town, a conglomeration of municipal seventies blocks of concrete, I walked into the main square, then crossed over and down a narrow street in the direction of the Bathurst estate. Set back from the road, the Fallons' Cotswold stone cottage, with its hanging baskets, crammed with flowers and weeping figs, brought a delighted smile to my face.

At the scrape of the latch on the wrought-iron gate, Robert Fallon opened the front door and ambled out to greet me. In his late sixties, a large man with soft benign features, he'd changed little since the days he'd lectured at Leicester University. Thinner on top, jowly, he still presented a commanding figure.

"Come inside out of the heat. Hope you don't mind eating salad. Iris thought it too hot for anything more substantial."

"Sounds lovely."

Sublimely cool inside, the Fallons' home smelt of geraniums. I gave Iris a homemade gift of peaches steeped in brandy.

Like her husband, Iris Fallon was well built. She had remarkably unwrinkled features and soft blue eyes that peered through tortoiseshell spectacles. Her mouth was small and dabbed with peach-coloured lipstick.

“You’re looking well, Kim,” she said.

Unable to tell whether it was a genuine compliment, or an ice-breaker, I pushed a smile.

Lunch was convivial, the conversation uncontroversial. Fallon listened with intensity when I spoke of my job in Cheltenham.

“Are you still involved in police work?” I’d wanted it to sound casual, but missed the mark.

“Not any more, my dear,” he said, meeting my eye. “My days of profiling are long over. Naturally, I still take a keen interest in criminology,” he added, as if he’d read the disappointment in my eyes.

After coffee, he suggested we took a stroll in the orchard.

“We can walk down to the river. It’s quite pleasant in the shade.”

Iris tactfully said that she would stay to wash up, declining my offer of help.

The heat blasted us as we crossed the garden but once we were safely under a canopy of trees, the air felt fresher. This was my big moment. This was what I’d come for.

“What do you know about stalkers?”

“Stalking is still uncharted territory. There is research but, as usual, it’s difficult to find funding.”

I pressed Fallon again.

“Why do you want to know?”

How eating disorders related to stalking was a fairly impossible sell. I looked straight ahead to better conceal the lie. “Academic interest.”

Fallon didn’t change step, didn’t miss a beat. “There are exceptions, yet most stalkers are men. They tend to be devious and extremely intelligent. Although the reasons for the behaviour are varied, there’s one common theme.”

“What’s that?”

"Rejection."

I lowered my head.

"They fall roughly into three groups," Fallon continued. "Former intimates who cannot accept that a relationship is over. The zealous type who's never met the object of his affection or has only come across her in passing, maybe a smile across a supermarket counter, or a brief exchange of conversation on the bus. Lastly, we have the deluded erotomaniac, who again has no prior relationship to his victim but is convinced that she's in love with him, or would be given the right circumstances. I don't need to tell you that human beings rarely fall neatly into any of these categories. There's some variation but, broadly speaking, that's the rough spec."

"Any evidence of personality disorders, psychiatric problems, schizophrenia, for instance?"

"Some, but not exclusively. My advice to anyone who finds herself in the unfortunate position of being stalked is to go to the police. Whereas it used to be put on the same disinterested level as domestic violence, it's now being taken seriously." He paused for a moment and turned towards me. "I take it we're talking about you, Kim."

"It's not that serious."

"Yet here we are having this discussion."

We carried on walking. The ground was pitted and dry and difficult to cross. Eventually the path curved gracefully as it made its slow descent to the river.

"Do you know who it is?"

I told him about Stannard, about everything that had happened to me, including Chris leaving. I confessed my uncontrollable feelings of anger towards the world. He lightly touched my back with his hand in the way a mother guides a child forward through a busy street.

"Then you know how your stalker feels."

I flashed him a sharp look. Fallon smiled. "It wasn't a vindication."

River trout splashed in the shallows. The ground beneath my feet softened slightly.

"You're certain it's him?"

I stopped in my tracks. For the police and for my friends to doubt me was one thing, but this was Robert, my mentor, someone I respected. But even he was not infallible. "Surely, after all I've told you . . ." My voice tailed off into the lengthening silence.

"Strangers stalk celebrities. Ordinary folk are generally stalked by people they know."

Chris leaving excluded him, didn't it? I wanted to ask the question but lost my nerve.

"At heart this is a power struggle," Fallon said. "Throw into the mix that he's both unpredictable and a fantasist."

"A fantasist?" I remembered Stannard's admission of daydreams.

"He wants you to be blank so that he can colour you in with all the attributes he finds attractive and appealing to him. He doesn't care if you crack up. It's a turn-on simply knowing that he can find ways to guarantee he's never out of your mind."

I let out a small exhalation.

Fallon continued softly, "In worst-case scenarios, it can culminate in abduction, rape, torture, murder. The flipside of love is hate. But you know this already, don't you, Kim?"

I nodded, taken aback by his ability to see right through me. "You're not making me feel any better."

When Fallon looked into my eyes his expression was grave. "I'm trying to make you see what you're up against."

Something rough caught in the back of my throat. "There must be recognisable stages of behaviour." It was like facing a terminal disease, each level signifying a critical escalation.

"The deadly stage is when he realises that he really can't have you."

"And when will I know he's made the transition?"

"He'll up the ante without warning."

And I will be prepared.

"You've come here to estimate your chances of success. Am I right?"

"I need to know if I can win."

"Only if you involve the police; you can't do this on your own."

It wasn't what I wanted to hear. Fallon sussed it. "Stannard, if that's who it is, presents you with the ultimate mind game and you're secretly fascinated by it…"

I almost stamped my foot. Hadn't Chris implied the same? "That's not true. I didn't seek this. I never encouraged it. I don't want it."

"You regard him as a challenge," Robert said, his voice stern.

"I've never run from anything in my life."

"I understand that, my dear."

Tears pricked my eyes. One trickled down my cheek. I pushed it away, hoping he hadn't noticed.

"*Don't* be seduced, Kim. If you go after your stalker in a blind attempt to convert him, you'll be playing straight into his hands. You already understand a little of what makes this man tick but always remember, in his eyes, he's doing nothing wrong. It's all quite rational within the context of his personality. He's really quite impervious to any form of deterrence. He enjoys what he's doing too much."

"So where does that leave me?" To my annoyance, my voice came out as a pathetic cry. "Do I let him carry on? Do I change my life? Move away? What do I do? I can't stand by and do nothing. I *have* to stop him." Crack him before he cracks me.

"Deep down, you know that's impossible. Has it occurred to you that maybe you want payback, not for what he's done, but for everything else that's gone wrong in your life?"

I was open-mouthed.

"You're a victim . . ."

"Oh Christ, Robert, not you as—"

He put up the flat of his hand. ". . . and you deserve to be listened to, but not by Stannard. Go back to the police. It's no longer regarded as a trivial offence. For all you know, he might have done it before."

"Really? Is that possible?"

"In common with the serial killer, a man or woman doesn't become a stalker overnight. There are grades of behaviour as he or she feels his way."

I swallowed hard. From the start, I was sure my stalker was male. Had I made the wrong call? Chris's words about Alexa reverberated: *She's practically stalking you.* No, it was absurd. Alexa was many things but she wasn't doing this to me.

"Take some leave, talk to a professional outside work. Don't, for God's sake, think that by talking to Stannard, or whoever your stalker is, he'll go away."

Who said anything about talking to him, I thought? I wanted to put the wind up him, embarrass him, shame him, fucking terrify him.

We were right down by the river's edge now. It was surprisingly fast moving, the colour of oily khaki. I imagined lying down on the bank, sinking into the grass, listening to the water and the lazy splash of river life.

"Think of this as a window of opportunity," Fallon said. "You've got a chance to let the police do something before it escalates."

"Do what exactly?" I laughed with derision. "They've dealt with the matter. It's closed. If I go back now, they'll say I'm making a fuss."

"Then talk to someone in higher authority; I could make some calls, pull strings."

I thanked him but declined. Call me stubborn. "Just suppose I go back to the police," I said, as if seriously considering the possibility, "and they nail him, then what?"

"The judiciary step in." He glanced away. I was quick to pick up on it.

"And do what exactly? Take him off the streets for six months?"

"A judge can sentence up to five years."

"But only if a stalker threatens violence. You know how it works, Robert. All Stannard has to do is appoint a sharp-thinking lawyer to defend his corner. Someone," I said, my brain hooked on Gavin Chadwick, "who will state that his client is innocent and misunderstood so that an out-of-touch judge will feel sorry for him and allow him to continue."

Fallon's response was late. "They're not all crusty old fools," he said eventually.

And that's supposed to be a comfort?

FORTY-SIX

I PARKED DOWN A side street and arrived at the apartment block shortly after three thirty. Lizzie's door was resolutely shut. I contemplated the outcome of the discussions that had taken place behind it. No matter what Lizzie said, they'd sell. I couldn't blame them. As soon as Stannard moved in, I'd have to sell up too—unless I could coerce him to pull out.

Entering the flat, the stench hit me as if I'd been pushed head first into a cesspool. Suspicion wired me for sound. The main room crackled with noise—air vents opening and machinery humming. Reduced to its essence by the heat, the smell was sour, rotting and faecal.

Clapping a hand to my mouth, I searched for the one thing that was wrong, my eyes fixing on a thick dark fog of bluebottle flies. Beneath, parked on the hearth, was a large black plastic bucket, the sort that might be used for coal or cleaning the car. Placed with precision, painting directly above, framed by the fake marble mantelpiece, it sat squat and glowering. I approached warily, thumb and finger pinching my nostrils. The flies lifted as one and buzzed around my head in a frenzied cloud. Peering inside, my jaw tensed to stifle a cry that, had it been born, would have ricocheted throughout the building. Filled to the brim, festering in the heat, were glistening intestines, guts and flesh, blood and hair and shit. A single eye from a dead animal stared up from the surface, like a grim piece of conceptual art.

I sprinted to the bathroom, resisted the urge to be violently ill, and splashed my neck and face with water. I wanted to be rid of his games, his twisted calling cards, HIM. Wrapping a towel around the lower half of my face as if I was about to run through fire, I tore back into the sitting room, picked up the bucket and, dashing back to the bathroom, threw the contents down the lavatory, flushing it three times.

Then gaped, open-mouthed, at what I'd done.

Anything he sends, bag it, Simon had told me in no uncertain terms, and in five fevered seconds I'd destroyed the best evidence I had, my instinct to wipe out the traces stronger than pragmatism. To do anything else had seemed unthinkable, and what was I supposed to do? Hang on to it? *Oh, excuse me, officer, I've just had a bucket of guts delivered.* Hysteria nibbling at my brain, I almost laughed out loud.

I shut down the heating, threw open all the windows, filled the bucket to the brim with hot water and disinfectant, and walked round, checking the points of entry for signs of break-in. There was no escaping the fact that someone had gained access to my flat. He'd already set a precedent by driving my car. He could easily walk in again, do what he liked, when he liked, only this time when I was there.

I left the apartment, walked quickly at first then, sure that I wasn't being followed, slowed down, sauntered almost, making sure that my movements did not betray my intention.

Cutting down an alley from Lypiatt Road, I crossed over into Tivoli and a short parade of shops that included two estate agents and a locksmith. Simmering anger gave in to eerie calm. Was it Stannard or, more creepily, was it someone else?

Hot on the heels of the guy fitting an alarm system, the locksmith promised to come out the next day. Next, I put calls through to Jim and to Bayshill, explaining that I was sorry but wouldn't be back until after the holiday. I didn't state that I was in Cheltenham.

"Any news on Chris?" Jim said.

"He's left me."

"God, I'm so sorry."

"No need."

"It wasn't what I was expecting."

What were you expecting? "It's fine."

"So you're on your own?"

Prickling with suspicion and hating myself for it, I said, "No."

"Good. This thing with Stannard . . ."

"Don't worry. He's back in the box."

"Really?"

"Yeah," and I hung up.

Crossing back into town, I decided on a process of elimination and considered the weapons at my disposal, which were:

Observation: know the enemy.

Knowledge: find out everything about him.

But the most powerful trick in my armoury was one I'd studied for all my adult life. I knew its stressors and what drove it to breaking point. The human mind was indeed the deadliest weapon known to man.

FORTY-SEVEN

Following up on Simon's information, I went online and discovered that Stannard had once been a model for Quartz, a top-end London agency, that his home in Wellington Square was a Grade II detached villa, and that Stannard Property Developments was situated adjacent to the town hall in Imperial Square, one of a row of three-storey buildings with both residential and commercial use. With the address in my hand, I set off.

Late afternoon, Stannard HQ looked like any other set of offices in Cheltenham with fine ironwork and Ionic-style columns.

The large window fronting the building was open and, from the street, I could see a green leafy potted plant, the outline of a female form, and a desk with a computer monitor. It looked honest and respectable.

Shortly after five, Stannard and his trademark sunglasses emerged. From the municipal gardens opposite, I watched him pause and gather himself against the wall of heat before trotting down the stone steps and turning right into Oriel Road in the direction of the city centre. Brushing off the grass from my jeans, I stood up and followed.

Dropping back far enough so as not to seem conspicuous, letting my attention be caught every so often by a piece of architecture, I experienced a swell of power and wondered if Stannard felt that same thrill of excitement.

At no time did he look round or break pace, nothing to suggest he was suspicious. His destination was a bar off the high street near Cambray Place. I went into another on the opposite side of the square, ordered a soft drink, and took a window seat. An hour later, Stannard emerged and I took up the chase at a distance as he retraced his steps to the office, where he spent fifteen minutes pacing, small cigar in his mouth, phone stuck to his ear before picking up his charcoal-grey Maserati from a reserved area behind the block. I made a note of the registration and, with the sense of a job well done, cruised back to my flat.

A fermented, slightly sweet odour clung to the furnishings in spite of my efforts to eradicate it. Without the locks changed and the alarm system yet in place, I spent the night on high alert, mobile in hand, half of me waiting for a light shining underneath the door, the disturbance of air, the smell of another. I woke early, eyes grainy from lack of sleep.

At half past eight, the alarm was fitted and a guy with a port-wine stain on his face came to change the locks. I made him tea and we chatted, and I felt the fleeting comfort of having a human being to talk to about nothing in particular, nothing that mattered.

By quarter to ten, I was sitting in a low-grade car rental agency with a bloke called Bill booking a dark blue Ford Focus for the day. An hour later I'd parked four cars down from Stannard's beautiful vehicle, waiting for the great man to go out and about his business. Fifteen minutes later, my vigil was rewarded.

I pulled out of the parking lot and followed the Maserati as it headed through town towards Pittville, a leafy enclave with a park and lake and lovely houses. The centre was dense with traffic, aiding rather than impeding my progress; the much faster car could not escape the Focus. Eyes boring into the back of Stannard's head, I attempted to read his thoughts, wondering what his next move might be. He rarely, if at all, looked in his rearview mirror, which suited me.

After half a mile or so, we passed the Pump Room, a surviving spa building, tourist attraction and, with its green dome and colonnaded façade, prime example of Regency architecture. The road opened up and the Maserati surged forward with a full-throttled, sophisticated growl. From the direction in which we were travelling, I estimated Stannard was heading for Prestbury, the site of National Hunt Racing, but the Masa veered off, making a sharp left, picking up speed, powering along a straight piece of road as though the Grim Reaper sat in the driving seat. About to stick my foot down, I was cut off by a courier. A quick exchange of horns and hand gestures, and the Italian stallion had faded to a speck in the distance.

Facing a crossroads, no car in sight, not knowing which route to take, I tapped the steering wheel with frustration. To turn left would take me back towards town. Turn right, out of town altogether. Had Stannard clocked me? Had he deliberately led me astray?

He specialises in old houses, does them up, full architectural spec.

I pulled forward and onto the Evesham Road with its constellation of old properties, as polished and polite as a middle-aged handsome woman. Scanning the driveways and restricted parking spaces, my hopes thinned and faded. Depressed, I pulled over with the intention of getting out of the car and stretching my legs. That's when I noticed the Property For Sale sign half obscured by a neighbouring home's scaffolding, and Stannard's car parked in the drive. Called Rowanbank, the house, a fabulous specimen of faded glory, looked tired, the roof worn, the windows giving every appearance of throwing themselves out of the brickwork and into the overgrown borders.

Suppressing a whoop of triumph, I noted the agent and, revving up the Focus, made my way back to the centre. Dropping the car at the rental company, I returned to the place I called home.

Lizzie was coming out as I was going in. Her cheeks flashed the colour of fresh meat. I didn't need to ask for the decision. It was already clear.

"I've spoken to Pete. No dice, I'm afraid. We're desperate to sell. Sorry." Lizzie's voice was like a guttering candle.

I nodded gravely. "When?"

"He wants an early completion." Lizzie shifted her weight from one foot to the other, her face tight. "What will you do?"

"I'm working on it," I said with a confident smile. "I don't blame you in the least. Better go. Stuff to do." I spun on my heel, walked away, leaving Lizzie to the heat and the prospect of a new start.

Back in the flat, I picked up the phone and called Fairweather and Co. They weren't particularly helpful. "Rowanbank is already under offer," the voice explained.

"That's not what the board says."

"We haven't had a chance to change it yet."

"But, until the property's sold, it's still up for grabs, isn't it?"

A disgruntled sigh coursed down the telephone wire. "An offer has been accepted by Mrs. Foley. To allow someone else to view at this delicate stage in the negotiations would be entirely improper."

I was getting the impression that Stannard was quite an important fish.

"Thanks for being so candid," I said, polite. I wondered what time would be best to catch Mrs. Foley at home.

FORTY-EIGHT

Taking a deep breath, I knocked on Heather Foley's front door the next morning a little after eleven thirty and stood back and waited. I felt supremely guilty for conning my way into the woman's home and reckoned I'd be given five minutes, tops, before being told to sling my hook. It was a risk worth taking.

A handsome-looking woman in her middle fifties, wide-hipped with an impressive décolletage, opened the door. Her polite smile broadened then narrowed into a grimace as the blue eyes zoom-lensed onto my neck and the injured side of my face. For a second or two, Mrs. Foley appeared unable to string a sentence together. Two words might have been written on her forehead: *freak show.*

I took a step forward, threw a bright smile. "Hope I'm not too early." I followed up with a firm handshake.

"No, not at all," Mrs. Foley stammered. She gestured to me to enter, walked halfway down a cavernous hall, and turned on her heel as if she'd had second thoughts. "As I explained on the phone, Rowanbank *is* under offer . . ."

"But you said you're unhappy with the terms."

Heather Foley ran a manicured hand through her tastefully tinted hair and seemed to crumple, suddenly weary and careworn. I was oddly reminded of my mother at the tearoom. "To tell the truth, I feel besieged, Miss Slade. It's not easy when you're a woman on your own." A lost look entered her eyes. "It's difficult to find people to talk to, people one can trust, which is why I decided to let you view. Most unethical, of course, but then I'm not too sure either my estate agent or my prospective buyer are quite as scrupulous as they would have me believe."

"You mean Mr. Stannard."

Heather Foley blinked in surprise.

"I'm afraid I wasn't as honest as I should have been when I called," I admitted, deciding to come clean. "I don't want to buy your house, Mrs. Foley. I want to talk to you about Kyle Stannard."

I watched the woman's startled reaction. The mouth widened into an O, her head thrust forward, knees bent slightly. Hands clenched into fists. "What a damned cheek."

"I couldn't agree with you more," I said with cool.

Mrs. Foley's eyes narrowed. "Are you a police officer?"

"I'm a psychologist."

"Now you've lost me."

"Mr. Stannard is causing difficulties for both of us. From what you've said, I think we could help each other. Naturally, anything you say would be treated in the strictest confidence."

Mrs. Foley gave me an appraising look, her face masked by uncertainty. "All right," she said slowly. "You'd better come into the drawing room. I've a feeling I may need to sit down."

"Call his bluff," I said stoutly.

I'd spent the past hour listening to Heather Foley's story: her failed marriage, her loss of confidence, her desperate desire to rebuild her life, including her hope of a face-lift, and Stannard's miserable attempt to beat her down. Once she'd started unloading, she was unstoppable. I empathised with her deep loneliness. From the torrent of words it was clear that this was the first time the woman had opened up about her abrupt change of circumstances to anyone—so much easier to confide all to someone you're unlikely to see again.

"But he might back out." Heather twisted her hands.

"He might, but you'll find someone else to buy the house, I promise you. If you're not entirely happy with Fairweathers, bin them. This is estate agent city. You could try one of a dozen other agents in town." I immediately thought of Simon. "In any case, I think, from what you've said, Stannard really is interested. You say he wrote a card."

"I've got it somewhere." Heather left the room briefly, her sharp footsteps reverberating down the hall. I got up and looked out of the window, admiring the row of wonderfully appointed houses on the other side. With a little TLC, Rowanbank could be magnificent. I couldn't fault Stannard's taste or business acumen.

Heather reappeared, brandishing the postcard. A picture of a grand double-fronted house on the front, an address in Wellington Square and phone number printed on the blank side. The handwriting was in black pen, large and fluid, the content polite. I read it twice, salted it away, and handed the card back. "He definitely wants it."

"But at a price," Heather said with frustration.

"At *your* price. Don't let him play games with you. You've already come down forty thousand, which more than compensates for the difference of opinion with the Highways Agency. He's trying it on, taking advantage of the fact you're a woman on your own. Don't let him."

Heather's eyes hardened. She sat up straight, bristling with new determination. "You're absolutely right. I'll speak to my lawyer today."

"This is your home, your future, your game," I insisted. "You set the rules."

Heather beamed. Her eyes radiated fun and youthfulness. She patted me on the knee, an expression of "all girls together."

"We must have a drink. I've got rather a nice Chardonnay chilling in the fridge." She got up, smoothed the creases in her skirt, her face flushed with excitement, and took two steps. Without warning, her face briefly clouded, a look of worry invading her features. "I'm so sorry. I seem to have done all the talking. It's such a relief, you see. You don't mind, do you?"

"Not in the least and you have my word it won't go outside these four walls."

"I suppose you're used to it, people's confessions, their anxieties. You never did say how Mr. Stannard upset you."

I looked up at her squarely. "I think we could do with that drink first."

I called Simon, explaining, without making any specific reference to Rowanbank, Stannard's method of operation.

"He's not doing anything illegal," Simon pointed out.

"It's sharp practice."

"Name of the game, I'm afraid."

"Taking advantage of a vulnerable middle-aged woman?"

"Happens all the time. She doesn't have to accept." Simon sounded irritated. I wondered if I'd gone too far and cast a slur on his new profession. "In fact the vendor could be accused of encouraging gazumping," he added. When a vendor accepts a higher offer after already agreeing to a sale price with a buyer, I registered. Simon was right, yet this was not what I wanted to hear. "I'm sure Stannard knows what he's about," Simon continued. "His stepfather's Gerald Mallory."

"Who?"

"The criminal defence lawyer."

So that's what Stannard meant by *moving in lawyerly circles*. No wonder he felt invincible. "Why didn't you tell me before?"

"I didn't know before. You're still convinced Stannard's your stalker?"

I hesitated. Did Simon still have Chris in the frame or did he have an ulterior motive? I realised I should let Simon and Molly know that Chris had left, but fearing a similar reaction to Claire and Charlie's, I chickened out. Truth was, Stannard no longer seemed to be ticking quite so many boxes. "Maybe," I said, evasive. "Where does Mr. Mallory hang out?"

"Works in London, though I think it's more part-time these days. He's got a huge pile near Bourton-on-the-Water, at Great Rissington."

"What about Stannard's mother?"

"Haven't a clue."

I wondered what had happened to Stannard's blood father. Simon jabbed through my thoughts.

"You're barking up the wrong tree, Kim."

Means I'll have to look closer to home then, I thought, as I said good-bye.

FORTY-NINE

I STOOD IN THE gated square opposite Stannard's home the next morning, an elegant villa, with shutters and sash windows and three stone steps and painted balustrade to the teal-coloured front door. As soon as he left, I crossed over to take a closer look at his habitat.

The air was close and sticky and gave every indication that, once the mist lifted, the day would be swathed again in brilliant sunshine.

A bit nervous, I glanced around. A cat stretched in the morning sun. Nobody about. No noise of human endeavour, only the sound of birdsong. Emboldened, taking quick steps, I sped across the herringbone-patterned brick drive, trampled a border, and peered inside a downstairs window. With minimal furnishings, no ornaments or keepsakes, no paintings adorning the wall, the vibe was Spartan. Crossing to the other side of the front door, I peered into another room, which housed an ultramodern glass-topped table, eight chrome and leather-backed chairs, and a light wood sideboard. Functional. Practical. No soul.

I slipped across the drive towards a wrought-iron side gate. Taking a swift look over my shoulder, I clambered over and dropped heavily onto a paved cutout area that contained a Cheltenham wheeliebin. Thick bushes and hedges formed a natural boundary with the property next door. Beyond, a walled garden was filled with borders, cascading rose bushes, and fruit trees laden with apples, plums, and pears.

A conservatory filled with rattan furniture jutted out from the main house. With double wooden doors obscuring the view further inside, I walked around the conservatory and tried the back door. Firmly locked, all windows closed.

Shielding my eyes with the flat of my hand, I squinted through a kitchen window, the glare of reflected sunshine temporarily distorting my vision and causing whiteout. I strained to focus. When I could finally see, breath exited my body in one great whoosh. Ahead were dozens of photographs, the cradle of his obsession. I expected to see my own image among them, but there was only one subject: Stannard. In black and white and colour. Stannard, as he once looked; Stannard, with his amazingly symmetrical features; Stannard, the beautiful. Shaken, I took a smart step back.

Something snagged my peripheral vision.

Heart rate quickening, I shot across the lawn and disappeared into a tangle of trees and jungle of hedge and shrubs, my gaze fixed on the apex of a roofline almost invisible from the house. The closer I got, pieces of an architectural jigsaw took shape and form—an upper elevation, stone, glass, wood—until a small, perfectly conceived stone two-storey detached coach house emerged out of the foliage.

What secrets did it hold?

Pressing my face to the glass, my jaw slackened. Strikingly, the room was empty; whitewashed walls bare apart from thee large framed photographic prints that stole my breath away. Oh God, I gasped, you really were drop-dead beautiful.

Deep in my groin, I felt a stir, a suppressed feeling of arousal that shook me to the core.

On the farthest wall, Stannard was bare-chested. Breathtakingly sexy, eyes narrowed, looking into the sun. A second print depicted a mean and moody Stannard leaning against the bonnet of a Jaguar convertible. By squeezing myself into the corner of the French window and twisting my head, I could make out the third: Stannard dressed in a suit, white open-necked shirt, head tilted back, throat exposed, mouth wide as if he were letting out a roar of laughter, his expression one of pure exhilaration. I could almost hear him and, in that sublime moment, I recognised his immense joy, his lust for life and blatant belief that he was invincible. It was like standing in a place of worship.

I lost all sense of time. Falling under his spell, I was transfixed.

FIFTY

EVENTUALLY, AS THOUGH COMING out of a coma, I took to my heels. Shooting over the gate, feet landing sure and firm, I fled across the road, out of the square, to streets bustling with sound and humanity. Skirting Fairview, I raced back into the hurly-burly.

Losing Stannard was not so easy. My brain coruscated. Stannard and the camera, standing alone, solitary by nature, a guy who told the outside world that he was sexy, no pushover, fun. This was the nature of the man, the makeup of his identity.

All twisted and crushed.

He must have suffered a great deal, I thought, almost colliding with a woman with a pushchair. Ashamed for dwelling on his former glory like a ghoul and voyeur, I was as certain as I could be that I'd read Stannard wrong. Speculation followed by assumption equals one hell of a mistake.

A bony hand clamped onto my right elbow. I let out a tight squeal and whipped round. Out of breath, an elderly woman with ruby-tinted cheeks and a painted mouth that exceeded her natural lip-line drilled into me.

"You were snooping."

"I don't know what you mean." I tried to extract my elbow from her fearsome grip. The fingers, like talons, dug deeper.

"I watched you. You were prying."

"I wasn't doing anything."

"Explain that to the police."

I froze. The old woman released her grasp, triumph in her eyes.

As I pounded through a crowd of shoppers, not looking back, her yell sounded over my head: "They're watching you."

The shock of Kim Slade's revelation had blown Heather Foley way off course. Her only knowledge of stalking was gleaned from a story line in one of the soaps she regularly watched on television. The memory of Stannard in the cellar now spooked the life out of her. What exactly had he been planning to do down there?

Having been put in the strange position of meeting both parties, she could understand the theory of Stannard's creepy fixation with the young woman. It came down to appearances. Curiously, it had pulled her up short. Here she was, considering cosmetic surgery on a perfectly good face when these two youngsters had no such choice. While she was sympathetic to Kim Slade, and it had been a relief to talk to the young woman about her problems, she worried about what exactly she was getting into.

This aside, pressure from both Fairweather's and Stannard's lawyers had increased by the day. Less inclined to sit on the fence, it was time to take a stand and go for broke. Before she changed her mind, she picked up the phone and called Stannard's number. Within seconds, his secretary came on the line.

"He's rather tied up at the moment, Mrs. Foley. Can I help?"

"I'd prefer to speak to Mr. Stannard personally."

"That might be difficult."

"Can you tell me when he'll be free?"

"Hard to say. He really is dreadfully busy."

We're all *dreadfully busy*, Heather thought with irritation.

"Is it connected to the sale of Rowanbank?" the secretary said. No, it's connected to his stalking activities, Heather thought cuttingly. "Only I'm sure your solicitor could sort it out."

Long pause. Heather realised that she was being stonewalled. "I don't want to speak to my solicitor. I want to speak to Stannard," she said, deliberately dropping his title.

Another pause. "I could pass on a message for you." It sounded as though an enormous favour was being bestowed. Heather suppressed a fresh flush of irritation.

"I'd be most grateful. Could you say that I'm doing nothing about rubbish, or the parking area that, apparently, belongs to the Highways Agency. If Mr. Stannard is consequently no longer interested in purchasing the property, perhaps he'd be kind enough to let me know within the next twenty-four hours. After that, Rowanbank will no longer be on the market. Good day."

FIFTY-ONE

CATHY VIEWED ME WITH surprise as I entered Ellerslie Lodge. "I thought you were in Devon."

"Splitting my time," I said. I needed hard information and there was only one person I could think of to supply it.

"Something wrong?" Cathy's expression pierced me.

I broke into a defensive smile. "No, not at all."

She looked unconvinced.

"Had to pop back to collect something," I said, bowling along, hoping that if I kept talking, the flimsiness of my excuse would stand up to scrutiny. "Is Kirsten around, only, as I'm passing, I'd like a quick word?"

Cathy's expression remained cautious. "I think so. Want me to go and see?"

I gave a no-rush, nonchalant shrug and waited. Minutes later, Cathy returned, Kirsten at her side, a look of sullen disdain on the girl's face.

"Sorry to drag you away, Kirsten, but I wondered if we could have a chat? We could sit outside on the lawn." I looked to Cathy for approval. She gave a brief nod, her expression indecipherable.

Kirsten mumbled "whatever" and loped towards the door. She wore sunglasses and a long dress with flowing sleeves that concealed her bony limbs. I threw an awkward smile and followed. We walked on past a bush of crimson-coloured flowers and towards a neatly trimmed lawn where Kirsten plumped down on the grass.

"Thought you were away." She drew her knees up to her chin, folded her arms, and fixed her gaze on the lawn.

"I am, sort of." I knelt down opposite her. "How are you keeping?"

"All right."

"The thing is, Kirsten, I need your help."

The girl looked up slowly. It was impossible to read her eyes behind the shades.

"You must have met a lot of people when you were modelling—photographers, make-up artists, agents, other models."

"Some."

"Did you ever come across a male model by the name of Kyle Stannard?"

"No."

"You're sure."

"Means nothing to me."

The words were clear, firm and loud. Kirsten's face showed no colour, no give-away facial tic.

"Maybe if I describe him to you."

"Tall, dark, and handsome, like thousands of others."

"So you *did* come across someone like him."

"All the time." Kirsten suppressed a yawn. I noticed the whiteness of the girl's knuckles, the way her hands twisted, as if separate from the rest of her. Brittle.

"This man was special," I said, emphatic. "Stood out from the crowd. He had presence and charisma."

Kirsten glanced away with a tight smile. "Have you any idea how many model agencies there are in London?"

"We're looking top end. Your notes state that you worked for Visage, one of the most select and successful modelling agencies in the country." From a professional standpoint, what I was doing was unforgivable. I was breaking every ethical code, yet I stood to lose everything if I didn't find out and establish the truth. "He worked for Quartz. Are you sure you never came across him?"

"Positive."

"He's not the sort of guy you'd forget. He has an aura about him. Still does even though he got his face kicked in."

Alarm chased across the girl's features. That got to her, I thought, not understanding how. "He's not in the game any more. Works as a property developer in town."

"Here?" Kirsten's limbs tensed. Her face pinched. "You know him then, this guy?"

"Kind of."

She fell quiet. The air hummed with heat. She pulled up a clump of grass and pressed the blades between her fingers. "Did he say he knew me?"

"No."

The aloof expression quickly resumed. I studied the girl's shrunken features and saw the buttoned-down misery in her expression. I'd hardly tapped the surface of what was going on in

Kirsten's mind. But Kirsten *was* hiding something, and secrets required a high degree of mental agility to conceal.

"Kirsten, I want to help you. But you have to trust me too. I get the impression that you're holding out on me. There's something you're not telling, something you feel bad about, maybe something you haven't even told your parents." Unethical in every aspect, I knew that not only had I crossed a line, I'd travelled a mile on the other side.

Kirsten wrenched up another handful of grass, her lips parted, and then she seemed to check herself and change her mind. She looked back at the Lodge. "There's nothing to tell and, if that's all, I'm due to see Jim. He doesn't like people being late."

FIFTY-TWO

The phone rang as I was thinking about preparing dinner. I picked up, Jim's voice at the other end of the line unusually frosty.

"I understand you came to see Kirsten this afternoon."

"Yes, I did."

"But you're on leave."

"Yes. I—"

"Would you mind telling me what was discussed?"

"We talked about Visage."

"The modelling agency she worked for?"

"That's right."

"Why?"

"Because it has a bearing on her current condition." I flushed at my own spin.

"We're all aware of that," Jim said, terse. "And?" He persisted.

"I didn't get very far."

"How far?"

"I think she's hiding something."

"What exactly?" Jim's tone was highly critical. "Can you be specific?"

"I don't think the modelling agency was responsible for precipitating her weight loss."

"Then what was?"

"That's what I'm not sure about." I wanted to tell Jim about Stannard and the way Kirsten reacted, but I recognised that it would be seen in a bad light. The bald truth was that I'd exploited my professional position in an attempt to find out more. I'd broken a professional code of conduct. But I'd underestimated Jim's sleuthing abilities.

"This wouldn't be connected to you, by any chance?"

"No, I—"

"I don't know what went on this afternoon apart from the fact that you hounded Kirsten about Kyle Stannard."

"Hounded?"

"What the hell did you think you were playing at?"

"Jim, please . . ."

"Whatever you said has had profound consequences."

This brought me up short and I stopped digging. "What sort of consequences?"

"Kirsten slashed her wrists half an hour after you left."

My heart somersaulted and leapt into my throat. "Oh my God, is she all right?"

"Fortunately, yes. Cathy got to her before she'd lost too much blood. She's in Cheltenham General in a fairly poor mental state. As you'd imagine, her parents are extremely concerned."

"Jim, I'm so terribly sorry. I don't know what else to say. Do you want me to talk to the Mathersons?"

"Good God, no."

"They have no idea I spoke to her?"

Jim deflected the question by asking another. "Why did you talk to her about Stannard?"

"I thought it might help," I said lamely, "what with them both involved in the modelling business."

"Help *you,*" he hissed in a withering tone. "If you have a problem, you go to the police, understand? You're supposed to be taking a break. You're supposed to be getting your act together."

"That's not fair."

"Neither is what you did this afternoon." I fell silent, braced for the next body blow. "Christ knows what will happen. Did the word *ethics* ever cross your mind? What are you trying to do, throw your entire career away?"

"I'm sorry," I said, mortified.

"I don't know what personal axe you have to grind, or how you think your situation has any bearing on Kirsten's, but don't you dare involve and interfere with my patients. Have you got that?" he barked.

"It won't happen again. Will you let me know how she is?"

"I think it best you stay off the case." His voice was full of winter chill. "I'm sure that's what the Mathersons would want. There will have to be an internal inquiry."

"I understand." I felt bleak and guilty. Never in a million years did I ever imagine that I would breach the professional code for my own personal crusade, yet that was exactly what I'd done. "Will you be speaking to the team at Bayshill?"

"I've already been in touch."

My stomach gave a queasy lurch. "What was the reaction?"

"The one you'd expect." He cut the call.

I dropped down onto a chair.

Stupid, stupid, stupid. What a terrible mess, and all my creation. Poor Kirsten. My crass approach had probably set the girl back weeks or even months. Understandably, my reputation was sunk and my job was on the line, but, measured against what I'd done to Kirsten, it was of little consequence.

I tried to focus, to analyse what Kirsten had said, more importantly, to read what her silences signified.

Snippets of Stannard's conversation reverberated through my head. *Secrets and guilt.* But whose and what?

If their paths had crossed, and I was pretty sure they had, Kirsten would have been around fourteen or fifteen years old, Stannard anything between twenty-five and thirty. Kirsten, a naive and impressionable teenager; Stannard, forceful, controlling, and arrogant.

Now what? I'd wanted a conversation with Kirsten in the hope that it would rule out Stannard as my stalker. Instead, he seemed even more suspicious. Jim wanted an enquiry into my conduct, in the light of which Bayshill were bound to reconsider my contract. My stalker was still out there. Somewhere. And if not Stannard …

Families were the best repositories for secrets. Stannard's ancestral family home in Great Rissington might yet hold a clue, but first I was going to London. I owed Kirsten that much.

FIFTY-THREE

THE VISAGE MODELLING AGENCY lay behind a darkened glass exterior in smart SW7. I walked up and down the street several times, mentally cranking myself up to enter. By asking for help from an organisation whose ethos I viewed as pernicious to the majority of my clients, I was selling out. Worse, I'd actually taken special care with my appearance. It's not what you look like that counts, I'd robustly maintain to clients, it's who you are. Yeah, whatever.

The vibe inside was plush and luxurious. Soft, caramel-coloured leather chairs rested against dark walls decked with starlets. The silence intimidated. I'd expected a place crawling with life. Maybe the inner sanctum was more vibrant.

A sultry-looking black girl in her late twenties, poised and stately, flicked her gaze up from behind a smart iMac. She looked through me and, sharp and focused, stared at my neck with something close to disbelief. At least I had her attention.

I counterattacked with a smile. "I wonder if you can help me." The girl responded by adopting a mask of impenetrability. I persisted. "You had a young model working for you a few years ago by the name of Kirsten Matherson."

No change in expression. No reaction.

"She would have been about fourteen or fifteen."

"I recall."

"You knew her?"

"Are you from the press?" Dark eyes thinned.

"No."

"Police?"

"No."

"So you are?" The tone was desiccating.

"Kim Slade, I'm a clinical psychologist and I'm treating Kirsten." I shuddered at the lie. If Jim had his way, I'd have nothing more to do with her ever again. Because of my folly there was the serious possibility that my career could be over. "Is it possible to talk to someone who knew her well?"

"You need to speak to Flick Sutherland."

"Thank you." I took a seat.

The girl resumed her duties. I waited, patient. She took out a pot of nail varnish and began to paint her nails. After a couple of minutes, she looked over at me. "Flick's no longer with the agency."

I stood up and, fixing a smile to my mouth, said, "Any idea where I might find her?"

"No." Lights off, nobody in, shutters down.

"It's important," I said. "Kirsten's not at all well. She's in hospital right now. I could really do with some help here."

Clearly unhappy with having pressure applied, she blew on her nails, which were a deep shade of emerald. "Flick left London a couple of years back."

"And you've no idea where I can get hold of her?"

There was a fraction's hesitation.

"Please."

The girl scowled, drew out a pad and scribbled a note. "Decided to get out of the rat race," she explained, handing it to me.

I glanced at it, suppressed surprise, and pushed the note into my bag. "Thank you so much, I really appreciate this."

The girl's expression slackened. "Is Kirsten really ill?" There was a tentative note of interest in her voice.

"She has anorexia. At the moment she's in hospital with her wrists slashed." And it's my fault.

"Bastard!"

"Excuse me?"

"That bastard's to blame." Her eyes gleamed with outrage.

"Who?"

"You don't know?"

"Know what?"

The girl's gaze travelled anxiously to the door. She leant over the desk, lowered her voice, as if afraid someone might hear. "Kirsten was raped."

Astounded, my skin erupted with cold sweat.

The girl cocked an eyebrow. "Should help some with your therapy."

"Raped by whom?" My voice sounded distant and detached from me.

"A male model; he worked for another agency."

"You knew him?"

The girl shifted her gaze to the door again and shrugged. "Everyone knew him."

I steeled myself, hardly able to get the words out. "Was his name Kyle Stannard?"

For the first time the girl looked me straight in the eye. "Yes," she said.

I headed for Gloucester Road tube station in a daze. Stannard had raped Kirsten. Stannard had raped Kirsten. I murmured it over and over again. And Stannard, Kirsten's rapist, was stalking me. Fallon's words blasted through my head: *For all you know, he might have done it before ... In worst-case scenarios, it can culminate in abduction, rape, torture, and murder.*

Kirsten's rape would play a massive factor in triggering anorexia. But, wait, why no mention in Kirsten's notes? Why hadn't the clinicians been informed? It didn't stack. Neither did it make sense that the police hadn't uncovered this important fact in their dealings with Stannard—unless they took the oh-so-reasonable point of view that he'd paid for his crime and was unlikely to re-offend. But surely they had a duty to warn me? With Kirsten underage, wouldn't he also be on the sex offender's register? The only other explanation I could come up with was that the crime was never reported.

Stannard's assertion, *People do as I say,* assumed new clarity. At the time I'd believed it was said to threaten me, but maybe he spoke the truth. His stepfather, the eminent Gerald Mallory, was in a perfect position to provide legal protection.

I got off and made my way to Paddington train station. A nasal-sounding announcement declared that the next train stopping off at Cheltenham was running late. Fed up, I went in search of a cup of tea, paid for it, and took it back to the platform and waited.

When I finally climbed on board the train, I pulled out the note handed to me and called Flick Sutherland. An articulate youngster, called Sky, informed me that her mother was out and was not expected back until late.

"Can I get her to call you?"

"She won't know who I am, but if she wouldn't mind. Can you tell her it's in connection with one of her models?" Thanking Sky, I left my number.

As soon as I got back, I checked the flat, poured a glass of wine and took a long swallow. Normally, I would have called Chris. Except Chris had gone. I took another pull of wine, briefly toyed with phoning Constable Grant, and just as quickly binned the idea. The cops were procedure merchants. They only dealt in hard evidence. Speculation, assumption, and rumour had no role to play.

But if Stannard raped Kirsten Matherson, people knew about it, and tomorrow I intended to find out exactly who they were.

FIFTY-FOUR

In my experience, waitresses and bar staff are invaluable funds of information. The staff at a local hostelry in Great Rissington proved no exception, the Mallorys' home swiftly located through a good-natured conversation with a genial barman.

I finished my Coke and stepped out into the car park. The sun was hot. Its rays, reflected from the Cotswold stone, bathed the village in a bright amber glow. I drove down a street, both sides bordered by pretty cottages and gabled houses, and out onto open road.

Oakridge House was some three and a half miles away, hidden by a long tarmac drive that shared a right-of-way with walkers and ramblers. I parked the car on a wide verge near the entrance and began the steep walk down.

Dense woodland flanked my right. Signs indicated public footpaths and wildlife, and stark warnings for dogs to be kept on leads at all times. To the left, the land gave way to rich pasture where a couple of dozen sheep grazed. At my approach, they scattered blindly.

The sun beat down upon my back. My head buzzed with heat and doubt. Had it really been such a good idea to come? I was there alone. Nobody walked pets. No mother with her children. No one taking the air. Perspiration gathered in the small of my back. Anyone could take me here in the undergrowth. Hurling the thought aside, I placed one foot in front of the other, kept going.

Roughly three quarters down the drive was a stagnant-looking lake, the surface a murky green scum. Winding around to the left and fenced by barbed wire, the way disappeared to a dirt track. There was no grass, only dense vegetation with little room for sunlight.

I kept to the main route, the drive wide enough to take a car. On either side, the cool green slipped away.

The entrance to Oakridge was marked by a fine set of gates. Open, they reclined against a bank of camellias and rhododendrons. I sneaked through, masking my arrival by staying close to the many bushes, flowering shrubs, and trees.

The house itself was not what I expected. Colonial-looking with a wooden veranda that would immediately betray the sound of intruders, it was large enough for a family and an army of servants. The upstairs room had white painted shutters fastened back against the outside wall. A gabled porch fronted the house and, as I drew near, I could see a flat green lawn with croquet hoops. The place exuded grandeur and fine living. The snapshot further jarred expectations. To my mind, stalkers like Stannard came from impoverished backgrounds. Falling prey to thinking in stereotypes, I recognised how stupid, mistaken, and ignorant I'd been. Neither breeding nor wealth insulated from personality disorders.

Skin suddenly clammy, I twisted around, screwing my eyes tight, scanning a line of trees and holding my breath until I thought I might burst. From somewhere I heard the distant sound of traffic. Turning, setting my face to the big house, a twig snapped and I let out a yelp of surprise.

"Impeccable timing," Stannard announced, with a half smile. He wore tight jeans and an open-neck shirt. I glimpsed a dark line of hair squatting on his chest. Fit and physically powerful, he was close enough for me to smell his distinctive aftershave, close enough to kiss him. The sheer magnetism of his presence shook me.

"We're about to sit down for lunch," he said. "I'm sure mother could squeeze in one more."

"You're mad." I felt annoyed for using such a loose and inadequate phrase to describe someone whom I suspected was psychotic.

"From where I'm standing, I'd say you're the crazy one." He gave my arm a tug. "Come on, she won't bite. My stepfather's rather a grouch but I'm sure you'll charm him."

I opened my lips in protest but my mouth went dry, and Stannard's hold was firm. He didn't say another word, but his intention was crystal clear. In his deluded way, he was taking me home to meet the parents. I don't know why but I stumbled forward. Stannard, meanwhile, kept up a steady stream of chatter about the house and its architecture.

A set of golf clubs adorned the hall together with a selection of umbrellas, walking sticks, and Wellington boots. A tall woman, gazelle-like, with classic bone structure, approached us. I estimated she was in her early sixties.

"This is Kim Slade, mother."

The woman looked vacantly from me to Stannard to me again.

"Olivia Mallory," she said. She did not extend a hand. Her mouth was a thin, disapproving line. I watched as the woman's deeply set eyes clamped onto my neck.

"She's my new friend," Stannard explained, casting me a cold-blooded look.

Olivia Mallory nodded apprehensively. "It's rather unexpected. Kyle didn't say you were coming."

"What's this?" We all turned and followed the voice, which had travelled from an adjoining room. A large, well-built man stepped into the hall. Dressed in a pair of casual tan-coloured trousers and a short-sleeved shirt, he had thin, greying hair, heavily hooded blue eyes, and an angular jaw that was beginning to slacken and show the signs of age. The man took one look at me and paled. Undaunted, Stannard ran through the introductions for a second time. The air crackled with tension. Gerald Mallory shot out a hand. I minutely shook my head and pressed my arms to my side.

"This isn't what it seems," I announced, my voice steely. The Mallorys viewed me as if I'd produced a gun. "Your son is stalking me."

Olivia Mallory let out a shrill cry.

Defiant, I stared at Stannard. He stared back, not with alarm, but with astonishing confidence. I suddenly felt as if I'd walked blindly into an ambush. "He's been following me, sending me stuff, threatening me."

"Then why are you here?" Gerald Mallory towered over me, the question asked in a forthright tone.

"Because I want it to stop."

"How dare you!" Olivia Mallory burst out. "How dare you come to our home and make false allegations."

"They're *not* false. Ask him," I said, tipping my chin in Stannard's direction. Gerald Mallory traded a look with his stepson, who let out a languid sigh.

"It's all nonsense. There's clearly been a huge misunderstanding."

"You call a pornographic image sent to my employers a misunderstanding?"

Mallory stepped in like a smooth-talking hostage negotiator talking down a hijacker. "If this is so, Miss Slade, then I suggest you go to the police."

"Do you really want your stepson to go to jail?"

Olivia Mallory let out a dry sob. Visibly shaking, she cast her husband a crooning look that said, *For God's sake, do something. This woman is nothing.*

"Miss Slade," Mallory said, stern edge to his voice, "think very carefully before you say something you may regret. Kyle has already spoken to me about you and your false allegations. As you're probably aware, making such serious claims and wasting police resources could land *you* in the dock."

I reddened. They were obviously colluding with him. "So he's always been a good boy, has he? Always treated women and the girls in his life with respect and decency? What about Kirsten Matherson?"

Stannard's skin drained to the colour of wood-ash. A vein pulsed in Mallory's temple. Olivia Mallory's eyes shrank to twin pinpricks of hate.

"Are you going to let her stand there, Gerald?"

Mallory took a step towards me. "I think it's time you left."

I stood my ground. I wasn't finished yet. "Your stepson raped Kirsten Matherson and now she's starving herself to death."

"You stupid little bitch," Olivia Mallory snarled.

"Mother." Stannard's expression remained grim. He looked genuinely shaken.

"She was the start of it all," Olivia Mallory continued. "If it hadn't been for her and her pathetic lies—"

"*Her* lies?" I said. "Why is it that everyone, other than your precious son, is lying?"

"My son," Olivia gasped. "My son was beautiful, really beautiful. He was the best, at the top-end of his career, but that money-grabbing trollop came along to spoil—"

"Olivia," Mallory warned, but she was gone, lost in recrimination and rage.

"Look at him," she screamed. "His face is ruined, his career destroyed, and now you come along with your filthy accusations. I'll see you in hell before you hurt my boy." The slap came hard and fast across my face. Cheek stinging, midgasp, I caught Stannard's expression of dismay and shock.

Gerald Mallory put an arm around his wife. "Get out," he ordered, "and don't come back."

I stumbled from the house and ran at break-neck speed down the drive. All I could hear were Olivia Mallory's screams smashing against my ears.

FIFTY-FIVE

I SPENT THE REST of the weekend wrestling my conscience. I badly needed to hear Kirsten's version of events, but contact was impossible. Attempting to stay in the loop, I called Cathy on Sunday morning to get an update, only to be told in wintry tones that Kirsten was *comfortable.*

On Monday, Alexa called. It went something like:

"Hi, Kim, which solicitor did you use for your divorce?"

I told her.

"Was she any good?"

I scratched my nose. "I couldn't really say. She did the job, but it wasn't complicated."

"I need someone with killer instinct."

"Do you?"

"I intend to clean Brooks out."

"Then I can't really help you—sorry."

With more pressing matters on her agenda, Alexa said good-bye. Part of me was relieved. If Alexa found a legal henchman to do her bidding, maybe she'd phone me less often.

Turning things over in my mind, I plucked up enough courage to risk ridicule and phoned PC Grant. He wasn't immediately available but I was assured he'd call back. I was making coffee when my entry phone rang. It was Jim. Oh shit, I thought, pressing the buzzer.

I let him in feeling like a sixteen-year-old capitulating to a parent after an almighty row. He looked grave and sad, and I feared the worst. I showed him into the sitting room. He examined my face in a way I recognised.

"If you've come about Kirsten, I can explain."

"It's not about Kirsten. It's about Kyle Stannard."

My chest tightened. Jim loosened the collar of his shirt. I noticed he was wearing a tie. It made him look strange and official. I invited him to sit down.

"When you told me that he was stalking you, you had my support and my sympathy," Jim began. "We were all behind you."

Were, I registered, picking up on the change of tense.

"Only now things are less straightforward. I've received a formal complaint from Gerald and Olivia Mallory. They came to see me first thing this morning. They maintain that you've been stalking their son."

"That's simply not true."

Jim continued, steadfast. "They say you followed him to their house and made a scene there on Saturday. They've threatened to go to the police."

It was all I could do not to put my head in my hands and let out a long low moan.

"I've managed to deter them for the time being, although I can't give you any guarantees. Mallory is a QC. He's not going to take this lying down. I take it from your silence that it's true."

I nodded, briefly dumb. Could I trust Jim? That was the big one. Finally, taking a chance, I said, "Jim?"

"Yes, Kim."

"Would you like coffee?"

He broke into a daft smile. "Long story?"

"Interminable."

———

I told him everything. He listened intently. His expression stiffened when I confessed to following Stannard. When I told him about the rape, his eyes widened, then narrowed.

"Nothing more than vicious gossip and allegations."

"But what if it's true?"

"Where's your proof?"

"Kirsten Matherson."

Jim's laugh was hard and hollow. "Now I really think you've lost the plot. Has it ever occurred to you that what you were doing was wrong?"

"Yes."

"That you might be mistaken?"

"Yes." I now recognised that I wasn't infallible. I harboured doubts. Had the receptionist fallen prey to malicious gossip?

"Well then," Jim said.

"But everything leads back to him. Everywhere I look, he's there with his irritating logic, his compulsion to grab my attention. My life was fine until Kyle Stannard came along to jinx it."

Jim took both my hands in his. "Chris would have left without Stannard's interference, Kim."

I drew away. I couldn't disagree. "What about Kirsten?" I said.

He gave me a level look. "Something as massive as this would be in her notes."

"You're really not convinced?"

Jim waited a beat. "The truth is, I don't know."

And neither did I. Not for certain. I could be looking at two entirely separate issues. What I needed were hard, incontrovertible facts. Noting the time, I wondered when Grant would return my call.

"In any case," Jim continued, "Kirsten's treatment is academic. The Mathersons want to move her back home as soon as possible."

I was despondent. The Mathersons lived on the wrong side of the Welsh borders, far away from an inpatient eating disorder unit. What would become of her? "How did you leave it with the Mallorys?"

"I promised to reprimand you, which I'm now doing. The real problem, Kim, is that the Mallorys have a point. Whether or not Stannard is your stalker, you've handed it to him on a plate."

I gave a sober nod of agreement.

FIFTY-SIX

THE ESTATE AGENTS CALLED me shortly after Jim left to inform me of a viewing scheduled for the following afternoon. I was asked whether or not I'd be at home.

"I'll be there," I said, an uncomfortable pull on my heartstrings; it was still a home of sorts. I'd no sooner put down the phone than it rang again. Taking precautions, I waited for the answering service to collect the call. It was Flick Sutherland sounding as though she was calling from a party—loud music, people laughing, the clatter of glass and cutlery. I picked up.

"Sorry," Flick said, in a throaty mid-Atlantic drawl. "It's the kids. They've got their friends round, celebrating break and all that. Turn the music down, someone," she blared, half deafening me.

The volume decreased a little. "Sky said you're some kind of shrink."

I explained my credentials.

"You don't say. I went to a therapist once. Best thing I ever did. Helped me get in touch with myself. The real me." The music erupted again. "For Chrissakes," the real me roared, the ear-splitting crash of breaking glass resonating down the phone line. This time the music died down to a low bass burble. Unfazed, Flick said, "How can I help?"

"I need to talk about one of your girls."

"I'm no longer in the business, honey."

"That's not relevant."

"Okay, shoot."

"Kirsten Matherson."

I heard a match being struck, the sound of lungs pulling on a cigarette. "What about her?" The zip had bounced out of Flick's voice.

"What's your connection?"

"I scouted her. What's yours?"

"Kirsten Matherson's one of my clients."

"Let me guess, eating disorder."

"Anorexia, unfortunately."

"No surprise with a mom like that."

Flick had my undivided attention. I waited for her to expand.

"She was always pushing the girl, nagging her, putting her up for any and every job. Kirsten had quite a look, popular at the time. Her mom wanted her to ride the wave while she had it. She insisted on as many castings as could be humanly fitted into a day."

"And Kyle Stannard?"

Flick's lungs drew heavily on the cigarette. I could almost taste the nicotine on my tongue.

"He was gorgeous and unique with good looks that last a lifetime. I'd have slept with him myself if I hadn't been pregnant."

I didn't need to muffle my surprise. After seeing those photographs in his house, I got it. "Tell me about him."

"He had the three Fs: flash, fun, fucking great in the sack—or so I have it on good authority. I lost count of the times girls cried on my shoulder because of Kyle. He was too damned charming for his own good."

Charming? "Did he have a temper, a bad side?"

"Sure, he was bad," Flick gave a throaty laugh. "He had an exotic lifestyle with a taste for cocaine and young women."

"Underage girls?"

"Not knowingly," Flick said, as though it wasn't that big a deal. "Hey, we girlies love that bad boy stuff, don't we? It's kind of intoxicating and wild. Truth is, Kyle had a love 'em and leave 'em philosophy that ruffled lots of little feathers."

I wondered uneasily whether the receptionist at Visage was one of them. "But was there a nasty side to him?" I no longer felt as surefooted. With every revelation, I was sucked a little deeper into Stannard's world.

"He was a perfectionist so he was quite capable of throwing a tantrum, but I never believed that stuff about him and Kirsten."

"You mean the rape."

"The *alleged* rape," Flick corrected me. "Kyle was the pinnacle of Marie Matherson's career plan for her daughter. That woman offered Kirsten to him like a sacrifice to the gods."

My heart thudded against my rib cage. "But she was only fourteen or fifteen."

"And looked a lot older."

"So what are you saying—that it was encouraged, it was consensual?"

I heard Flick exhaling. "Who knows what goes on behind closed doors? All I can tell you is that there was a lot of chatter, rumours flying around but, at the end of the day, the case was dropped."

"It never went to court?"

"Damn right."

"And afterwards?"

"Plain tragic."

"You mean Kyle?"

"Must have been seven or eight months afterwards," Flick said, sombre now. "Kyle was walking down the street at night and got jumped by muggers. They stole his wallet and watch. He put up a fight and they smashed his face in. Last thing I heard, he was having reconstructive surgery. I left London not long afterwards, moved to Cornwall."

"Because of what happened?"

"Nah, I had my own demons to flee."

We all have those.

FIFTY-SEVEN

GEORGIA WASN'T KEEN. I couldn't blame her. Risking everything, I'd be finished if we were caught. By implication, Georgia would bear a heavy share of responsibility.

"I only want ten minutes," I said. "Ten minutes when I can talk without her parents coming in and blowing me out."

"Remember what happened last time?"

"You'll be there. You can monitor it."

"What about Jim?"

"He won't know unless you tell him."

Georgia stuck her hands in her pockets and said nothing—default position for the exasperated.

"Kirsten's in denial," I pointed out, "and it's not going to go away. She can will herself to starve but she can't will away the past. She won't get better unless she confronts it."

"That's your professional opinion?"

"Yes."

Georgia shook her head. "Insight isn't always a cure, as well you know. It's too risky."

"So is doing nothing."

Stony silence.

"Please, Georgia."

"Kim, this is about you," she hissed. "It sure as hell isn't about Kirsten."

"It's about both of us. Come on, Georgia, my career's on the line, but Kirsten's life is in the balance."

Georgia's face darkened. She looked at the wall then looked back at me. "You really reckon this Flick woman knows what she's talking about?"

"I do."

"Ten minutes?" Georgia said at last.

"Tops." I beamed. "And thank you."

"Don't thank me." Georgia glowered. "This is probably the most stupid decision I've ever made in my life. Meet me at the entrance in an hour."

Kirsten Matherson, bandaged arms resting in her lap, sat on a wicker chair, her face tilted towards a window revealing a thoughtfully arranged garden. Entranced by sparrows taking a water-bath in an ornamental trough, she didn't move as we entered the room.

Georgia took up a position by the door like a sentry. She spoke first, gently reminding Kirsten of my visit. Kirsten gave an imperceptible nod as I sat down next to her.

"I'm so very sorry for what happened," I began. "I never meant to upset you." A faint smile played on the girl's bloodless lips. "Are you feeling better?" I asked.

"A bit."

"All right if we talk about stuff?"

Kirsten's bony shoulders relaxed. "I guess."

"Your parents are right to be angry," I said.

"It's my dad. He's protective of me."

"As all good fathers should be," Georgia cut in lightly, catching my eye.

Kirsten twitched a smile. "Yeah," she said, dreamy.

"Tell me about him," I said.

The girl shrugged. "He's great. He's a bit strict, but he looks after me and my mum," she said, big-eyed. "They both want the best for me."

"And you've got two older brothers, Robert and Stephen, that's right, isn't it?"

Kirsten braced. "What about them?"

"Nothing. I have two of my own." I smiled. Always would have to my mind, despite the fact that Guy was dead. "Sometimes it's a pain being the only girl, don't you think?"

"I suppose. I don't see much of them," Kirsten said briskly. "They're working out in Australia."

"Visit much?"

"Once, not lately." A sudden, hunted look appeared on the girl's face. Her limbs tensed, shoulders straightened.

"Are you getting tired, Kirsten?" Georgia broke in, throwing me a warning look.

"A little."

"One last thing, and I know it's hard," I said, avoiding Georgia's furious expression. "We talked about Kyle, remember?" I held my breath in an agony of frustration. "You knew him, didn't you?"

Kirsten looked past me to a faraway point that only she could see. "How is he?"

"He's fine."

"I'm glad."

Georgia traded a baffled glance with me.

"Can you tell me what really happened?" I said softly.

"I fell in love."

"With Kyle?"

Kirsten nodded.

"And he broke it off?"

"He broke my heart." Kirsten's eyes glistened.

So that was it. I wished I could put my arms around her and give her a hug. "And then what?"

"It was my mother's idea." Kirsten's expression was pleading. "I knew it was wrong but I was so hurt, so broken. You've no idea what he was like. He was funny and wonderful and kind. When I was with him I felt like a princess." She spoke as if her voice had harnessed all the energy from her body. "All the other girls were jealous of me. Then …" She stumbled, big tears in her eyes. "When he told me it was over, I thought I'd die. You've no idea how it feels to be crushed and rejected."

I smiled sadly, laid a hand on Kirsten's arm, and recalled Flick's account of Marie Matherson's ambitions for her daughter—ambitions that were thwarted. "So your mother came up with the rape story?"

Georgia's eyes shot wide with surprise. Kirsten looked down, licked the corner of her mouth. "It seemed a good idea at the time," she said unconvincingly. "I didn't know what would happen. My mother made me promise not to breathe a word, especially not to my dad."

"What was his reaction to the alleged rape?"

"He went ballistic. There was so much pain in the house. I felt swept along by it. Will I get into trouble?"

"No," Georgia cut in. "This isn't your fault."

Kirsten twisted her hands. She looked anguished. "Once you make up a lie, you need another to back it up. I kept changing my story to keep ahead of the game. In the end it was my word against Kyle's."

Your lie against his truth, I realised with a jolt.

"There was no physical evidence," Kirsten shivered, "and it got more and more difficult. The police warned me what might happen in the witness box and I thought then that, no matter what my mother said, I couldn't go through with it. Not for my sake but for his. The worst that could happen was that Kyle could be done for underage sex. In the end, I refused to press charges, and the case was dropped."

"But mud sticks," I said.

"Yes." And with deep sadness in her voice, she added, "And my dad never forgave him."

I left the hospital. The thread of evidence on which I'd tugged had unravelled and exposed a grave mistake. Mine. No wonder the Mallorys were furious.

But now I more than sensed that Stannard was innocent of stalking me because Stannard had not raped Kirsten.

I replayed events in my head, thinking back to the time I hung back outside the bookstore. I'd raised my hand to get a signal for my phone. Was that what Stannard mistook for a wave? His cold denials, his justified horror at yet another false allegation, and I'd been deaf, dumb, and blind to them.

I didn't doubt that Stannard had been all of the things Flick Sutherland described. And yes, he'd bugged me, pursued me with relentlessness, eager to talk out his fears and obsessions, but he was not the man who'd turned my life upside-down. This was a guy who'd been set up, his reputation destroyed and then, when life was returning to normal, thugs had mercilessly beaten him up. Life had indeed dealt him a bad hand of cards and, as I considered this, I discovered that, although he'd complicated my life to a terrible degree, my compassion for him and my empathy with him ran deep. How could I have behaved in such a morally bankrupt way?

It left wide-open one last question: If I was so off-beam, so out of whack, who was the real scary bastard?

FIFTY-EIGHT

Someone you *know*, Fallon said.

With no appetite either for food or retail therapy, I idled in the direction of Cheltenham's very own Left Bank and centre of bohemia—the Bath Road—and bumped into Molly.

"Kim, you look dreadful."

I supposed I did. My friends considered me crazy. I'd lost credibility at work. I'd lost faith in my own sense of morality and judgement. I planned a move to God knows where, to a place my face, no doubt, would be gawped at. I had no idea who my stalker was, other than it wasn't Stannard. No pressure.

Molly linked an arm through mine and propelled me in the direction of Morans eating house and wine bar. Grabbing a table for two, Molly ordered for both of us and over wine and food, and under Molly's merciless inquisition, I told her enough edited highlights to satisfy my friend's curiosity. Molly's eyes grew wider with each revelation.

"My God, you poor thing, how absolutely awful for you."

"I'm selling up. I've got a viewing at the cottage tomorrow afternoon."

Molly's shock translated to disapproval. "Do you think it wise to sell? You're quite safe there. After all, the nutter following you has no idea about your other home, your other life."

What other life? "It's only a matter of time."

Molly slipped out a lipstick and compact from her bag. "I'll have a word with Simon."

"What about?"

"Your house sale, silly."

"I've made up my mind, Moll, and I've appointed a local estate agent."

"You can be so stubborn," Molly said, applying a generous coat of lipstick. "You should listen to good advice." She snapped the compact shut.

We paid and walked back through town together. Pausing to go our separate ways, Molly kissed me on both cheeks. "Sorry about Chris," she said. "We never really—"

"I know," I jumped in.

Molly threw an awkward smile, told me to take care, and left.

My heart flipped with surprise at finding Grant and Cunningham waiting for me back at the apartment.

"I didn't expect you to come round. A phone call would have been fine and erm … I've sorted things out."

Grant's face was set like weathered granite. "Your sorting out has resulted in a complaint."

"So you freely admit it?" Grant said, once we were inside.

"Yes." No point in denial.

"You entered his property?"

I felt only a moment's contempt for the old lady who'd grassed me up. I was in no position to take the moral high road. "I went onto his land. I was fed up, frightened, and wanted to take the law into my own hands. I was wrong. I made a mistake," I said, chastened.

Grant slowly shook his head in disbelief. "What if you'd been right? Do you realise the risk you were running?"

"I didn't think I had much to lose." I bit my lip. The moment the words left my mouth, I knew it sounded spiky and wrong.

Grant glanced at Cunningham in irritation. He obviously took my comment as a direct criticism. "Has anything else happened, Miss Slade?"

"Nothing." I could have told them about the threatening card and the bucket of rabid flesh, but it would only sound dubious in the current circumstances. They'd think I was making it up. Best to admit to what I'd done and take the rap. "What happens now? Do I receive an official caution?"

"Not this time."

"Quid pro quo," I said, referring to Grant's previous chat with Stannard.

"Consider this a reprimand," he said, unmoved. "If anything else happens, you report it to us first. You do not try to take the law into your own hands. Got it?"

I nodded obediently.

Once they'd gone, I took a shower. Standing in the kitchen later, I opened a tin of tuna and mechanically ate the contents. When the phone rang around quarter to nine, I listened, heard the click, then the recorded message followed by the sound of breathing. I went over to the window and looked at people slipping by. The phone went several times, each time the caller staying on the line for around ten seconds, no more, no message left. I was no nearer to knowing his identity.

And he didn't give a damn.

Who the hell was it?

FIFTY-NINE

I ARRIVED AT CORMORANTS Reach at midday. For an irrational moment, my heart swelled with hope as I imagined Chris standing at the entrance. But gone is gone, I reminded myself. Time to get a grip.

My feet halted almost before my body at the sight of the front door ajar. I pulled out my phone to call the police and cursed, not for the first time, the absence of a signal. Briefly looking around for something to use as a weapon, I stole back to the car. Opening the boot, I took out the jack, returned to the house, and eased the door gently open. It protested with a loud whine.

Grinding with nerves, I waited a beat then zipped across the living room floor, peered into the study, and moved soundlessly down the steps into the kitchen.

There, I saw him. He had his back to me. I swung the jack. He turned, eyes wide and white.

"Charlie," I gasped. "What the bloody hell do you think you're playing at?"

He put both palms up. "Are you going to put that thing down?"

"Not yet." I ground my jaw so hard I thought my teeth would crack.

"Simon asked me to look in."

"Simon?" This was getting more bizarre by the second.

"He said you've got someone viewing your house this afternoon. He thought it would be a good idea if a bloke was with you."

Molly must have told him. "Then why didn't you phone?"

"I didn't think it would be such a big deal. God, Kim, you don't seriously think..."

"Where's your car? Why isn't it in the drive?"

"Because," he said, his voice loud, "I came in the Land Rover and the handbrake's not that clever. It's parked down at the creek where it won't roll away."

Eyeing him, I backed off, awkwardly laying the jack down on the kitchen table. Charlie sat down hard on the nearest chair. I smelt the fresh tang of cow shit on his clothes.

"I think Simon had a point," he snapped. "You need protecting from yourself."

I glared at him. "You still haven't explained how the hell you got in." Keys, I thought, Charlie would have had ample opportunity to "borrow" mine and get a copy made. My eyes travelled to the kitchen table.

He expelled an exasperated sigh. "The door was already open."

"Impossible." Deliberately, I let my gaze rest on the jack. Charlie picked up on it and scowled.

"Are you absolutely certain you locked it when you left? You do seem to be in a fair old state," he added, his voice caustic.

"Which is why I'm very careful about my security," I flashed. He locked eyes with me, as if saying *screw you*. "There's really no reason for you to stay," I said haughtily. "The agent is accompanying the viewing."

Charlie's face expressed a variety of emotions, mainly anger. "What the devil's got into you? I'm trying to help."

"I don't need your help," I bit back. "Or anyone else's."

"If that's the way you feel about it." Ugly-faced, he clambered to his feet.

Yes, I did. I didn't trust him. I didn't trust anyone anymore. They were all too damn close.

Charlie marched past. I followed him out. He suddenly turned, his weathered face very red and close to mine. "From what Simon's told me you're sailing pretty close to the wind. It won't bring Chris back, you know. He's gone for good. And I can't say as I blame him."

The viewing was a pointless exercise. To be fair, the agent acted with suave sophistication, talking the cottage up, throwing in the odd amusing anecdote, using the right amount of carrot and stick. I guessed the viewers were a second marriage. The husband was old and dishevelled-looking in spite of the effort to dress in a trendy fashion—trousers with spanner pockets and a baseball hat; the wife was young, skittish and strident, as were their two little girls. Within minutes, the children were left to roam and wreck. While Mummy and Daddy amused themselves by comparing the small rooms with the *much larger* proportions of a property they'd seen earlier, I spent my time deterring Tamsin and Lily from throwing themselves into the creek.

"Why are you leaving such a glorious place?" the husband asked.

"Personal reasons," I answered evasively. *Personal* covered every crisis under the sun. Chris had cited the same excuse, I remembered.

"That went well," the agent said as we watched the family disappear in their powder blue Volvo.

I issued a brief, cynical smile. "They won't be back." About to return to the cottage, I heard the crunch of tyre on gravel. I looked at the agent. "Did you schedule in someone else?"

He shook his head. I watched two men step out of a BMW and ran through the stock-list of possibilities—Jehovah's witnesses, door-to-door salesmen, lost tourists—and found myself coming up empty. Something in the way they approached chimed with a grim and distant memory of police officers on a mission.

The older of the two men—a lean, wiry individual with close-cropped sandy-coloured hair—walked a couple of paces behind the other, his line of vision scoping the cottage and its surroundings with a professional eye. The younger—tall, blond, and with a heavier build—was, by contrast, entirely purposeful. His eyes locked on me with a kind of ruthless determination. He flashed a warrant card announcing he was Detective Sergeant Martin Hatchet. The older man gave a curt smile and introduced himself as Detective Inspector Malcolm Darke. Even in my surprised and tense state, I thought it odd that the man with the lower rank asked the first question.

"Are you Kim Slade?"

I nodded, a sudden sensation of dread crushing the centre of my chest. Hatchet eyeballed the estate agent.

"Is there somewhere we can talk in private?"

"I was on my way out," the agent said, his expression one of febrile curiosity. I imagined he'd have a lot to gossip about in the office on his return. "Speak to you later, Miss Slade," he threw over his shoulder with a little too much swagger.

My mind racing, I took them inside and showed them into the sitting room. I'd hoped that the business with Stannard was officially cleared up. Oh God, I thought, the Mallorys. Even so it seemed a ridiculous waste of police resources for two detectives to come all the way to Devon to charge me, or maybe these were local boys. I guessed they were going to do me for harassment. How paradoxical.

"I understand you lived with Christopher Beech," Hatchet said.

Confused, I looked from one to the other. Darke's blue eyes remained steady though I could see, by the way Hatchet leant forward, my response carried significance. "We split up."

Hatchet regarded Darke. I saw the tightening of the jaw. I could smell impending disaster. "What is this? Is he in some sort of trouble?"

"I'm afraid we have bad news for you, Miss Slade," Darke said. "Christopher Beech is dead."

SIXTY

Someone had done the equivalent of chucking me onto a roller-coaster ride and thrusting the gear in reverse. After an initial, "Oh my God, oh God," I was clean out of words. Body rigid, hands twisted, I tried to concentrate. Beads of sweat pocked my skin. My jaw ached. I felt such an immediate, plunging depth of misery.

Suddenly, blood surged in my ears. Nausea enveloped me. I pitched forward. An arm shot out as my legs buckled and gravity took its toll. Later, someone, blurred and indistinct, placed a glass of water in my hand, and a mug of sugary tea. I took an eager sip. Time coalesced. Darke was talking and talking, his words far away and obscure, as though he were speaking from an underwater cavern.

"Are you feeling better?"

How could I answer a question like that? I sat and stared but saw absolutely nothing.

"His body was found by walkers yesterday," he said gently.

"Walkers?"

"On the moor."

"Dartmoor?"

"In a remote forested area, near Sittaford Tor."

"I don't understand. What was he doing there?"

"That's what we're trying to find out."

Spun out, I said, "Some kind of accident?" I tried to strike the hopeful note from my voice. Accident was comprehensible, something else wasn't.

Darke lowered his gaze. "I'm afraid not."

I gasped. "Are you sure?"

"Yes."

Pain assailed me. Slow tears rolled down my face.

"He was found in his car. Some effort had been made to set it alight."

Involuntarily, I gagged and clasped a hand to my neck, shielding the skin. *These are old burns,* I wanted to tell them. *These are unconnected to now.*

"Probably as a means to cover the crime," Darke explained.

"Lucky not to have set the woodland ablaze," Hatchet added.

I felt as if they were both looking at my disfigurement. "How did he die?"

"Can't say," Darke said. "There will be a post-mortem and lab reports."

"And this happened yesterday?"

Hatchet and Darke exchanged glances. Darke answered, "Time of death is uncertain. There was some decomposition."

I stared incredulously. Chris was never going to return, but this ... I clutched the mug tightly with both hands. My nose streamed and the slow drum roll of tears increased. They splashed down my face. Darke handed me a tissue.

"We'll need to take a formal statement."

"I understand."

They waited as I made a not entirely successful attempt to pull myself together.

"So when did you last see him?" Hatchet asked too casually.

I frowned. So much had happened. "It's hard to say exactly. Must have been two weeks ago." Was it? I honestly couldn't remember. "Yeah, a Monday morning," I added more confidently. "I was on my way back to Cheltenham. If I look on the calendar, I can find the date."

"Later will do. What were you doing in Cheltenham?"

"I work there. I'm a clinical psychologist."

"And Christopher?" Darke interposed.

"Chris. Just Chris. Um, an English teacher."

"Where?"

I wondered why he'd asked the question. Surely they'd discovered that already. Maybe it was a method of getting me to talk, to cross-reference facts.

"At the secondary school," I said.

"How did Chris seem on that Monday?" Darke enquired.

I lowered my gaze. I didn't want to remember. Somehow I managed to force an answer. "He was pensive, thoughtful."

"In what way?"

"I don't know." Fresh tears pricked my eyes.

Hatchet made a note. It put me on edge. I wanted to slink away and dig a hole and hide in it.

"When did you speak to him last?"

"That morning before I left." I looked from Darke to Hatchet. "I phoned him as usual when I arrived in Cheltenham but he didn't answer."

Darke glanced around the room. "You phoned him here?"

"Yes, and I tried his mobile, but it was switched off. I was worried so I contacted the school and discovered he'd phoned to say he wouldn't be in."

Hatched looked up. "When did he make the call?"

"The same day I left."

"Any idea of time?"

"Before lessons, I presume."

"But he didn't tell you of his intention?"

"No."

"Was he ill?"

"Not that I knew of."

Darke nodded for me to continue.

"So I came back," I explained.

"When?"

I told him I'd come back to Devon on Tuesday.

"And that was unusual?" Hatchet's face was without expression, intimating that he was a fact-gatherer, pure and simple.

"Yes. I left several clients in the lurch."

"Go on."

"He wasn't here. He'd cleared out. He'd left me."

Darke's eyebrows drew together. "Left you?" I nodded, unable to hold my distress at bay. He looked genuinely sorry. "Do you need a break?"

I shook my head, wiped my nose with furious irritation. "I want to help. I do, but I can't believe it's happened. I can't think who would do this to him." Except, I could. Blood rushed through my head like a flash flood. Should I tell them? Would they believe me now that I'd been so utterly discredited by the police in Cheltenham?

"Take your time," Darke said. "How long have you known Chris?"

"We'd been living together for almost four years."

"What was he like?"

I looked at Hatchet, taken by surprise. I wanted to do the best by Chris, but it wasn't simple. I let out a breath, fudged the question. "He was very private. Hard-working, well-liked by colleagues." God, it sounded like a reference.

"Friends?" Darke said.

"He didn't have a huge circle. My friends were his friends." My nerves tightened. "There were people he went drinking with from school. His best mate's Andy Johnson, another teacher. Andy's known him longer than me."

"It would be helpful if you could provide us with a list of associates," Hatchet said, tapping the tip of the pen on his pad.

"Of course."

"What about family?" Darke said.

I shook my head. "He was put into care. Spent much of his early life in foster homes." My voice sounded halting, false and business-like. I didn't want to tell them about his brush with criminality, the violent temper. He'd never used it on me so why should I?

Hatchet clicked his tongue. "Not what you'd call an idyllic upbringing."

Darke threw him a reproachful look. "Did he have any enemies, Miss Slade?"

"None that I can think of." I thought of Simon and Molly, Charlie and Claire, their barely concealed dislike. "Nobody close who'd want to kill him," I stressed.

"He wasn't in debt or had any drink or drug problems?"

"No."

In the briefest of silences, I sensed that they were regrouping.

"You say Chris left you," Darke said.

"Yes."

"The split, was it completely out of the blue?" He leant forward a fraction. His eyes looked black instead of blue, the pupils enormous. "Did you see it coming?"

"No, no, I didn't." I briefly shut my eyes, braced for the inevitable.

"So you don't know why." There was an upward inflection in Darke's voice.

I gathered the remains of my pride and looked straight at him. "He left me a note. There was another woman. He …" I stopped. In their eyes, they now had a motive. The increase in tension in the room was tangible. I could taste it and it tasted bitter. Nobody said anything for a moment.

"Do you have the note?" Hatchet said.

"I threw it in the creek." To my own ears, I sounded dodgy.

"Have you got the pad it was written on?"

"It was typed on a computer. Chris had appalling handwriting," I explained.

"But he signed it?"

"Yes."

"You're sure it was his signature?"

"Yes." Unmistakable.

"Do you have a computer here?" Hatchet's expression was penetrating.

"In the study, but Chris rarely used it. He had his own laptop for work."

"Worth checking out," Hatchet said to Darke who nodded.

“We’d like to search your home,” Hatchet told me. “It’s standard procedure and entirely voluntary but if…”

“Yes.” They’d do it in any case. I rubbed the top of my arms although I wasn’t cold.

“The identity of the other woman.” Darke dropped the remark delicately into the conversation.

I made eye contact with him. “Chris didn’t say.” I wasn’t sure why I used the truth to conceal a lie.

Darke returned my gaze with a searching expression, his eyes two black orbs. “You said on the morning you last saw Chris, he was troubled.”

“I said pensive.”

“Because of his extracurricular relationship?” Hatchet said, smart with it.

“I assume so.”

“And you had no idea?”

“I already said. None.”

Hatchet scribbled some more, head down. “Any idea what time you left the house that morning?”

“I was running late. I’d overslept. I suppose it must have been around half past seven. I don’t really remember exactly.”

Scribble, scribble, scribble. “So you arrived in Cheltenham at what time?”

“Around quarter to twelve.”

Hatchet’s eyes shot up to meet mine. “Four and a half hours?”

Looking into his face, I had the horrible realisation that this was a game changer.

SIXTY-ONE

Before I could answer, Darke intervened.

"What were you driving?"

I told him. "Traffic was slow and I had a puncture," I added.

"Where?"

"Outside Loddiswell."

"What did you do?"

"Changed the tyre."

Hatchet raised his pale blond eyebrows in disbelief. "You didn't call Chris?"

"Why would I? I believed he was going to work. I'm perfectly capable of changing a wheel." I tried to laugh, but it got choked off somewhere. "I called Cathy," I said, a light pinging on in my head.

"Cathy?"

"Cathy Whitcombe at Ellerslie Lodge, where I work. I told her I was going to be late. You can check."

"How long did it take to sort the puncture?" The question sounded clipped.

"Forty-five minutes."

Hatchet's eyes fixed on mine once more. "Anyone see you?"

"I don't have a clue. I don't think so. I was concentrating on what I was doing. Look, do we have to do this now?" I said, suddenly tense with exhaustion. I understood they had a job to do. I genuinely wanted to help, but I wasn't ready for being shoved under a microscope yet. More importantly, I needed to think, to process the horrible news.

Darke was more solicitous. "Is there a friend you could call to come and stay with you?"

I immediately thought of Claire and wished I'd been more civil to Charlie. "I'll sort something out," I said, eager to be rid of them.

"We'll need you to come to the police station tomorrow to formalise things," Hatchet said, "and resume our discussion," he added pointedly.

Oh God, I thought. "What time?"

"Eleven."

"Should I have a lawyer with me?"

"You have the right to have a solicitor present. Up to you. We'll be sending a team round to search the cottage and you'll also be assigned a family liaison officer."

Someone to check up on me. I walked with them to the door. Darke paused. "I see you have the cottage on the market. How long's it been on?"

"Not long."

I didn't dare analyse the expression on his face.

I stumbled back from the closed door and slid down onto the floor. I wanted to reel the footage back, to discover that it was all a mistake, anything to deflect the desolation. Chris had betrayed me, but now that he was dead I felt bereft and stricken. I closed my swollen eyes, tears seeping out between the thickened lids, sat absolutely still, constricted.

To die like that...

The thought of him not being quite dead before the fire started tore into me. And what if he hadn't been? The grim thought made me crawl inside.

Fire. The word alone conjured up a primitive and elemental fear. I knew its strength. I understood the terror it engendered, the pain it caused, its ability to scorch and disfigure. Mystical and sexual, it symbolised both death and rebirth. For arsonists it was a turn-on, the ultimate power, and means to create impact. Whatever the reason for setting Chris's body alight, I doubted it was simply a means to cover the evidence. There was a message in the murder. For me.

And the cops were hunting Chris's killer in the wrong place.

SIXTY-TWO

ANDY LIVED IN ONE of a row of cottages in Eastern Backway in Kingsbridge. Situated in the cleft of a steep road, the little home vibrated with the permanent sound of cars slowing down and changing gear. The front aspect looked out onto a park and fire station.

The sun beat down on the yard outside his front door and welded me to the concrete.

As soon as I saw Andy, I knew he'd heard. Red-rimmed eyes accentuating his pale skin, he held his arms out to me like a child asking for a carry. We fell into each other. He gave a low groan. I'd no idea how long we stood there, propping each other up.

Eventually, we went inside. Same jumble. Same smell of Chinese takeaway. A vase of fresh flowers was the only clue that a woman had made a recent visit. I commented on them. "Jen," he explained. As if on cue, she popped her head around the door.

"Hiya, want a cuppa? That's all I've done since we heard the news. Terrible, isn't it? Everyone's talking about it. They're saying it's murder. Sugar, milk?" she said, coming up for air.

"Tea, no sugar, thanks," I said, feeling awkward. I'd wanted to speak to Andy alone, without interference. We sat down together on the one available sofa. It was covered in cat hairs.

"How did you hear?" I asked him.

"South Hams Radio. Wasn't specific at first, but it didn't take long to work it out. Half the school is in shock. He's going to be badly missed."

"Have the police seen you?"

"Not yet. It's true, then?" Andy's voice cracked.

I took his hand in mine. "I'm sorry, Andy." Without warning, a wave of tears erupted. He put his arms around me. I buried my face in his shoulder, soaking his shirt, and he stroked my hair.

"That's right, you have a good cry," Jen said, emerging from the kitchen. "That's what my mum says. No point in keeping it all in."

We pulled apart. I felt Andy bristle beside me, Jen blundering through our grief like a cheerleader at a funeral service.

"There you go. A nice cup of tea and a plate of biscuits."

"We're not hungry," Andy said, speaking for both of us.

"Got to keep you strength up at times like this," Jen said. "So what's the craic?"

"Fuck's sake, Jen," Andy burst out. "Just listen to yourself. Will you stop fucking talking—please?"

"Oh," she said, big eyes wide with hurt. "Sorry. I always talk too much, especially when it's serious. It's me. My mother's always telling me to button it. I didn't mean …"

"It's all right, Jen." I gave a tired smile, wishing I had a remote to switch her off.

"Why don't you go and get a pint of milk or something?" Andy said, casting Jen a meaningful look.

“Fine,” she said, reaching for her bag. “Anything else you want—sweets, a newspaper, magazine?”

“No,” Andy snapped. “Take as long as you need,” he added more gently.

We fell silent while the door opened and shut.

“She’s completely doing my head in,” Andy muttered in apology.

“She’s trying to be helpful, that’s all,” I said, realising that we were all overwrought. Jen couldn’t help being an emotional illiterate.

“I know,” he said, apologetic. “We were supposed to be going off in the camper van together today, but this has changed everything.” He took a drink of tea. “So what actually happened?”

“Andy, I …”

“I need to know.”

I told him.

“Christ almighty.” He put his hands to his face.

“And the police think I had something to do with it.”

He looked as if I’d handed him a gift wrapped in barbed wire.

“The police know that Chris left me for someone else.”

“What’s that got to do with anything?” he said, indignant.

“*Crime passionel*, revenge. Don’t you see, it looks like I have a motive.”

“That’s bollocks.”

“At the moment they don’t know about Carolla Dennison.”

He gave me a sharp look. “You think she was involved?”

“Definitely on a sexual level.” I failed to push the bitterness and resentment out of my voice. I knew Chris. I knew his needs.

Andy shook his head slowly. “I wouldn’t have put Carolla Dennison down as a murderer.”

Jury was out. Even if she were innocent, Carolla might provide a lead. "Is there any way I can get hold of her?"

"Is that wise?"

"I only want to talk. She might be able to help."

"How?"

"She knew Chris. She might have seen him with someone, someone who had it in for him."

"Right, I see where you're going with it."

I didn't spell it out. We both knew I was talking about my stalker. "What about the place she's living in?"

"She was renting somewhere in Thurlestone, but I'm not sure she's still there, or whether they'll give a forwarding address. Pat Emerson might be a better contact, but he's on holiday."

Of course, the Head was bound to know how to get in touch. "What about other work colleagues?"

Andy brightened. "She was quite pally with Jo Sharpe. She lives in Saffron Park."

"Number?"

"Can't remember. Wait," he said, putting a hand to his temple, "the house is called Fallowfields."

SIXTY-THREE

"Are you Jo Sharpe?"

Small with short brown hair, green eyes, and a deeply freckled face, the woman nodded and got up from the border she was weeding. Rubbing her hands against her jeans, soil trickled through her muddy fingers. I introduced myself.

"Chris Beech's girlfriend?" The green eyes gleamed in apprehension.

Not really. Not anymore. "That's me."

"Christ," Jo let out.

"Can we talk?"

Jo tilted her head, looked at the sky as if she'd thought about such a moment but never believed it would happen. "I don't know. I'd rather not get involved. I'm Carolla's friend," Jo said in response to my searing expression. "I know she behaved badly but in the end no one got hurt."

I checked a verbal response and looked in open amazement. Embarrassment flooded the other woman's freckled features.

"You don't know what's happened, do you?" I said. "You don't know about Chris."

Jo wrinkled her nose. "Know what?"

"He was found dead. The police think it was murder."

We sat in Jo's cramped kitchen. Tension either makes you talkative or clam up. Jo was a gabber.

"I don't know how much you know about Chris and Carolla. I can guess what you're thinking, but it really wasn't like that. Not far off, I know. More like having sex with all your clothes on."

"Frottage," I said. Hell, what a comfort.

Jo looked blank.

"Having sex with … oh, never mind."

Jo gave another slight mystified nod. "See, there was a group of us who'd meet up midweek for a drink after work, usually at the Hermitage. It got to be quite a regular event. We'd drink far too much and end up at the Balti House."

This was news to me. "Who exactly?"

"Carolla, me, Paul Hammond …"

"The history guy?"

"That's the one. Faye Hannaford, the new Chem teacher, Andy and his new squeeze, Jen, Chris …" I briefly tuned out. Chris the loner, Chris the friendless, Chris who liked his own company best of all. Chris, the man I barely recognised.

"They used to go to the cinema a fair bit."

"What, Chris and Carolla?"

"Yeah, she complained to me once that she didn't like his choice of films. She was more into comedy, romance, you know the thing?"

Crawling inside, I nodded. I'd thought films were *our* thing. I'd no idea he'd shared his passion with someone else.

"Anyway it was never going to happen with you on the scene. Sure, there was a deep attraction there right from the off. Any fool could see that. You'd only have to walk into a room and you could sense the sexual tension, but it came to nothing."

"How do you know?"

"He felt too guilty. You were the stronger pull, I guess. Not that Carolla told me every little detail. I mean, she wouldn't, would she? My God, I wonder if I should tell her. She'll be devastated."

She has no bloody right to be devastated, I railed inside. "You said it came to nothing."

Jo tilted her head. "Shouldn't you be at home, or something?"

"I need to know the truth."

"Why torture yourself?"

Because the alternative is too horrible to contemplate. "How much did Carolla really tell you? Did she tell you that Chris was leaving me? Did she tell you that he was going to fly with her to the States?"

Jo's denial was more a shout of alarm.

"I don't think you know your friend as well as you think," I said.

SIXTY-FOUR

I RACED BACK TO the cottage. The phone kept ringing with messages of condolence from Chris's midweek drinking pals and colleagues. I let the messaging service collect the calls, poured a glass of lemonade, and took it outside. In the early evening sun the water was the colour of copper, the air still and quiet. Not so my thoughts, which were like a couple of rampant poltergeists in my head. The truth, such a flexible commodity; it all depended on whose truth I believed. Nothing to write home about, Jo would have me think, yet even she'd been forced to admit to the existence of stolen kisses, secret meetings, simmering phone calls, sexual fucking tension. So it wasn't all a one-way street then, I'd pointed out tersely. And in the end Carolla had won, not me. The final good-bye letter proved it.

Obsessively, I wondered exactly what had gone on between them. Had he fucked Carolla like he'd fucked me? Why hadn't Carolla reported him missing if they were such an item? Even if I got to speak to my love rival, I'd only be scratching the surface, getting Carolla's nicely sanitised version of events. And it all depended on Jo getting in touch with Carolla, and Carolla contacting her, and why would she? I certainly wouldn't if I were in her shoes.

I ditched the lemonade and went to the drinks cupboard, the standard Slade response to a crisis, and found the remains of a bottle of cheap cooking brandy. Pouring a small measure, I drank it neat. Whatever I did now, I couldn't afford to make the same mistake again. This time there must be no assumptions, only facts. I had to weigh them up against cast-iron evidence, and apply Gavin Chadwick–proof rules. My stomach lurched. The police were going to interview me the next day. I could have a solicitor with me. My choice. No sweat. They hadn't said as much but I knew the bottom line. They meant business.

I poured out more brandy, took a gulp, the heat warming my insides as I tried to work out whether it would be better to have a lawyer with me, or not. Having one might be viewed as an admission of guilt. I hadn't the faintest idea who to lobby, how to go about it, criminal lawyers being outside my field of experience—a shitty dinner party with Gavin Chadwick didn't count.

I wandered through to the study and played the first of several messages. Claire's voice was strained, not like Claire at all, which, I supposed, was understandable. Grief mixed with guilt is toxic. Claire's message was an open-ended invite to stay at the farm until things *died down*.

The next message was from Detective Sergeant Fiona North, a family liaison officer. Announcing she'd already called at the cottage but not found me in, North suggested I might like to phone her; the third, from Andy, no message; the fourth, from Molly, breathy, tearful, compassionate; the fifth, from Alexa, who called to say that she'd found the lawyerly equivalent of a pit bull. The last was from my estate agent, stating the obvious: no offers but endeavouring to get more punters round. I swallowed a mouthful of lemonade.

Not now you can't, I thought. Death puts people right off.

SIXTY-FIVE

Fiona North was not what I expected. Slim, with blond hair that she wore clipped back into a low ponytail, she had baby-blue eyes and, in her casual trousers and shirt, looked about nineteen and too young to be delving into murder.

Barely eight in the morning, I scratched my head, wondering why on earth she needed to arrive so early. Maybe it was designed to catch me out. "Come in. I'm not fully functioning yet."

"Don't worry. I'll make us a pot of tea, or would you prefer coffee?"

"Well, I …"

"I'll put the kettle on while you think about it," North said, heading to the kitchen as if guided by a homing device. "How are you feeling, sleep all right?"

"No." I sat down, studied the grain of the kitchen table, and listened to the clatter of someone else taking over my life.

North rested her back against the worktop. "We could have a word with your GP. Maybe he could prescribe something to help you sleep."

I winced. I didn't like *we*. Neither did I like the fact that I felt as if I were sitting in *her* kitchen. "Thanks, but no, I'm not keen."

The baby-blue eyes didn't waver. "I'm very sorry for your loss. You're understandably upset, deeply upset, but I'm here to help. Look on me as a bridge between you and the police side of things. If there's anything you want to tell me, or anything you don't understand, or something you wish to ask, then fire away. I want you to look on me as a friend. Call me Fiona, please."

Mentally, I thought, spy. I nodded and forced a smile. "Fine."

Fiona beamed, glad, it seemed, to have got the lowdown out of the way. "Tea or coffee then?"

I settled for coffee and expected a torrent of questions, or at least to be actively pumped for information. Instead we talked about Fiona's background and growing up years spent in Solihull. It's what I would call finessing. When I found myself talking about my own family, I realised that Fiona was smarter and more experienced than she looked.

"So you've not seen your mother since?" Fiona said.

"No."

"You don't miss her?" Fiona's expression failed to conceal her fascination.

I looked at the wall. I missed the fact that I'd had nobody to shop with, to discuss clothes with, to talk to or confide in when I was growing up. Had my mother stuck around, I doubted I'd have been cast into a boarding school. I hoped that she might have defended me, stuck up for me, understood me. With her on my side, I suspected that my life would have turned out quite differently. Who knows, I might have escaped the perils of the bonfire. For me, the big heartache was that it didn't matter how many people were in the house, there was always one missing, always a grave sense of loss. I didn't say this. I gave Fiona a highly edited answer.

She listened, hand under her chin. She wasn't taking notes exactly, but I could see the information being stored behind those sweet little eyes, slotted in and measured against the evidence.

"It must have been difficult."

"Let's not overstate it."

"You must have felt lonely and rejected."

Her observation didn't come close. As soon as the words left her mouth, I could almost see a light shine on in Fiona's head. She was making the link between the earlier abandonment of my mother and then my lover. Sharpened emotions and powerful feelings equal crime of passion. Added to my gaffe with Stannard, I felt practically convicted already.

"What will happen to Chris?" I asked, trying to shift the focus.

"There'll be an inquest. His body can't be released for burial yet because of the investigation."

"Are they're still running tests?"

"There are certain procedures."

I cleared my throat. "And what are the mechanics of the police investigation, or aren't I allowed to ask?"

Fiona flicked a reassuring smile. "We need to establish timelines."

"You mean when Chris was last seen, time of death?"

Fiona nodded and took a sip of coffee. She moved gracefully, a bit like a Siamese cat.

"How do they establish that?"

"Forensics. Witness statements. House-to-house enquiries."

"There are no houses. My nearest neighbour is the other side of the creek." The fact that the vacationing population was in constant flux would hardly help.

Fiona looked at her watch. "You remember you're due at the police station at eleven?"

How could I forget? "No," I said with the ghost of smile. "I haven't forgotten."

"I could drive you there, if you like."

"Well . . . erm . . ."

"Only the forensic team want to come and check out the cottage. If we leave soon," Fiona said, pulling out a mobile phone, "they could be finished by the time we get back."

I'm being hustled, I thought. I imagined a load of men in white zipped-up suits, kitted out with gloves and special footwear, poring through and ransacking my things. "All right," I said, thinking it was better to get it over with. "Any idea where to kill a couple of hours?" *Kill.* I blushed.

Fiona gave me a *Doesn't matter* smile. "Lovely day for an amble along the beach."

"But it will be packed with people." Some I'd know, or would know me. I didn't relish the pitying looks, the tongue-tied words, and the suspicion.

"Not where we're going," she grinned, almost playful.

I had to admit I rather liked her.

SIXTY-SIX

FIONA WAS RIGHT. HIGH brambly hedges, zigzagging road, no passing places or ice-cream vans—an unlikely place for the modern tourist.

She parked the car in one of only a dozen possible places and we got out and walked. It took ten minutes to reach the raised beach at Prawle Point. There, we found a family of adders sunning themselves on rocks.

Fiona very smoothly manoeuvred the conversation round to Chris. I saw it coming, watched the moves, the seeming indirectness, and rapidly readjusted my earlier take on the baby-faced liaison officer. This was one smart individual.

In answer to her questions, I told her the truth. Why not? If Fiona were sophisticated, she'd recognise that no relationship is perfect, that there are flaws beneath even the most successful partnerships. I didn't play down Chris's moods, his ability to irritate others, his mercurial manner.

"Did he make enemies?" Fiona probed.

"No. But he didn't make friends easily either." Except was that strictly true? Jo had given a different impression. What about all those people who phoned to express their sympathy?

"Apart from Andy?"

Good memory, I thought. She'd obviously been well briefed. "Andy's outgoing, happy, brash really. I guess it's a case of alter egos."

"And there was no one from Chris's past?"

"It's possible," I said, reflective. "Before coming to Devon he'd worked in London in an inner-city school where teachers were regularly threatened by parents and pupils. I guess it might be a line of enquiry worth looking into."

"And the other woman?"

"That's also worth investigation." I attempted to suppress a strong streak of jealousy.

Shortly after half past eleven, Fiona drove me to the police station in Kingsbridge. Set back from the road, it looked neither unprepossessing nor extraordinary, simply a rural cop shop in a market town.

Darke greeted and thanked me for coming. Wearing a navy lightweight suit, pale blue shirt, and red tie, he looked more official than the day before. I wasn't sure if it flagged something up, whether I was going to be treated less as a victim more as a suspect. My scant knowledge of police interview techniques based on television dramas meant I worried that I might be in for an aggressive line of questioning. As it turned out, I had nothing to fear. Not at first.

After submitting to a voluntary DNA test by giving a simple mouth swab, I was taken into a bleak, sparse interview room with moulded plastic chairs. It reminded me of consulting rooms in poorly funded regional hospitals. Darke explained the proceedings while waiting for Hatchet to join us. I was told the identity of those present. Under caution, and the interview recorded, I was asked to run through much the same ground covered the day before. Darke smiled sympathetically. It occurred to me that he wanted to be liked and trusted, which wasn't that difficult. He gave the impression that we were working together, part of a team, although I'd stop short of suggesting that he was batting for me. I didn't feel threatened, which was why I decided to expand one of my answers. I took a deep breath. If I didn't tell them now, they'd find out later and then it would look even spookier.

"Yesterday, when you asked me about Chris's state of mind, I said that he was pensive."

Hatchet jumped in. "Because of the other woman." Darke's reproving look connected and glanced off his police colleague.

"Because I was being stalked."

Darke did his best to look matter-of-fact. His eyes gave him away. They shone.

"The police in Cheltenham know all about it," I said. "If you talk to PCs Grant and Cunningham, they can fill you in."

"This person stalking you," Darke began.

"I don't know who it is but, don't you see, the person stalking me could be Chris's murderer." I looked at both of them, waiting for them to make the link.

Hatchet exchanged a look with Darke who shrugged.

"Have you experienced problems in Devon?"

"Well, no."

"So whoever was stalking you in Cheltenham knew nothing of your life here?"

"I don't know. Assume nothing, surely?"

There was a brief silence, broken by Darke. "Thanks for being so candid."

Is that it? No more questions? No new leads? Cold assailed me in spite of the stuffiness of the room. Was it possible that I was suffering from false memory syndrome? Had I made everything up, my disordered home life with my dad and brothers included? I pressed my hands underneath my thighs, dug the nails into the soft flesh to prove to myself that I was real, that I existed.

Darke stroked his chin, casual. "Does the name Carolla Dennison mean anything to you?"

I struggled to recover and keep my gaze steady. "She's a games teacher at the school where Chris worked."

"Have you met?"

"Once, maybe twice."

"Did you suspect that she was the other woman?"

"Suspect, yes, but—"

"You didn't mention her *yesterday*," Hatchet said with heavy emphasis. His blue eyes felt as if they were boring into me, unearthing buried secrets from my mind. "You didn't tell Fiona of your suspicion," he added, his voice laced with accusation.

"It was only supposition. I didn't know for a fact." I blindly wondered whether Jo Sharpe had told the police of my visit. If she had, oh my goodness…

"Didn't you?"

"No," I lied.

"And *now* you know," Hatchet said slowly, "how do you feel?"

I looked from one to the other. I was tempted to say *murderous* to see how they'd respond. "Betrayed," I said.

"Betrayed by Chris, too," Darke said intently.

"But not enough to kill him, if that's what you're driving at."

SIXTY-SEVEN

I HAD THE MOTIVE. Because of that silly puncture, I had the opportunity. And they'd caught me in a lie. If Fiona knew what line of questioning they were taking, I thought as I staggered out of the interview room, she kept her cards close to her chest. All Fiona asked with an eager smile was whether I was ready to leave. Had the time come to get a lawyer?

"Did it go all right?" Fiona said when we were back in the car.

"Mostly." My voice was flat, drained of expression.

Fiona gave me a quick sideways glance. "What do you want to do now?"

Prove I'm innocent. Find Chris's murderer. Nail him. "Will they be finished at the cottage?"

"Probably not."

I put a hand to my face. I felt dirty. My hair needed washing. God, I was tired to my bones. "What exactly are they looking for?"

"Forensic evidence, any clues to Chris's plans, people he was going to meet, that kind of thing."

I scrunched myself up in the seat, trying to make myself as small and inconspicuous as possible. Nothing was said for the next mile. I didn't even register in which direction we were driving. Too busy dwelling on the fact that the police seemed unsurprised by my disclosure. Had they already done their homework? Had they already discounted my theory? If the police weren't going to make the connection between Chris's murderer and my stalker, I'd have to do it for them.

"You should eat," Fiona pronounced.

"I'm not hungry."

"But I am."

She pulled up outside the Church House Inn at Stokenham. The place was rammed inside and out with couples with shiny-faced toddlers, families wading through seafood platters and Ploughmans, and gaggles of teenagers larking about, stuffing down chips. I dodged a swarm of wasps attracted by shoals of sticky empty glasses. Somehow Fiona managed to commandeer a small table under an apple tree, set back from the rest of the diners.

Ten minutes later, I had a glass of white wine in my hand, Fiona a soft drink, "Since I'm driving," she explained.

And on the job, I thought, taking a tentative sip with a discerning smile. Perhaps the alcohol was a base method to loosen my tongue. I half closed my eyes, tipped my face to the sky, letting the sunshine fall on the good side. Might as well come out with it. "They think I did it." I opened my eyes and looked straight at Fiona to better gauge her reaction.

Fiona took a drink. "They have to pursue all lines of enquiry, Kim. You're only a strand."

"More like a thick piece of rope."

The blue eyes suddenly went very pale, very cool. "Did you do it?"

"No."

Fiona waited. I held her gaze. "You're bound to feel under the spotlight," she said with a level look. "Unfortunately, nearest and dearest always come in for special scrutiny. It's a sad fact that most murders are committed by people we know."

"Then why not investigate the other woman?"

Fiona shrugged. No quickening of interest.

"What about the guy stalking me?" I locked on, read the same vapid expression in her eyes, and smiled. "I get it. You don't believe my story."

"It's not about belief. It's about evidence."

I frowned. "What aren't you telling me?"

"Nothing." Fiona's face had a closed expression.

I took another cautious sip of wine. "So how did you get into all this?"

"All what?"

"The police."

"By accident." Fiona's features loosened. A smile hovered on her lips. This was easier terrain for her, her expression intimated. "After my degree I wasn't sure what I wanted to do. There were several avenues I could have taken but none of them felt quite right. On a whim, I applied for the police service. They were having a major drive on recruiting graduates at the time. It seemed like an attractive package. There were incentives."

"Fast-tracking?"

"Uh-huh."

"So what was your degree in?"

Fiona smiled sweetly. "Psychology."

SIXTY-EIGHT

On the surface the cottage looked pretty much the same. No obvious evidence of disturbance. No paw-marks from sniffer-dogs. Only when I opened drawers and cupboards did I find things put back in the wrong place, or not put back at all. The boxes carefully packed in preparation for a move were unpacked, the computer gone. I couldn't imagine Jim Copplestone's reaction to the fact that I was now at the centre of a murder inquiry.

Fiona had left earlier, stating that she would pop in some time the following day, though she didn't specify when—a ploy no doubt to keep me on my toes. I thought about driving over to Claire and Charlie's but didn't have the energy, or at least that was the line I sold myself. Instead, I phoned Andy. He sounded flat and depressed. I invited him round, but he said Jen was popping in to see him. I didn't know whether this pleased him or not.

"I'm glad you've got company."

"I feel bad for being horrible to her. She's trying her best to be supportive, but I wish she wouldn't fuss so much. I'm bloody drowning in caffeine."

"She means well."

"I know. She's a decent salt of the earth Devon girl."

"Don't knock it."

Neither of us spoke for a few seconds.

"So what's the latest?"

"I've given a statement. The police have searched the cottage."

"What for?"

"It's standard procedure," I said, skirting the nitty-gritty. "How about you, have the police called?"

"The body-snatchers arrived first thing this morning."

"What?"

"Two coppers, Darke and Hatchet."

So they'd visited before my interview. "What sort of questions did they ask?"

"They wanted to know when I'd last seen Chris. How he seemed. How we got on. How long we'd been mates. What I knew about his relationship with Carolla Dennison—precisely zilch. About you …"

I started. "About me?"

"It's all right," Andy said, a trace of humour in his voice. "I didn't tell them you were a foot fetishist, or anything."

I smiled.

"I answered stuff, really," he said, vague. "Not sure I was that much help, to be honest."

"And how are you feeling?"

Andy let out a sigh. "Dunno. Frozen, I guess. I haven't really taken it in. What about you?"

"Desolate." Yet determined, if that were possible.

There was a bit of an awkward silence. A question needled the back of my mind. "Andy, did you speak to the cops about the stalking business?"

"Yeah, I did."

Shit.

"Did I do the wrong thing?"

"It doesn't matter. They were going to find out sooner or later." But I wish it were me who told them first.

SIXTY-NINE

I CLEANED, SCRUBBED, POLISHED, and hand-washed a pile of clothes that lay in a dirty heap in the spare bedroom, the standard woman's response to emotional turmoil. I lumped together the kitchen gadgetry and boxed it all up, stacking the cardboard containers side-by-side on the work surfaces. I changed sheets, moved round furniture, and tried to watch television. A police procedural flashed onto the screen—art imitating life. I switched it off, returned Molly's call, and got caught up in a three-way conversation, Simon perched in the study, Molly in the kitchen. Once the condolences were offered, I found myself on the end of an interrogation. Yes, the cops had paid a visit, asked lots of questions, the place had been searched, and I'd given a statement.

"Do they know about the stalker?" Simon said.

"It's irrelevant to the enquiry."

"Did they say that?" I couldn't tell whether he was surprised, or something else.

"They acted it."

"You know you're a bloody fool to go after Stannard."

"Simon!" Molly burst in.

"Well, it puts her in a helluva bad light."

"*Her* is quite aware of that," I said, crestfallen.

"Sorry, Kim," Molly said. "I'll kick him for you."

It was lovely talking to Molly. I missed the familiarity, the rough and tumble.

"So do the cops have any idea who did it?" Simon asked, relentless.

"Yes, me."

"Absurd," Molly snorted. "You're having us on." There was a nervous feathery ring to her voice.

"I wish I was. I had the motive. I had the opportunity."

"But you couldn't..." Molly's voice faded.

"In theory, she could," Simon said, frank and businesslike.

"Thanks for the vote of confidence," I said with a jittery laugh.

"I'm simply stating that the police are only doing their job. They have to explore every possibility, every avenue."

"Even if they're peering down a cul-de-sac and I'm at the end of it?"

Simon didn't offer any reassurance. "Who do you think it is?"

"It could have been the woman he was having a fling with," Molly said.

I suppressed a sharp intake of breath. The thought had already crossed my mind. Could it be?

"A long shot, maybe," Molly continued. "But *cherchez le femme*, I say."

Simon didn't say anything at all.

SEVENTY

Carolla Dennison.

Was it possible?

I half slept, part of my brain tuned to the sound of a latch dropping, the sigh of door against carpet, the noise of footsteps on the creaky stair. A tawny owl had taken up residence outside across the creek, hooting a warning. Foxes screamed in rapture. At last, plunging into the sleep of the unconscious, I was disturbed by a loud rapping at the door.

I stumbled out of bed, grabbed a robe, and went downstairs. Making sure the chain was secure, I opened the door a crack. Fiona North stood on the step with a large bag of shopping in her hand.

Dispirited, I let her in. Fiona looked more corporate in a cream-coloured short-sleeved shirt and matching skirt. Her legs were shapely, smooth, and lightly tanned. The sandals looked Italian, not too high. Nice. I wondered anxiously whether the businesslike image came with a businesslike message.

"What time is it?" I asked, my words slurred with sleep.

"Time you were up."

"Has something happened?" I was alert now, cued by the edge in Fiona's voice.

"Darke wants to see you."

"Here?"

Fiona shook her head. Again, I ran through the pros and cons of having a lawyer. For a second time I ruled out the idea. In my head, appointing one made it seem as if I had something to hide, as if I were guilty.

"I'm not dressed or anything," I protested. I hated anyone seeing me without my make-up on. It made me feel exposed and vulnerable.

"It's why I brought breakfast with me," Fiona smiled, a check-mate expression on her face. She emptied the bag onto the kitchen table. Croissants, a pot of jam, butter, and a litre of fresh grapefruit juice spilled out. "You go and shower. I'll warm these up."

I took longer than I needed. Over croissants and coffee, Fiona mentioned her current boyfriend. I spotted it as a warm-up to find out about any of my previous relationships. Sure enough, the question was slipped into the conversation. Glad to be one step ahead, I gave Fiona a brief resume, mainly because any past serious liaisons were few. After a while it dawned on me where Fiona was going with it; she wanted to explore if my disfigurement was a bar to members of the opposite sex. Failing to elicit an enlightening response, Fiona came straight out with it.

"I noticed you have a scar on your neck. How did you get it?"

Not subtle enough. "A childhood accident. I'll go and give my teeth a clean." I smiled, firmly concluding the conversation.

We arrived at the police station shortly before half past ten. This time I was asked to take a seat in a lobby. Fiona said she'd be back later and disappeared. An elderly lady with a marked stoop came in to make a complaint. A middle-aged man handed in a driving licence that he'd found in a gutter.

Darke entered. He flashed a smile that looked more like a grimace. He invited me to follow him. I was shown into an incident room. This time there were more people. Hatchet was already seated. A young police officer stood by the door. I sat down and drew my chair close to the table rather than sitting isolated away from them. I wanted to create an impression of full cooperation and civic responsibility.

Darke went through his usual routine, stating those present and the time. He turned to me with a strained smile, which I found faintly worrying.

"The post-mortem report suggests that Chris suffered extensive head injuries. The damage caused by something heavy, maybe a hammer."

"God," I burst out. "So the fire was definitely a cover-up, a means to destroy evidence?"

"It would seem so. We've been trying to establish timelines. We know that friends of yours, the Lidstones, had dinner with you on the Saturday evening you were last in Devon with Chris. We're also aware that Andy Johnson popped in to see you the following Sunday morning. We know Chris made the call to school at seven fifty a.m. on Monday."

"Shortly after I left."

"Yes," Darke agreed. "After that the trail goes cold. We can only conclude that you were the last person to see him alive."

Instantly, I realised its significance. "What about Carolla Dennison, the woman he left me for?"

"He didn't, Kim." Darke's voice was marshmallow soft.

"What do you mean?" I sensed that they were holding something back.

"Carolla was already in the States."

"In America?" I said stupidly.

"Carolla Dennison boarded a flight to New York on the Saturday," Hatchet stated, loud and slow, as though I were deaf. "She travelled alone and was already in the air by the time you sat down for your main course."

So Chris never left with her, I thought incomprehensibly.

"There was no ticket registered in Chris's name either," Hatchet added.

"Then why the note?" I said in angry confusion. "Why the hell did he tell me he was leaving with her?"

"Maybe he changed his mind," Darke suggested.

"Or was using her as an excuse," Hatchet said.

"But the affair," I said.

"Depends how you define it. Carolla firmly denies they ever had a serious relationship."

"You've spoken to her?'

"We have."

"Sexual equals serious, doesn't it?"

Neither police officer responded. "Sexual tension. Her best friend said so. Everyone said so," I flared.

Darke exchanged glances with Hatchet. "Where's the evidence? People gossip. You know what the place is like."

Before I could respond, Hatchet said, "Were you jealous?"

You bet. "Maybe you should be asking her that question."

Darke frowned. "Would you like to explain?"

"Maybe Carolla was stalking me."

The lines in Darke's brow deepened. I could tell he simply didn't buy it.

Words like worms slithered inside the frontal lobes inside my brain. I'd no idea how many minutes passed, or if they were seconds. I was asked if I was prepared to continue. I agreed, although I would have preferred to request an adjournment.

Darke started speaking again. "At the moment we've got the date Chris was last seen and heard, and the date he was found dead. We need to narrow the gap. I don't know if you're aware of this but when a body is left outside in the heat, especially in the kind of temperature we've been enjoying at the moment, the rate of decomposition is difficult to gauge. To try and pin down a time of death, we brought in a specialist, an entomologist."

Insects, I registered with a shudder.

Darke kept talking, his voice strangely melodious, perfectly pitched, and a cover for the horror of what he was describing. "Scientific deduction points to the fact that Chris was killed at least a week before his body was found."

Was that it, I wondered, had they delivered their final blow or was more in the offing?

More.

Hatchet took up the story. "We've spoken to PCs Cunningham and Grant at the Gloucestershire constabulary."

Believing this to be good, I nodded.

"They say that the person stalking you was never identified."

"That's correct."

"But you had an idea who it was. Did you believe it to be Carolla Dennison?"

I shifted position. This was getting worse. I wished I'd never mentioned Carolla. "I thought it was someone else, actually. It turned out I was wrong, a dreadful mistake."

"We know that," Hatchet said briskly.

Darke thrust him a warning look and picked up the thread. "When we were downloading your computer we found the note from Chris to you."

"My computer? But Chris never used it." I looked from one stern face to the other, tumbling to exactly what they were thinking.

"We also found something else," Darke said. "You remember the anonymous letter you received after your car was taken?"

I gripped the seat, anchoring myself, as if preparing for a tornado.

"We found that on your computer too."

"But that's not possible. That would mean Chris was my stalker."

"Or you wrote the letters yourself," Hatchet said.

SEVENTY-ONE

"That's plain ridiculous!"

"Which—Chris stalking, or you writing the letters?" Darke's voice was metallic.

"Both," I said, with fury.

Hatchet pushed a sheet of paper towards me itemising the times and dates when the letters were written. I studied them, breaking into a thin smile, and pushed the sheet back.

"I can prove categorically that I was in Cheltenham. You can check with the Bayshill Clinic, check with the Lodge."

"What are your technical skills like on a computer?" Hatchet said, unstinting.

"Not good enough for what you're suggesting."

"Still doesn't rule Chris out," Hatchet said doggedly.

"Yes, it does," I insisted. I didn't know whether I felt relieved the spotlight had shifted from me, or not. "Psychologically it makes no sense."

"A high proportion of stalkers are ex-partners."

"The crucial word is *ex*. We were still together."

Hatchet shrugged as if it made no difference. Darke opened his mouth to speak.

"Wait," I said, brain electric. "The timeline."

"What about it?"

"You say Chris died at least a week before he was found."

"That's our working theory."

"Then he couldn't have delivered a bucket of crap to my flat in Cheltenham. It was left *after* I had the note from Chris. Don't you see?" My heart roared with excitement.

"A bucket of crap?" Hatchet said, his eyebrows meeting in the middle.

"Flesh and faeces."

"Flesh?" Hatchet's reaction was visceral. He paled, his disgust clear.

"Animal, not human," I said pointedly.

"When was this?" Hatchet said, rallying.

"After I discovered Chris had bailed out."

"Perhaps it was already there," Hatchet said. "Perhaps he planted it."

It was difficult not to eye him with disdain. "I think I'd have spotted it."

"Because of decomposition, we only have an estimation of time of death," Hatchet pounded back. "It's not absolutely certain."

I glared at him. Hatchet's nasty tendency to cherry-pick bits of so-called evidence to suit his argument made it virtually impossible for me to counter his accusations.

"Did you report the incident?" Darke said.

I coloured up and confessed that I'd chucked the contents down the lavatory. They both looked at each other, the unspoken exchange revealing to me that they were dismissing it as an unlikely tale. Darke took hold of the reins of the conversation once more.

"As a psychologist you must be aware of the dynamics that govern relationships?"

"We all play games to a lesser or greater degree," I said. "It doesn't necessarily mean we're dysfunctional."

"But you'd concede that some guys can be controlling and manipulative."

"So can some women." I made direct eye contact to let Darke know that I had nothing to hide.

"What kind of a relationship did you have with Chris?"

"An equal one." We both had emotional wreckage stuffed into our closets.

"Which one of you was more dominant?"

I locked eyes with his. "I've stated it was equal."

Darke glanced away for a moment. "Your career is obviously important to you."

"It is."

"But you were prepared to jeopardise it."

"No comment." What the hell had they unearthed? Had Jim told them about Kirsten?

"Was Chris jealous of your work?"

Had there been an undercurrent? "No, absolutely not."

"So he wasn't a jealous man?" Darke persevered.

"Not in the least."

"Maybe he was plain bored," Hatchet said, eyeing me with contempt.

SEVENTY-TWO

THEY LET ME GO. I'd no idea why. After the grilling, I thought they'd detain me. Perhaps it was a case of too much circumstantial evidence, not enough of the hard stuff. I said nothing on the way home and was glad when Fiona left.

By the time I got back, the post had arrived. At a glance I could tell there were a number of sympathy cards and put them to one side to be opened later.

I made strong coffee and took it into the dining area, an alcove off the kitchen separated by an ornate and battered Chinese screen. It was dark and quiet inside. The view from the single low window extended to the thick leafy smudge of trees on the opposite side of the narrow road. One of Chris's favourite places, he would often hive himself off there to mark papers.

Setting the coffee down, I went into my study, found a note pad and pen, and returned.

The police had two theories: I had fabricated the stalker story and killed Chris, or Chris was my stalker and I'd found out and killed him. Lose-lose.

If the police couldn't be precise about time of death, the bucket incident was no longer a deal-breaker. Was it possible that he'd stalked before? Surely, the police would have checked.

Our separate lifestyle gave Chris the perfect opportunity to hound me, but what about the logistics? I was sure the timing was off. Chris simply couldn't have been responsible for all those incidents, not without exhausting himself or clocking up enormous mileage on the car. With a jolt, I remembered that he'd got rid of the old one to buy the Alfa. He'd made a joke of it. Maybe it was to cover his tracks. Then again, maybe he'd used the Triumph.

Back to square one.

I tore off a sheet of paper and started another. It still didn't answer the question: who had murdered Chris? *Most murderers are people we know*. And the people Chris knew were my friends. I couldn't imagine any of them killing him. Not like that. Not by stoving his head in. Not by fire. So what about people at work? There was Andy (absurd idea), Pat Emerson (hardly), other teachers (professional jealousy, perhaps?), or what about pissed-off parents, pathological pupils? No, no, no.

The call to the school office was the last official sign of Chris alive. Some time during the next twelve hours, he was killed. But what happened in between?

I tried to put myself in his shoes. Maybe he felt conflicted, regretting his choice to stay, sad even at Carolla leaving. It would explain his constant need to check his phone for messages. So what would he do? Go for a walk, wander down to the beach, get some sea air in his lungs, feel the wind in his hair. Along the way he meets someone.

No, that wouldn't work for one very simple reason, I realised. There were literally scores of people crawling the lanes in high summer. He would have been seen and, more importantly, whoever was with him would have been seen, too.

A pain gnawed at my right eye. I got up, rolled my shoulders to break the accumulated tension in the muscles, stretched my arms above my head, and caught sight of something askew on top of the dresser. Pulling out a chair, I stood on it and reached down for a spiral-bound photograph album. A little scuffed, clearly handled by unseen hands, my name was written in capitals on the front in Chris's writing. Below, a photograph of me aged about three. I had a crooked goofy grin and a cute look on my face that proclaimed I was not camera shy. I marvelled at the perfect skin, plump and smooth, and felt an intense pang of loss.

I flipped the front cover, the page faintly creased, presumably by a crime scene officer. Then my jaw slackened, eyes widening at a photograph of myself holding hands with a young and pretty woman. I'd never seen it before, and God alone knew how Chris had got hold of it, but I recognised from the set of the eyes and mouth that the young woman was my mother.

Dropping down into the nearest chair, I ran my fingers over the print, riveted by the story unfolding in front of me. I turned the pages. Pictures of me gap-toothed with Guy and Luke scoffing, ice cream with our father on holiday in Bournemouth, school photos where I looked sullen and afraid, a birthday party in a garden at Claire's mum's, me on a pony, me proudly wearing a gown and hat, holding my degree. There was even the photograph that I made

Chris promise to destroy with a *Sorry!* scrawled next to it. On the very last page there was … nothing. I stared at the empty space for ages, my heart leaping with hope. If I'd stumbled across a scrapbook of crude and jumbled images, Darke's theory would be conclusive, but this book, this wonderful gift, was hardly the work of a man who hated and wanted to control me. This was the work of a man who had loved me, who wanted to say that he was sorry, that he'd been a fool, that in the end, even after temptation and struggle, he'd chosen me.

I was glad.

I went back to the beginning of the album and journeyed through my life story for a second time. As I came to the final, empty page, I realised what was missing: the day on the beach when I'd stretched out on the rocks and felt radiantly happy. Chris never had the opportunity to process the print because his life was taken. Its absence held a clue.

Without considering the time, I called my big brother. I should have called him and told him absolutely everything before.

SEVENTY-THREE

I DROVE UP THE motorway half expecting a police car to scream up behind, siren wailing. Nerves shredded, I'd had the mental equivalent of a smack round the head.

According to Luke, Chris had phoned two months previously and told him about his novel idea for my birthday.

"I'd clean forgotten about it when you called," Luke said. "I guess I was too shocked. I thought the break-up was a blip and that he'd come back."

If only. "So when did you send him the photographs?"

"Must have been a week after that. He phoned to thank me. He was really made up by them."

The same time he was supposed to be stalking me.

I switched into the faster-moving outer lane and arrived back at the flat in Cheltenham around half past five. Up the stairs, boldly unlocking the door, I scoured the carpeted floor for a note or an envelope, ears straining for the beep of the answering service. Nothing.

Into the sitting room, I expected to find something amiss. I sniffed the air. No foul smell. No unusual fragrance. No graffiti or writing on the wall. The kitchen told the same story. I peered inside the fridge, opened the cupboards and, finally, retrieved the notebook I'd kept on Simon's orders. Flicking through the entries revealed nothing I didn't already know.

I checked the bedroom and bathroom. Only when I was really, really certain did I slump into the nearest chair.

Whoever was stalking had stopped. I'd waited and waited for such a moment, longed for it, but now that it had, I felt a stab of cruel disappointment. If I went to the police with my latest finding, I knew what they would say: that the album was an elaborate subterfuge, that Chris was my stalker after all. With his death, his stalking activities were finally over.

Lids heavy, I closed my eyes. Drifting, it was like looking into polluted seawater. The oil-stained surface ripples. You think you see something. Extinct marine life, maybe. Something floats to the surface and then, whatever it is, dead fish or gull, it falls away, lost in the murky depths.

Robert Fallon had talked of a critical period when the ante was upped. Chris's murder fitted the pattern. It marked the beginning of the endgame.

My eyes opened and fell on the painting. There are three: stalker, love object, rival. Two men. One woman. Both want her. So one destroys the other. Then what? Game over. Winner takes all. Except, he doesn't. He can't, I realised with shock. That's not what he wants. His goal is annihilation. Hers. He wants to crush her. He wants to reduce her to a nothing. So he leaves her out in the cold. He *frames* her. He lets her take the rap for a crime he committed. Destruction complete.

I waited, hoping the phone would ring, but it didn't. Five minutes later, I switched off the light and fled.

SEVENTY-FOUR

"Look, it's not really a good time," Claire said. "I'm taking the kids out for the day, picnics to pack, you know how it is."

Oh yes, I was rude to your husband and now I'm a murder suspect. I know exactly how it is. I know precisely how I came across: mouthy, manic, neurotic, and uptight. How long would it take for the local gossip machine to swing into action, I wondered?

"It won't take long." I smiled, praying the warmth of my voice would transmit down the line. "Could you give me Gavin Chadwick's number?"

"God, are you sure that's a good idea?"

"I haven't had a better one," I answered truthfully. If his lawyerly expertise was as robust as his debating skills, he no longer seemed like a rubbish bloke to have onside. His warning of the perils of lack of representation, so far, had rung true.

"Are you all right, Kim?" The tone was exploratory, reminding me of the many times Claire had asked the same question after one of my frequent and distressing trips to hospital, prior to my return to boarding school, or when another of my father's women breezed in and took over.

"Yes." The answer had been my default position for as far back as I could remember. "I'm fine."

"Sounds as though you're in a rather a mess," Gavin said, in answer to my request. "I was going to dig up the garden—not that I've a clue what I'm doing. Lottie's the one with the green fingers. I'm the hired hand. Better come over right away."

I drove to Harbertonford, a village near Totnes prone to flooding in winter. Following Gavin's precise instructions, I turned left towards Fine Pine and followed the road back round for a quarter of a mile through leafy countryside, eventually turning off down a lane no wider than a dirt track.

Badgers Leap was the kind of place you only stumbled across. A long, low traditional Devon longhouse, it sprawled out in the countryside like a lion in high grass.

I turned into the driveway and got out, my entrance marked by an inquisitive look from a boy of about fourteen years of age. He was tall and thin and wore spectacles.

His skin had an adolescent crop of spots. He looked deeply serious.

"You must be Milton."

"My friends call me Milt," he said, scrutinising me.

"Is your dad about?"

Milton nodded, the serious look remaining. "Pa's in the study. Do you want coffee or anything? Mum's out but my sister's pretty good in the kitchen."

I laughed. "It's a bit sexist, isn't it?"

"S'pose," he agreed without humour. "If you follow me, I'll show you the way."

We passed through a long maze of rooms interconnected by narrow corridors. It was dark, cool and warrenlike. Although the sun was up and shining brightly, it only seemed to penetrate so far. With its wood-burning stoves and small rooms, Badgers Leap was more of a winter retreat.

The study was an impressively sized room with a large, leather-topped desk, ladder-backed chairs, and floor-to-ceiling bookcases containing thick, intimidating-looking tomes. On a side table rested a decanter and several glasses. Silver-framed photographs of Lottie and the children adorned one wall.

Gavin Chadwick greeted me in full European style. In his open-necked striped shirt and chocolate-brown trousers, he looked less lawyer and more landowner.

He invited me to take a seat. "I'm terribly sorry to hear the news about Chris. We both are. Must have been a tremendous shock." He sat down behind the desk and rested his hands on the leather.

I could take a verbal detour. I could tell him my story from beginning to end. I could hope that he would see the terrible predicament I was in by osmosis. Why mess about?

"The police are looking for a motive for Chris's death. I fit the bill."

Chadwick picked up a gold-plated fountain pen, unscrewed the top, and leant forward. "You'd better tell me everything." A hint of a smile played on his lips at the prospect of a shared joke. "Communication is the key, isn't that right, Kim?"

Chadwick's smile had long disappeared. "A pity you didn't think to bring me in sooner."

"I thought it would look like an admission of guilt."

He shook his head in disbelief and made another note. "Have the police had the results back from the search?"

"If they have, they haven't informed me. Does it make a difference?"

"It depends whether Chris was killed at the cottage, or not."

My blood froze. "He was killed in his car."

"Did the police state that?"

"Well, no. It's what I assumed." Chadwick's expression remained grave. "If he was," I said, "it looks bad for me, doesn't it?"

"Not necessarily," Chadwick said, a bit too airily, I thought. "Forensics may shine a new light on an enquiry, but it has to be a part of the process."

"But my DNA will be all over the place."

"True, but they're looking for solid evidence, causal links. If they find blood in the cottage, they'll have to first establish whether it belongs to Chris. If that's the case, the cottage will become a crime scene and . . ."

"I'll be in the police station and interviewed as their prime suspect."

Chadwick held my gaze, unflinching. "Yes."

"Meanwhile the murderer goes free."

He didn't say anything, gave me a searching look. "Tell me about the stalker again."

I ran through the lot, blow-by-blow, including my own shabby part in following Kyle Stannard.

He frowned. "Not very smart."

I agreed.

"And the police are convinced Chris was your stalker?" he said.

"Or I fabricated the whole thing."

"And the letters on your computer?"

"I can prove that I was in Cheltenham when they were written."

"That's a start," Chadwick said crisply. "And you're not being stalked anymore?"

Embarrassed, I dropped my gaze to my hands. "I know how it looks."

Chadwick tapped the side of his nose with the pen. "Setting aside the identity of the stalker, what do *you* think happened to Chris?"

"I genuinely don't have a clue about the chain of events, but I'm sure my stalker and his murderer are one and the same."

He nodded silently. For the first time I felt as if someone was actively considering my theory. It felt good.

"The police appear to believe that Chris was killed on the same day you returned to Cheltenham, right?"

"Yes," I said.

"Reason?"

"Blowflies and maggots—forensics."

"Which can be open to interpretation in cases of decomposition." He nodded for me to continue.

"Someone stoved his head in with a heavy instrument, a hammer odds-on favourite."

Chadwick's eyes fastened on me. "Did they tell you that?"

"I think so. Yes, I'm sure they did."

"Which part of the head?"

"I don't know. Does it matter?"

"Rather. Was he sneaked up from behind or was it a full-frontal assault?"

He meant was it male or female, I thought. If it were full on, Chris would have defence injuries, and bits of the murderer's DNA would be underneath his fingernails. I felt a rush of euphoria as if, after struggling for days, I'd found a piece of jigsaw that fitted into one of the numerous pieces of sky. "If full on, it couldn't possibly be me."

"But if the reverse were true ..." He floated the question. It hung in the air like a kite on the breeze. Was this the point, I thought, where a lawyer entertains ideas about his client's guilt in spite of knowing that he has to defend him? My newfound confidence evaporated.

"Then a woman could have carried it out," I admitted.

Chadwick got up, walked over to a window obscured from light. "You say you had a puncture that morning. Did anyone see you pulled over?"

"I was so busy struggling with the wheel-nuts I didn't notice."

"Pity." He drew breath in through his nose and let out a long sigh. "As I see things," he said, at last, "the evidence so far is circumstantial. There is no smoking gun. One of the easiest traps detectives can fall into is developing a theory about what happened and forcing the facts to fit. A lot depends on what, or if, they find conclusive evidence at the cottage. As far as the police are concerned, you had the motivation. Hell hath no fury, et cetera."

"So even if Chris wasn't the stalker, I'm still in the frame?"

He turned sharply towards me. "You're still convinced of Chris's innocence?"

I bent down, pulled the photo album from my bag, and handed it to him. "Does that look like a man hell-bent on destroying me?"

SEVENTY-FIVE

I DROVE BACK IN the direction of Kingsbridge. It came down to behavioural psychology versus forensics. That's what I was up against.

It didn't matter that the stalking had stopped, and it didn't count that the stalking arena appeared to be in Cheltenham. That was only the playground in which the guy chose to amuse himself. Devon was the place he played hardball. He'd come. It was simply a question of when.

I parked the car in the bottom car park near Creeks End, a bar and café at the head of the estuary, and headed up Fore Street.

I should have felt at home, should have felt safe. This was my old stamping ground yet I was a stranger. Among the faces of tourists, of people I didn't know, many I did. Only a few came near. In the fruit and vegetable shop, close to the entrance to the Baptist Church, I was given a warm reception as always. Others outside crossed roads with paralysed expressions. Some watched. Some whispered. A few walked away. This wasn't paranoia; the air was thick with rumour. And I, not Chris, was at the centre of it.

Visibly irritated, her normally soft, flattering contours sharpened into lines, Fiona North was waiting by my car on my return.

"Where have you been? You can't take off without telling me. I've been trying to get hold of you."

"Sorry, meeting with my brief," I said, falling irresistibly into cop-drama jargon.

"You'd better give him another call," Fiona said, grim. "Darke wants to see you. Now."

I had visions of Chadwick stepping in every five minutes with either a cauterising remark or the immortal line, "My client is under no obligation to answer that question." It didn't work like that.

There was no sign of Hatchet. Instead, they'd drafted in a bottle-blond female in a sharp suit and heels. "I'm Detective Superintendent Hayley Niven," she said, shaking my hand. You didn't have to be a shrink to work out that the inquiry had stepped up a gear. I was glad I'd got Chadwick batting for me.

Niven ran through a rough summary of events as described by me on the morning I last saw Chris. I nodded my way through so comprehensively that I almost missed the trick question.

"So you didn't return for anything?" Niven said.

"No."

Niven gave an easygoing smile. She had a large number of teeth crammed into a small mouth, an orthodontist's nightmare. "How did you feel about Chris breaking off the relationship?"

"As one would expect," I replied evenly, "upset."

“It must have been especially difficult believing that there was a third party involved.”

Here we go, I thought, a show of female solidarity to suss out whether my tears were for Chris or for myself. Aware of Darke and Niven looking at me, and the need to say something, I muttered in agreement.

“It would be natural for you to feel angry,” Niven said with false sympathy.

“I wasn’t—not with Chris, at any rate.”

“But you *were* angry?” Niven leant forward a little. Her eyes were cold-rolled steel. I met her gaze, knowing that I was being given a get-out clause. I could write the script. *Perfectly normal to feel anger and betrayal in the circumstances. Quite understand how you lost your temper and lashed out.* Except, I didn’t.

“I was deeply upset. There’s a difference,” I said as evenly as I could.

Niven gave me an acid stare. “I see your cottage is on the market. Is that a recent decision?”

It would be easy enough to check with the estate agents. “As I already told DI Darke, yes.”

“Rather sudden, isn’t it?”

“It’s not unusual to make a hasty decision after a traumatic event.”

Niven raised an eyebrow. “Traumatic?”

“Divorce, bereavement, losing one’s job can all be classed as life-changing events, as can the break up of a major relationship, with or without marriage.”

Niven smiled agreement, glanced down at her notes. “You’ve been married before, I see.”

"Yes."

"What happened?"

"It didn't work out."

"And did you wish to marry Chris?" Niven inclined her head in a grotesquely coquettish fashion.

"It was never discussed."

"But was marriage something you ..."

"I fail to see where this is leading," Chadwick intervened, his voice piercing the air like an arrow in flight. "I would remind you that my client has already covered similar ground in an earlier interview."

Niven fixed him with a cold-blooded look. "I'm merely suggesting—"

"That I was distraught enough to kill him," I said with horrible calm.

"And were you?" Niven locked eyes with mine.

"I was not."

Darke shuffled. Niven waited. Chadwick tapped a finger on the table. First round over.

"For the last couple of months"—Niven smiled, adopting a more solicitous tone—"you were under a great deal of pressure."

I didn't say yes or no.

"Could you tell us about the period of time during which you allege you were stalked?"

"I've already given a detailed account to the police in Cheltenham."

"We'd like to hear it again from you."

I gave as full a picture as possible.

"When was the last time you were harassed?"

I appealed to Chadwick. "I've already been through this."

"It will help clarify things for me," Niven said with a cool smile, as if she was asking me to do her a favour. Chadwick conceded with a small wave of his hand.

"When someone left a bucket of crap in my flat."

Niven remained unfazed, stone-faced. "Yet you failed to mention this particularly abhorrent incident to the police in Gloucestershire." She looked down at her clipboard. "It says here that you received a number of silent phone calls, a pornographic image was sent to a computer at work, and that your car was moved."

"Yes."

"Why no mention of the bucket? Seems a very odd thing to forget," Niven said, looking up.

"I didn't forget. I wasn't sure of the response, that's all."

Niven locked eyes again. I felt myself automatically colour up. "We have reason to believe that Chris was killed in another location, his body dumped later the same day at Sittaford Tor. Forensics suggest Chris was killed by several blows to the head," she continued effortlessly. "He sustained no defence wounds and, from the trajectory of the injuries, the blows were delivered from behind."

I felt Chadwick bristle beside me. I maintained eye contact with Niven. "By someone taller than me."

"How do you know?"

I addressed Darke. "How tall are you?"

"Er ... six-two?"

"Stand up."

Darke looked at Niven, seeking permission. She let out a weary sigh and motioned for him to stand. I stood up behind him. Niven described the action for the benefit of the tape. I made a fist and reached up. "Even with a hammer in my hand, my blows would have fallen on top of your shoulders, or neck. To hit Chris, I'd have had to be standing on a box." I sat back down.

Niven issued a smug smile. "Unless he was sitting or bending."

"No doubt your lab team will be able to confirm," Chadwick said. I did my best not to appear rattled.

"They already have," Niven said. "He was bending over."

Chadwick asked for a break. Stunned, I nodded, then, as if I'd snapped out of a hypnotist's trance, demanded, "Where?"

Niven flashed confusion.

"Where was he bending over?" I persisted.

"We thought you could answer that."

"I'm afraid I can't."

"Can't or won't?"

Anger balled in my stomach. I swallowed, did my utmost to control my voice and stop it from shaking. "You've done a search of the cottage. What did *you* find?" I looked from Niven to Darke, seconds grinding. The air crackled. I could hear Chadwick breathing fast in anticipation beside me.

Niven forced a thin smile. "We found nothing, Miss Slade. Nothing at all."

SEVENTY-SIX

Fiona offered to take me back. I declined

Afterwards I stood with Chadwick. He looked pleased with himself, sly even, though I couldn't think why. As the hunted, it was me who'd made the running.

"Forensics is playing in your favour," he said, with a self-congratulatory smile. "They've got nothing on you, Kim. No bloodstains at the cottage. No DNA under the victim's fingernails."

The victim? It's Chris, I wanted to cry. "They'll keep on trying," I said with heavy resignation. "Like the argument on WMDs, it may prove impossible to obtain the evidence but, as far as they're concerned, it doesn't mean it's not there." I wondered how long it would be before they commandeered my car. I asked Gavin.

"Does it worry you?" His look was penetrating.

"Of course not."

He visibly relaxed. "To be honest, they can afford to take their time. Bloodstains are not easy to remove. Obviously, if you make any attempt to clean the inside of your car, or sell it, the police are going to pay you very serious attention."

"Thanks for the advice," I said, sober.

He inclined towards me in a confidential tone. "I gather there are other lines of enquiry." Did he really know or was he making a presumption? "They certainly don't have anything near enough to charge you with," he assured me.

I drove back to Cormorants Reach. It was hard to describe my feelings of relief. I couldn't bear the place I'd known as home to be a violent scene of death. It would have been a gross violation.

I ran back to the point in the conversation when Niven talked of third parties, meaning the other woman. In the drab light of the interview room, it seemed like a possible lead. Was there an outside chance that Chris played both Carolla Dennison and me for fools? Had there been *another* woman? An obscure thought flittered into my mind and flittered back out again. Deep down, I felt I was within reach of something, yet I couldn't quite catch hold of it.

The house phone was already ringing as I crossed the drive. Immediately on alert, I charged for the door, thrust the key in the lock, threw it open, and listened hard to the recorded message. On hearing Jim's voice, I snatched up the receiver. He ran through a standard *How are you bearing up and everyone sends their best* routine. Once that was over, he told me about the visit he'd received from the police.

"They're checking you out."

I wondered what Jim had told them. "That's what they're supposed to do," I said mildly.

"It would seem they have an agenda."

"In their eyes, I had the motive and opportunity."

I hoped he'd protest strongly. He didn't. He asked if they'd found the murder weapon.

"Not that I know of."

"Let's hope they do," he said. "It might put you in the clear."

Might? "Only if it has a big label attached to it saying this was not handled by Kim Slade." Pathetically, I tried to sound funny. He gave a snort of mirth, which he quickly stifled.

"Jim, what's the news on Kirsten?"

"She's gone home. No lasting physical damage." He lowered his voice. "You have enough to worry about without piling on any more. About coming back to work," he said briskly.

"Yes?"

"Unfortunately, the press have got hold of the story and that's not good for the clients."

"I'm sorry. I should have anticipated..."

"We, therefore, think it appropriate to suspend you."

My world turned several shades darker. "For how long?"

"Can't say."

I went for a walk to clear my head. Following the road to Mill Bay beach, I crossed the car park and meandered up a narrow, secluded track flanked by fields and woodland. The air smelt earthy, a hint of autumn in the summer sun. I tried very hard to be lost in the moment and enjoy my surroundings. I didn't want to speculate, to guess what Jim was really thinking, to fog my already overloaded brain with thoughts of hammers and motives and people.

From nowhere, I heard the definitive sound of a branch cracking behind me. I stopped walking and turned round, expecting to see a man with a dog, a couple hand in hand, a family returning, hot and sweaty and bad-tempered, from a day on the beach; but no one was there. I peered through the trees. "Who's there?" No reply.

I turned back and hurried on.

Had he come?

Was he here?

In Devon?

No longer a beautiful piece of scenery, the leafy track joined a farm trail. By the time I reached it, my muscles screamed, nerve endings on fire. Rather than cross and rejoin the woods, I took the wider and longer route out onto the road and passed through Rickham. That way, there were houses and more chance of being seen by a random driver or farmer ploughing a field.

Back inside the cottage, I searched the downstairs and upstairs rooms, took a shower, dressed, and poured a cold drink. It took mental strength to resist paranoia. Trees *did* make a noise, breeze or no breeze. Twigs snapped. Could have been a stoat or a fox. He would come all right, but not yet. The timing was off.

Cooler at the front of the house when the sun moved around, I opened the door and sat on the step, legs stretched out. When the phone rang, it didn't freak me. I refused to let it. I got up slowly and with determination and walked into the study.

"Hi, is that Kim Slade?" The voice was breathy, female, Trans-Atlantic.

"It is."

"This is Carolla Dennison."

I reached for a chair and sat down with a thump. "I appreciate the call."

"I shouldn't really be talking to you. It's not allowed," Carolla rushed on. "But I wanted you to know how sorry I am."

I prickled. For what exactly?

"When Jo told me I felt so bad."

Did she realise that every time she opened her mouth, something rotten slid out?

"I, or rather we ... oh dear, I don't know how to describe what happened."

"What exactly are you trying to say?" I said, contained.

"Chris and me, it wasn't what you think."

That's what Jo said, I recalled. Seemed like the pals were reading from the same script. "Look, Carolla, I don't know why you phoned." *Spare me the bleeding heart routine* was what I really wanted to say. "I don't need protecting. I don't want my sensibilities respected. I simply want to know whether you're aware of anyone approaching Chris, anyone odd, anyone you noticed hanging around and he didn't."

"No," Carolla said. "Can't say I did."

"Are you absolutely certain? Did he mention anything that was strange, an incident, something not quite right?"

She seemed to think about it. "No," she said, finally. "He never mentioned anything like that."

"Right," I said, in a way guaranteed to finish the call.

"I thought you'd want to know the truth," Carolla said.

"What truth?"

"About us, about our fling."

I felt as if someone had shot me. I'll be all right, I told myself. A fling was nothing, sex without love, that's all. Happened all the time.

"We only slept with each other half a dozen times."

Only? "Why are you telling me this? What the fuck do you want—absolution?"

"I don't blame you for being angry. I'm ashamed to admit it, but I was ruthless in trying to take him off you. I bombarded him with texts and messages, pretty much *stalked* the poor guy, even after he'd finished it." Had I not been sitting down, my legs would have buckled. "And, yeah, he got tempted to run away, but in the end Chris broke it off."

"And that's supposed to make me feel better?" I was rabid with rage and pain. "He broke off with me too, and it was your fault."

"But he said he couldn't give you up," Carolla said in astonishment.

My brain felt full of porridge. Nothing made sense. "Did he ever tell you that he was leaving me?"

"No way."

"He never said he wanted to go away with you and start a new life?"

She hesitated. My heart creased with pain. "In the first flush of lust, sure he did," she said. "Later, no."

"And you told the police this?"

"Yes."

"Did he ever talk about another woman?"

"Are you crazy? He adored you. And do you have any idea the kind of hours the guy worked?"

"So there was no room for anyone else in his life other than you and me?" I had to be absolutely certain.

"Only you."

SEVENTY-SEVEN

I MADE ANOTHER CALL. It rang for an age. At last he answered. His voice sounded sleepy.

"Yeah?"

"Andy, it's me."

A noise, like twanging bedsprings, echoed down the line. I mused on what I'd interrupted. "Sorry, is Jen with you?"

"Not anymore."

I could almost hear him surface from postcoital unconsciousness. "I'll call back."

"No, you're all right. What was it?"

"Carolla Dennison called me. Look, could we meet for a drink later?"

"We could, but I'm supposed to be seeing Jen."

"Oh," I said foolishly. "Never mind."

"She can tag along. With the amount of time she spends in the Ladies, we could have the whole case wrapped up."

"No, it's fine."

"It's not fine. I'll put her off."

"Don't do that."

Andy was having none of it. "Shall I pick you up?"

"Probably better if I come under my own steam. Are you sure she won't mind?"

"'Course not."

"Let's meet somewhere out of town," I said.

"Suits me."

"How about the Sloop—nine o' clock?"

"Great. See you then."

I put down the receiver, went to get up, and stopped. I'd left the front door open to the large porch. I swore a shadow moved across the entrance. Fool, I cursed under my breath. After my walk I'd failed to take the most basic of precautions and now someone was inside the cottage. Someone uninvited. If it were a friend, they'd surely call out, but there was no sound other than someone moving about. I raced into the sitting room and grabbed the poker. The shadow moved.

Flattened against the wall, banking on the element of surprise, I listened and heard whoever it was quite clearly now. Footsteps and small shallow gasps punctuated the air. Mine. This was the someone who'd followed me, the someone who…

The door flew open. I lunged. Thrown face down upon the carpet, skidding across the pile, my cheeks burnt with friction, the poker tumbled from my grasp. Gripped by one wrist, I let out a terrific scream and lashed out. A hand released me almost immediately and I struck out hard with a fist.

"It's me. It's me, Simon," he said, grabbing both my hands, pinning me down.

"Let go," I struggled. "Get off me, you fucker."

His arms fell to his sides. He shot back on his haunches and scrabbled to his feet. "I didn't mean to startle you."

"Are you crazy?" I rolled onto my knees and, one hand flat on the floor, pushed upright. "What are you doing here?" I tried to blot out the intense pain in my arm, my stinging face. I didn't want to put a foot wrong. It seemed that this bloke, my friend, an ex-soldier, could quite easily kill me.

"I came to make sure you're all right."

I gawped, bewildered. Like you instructed Charlie, I thought.

Simon suddenly paled. "Jesus, you think I came to hurt you."

"You gave a damn fine impression."

He spread his hands, brow furrowed, a hurt expression in his eyes. "Kim, surely you can't think that of me?"

Yep, I could. Whether or not I was right was another matter. Lately, anything was on the cards. "Like a drink?" Nice and easy.

"Good thinking." He scoped the room in a professional manner.

I made a play of going through the motions, finding the bottle, locating the corkscrew, popping the cork at the same time as pinpointing my mobile phone. I also slipped out one of the new knives from the kitchen block, and slid it under a magazine, in case. Sly.

I handed Simon a glass and watched his eyes. This is an old friend, I reminded myself, taking a long swallow. *Someone close.*

"So you're all right then?" He eyed me over the rim of his glass. I didn't care for it.

"Yes."

"You haven't been harassed?"

"Do the police count?" I said, making a weak attempt at humour.

"That bad?"

"I've got nothing to measure it by. At least I've found a decent lawyer."

"Sounds like a contradiction."

I smiled clumsily and snatched at my drink. "Simon," I said, treading with caution, "you did rather overreact."

His eyes connected with mine. "Instinct. It's what I'm trained to do. I see someone coming at me with a knife ..."

"A poker," I corrected him.

He flashed a brilliant smile. "And off I go. Is your arm okay?"

"Badly bruised. It isn't broken, or anything." I tried to reciprocate his smile. It probably came out as a grimace.

"Sorry." He tugged at his drink.

"Is something wrong?"

Another smile. "Astute as always."

Something fragile ripped inside me. I inched closer to the magazine.

"Things aren't working out, Kim." His expression was straight and direct.

"No?" I measured the distance between me and my means of self-defence.

"Since leaving the regiment, my life seems to have lost all meaning. I know this sounds awful but your bit of bother, well, it's about the first time for a while I've actually felt alive."

"And how does murder score on the excitement scale?"

He visibly cowered and hung his head in shame. "I'm really sorry, Kim, crass of me."

Hot air escaped through my nostrils. My life has been turned upside-down. He finds it a turn-on. Terrific. I did my best to haul the conversation back on track.

"I thought you were doing fine. You seemed happy enough last time we spoke. Job going well…"

"Do I *look* like an estate agent?"

"No, no, not really," I said, surprised by the sudden burst of aggression.

"Sorry." He ran a hand over his stubbly chin. "Shouldn't have spoken to you like that. I didn't mean to be short, not with you of all people, not after everything you've been through."

Is this him? Is this the real Simon or the one I don't know?

"Truth is I feel like a fish out of water. Doesn't matter what kind of a job I do in Civvy Street, it doesn't give me the same buzz."

"It's bound to take time."

He looked lost. "I don't think I'll ever get used to it. Not really."

"Couldn't you get a job in security or protection, or something? There must be openings for someone with your expertise. Why don't you join the Territorials?"

"I'd love to, but it's not what Molly wants."

"Have you discussed it with her?"

"There's nothing to discuss. Molly wants me in a safe job where my life's not on the line. She's never been more pleased than the day I came home for good. She'd feel so disappointed if she thought I was unhappy. The trouble is I'm addicted to chasing danger."

First he attacks me, then he apologises. Now he seems suspicious as hell. "Does Molly know you're here?" I tried to make it sound casual, as if it were no big deal, either way.

"Sure."

"Shouldn't we give her a call?"

"Go ahead."

I crossed the floor and picked up the kitchen phone. If Simon had another agenda, he wouldn't be keen on me contacting his wife. Molly answered after two rings. "Is my lovely husband with you yet?"

"He is." I kept my eyes firmly on Simon.

"Are you all right, Kim?"

I am now. "I guess so."

"We're worried about you, honey. Simon thought you were such a freaking nutcase going after Stannard. He's concerned he might come looking for you—you obviously bring out my hubbie's protective instinct," Molly said, clearly finding it endearing.

"Sweet," I said with a fixed grin.

"You know Simon," Molly said proudly, "he can't resist the lure of danger. I sometimes think he misses the old days. Shall I have a quick word with the lord and master?"

I gratefully passed the phone over.

"Hello, sweetie," Simon said.

I retrieved my mobile, pretended to check a call, and punched the emergency number into contacts as a standby. Simon continued to chat with his wife and I watched and listened and, minutes later, ached inside. I didn't enjoy suspecting my closest friends.

After a couple of minutes Simon put down the phone and broke into a cheeky grin. "She says I mustn't lecture you."

"Good for Molly. Have you eaten?"

"No, and I'm starving."

While I cooked, Simon offered to check the security. "It's actually rather good," he pronounced. "Water one side, good solid door on the other, and the locks are quite sturdy. The only problem you've got is that you're quite cut off should he manage to get in."

We ate omelettes filled with bacon, mushrooms, and cheese, and a side salad of freshly picked sorrel and tomatoes. We talked about the old days, Simon's chequered career path, and his hopes for the future. One hour lapsed into another. I began to relax.

"Don't you have any sort of counselling or advice before you come out of the forces?" I said.

He gave a dull laugh. "The nearest you get to psychology is eight pints of lager followed by whisky chasers. Supper was lovely, by the way," he said appreciatively. He stretched in a way that was faintly reminiscent of Chris.

"Coffee?"

"Please. Then I ought to be heading back. Is that your motor outside?"

"The Celica?"

"Nice heap of metal."

"Yes …" I stopped, mind scrabbling for a mental foothold. I'd heard the phrase before. No, not heard, *seen*. "What did you say?"

"Your car. It's nice. We only ever see you on foot in Cheltenham."

"That's not what you said."

"Didn't I?"

"You called it a nice heap of metal."

"I'm a petrol-head, remember?" Then he broke into a sudden, intoxicating smile. He put his hand on my bare arm. The palm felt warm, moist and greasy at the same time. I prickled with alarm. "You look like someone's walked over your grave."

"I …"

"It's okay, Kim, you don't have to explain. Not to me."

He left forty minutes later. "Don't waste energy worrying about me, will you?" he called, craning his head out of the car window as I hovered on the porch. “I’ll figure it out. Maybe I’ll take up flying, or extreme sports, or something.”

I double-locked the door, the smell of burning rubber all that was left of his Audi TT as it vanished from sight. Double shit—I’d forgotten all about Andy and it was now after midnight.

SEVENTY-EIGHT

I couldn't sleep, and it wasn't the compressed heat, creaking doors, or the hooting owl. I got up, made tea, and took it upstairs. Creeping back into bed, I closed my eyes and lay ramrod still. My mind refused to shut up: Simon, heap of metal, stalker.

At some stage, I fell asleep.

The next morning I phoned Andy first thing but there was no reply. Feeling bad, I decided to brave the gossips and go into town. On my way out, the phone rang. The messaging service kicked in. It was Fiona North. I kept on walking.

Parking in the lower car park, I walked across the pedestrian crossing and past the newsagents and bumped straight into a now definitely pregnant-looking Claire. For once, she had no children with her.

"Hiya," I said, grotesquely upbeat.

Claire smiled an awkward greeting. Her eyes glanced away as if she had something of more pressing importance. "I came in for a doctor's appointment," she explained. "Thought I'd do some shopping."

"Have you time for a coffee?"

Claire made a play of looking at her watch. I spotted the excuse already formulating on her lips. In desperation, I dropped all pretence.

"Please, Claire. I need a friend."

Our eyes levelled. Claire's expression lightened into one of sympathy. "All right, but I really mustn't stay long."

We went to an upstairs café with views over the town and sat at a corner table with a surface sticky with spilt drink, cake crumbs, leftover cups and plates. A waitress cleared away the debris and I ordered an espresso. Claire asked for herbal tea. When it arrived it looked like the contents of a goldfish bowl.

"I'm sorry I haven't been to see you," I began hesitantly.

"S'okay, I understand." Claire kept her eyes on the pallid-looking tea.

"Did Charlie mention our last meeting?"

Claire looked up, eyes flashing with rebuke. "Why do you always push people away who try to help you?"

"I shouldn't have bitten his head off," I mumbled. "Bad habit. I'm sorry."

"You threatened him."

"Claire, I really didn't. I was frightened. He was in my home unannounced, for goodness sake. Oh my God." I lowered my voice. "Is that what he told the police?"

Claire looked towards the door. I pressed the cup firmly to my lips. The coffee tasted bitter and stale.

"Everyone's talking about it," Claire murmured. "They're saying…" Her voice faded.

"What are they saying?"

Claire shrugged and looked down. "I don't listen to gossip."

"No smoke without fire, is that what you really think?"

Claire looked up. I wondered what she wasn't telling me and whom she was protecting.

I raced up the road to Andy's. Cutting through an alleyway near to the Nat West Bank, my phone trilled

"Did you get my message?" It was Fiona North.

"No."

"Where are you?"

"Town."

"That's handy. Did you come by car?"

No, I walked. It's only ten miles, after all, I thought with sarcasm. "Yes."

"Can you meet me in half an hour? Bring the car."

"Why?"

"We need to discuss things."

Discuss what precisely? "Where?"

"At the police station."

"Fine. I'll call my lawyer." I cut the call and phoned Gavin on his mobile number, explaining the situation.

"Probably a new development," he said with authority.

"She asked me to meet her in my car."

"They want to search it."

"Then they're wasting their time."

Chadwick made no comment. "I'm in Totnes at the moment but I can drive straight over. Be with you in twenty minutes."

I was certainly getting a royal service, I thought, as I knocked on Andy's door. With a sigh, I wondered how much it was costing.

Andy's face was without a trace of expression. He stood with his arms crossed, pissed off by the look of him.

"Sorry about last night," I said. "Can I come in for a second?"

He opened the door wide. I stepped inside. Mess as usual. The only area that looked sane was the bit around the computer. The desk was tidy. Below, on the floor, were two piles of neatly stacked newspapers. I scanned the top copies, my eyes fixing on the headline blasting from the latest edition of the *Kingsbridge & Salcombe Gazette*: LOCAL TEACHER MURDERED.

"I should have phoned," I said, wanting to go and pick it up and read it. Hang on, I thought, turning to him. "But then you didn't call me either."

"I gave it until ten, figured you weren't coming, and called Jen. We had quite a good evening. So what happened?" His arms remained folded.

"Don't be mad at me."

"I'm genuinely not." He gurned and made me laugh with relief.

"It's rather complicated. The thing is I can't stop. I'm due at the cop shop. Look, how about dinner, my place this evening, by way of an apology. Bring Jen with you."

He cracked a smile. His arms dropped to his side. "I can't do tonight."

"Tomorrow?" If I hadn't been taken into custody, or whatever they did, by then.

"Cool. I'll let Jen know."

"The truth is, Andy, I could do with you guys around."

He looked concerned. "You haven't had any more trouble?"

"Not exactly, I'll explain tomorrow."

"Shall we bring anything—wine, chocolates?"

"Either." I'd been forgiven and gave him a peck on the cheek.

Hurtling back down Fore Street, I crossed the road, passed a pub, and stepped into the car park. The traffic was solid and it seemed to take forever to drive up the hill to the police station.

Fiona was waiting, along with Darke and a couple of other officers. They looked like a posse and, for a horrible moment, I feared I was under arrest.

I tipped up on the balls of my feet, furiously casting around the car park for Chadwick. There was no sign of him. Trying to look relaxed, I walked over and offered an easy smile.

Darke was courteous. "Thanks for coming in. This won't take long."

"What won't?"

"Searching your car. DS North will run you back home later and collect you when we've finished with it."

"Couldn't someone have told me rather than all this cloak-and-dagger stuff?"

It didn't amuse him. "There are other issues we want to discuss."

"Issues?"

Darke looked evasive. "Things you should know."

"But my lawyer isn't here yet."

"We can wait."

Then it really was serious, I thought. We waited for almost forty minutes. I handed over the keys and, in consternation, watched my car being loaded onto a low-loader. Fiona made small talk. Someone gave me a plastic cup of hot coffee that burnt my fingers and tasted vile.

Chadwick phoned. "My car's broken down—something to do with the alternator. I've got the tow guy with me now."

"How long will you be?"

“Not entirely sure. What’s the latest?”

“You were right. They’ve taken the car.”

“That it?”

“They’ve got new information.”

“No sign of the Super?”

“Haven’t seen her.”

“Then I’d better speak to Darke.”

I called him over, explained, and handed him my phone. He took it. I could hear Chadwick’s voice booming from the other end. Darke muttered an affirmative, turned on his heel, and walked off a little. Then he returned, a sheepish look on his face, and handed the phone back to me. Chadwick was still on the line.

“It’s all good. Go and get some lunch. I’ll be with you quick as I can.”

“Thank you.” I wasn’t hungry.

SEVENTY-NINE

Hair freshly cut and coloured, Detective Superintendent Niven sat at the table with a clipboard in front of her. She wore a sober pale grey suit with a white shirt that made her look like a conference official. She offered Chadwick and me a brief smile and gave a limp wave of her hand, indicating for us to take a seat.

"Thanks for coming in, Kim."

Interesting use of Christian name, I thought—could be a softening up tactic or, wildly optimistic, I was viewed as less of a suspect.

"We've had detailed analysis back on Chris's car. Bloodstains were found in the engine compartment. It would seem that he was bending over as one does to check the oil…"

"He wouldn't need to check the oil. It was a new car," I pointed out, clearly ruining her opening gambit.

"I'm simply giving an example." Niven's smile was cold. Her teeth glittered like specks of ice. She waited a beat. "You don't really like women, do you? You find them tricky, difficult to connect with."

Winded, I opened my mouth, but no words emerged. Fortunately, Chadwick did the talking for me.

"I really must protest."

Niven continued unabated. "You're quite a spiky individual, Kim. Would it be true to say that you are a woman who lives on the edge?"

"I don't…"

"Presumably, you muzzle your anger while at work."

"That's not true," I choked, only too aware that Niven's incisive assessment contained more than a grain of truth. It wasn't that I disliked women—my close circle of female friends proved otherwise—but I knew myself well enough to know that I had issues with trust after what my mother had done to me.

"I fail to see how your barbed opinion of my client is connected to the case," Chadwick said.

Niven ignored him, her full attention on me. "As you are aware, Kim, we've already established Chris was hit from behind. The initial blow would have been enough to knock him off his feet, pitching him forward. The second and third blow would have rendered him unconscious. Do you know what happens to people with head injuries?" She inclined her head, a thin smile on her pale coral-coloured lips, the question rhetorical. "The brain swells and, as it expands, it pushes down on the brain stem, shutting down the mechanisms that control breathing and heart function."

Without waiting for me to digest it, Darke fired a question.

"You were born and brought up here, weren't you?"

"Yes."

"Would you say that you have a fairly good geographical grasp of the area?"

"Yes."

"Do you know the area around Sittaford Tor?"

"Not intimately."

"But you've been there?"

"Yes."

Niven leant forward. Her hands were clasped, not tightly, but in a relaxed fashion. "I understand that Charlie Lidstone is a friend of yours."

"That's right." This was a hell of a switch in the conversation.

"Known him for long?"

"About ..." Goodness, I thought, was it really that long? "Fifteen years or so."

"Good friends then?"

"I'd say so."

"Yet only days ago you threatened him with a car jack." Niven cocked an accusing eyebrow.

Chadwick twitched beside me. "That's not strictly true," I said. No wonder Claire was edgy.

"Which bit isn't true, Kim?"

Sod, I wish she'd stop calling me by name. "I didn't threaten him."

"You deny it?"

"Strongly," I protested. "He was in my house, uninvited. I was protecting myself. He could have been an intruder."

"Ah, back to the stalker."

"You make it sound as if I'm making him up." My voice shook. I wanted to get up and flee and never come back. Sensing it, Chadwick shot out a steadying hand.

"You were afraid?" Niven said evenly.

"Yes."

"Because you've been stalked?"

"Yes."

The coral lips twitched into a nasty little smile. "Did you get the stalking idea from your friend Alexa Gray?"

My eyes shot wide. "I'm not sure I follow you."

Niven looked to Darke, who spoke. "We understand that you know Alexa Gray."

Had they been checking my phone? I supposed they must have. "Well, yes." Dizzy, I thought the floor might suddenly rush up to meet me.

"Did you know that a friend of Mrs. Gray's went missing?"

"Gaynor Lassiter, yes, I know about that." I looked helplessly at Gavin, who looked as perplexed as I felt.

"Mrs. Lassiter was allegedly stalked before her disappearance," Darke said.

I shot forward. "That's it then. It can't be a coincidence."

"It was never established."

"But don't you see," I said, Robert Fallon's words ringing in my ears. "There has to be a connection."

Niven frowned. "A connection?"

"To me," I said exasperated. I looked from Niven to Darke, begging them to grasp what I was saying.

"There's no evidence, whatsoever, to suggest a link," Niven said, stony.

I viewed her with real dislike. Whatever I said, she'd twist my words. They had me down for a fantasist.

"Do you approve of taking the law into your own hands?" The barbed smile returned. We were back to my alleged threat to Charlie.

"No, of course not," I said, exhausted, "but, last I heard, it's perfectly acceptable for a householder to defend himself from intruders."

"I was referring to your conduct with Kyle Stannard."

I took a breath, trying to resist rising to Niven's bait. "It wasn't like that," I said as pleasantly as I could.

"We understand you were quite zealous in your pursuit of Mr. Stannard. You went to his parents' home, isn't that right?"

"No comment."

Niven paused for effect. "Would it surprise you to know that we've identified the weapon used on Chris?"

Clever switch of emphasis, I thought. "You've found it?"

"Not yet, but we know from the type of injuries what was used."

"You said it was a hammer."

"Did we? I thought we said it was something *like* a hammer."

I felt Chadwick's eyes bore into the side of my head. "Maybe," I said, bullish. "I don't remember for certain."

"Are you sure you don't remember? You see, it was a car jack, Kim, exactly the type of weapon with which you threatened Mr. Lidstone."

Chadwick immediately asked for a break and whisked me off to a side room.

Once inside, his gaze hardened. "They're giving you an opportunity to change your story."

"I don't want to change my story," I said, desperate not to cry. "I used my jack to change the wheel on my car. I grabbed it when I thought I had an intruder. I did *not* use it to kill Chris."

Chadwick's cool eyes fused on mine. "Tell me more about Gaynor Lassiter."

"I hardly know anything about her. She's a friend of a woman I used to go to boarding school with. Until today, I'd no idea that the missing woman had ever been stalked." Made me wonder why Alexa had failed to mention it.

Chadwick nodded in the way people do when they dismiss a theory. Sledge-hammered with new information, I was on a knife edge and dangerously close to slipping into a fugue state.

"And Charlie?"

Surprised, I told him what happened.

"Do you reckon Charlie laid it on thick to the police?"

"It would seem so." I really didn't want Charlie getting into any more trouble. "I had coffee with Claire this morning," I explained.

Chadwick tapped the side of his nose, a perplexed expression on his face. He didn't say anything immediately. "What was Charlie doing in your house?"

"He came to sit in when I had a viewing. I'd no idea he was going to show up, so it was rather a shock."

"Did he have a key?"

"The door was open."

"Who said?"

"He did."

Then I gabbled on about Simon, his reference to my car as a nice heap of metal, how it fitted with the anonymous note. Before I ran out of steam, Chadwick had a strange expression on his face, as if he were saying *All these men, all these red herrings.* "Sounds as if you're grasping at straws."

"You don't think his choice of words significant?" I was practically pleading with him.

The way he was looking at me, it was a distinct possibility that a psychiatrist would rock up and spirit me away under the auspices of the Mental Health Act.

"They won't find anything incriminating in the car, will they?" he said, slicing through my thoughts.

"You already asked me that," I said. "Not unless someone's planted evidence."

Chadwick's eyes darkened. His voice was sharp. "This is real life, Kim, not an episode of *Murder She Wrote*." He opened the door, popped his head round, intimating that we were ready to resume. "Leave me to handle this," he hissed as we walked back inside.

"My client feels there's nothing to add to or retract from her original statement," Chadwick said, like a QC summing up for the defence. "I think it's fair to say that my client's professional life is exemplary. Her work, specialising in eating disorders, is highly regarded both by her peers and patients alike. She has a livelihood and a reputation at stake."

With a rush of guilt, I remembered Kirsten Matherson.

"I would also point out that she has roots in this community and is therefore not likely to flee."

He's persuading them not to detain me, I realised, my eyes trained on Niven's inscrutable face.

Darke looked at Niven, who looked at me. "Surrender your passport and you're free to go," she said with a deadly, self-satisfied smile.

EIGHTY

I ASKED FIONA TO drive me to an off-licence. In preparation for the following evening, I bought a mixed case—South African white, French and Chilean red—and a pack of lager because Andy preferred it to wine. A concession to responsibility, I also bought two litres of water, one still, one sparkling. I hardly spoke on the drive back to the cottage, deflecting any question with a monosyllabic answer.

I carried the case of drink to the door. With one foot on the step, I stopped. Fiona, behind, barrelled into me.

"What's up?"

"Listen."

She took a step forward, put her ear to the door. "Music playing."

"Yes."

"You must have left it on."

"No."

"Are you sure?"

"Certain."

"You wait here. Give me the keys." Fiona unlocked the door and walked inside. I rested the box down and sat on the step, waiting for something but not sure what. Seconds later, the cottage fell silent. Fiona reappeared. "Coast's clear."

I followed her in.

"It was on a loop. Do you recognise it?" Fiona held up a CD.

Of course I did. U2. "Love Is Blindness." Three-in-the-morning-drunk, lyrics sucking me in, sexy riffs epitomising a dark, obsessive theme. I didn't know my stalker's identity, but I knew now what drove him. Therein lay the fear and the anger. And I knew about that, too. Mine.

I looked at Fiona squarely. "Dead men don't stalk."

"What do you mean?"

"He's back. He's here. Like I always knew he would be."

"But Chris ..."

"*Not* Chris," I hissed. "Here, let me show you." I led Fiona to the dining room and showed her the photo album.

"We've already looked at it," Fiona said.

"But you didn't know what you were looking for because it wasn't there. You didn't realise its significance." I told Fiona about the missing photograph, what it meant. "This is the real Chris. Don't you see, psychologically speaking, this can't have been the man stalking me."

I watched Fiona's pensive expression. "Maybe it's the impression he wanted to create," Fiona said. "To come across as the attentive, caring lover, but underneath something else was at play."

I shook my head, vehement. "*What* was at play? *What* motivated him? He had an affair. He had an exit strategy already lined up and then changed his mind and decided to stay."

Neither of us spoke. Fiona touched the photograph lightly with her fingers. There was hesitation in her manner. I picked up on it. She was weakening and coming round to my point of view. I pressed home my advantage.

"Chris was already dead when someone entered my flat in Cheltenham and left a revolting calling card. Now this." I glanced in the direction of the CD player.

"You say your brother, Luke, can verify that Chris called him?"

"Yes."

"How do you explain the letters?"

"The computer can't tell you the identity of the letter writer."

"What about the dates? What about his signature?" The blue eyes filled with concern.

"They must have been forged." To my mind, Fiona was outgunned, but she still didn't look convinced.

"Would you like me to stay?" she said as if to appease me.

"No, I want you to go." It won't end unless you do.

EIGHTY-ONE

I CHECKED MY PHONE, noticed I had three missed calls, put the lager and two bottles of white wine in the fridge, and exchanged my sandals for a pair of sturdy ankle boots, my thin jacket for leather. I scrunched back my hair into a ponytail. It wasn't a style I liked because it exposed too much the damaged side of my face, but it was practical.

Snatching my crash helmet from the cupboard, Chris's keys from the drawer, I went outside and crossed the gravelled drive to the garage. Chris's metal-grey bike sat inside, ready for a fast exit. I let out a low moan and a rush of grief stormed me as I remembered better times. I don't know how long I stayed, shoulders shuddering, my face hot and wet with tears, head splitting. Could have been a couple of minutes. Could have been more. When the worst was over I pushed aside the illegality of what I was about to do and, with both hands on the high handlebars, I swung onto the saddle. Flicking the kickstand up with my boot, I stabbed the key into the ignition. Immediately the dashboard lit up, the neutral light glowing green. As Chris's ghostly voice whispered the moves in my ear, I punched the kill switch, pulled the clutch in, pressed the starter button to fire up the engine, then flexed the twist grip and short-shifted through the gearbox, as Chris had shown me. One down and five up through the six-speed gearbox, the accompanying growl from the nonbaffled exhaust providing the bass rhythm for the roar in my heart. I'd no idea if I could handle such a powerful machine. I'd only ever test-ridden the Tiger on lonely country lanes; a motorway was a very different story.

Before I lost my nerve I shot out onto the drive and headed straight to Kingsbridge, concentrating hard on not taking the bends too fast. Once there, I stopped at a payphone near Dodbrooke Church, where I called Alexa.

"Kim," she exclaimed on hearing my voice. "I've been trying to get hold of you. I've had a visit from the police."

"I know."

"They said that Chris has been murdered."

"Yes," I said dully.

"My God, so that's why they were asking all sorts of questions."

"About me?"

"And Gaynor. I'm not sure I follow the connection."

My wits sharpened. The police maintained that there was no link. Niven had been adamant. Was her intention to use the information about Lassiter to discredit me, or was she genuinely following a lead?

"Do you remember the names of the officers who talked to you?"

"A guy called Darke, and a woman whose name I forget. I got the impression that she was senior to him. I didn't like her, actually."

"Alexa, I don't remember you ever saying that Gaynor had a stalker."

"What?" The pitch of her voice was so high she couldn't be faking it.

"You didn't know?"

"I had absolutely no idea. Is that what the police told you?"

"Yes." I scratched my nose, trying to assemble my thoughts. It wasn't so strange that the police had another agenda because they thought I was responsible for Chris's death. Then it hit me. "Gaynor's husband would know his wife was being stalked, wouldn't he?"

Maybe the stalking element was deliberately held back from the public and press so that it wouldn't elicit a load of calls from cranks and hoaxers. Either that, or the police lacked concrete evidence. The very nature of stalking meant things often happened in secret and only held significance for the victim. Perhaps the police had been as sceptical of Gaynor's stalker as they had of mine. "Does Gaynor's husband still live in Bristol?"

"Ivan moved to Exeter."

"Do you have an address, a phone number?"

"He won't talk to you."

"You don't think so?" I failed to hide my dismay.

"He had a rough ride with the media. The press practically camped outside his door for twelve months."

"Give me his number and address anyway."

EIGHTY-TWO

Ten minutes later, I was tearing along the A38, the bike opened up enough to set my jeans on fire.

Alexa was right. Ivan Lassiter had picked up the phone and, half-way through my staggered pitch, told me he had absolutely nothing to say and hung up. I got the impression that he was an exhausted man rather than a guilty one, which is why I decided to see if a personal, face-to-face plea would persuade him. Realistically, I was running out of options.

I arrived in Exeter around seven in the evening. Ivan Lassiter lived in a large historic-looking building close to the university where he now taught. I looked up at the vast expanse of red brick and arched windows, solid and dependable, and prayed that my journey had not been in vain.

Parking in the visitors' slot, I sneaked in as a young foreign student came out and found myself in a vast communal hall with high ceilings and echoey wood-panelled walls adorned with portraits of eminent individuals. A wide staircase ran up two sides of the building. It reminded me of school. Armed with only a name and number, I took the right set of stairs, travelled to the third and highest floor, and rapped on the front door of Lassiter's apartment.

The door opened and in the entrance stood a serious-looking man with tinted spectacles, thick sideburns, and thin lips. Around Chris's height, he carried less weight, as if he devoured books instead of food. His clothes were rumpled, his trousers a flappy size too big and his neck, rearing up from his shirt collar, reminded me of an ostrich. Everything about him revealed that he was a man who lived alone and wished he didn't. From somewhere deep inside the room, I heard a snatch of Vaughn Williams.

"*Fantasia on a Theme of Thomas Tallis*," I smiled.

Perplexed, he blinked and inclined his head. "Should I know you? Your voice..."

Shamelessly, I turned my less attractive side towards him. "I called you earlier. I understand why you don't wish to talk to me, and I really don't want to rake up the past, but I'm desperate. Will you help me? Please."

He stood stock-still. We both did. I couldn't read the expression behind the lenses. When he asked me to step inside I realised I'd been holding my breath.

We sat down in a sitting room with terrific views over the city.

"How far have you travelled?" he said, glancing at my crash helmet.

I told him.

"You must be thirsty. Can I get you a drink?"

"Water would be lovely, thank you."

While he was gone I looked around me. Everything was grey—the sofa, chairs, carpet and walls, even the granite-topped coffee table. I wondered if it had always been so. Had everything lost its lustre and colour when his wife disappeared? My gaze fell onto a framed photograph on the window ledge. I got up, crossed the room, and picked it up. It was a shot of a younger and more rounded Ivan. The woman with him was laughing. They both were. A palm tree behind them suggested that it was a holiday snap. I studied her face. She had lovely hazel-coloured eyes, a neat nose, and a mass of dark brown hair, but this was not what caught my attention. Briefly, and with a jag to my heart, I wondered if I were dreaming.

"That's Gaynor," Ivan said, handing me a glass. Sweetly, he'd added ice and a slice of fresh lime.

"She's very pretty," I said.

"Yes," he said, "and a gifted musician."

"Professional?"

"No, she worked in medical research." He took the photograph from me and placed it back on the sill. "Happier times," he said, the shine gone from his voice.

We both sat back down and I took a deep drink.

"I'm afraid I only half listened to what you told me on the phone," Ivan said. "Do you mind running through it all again?"

I first explained my connection to Alexa then started back at the beginning. I told him about my stalker, about Chris, about the police and my fears.

When I finished he leant back into the sofa, clasped his fingers together, and touched his chin, thoughtful. For the first time here was someone who understood and who'd listened to my story without either cynicism or disbelief. "And you think there's a link between what's happened to you and Gaynor's disappearance?"

"It's a long shot, I know."

"Then why did the police turn up at my door yesterday? You're aware I had a visit?"

"That's what tipped me off. You see, Alexa never mentioned that Gaynor had been stalked."

Ivan flashed a smile. "You know Alexa Gray well?"

"We went to school together."

"How do you rate her?"

I paused, the complexities of Alexa's personality a diversion. "Well, she's a little highly strung…"

"Precisely. She really wasn't that close to Gaynor."

"Oh, I see." At least, I thought I did.

"She's the last person I'd mention stalking to."

At least Alexa was telling the truth.

"What troubles me," Ivan said, "is that the police mentioned it to you."

"They had their reasons." Although not the ones you might think, I thought.

"To be honest, I had a tough time convincing them myself."

"That Gaynor was being stalked?"

He nodded. "Understandably, the police are evidence-based and not very adept at factoring random events into an investigation. So much of what happened to Gaynor could be explained away as fantasy or false memory or getting things muddled up. It didn't help that Gaynor wasn't keen to make a fuss and ditched anything that could have provided them with a lead. She thought if she ignored it, it would stop."

A woman like me. "So they decided to withhold the information from the public?"

Ivan nodded.

"What form did the stalking take?"

"Her car was moved at work." I did my best to keep my expression steady. "The phone would ring," he continued. "If I picked up, the caller would hang up. If Gaynor picked up, he'd stay on the line. We did all the usual stuff, reported them as nuisance calls, tried to phone back but the calls were untraceable and the best the phone company could do was offer to change the number."

"Did the police check out her phone records?"

"As part of the investigation, but they never managed to trace the caller."

"Anything else?"

"She had gifts sent to her at work."

"Cards, chocolates?"

Ivan nodded, twitched a smile. It seemed as if it was a relief for him, too, to talk to someone who'd experienced something of what his wife had suffered.

"And you never had a clue who it was?"

He pressed his hands to his face, tipping the spectacles up onto his head, and rubbed one eye. "No." The glasses flicked back down. "The energy we expended trying to find out could have fuelled the grid for a month."

"It turned your life upside down," I murmured.

"You understand," he said, his expression bleak.

"So what happened in the end?"

"She didn't come home." He looked as mystified and hurt as he must have done at the time. "She went to work. We were supposed to be meeting for a drink and she never arrived."

"I am very sorry." Next, I needed to ask the million-dollar question. "Do you think the person stalking your wife abducted her?"

"I'm convinced of it."

I fell into a respectful silence.

"We're into our second year. Deep down I know she's gone. But the only way I keep going is thinking she's alive, that we still have a life together. Does that make sense?"

I nodded sadly.

"That's why I couldn't cope with the press intrusion. Every time I had a knock at the door or a message shoved underneath it with invitations to sell my story, I knew we'd moved from missing wife to murder victim."

"Is that why you moved?"

He nodded. "I still get the odd phone call, but with nothing like the same intensity."

A light went on in my brain. "Did the local press in Bristol cover it?"

"*Bristol Evening News*. I even remember the guy's name, Josh Brodie. Why do you ask?"

"I'd like to talk to him."

Anxiety etched Ivan's face. "Are you sure? Do you realise what you might unleash?"

Too late to worry about that. I smiled. "I'll take my chances. I don't suppose you happen to have his number?"

Reluctantly, Ivan agreed. "Give me a moment then."

He disappeared and reappeared with a business card, which he handed me. I glanced at it, thanked him, and pocketed the card.

"One last thing, did Gaynor ever receive anything strange on her computer?"

"No."

"Are you certain?"

"I'm positive. It was mostly out of commission during that period. She had repeat problems with the hard drive, an absolute pain. The computer was constantly booked in for repair."

"But the police did take a look at it?"

"I believe they did, yes."

I couldn't think of anything else to say. "I'm sorry to have taken up so much of your time."

I got up and Ivan walked me to the door. "Apologies for earlier. Will you let me know how you get on?" he said.

"I will."

We both hovered awkwardly by the entrance, neither of us sure how to say good-bye. Impulsively, I stuck out my hand. "Thanks for relenting."

Ivan's smile was ringed with sadness. "You reminded me of my wife. You struck a chord."

EIGHTY-THREE

I FOUND A PUBLIC phone box and called Josh Brodie's mobile number. It rang and rang and I almost gave up, then a voice said "Yep," and I pushed in some coins.

"Are you Josh Brodie?" I said.

"The one and same." His raspy voice indicated a twenty-a-day habit. In the background I could hear the noise of glasses clinking, conversation at full throttle.

I explained who I was. "I've just spent the past hour with Ivan Lassiter. He—"

"Gaynor Lassiter's husband?"

"Yes."

"Go on."

"I've got information that might interest you."

"Yeah?" The phone crackled. I assumed he was walking to somewhere quieter. "That's better," he said.

"It would be best if we met."

"Maybe," he said, not sounding that committed. "Are you in Bristol?"

"Down the road, Exeter."

"I don't have my diary on me."

"What are you doing now?"

"I'm at an awards ceremony in town. Can't duck out, I'm afraid."

I glanced at my watch. It was eight thirty. "I could be with you within the hour. How about afterwards?"

"That won't work for me. It could be an all-nighter."

"Mr. Brodie, my boyfriend has been murdered. Gaynor Lassiter was being stalked and so am I. I think the same person who abducted her is out to get me."

Noise on the phone told me that my time had run out. I scrabbled in my pocket and thrust another load of coins into the slot.

"Are you still there?" I felt perilously close to meltdown.

He didn't answer my question, but posed another. "I know this sounds strange, but have you got any marks on your face?"

"Will scars do?"

"Perfect," he said. It was the same reason Ivan Lassiter had let me in his door. "Meet me at the Marriott on College Green as soon as you can. Ask for me at Reception. I'll brief them that I'm expecting you."

EIGHTY-FOUR

I SPED UP THE stone steps to the hotel, a grand Victorian building, navigated my way past a group of smokers, and entered through a revolving door that opened out onto a wide foyer smelling of polish and fresh flowers. As I approached Reception, I heard a ripple of applause from deep within and, close by, the sound of a bar working at full belt. I gave my name, stated I was meeting Josh Brodie, and was asked to take a seat, which I did in an alcove by a window. Minutes later, a man I assumed to be Brodie strode towards me. His bowtie was undone James Bond style, and he had an eager look in his hangdog eyes. He was younger than I'd imagined, nearer forty than fifty. He had short dark hair spiked upright with gel. Incongruously, he wore trainers. Not a good look with a dinner suit.

I stood up to greet him. To my consternation, he crooked one finger under my chin to better examine my face, studying it as if it were a fine work of art. When I'd met with his approval, he invited me to sit down, which I did.

"Drink?" he said.

I shook my head. "I'm driving, but don't let me stop you."

"No, I can wait."

I cut straight to the chase. Josh was already halfway there with my story. All I had to do was fill in the detail. Like a true hack, he interrupted when he wasn't quite clear and went over a couple of things, like the computer image, presumably to verify exactly what it entailed. He also asked me about Stannard even though I'd discounted him.

"You've obviously followed the Bristol case," I said finally. "What I need to know is whether there are any other similarities, something else I've missed, a seemingly minor detail—anything that connects me to Gaynor."

He studied me for a moment, as if weighing something up, then took out a fresh pack of cigarettes and pulled off the wrapper.

"Mind if we go outside? I think better when I smoke."

"Not a problem," I said.

Fortunately, other smokers had left so it was just the two of us leaning over the spotlit stone balustrade. I waited patiently while Josh went through the ritual of lighting up. He took a deep drag and a thin stream of smoke puffed out into the night.

"Better," he said, happy now. "How are the police dealing with it?'

I let out a giddy laugh. "They have me down for a murderer and believe I made up the stalking story to deflect the limelight."

"I'm surprised they haven't banged you up."

"It's only a matter of time."

"Got a good lawyer?"

"I believe so."

Josh took another drag. "What you have to remember is that the police hate linking cases, particularly if it involves another constabulary. It goes against their copperly DNA," he added irreverently.

"I think I'd worked that out," I said with a shaky laugh.

"They also won't make a connection between Gaynor Lassiter who disappears in Bristol, Chrissie Taylor who commits suicide in Holmes Chapel, Cheshire, Anita Finch in Birmingham and Melanie Simpson in Presteigne, Wales, both of whom vanished."

My heartbeat didn't quicken. It pulsed at full tilt. "And were they stalked?"

"Can't confirm in the case of Melanie Simpson, although I think it likely."

"And who was the first?"

"Chrissie."

"And she screwed up the grand plan by killing herself," I said thoughtfully.

"That's my guess."

"How did she do it?"

"Pills. Died of a massive overdose."

"When?"

"Eight years ago."

Which means he's been improving his game for some time. "And what do you think bonds us together?" I knew, but I wanted Josh to spell it out.

"Every single victim had some kind of facial defect."

The confirmation of what I most feared made me flush with heat then icy chill.

"Sick, huh?"

I nodded, rubbed the tops of my arms to stave off a shiver.

"Chrissie had badly scarred skin as a result of teenage acne," Josh explained. "Anita had a port-wine stain on her right cheek; Melanie Simpson suffered from a rare skin condition. Gaynor …"

"A large birth mark." I remembered the raised cluster of brownish marks on her face. Congenital nevi, at a guess.

Josh nodded. "And then there's . . ."

"Me," I said. "Have you spoken to the police about your findings?"

"I gave up. Not enough evidence, apparently, and the families were not always supportive. Can't say as I blame them," he said without rancour. "It must be torture."

I was refreshingly surprised. I always thought journalists put the story ahead of sensitivities. "Are there any other similarities? You appeared to take an interest in the computer image."

"In two cases, the girls had answered classified ads for computer recycling."

"Which girls?"

"Chrissie and Melanie."

And then there were Gaynor's computer repairs, I remembered. "What's your take on the perpetrator?"

"Someone who has the freedom to travel," Josh said. "Could be a lorry driver, a sales representative, someone with plenty of time on his or her hands."

I grimaced. "Her?"

"Statistically, it's more likely to be a male, I grant you. The victims are all female and disappearing folk is a masculine pursuit but, I don't know, it's such a weird one, maybe a woman is responsible. Women are more concerned with their appearance than men, aren't they?"

I lapsed into silence. Josh punctured my thoughts. "Would you let me interview you? We could strengthen your case."

I was aghast. "I don't know. I haven't thought it through. It's not what I came here for." Irritation crackled behind his eyes. As far as he was concerned, I was an exclusive and, now that I'd got what I came for, I flitted out of reach. Keen not to disappoint, I said, "Give me twenty-four hours to think about it."

"Fair enough. What's your number?" I hesitated. The last thing I needed was a crime correspondent hounding me. "In case I think of anything else," he said with a slack grin.

I relaxed, told him, and watched as he shambled back inside followed by a wispy trail of cigarette smoke.

EIGHTY-FIVE

THE JOURNEY BACK WAS fraught. In spite of the halogen driving lights, I was unaccustomed to travelling in the dark on the Triumph, and found myself constantly misjudging distances. On the outskirts of Exeter, the low-fuel light shone and I worried that it could have been on for some time. To try and conserve what petrol I had, I decreased speed and rode in the slow lane. It felt as if I'd painted a bull's eye on my back. I fully expected the traffic police to rock up and signal for me to pull over.

By the time I reached Cormorants Reach, it was well past two in the morning. Every muscle and sinew hurt. My eyes were practically bleeding with strain. As the tyres crunched across the gravelled drive, I experienced a profound sense of dread. Was someone lurking inside, armed for my return?

Impossibly wired, it took me a long time before I dropped off to sleep. Some time later, loud rapping at the front door roused me from unconsciousness. I shrugged off the duvet, dragged on a robe, and sleep walked to the open window. Pushing back the curtain, a shaft of bright sunlight prised open my eyelids. My bleary, stumbling gaze focused on Fiona North, who was looking straight up at me.

"Sorry, were you asleep?"

I mumbled a reply to the effect that I was exhausted. Her secret smile inferred that she was pleased—meant that I was in no fit state to argue.

"Your passport," she said. "I should have collected it yesterday."

"I'll be right down."

"No hurry."

I took her at her word and took a detour. After having a pee, I splashed water over my face and went downstairs to let her in.

"What time is it?" My mouth was furred with fatigue.

"Lunchtime." She glanced at her watch. "Ten minutes past one, to be precise."

I'd slept for almost nine hours straight and had to check myself from saying so.

"Are you all right? You look a bit peaky."

"Tired," I burbled. I asked Fiona to hang on while I fished out my passport from a drawer in my desk, probably not the best place to keep it, I now realised.

Handing it to her, I said, "That it? No more interviews?" I guess I sounded facetious because her responding look was cool and professional.

"Not today." Which meant tomorrow.

"I've been thinking," I said, wrapping my dressing gown tightly around me. "Perhaps he's done it before. Perhaps there are other victims."

"Why do you say that?"

"Chris's murder infers a different type of offender."

"Go on," she said, her blue eyes locked on mine.

"Someone who has gradually worked his or her way up the criminal ladder, someone who might have started out with harassment or stealing, or…"

"Are you suggesting the alleged individual is a serial offender?"

"It's possible, isn't it?"

Fiona looked sceptical.

"Chris's murder is almost incidental. It's not the point of it all, don't you see?"

From the look on her face, she clearly didn't.

"Gaynor Lassiter had a birthmark on her face," I burst out.

Her eyes narrowed. "How do you know?"

"Alexa Gray told me," I lied.

"All right," she said slowly. "You're saying that there is a tenuous connection to you."

"It's not tenuous," I said, appealing to her. "The stalker and murderer is driven and turned on by disfigurement. That's his bag. It's what grabs his attention." Other than that, I had little idea about the exact psychopathology behind the symbolism.

"Ridiculous speculation."

I shook my head in an agony of frustration. "What if there were other victims?"

"What others?" She looked genuinely take aback.

I reeled off the list. Fiona looked at me as if I'd announced I was about to self-immolate.

"Where on earth did you find this out?"

I swallowed. "I contacted a journalist whose been working on the Lassiter case. He—" I stopped. Fiona's expression said it all. Journalist equals trial by media equals rubbish.

Wildly out of character, I grabbed the sleeve of her shirt. "Will you pass on what I've told you?"

She patted my hand and framed her mouth into a smile. "Of course I will. Shall I make you a nice cup of tea? You could take it up to bed."

Lost, I smiled back, obedient. "That would be lovely—thanks."

I let Fiona faff about. I promised to rest. When she offered to stay I said, "I'll only be asleep, no point." I had to send her away. I couldn't flush the perpetrator out unless I was alone. Cranky to an outsider—I was putting my life at risk—but without taking it to the limit, the game would never be over, never won.

As soon as she'd gone I showered and dressed and carefully put on my makeup. My mind was electric, consumed by the thought of the other women—what they had endured, the depths of their despair, the twisted way in which the stalker, abductor, and now murderer was turned on by our physical imperfection. Next, I thought about me. *Nice heap of metal*, Simon had remarked. *You're sailing pretty close to the wind*, Charlie had accused. *You shimmer with sadness,* Stannard had said. His perspicacity had amazed me. Was my stalker also turned on by my fragility, the sense that for all the show I had not quite transcended the consequences of an unfortunate accident?

Then it clicked.

Purposeful, I picked up the phone and called Carolla Dennison's close friend, Jo Sharpe. There was something I needed to ask her.

EIGHTY-SIX

ANDY ARRIVED SOONER THAN planned.

"No Jen?" I squinted over his shoulder.

"She got as far as my place then threw up on the sofa."

"About time you had a new one."

"Ha-bloody-ha!"

"Poor woman—what was it, something she'd eaten?"

"She muttered about a dodgy prawn sandwich at lunchtime."

"Not nice."

Wearing a cream linen shirt and stone-washed jeans, he looked smart and clean and composed.

He chucked his jacket, a lightweight sailing affair in navy blue, onto a chair and handed me a bottle of wine and a box of chocolates, oblong-shaped and gift-wrapped in a harlequin design. "Don't open them now," he said. "They're for later."

I thanked him. "I thought we'd have a drink on the terrace. I haven't started cooking yet." I took hold of the corkscrew. "Wine or lager?"

"Wine first."

I popped a cork and poured out.

"I feel guilty," he said.

"Why?"

"Here we are about to share a lovely meal and Chris is dead."

"Survivor guilt," I said. "Best cure is to make this a celebration of his life."

"I'll drink to that," Andy said. "To Chris." We chinked glasses.

"Are you hungry?" I asked him.

"Not especially."

"Good. We'll drink then. I can cook later—I promise not to get drunk," I added with a knowing smile that made him laugh.

We went outside. I was glad of the fresh air. Andy sat down and spread his feet apart. I sank into the nearest chair. I hadn't had time to properly take on board what Jo had said. Something that had appeared impossible for thirty different reasons was now credible. I gazed across the water, listened to the sound of birdsong.

"You look preoccupied."

I twitched a smile. "I've been thinking a lot about when I was growing up, places I visited, people I knew, family," I said. "I guess that's what happens when someone dies. You start looking at your life in a different way. You see the constant themes, the things you should have changed but never quite got around to, what you should have said or, more often, kept quiet about. Sorry," I said, "I'm dribbling on."

"No, you're all right. You said you wanted to talk."

"Yes, I did."

"About?"

My pulse rate stammered. I fell momentarily silent.

"Kim?" he prompted.

"About you."

"Me?" He tossed his head back and laughed. "You're so damn enigmatic. Is that the right word?"

"Probably." I forged a smile, took a drink. I ought to listen.

"Nothing to tell that you don't already know." His grin was off-centre. Fleetingly, he reminded me of Stannard.

"There's lots of stuff I don't know about you."

"Like what?"

"What your parents do for a living."

Andy's grin split wider. "My dad's a retired accountant. My mum's a homemaker and world-class bore."

"See, I don't know everything." I took a sip, eyes fixed on the silvery water. "You're an only child, right?"

"Yeah, but I wasn't spoilt."

I chuckled, as if sharing the joke. "Didn't you move from Cheshire to Plymouth?"

"Yes."

"Ever go back to Cheshire?"

"Why would I?"

"No reason."

"We hadn't always lived in Cheshire," he said.

"Really?"

"My dad had a job in Kingsbridge, would you believe? We lived at Stentiford Hill for a short time."

"How old were you?" I took a drink to avoid his sly gaze.

"Why?"

"Getting my bearings."

Andy blinked rapidly. "Twelve, thirteen, I forget."

"We might have gone to the same school if I hadn't been sent away."

"And I hadn't moved back to Middlewich," he reminded me.

"When was that?"

"When I was almost fifteen."

"Odd time to leave," I said. "You must have been in the middle of your GCSE exams."

Darkness entered his expression.

"This is your cue to rattle on about your school days." It was meant to sound playful. I wasn't sure that I'd struck the right note.

There was no return smile. His look was stark. I recognised common ground. "I hated them. It's why we relocated."

This was big news to me. "Yet you teach in the same school."

"Payback," he said abruptly.

"For what?"

"Being bullied. I hadn't grown up with the other kids. I didn't sound like them. Walking the same corridors where I was teased and taunted gives me a sense of triumph, of power. I've mastered my demons." A strange light crept into his eyes. I couldn't distinguish whether it was the slant of the evening sun or if it came from deep within.

"Did Chris know about it?"

"No one knows."

"Except me."

"Except you." He held my gaze a fraction longer than was comfortable.

"Seems like neither of you confided too much in the other."

He was dismissive. "Guys rarely confide."

I knew and issued a direct look. "You discussed Carolla Dennison, didn't you?"

"Well, yeah, although I didn't know about his fling," he said quickly. "Babe talk, us blokes do that kind of thing."

"And there's me thinking that gossip was solely a female pursuit."

He laughed a little, took another drink.

"It must have given you quite a buzz to be the first with that piece of news." The crispness in my delivery was provocative.

"I didn't tell anyone about Carolla." He sounded appropriately defensive.

"Yeah, I remember. So who *do* you confide in?"

Andy tensed. "About what?"

"Things that bother you."

"I'm not the neurotic type."

"I didn't say you were."

He took out a pack of cigarettes and unwrapped the cellophane. "Something else you don't know about me," he explained with a rakish smile, taking out a cigarette, tapping it on the pack, putting it in his mouth. "Does it bother you?"

"We're outside. Go right ahead." He lit up, slowly, methodically, ritually, some might say pedantically. I thought of smoke in the night, the figure standing in the lamplight outside my flat. "What about Jen?"

"What about her?"

"Do you two talk?"

"It's not that kind of relationship," he said with a sly *Know what I mean?* grin.

I looked out across the creek at the shivering light, the way the vegetation disappeared into the shadows.

"Did you always teach IT?"

Andy shook his head and blew out a thin wisp of smoke. "My degree is in mathematics. IT was a natural progression—both subjects require logic."

Logic and logistics and getting from A to B. "You don't find it dull dealing with machines instead of people?"

"Machines are way easier to manage." A smile spread across his face.

"And repair."

"Well, yeah."

"And control," I murmured.

"Saves a lot of hassle." He flicked some ash.

"Is that how you view people—as a lot of hassle?"

"Can be," he said, clipped.

"Doesn't that make life lonely?"

His jaw tensed. "I've got lots of friends. You missed some great nights at the Hermitage, by the way."

"So Jo told me." I took a drink for courage. "Is that your story, Andy?"

"What?" He smiled, but his eyes, glinting with suspicion, didn't match the set of his jaw.

"Lots of friends, no deep relationships."

"I'm not sure Jen would be happy with your assessment."

"Ah, the elusive Jen, I was forgetting."

"She's sick for one night and she's elusive? What are you like, then?"

"It's okay," I said. "Not everyone is ready to settle down."

"Nothing wrong with that."

"I agree. We're all different. We each have our individual characteristics," I said, flicking a lock of hair back from my face, giving him the full effect. Did I imagine a facial tick, a tiny shudder? "Every one of us has a different story to tell."

"Not me. My cupboard's clean."

"I never suggested it was dirty."

"Got any lager?" he said, draining his glass.

I got up on tired legs, went inside, cracked open a can, and handed it to him. Moving the chair away a little, I perched on the edge. He flipped down some lager, took another drag of his cigarette.

"As you were Chris's friend, his *best* friend, his mate," I said, with blood-freezing clarity, "I thought I'd test out a theory on you."

He looked at me with slow eyes. "Go on then."

EIGHTY-SEVEN

"THE POLICE THINK CHRIS was my stalker."

Andy's eyes widened in disbelief. "You're joking. That's impossible."

"Yes, it is, for all sorts of chronological reasons."

"Poor Kim." His face was a picture of pity. "But what about that guy you were telling me about?"

"I was wrong. It landed me in a heap of trouble, but that's another tale." Feeling gutsy, the way in which my dad had trained and hardened me, I leant dangerously towards Andy. "Don't you see, the guy stalking me is the same person who killed Chris."

Rock solid, Andy didn't move a muscle. "Makes sense."

"I've often wondered about him, what he's like, whether he's some pathetic creep, no friends, a loner, you know the type. I thought there was a fair possibility that he was mentally ill, but lately I've come to feel quite differently about him. He's sophisticated, manipulative, and smart. Systematic in his approach, he has what you'd call a methodical and logical mind."

Andy's eyes glistened. "I'd guess you'd know."

I waited, watched his hands. Hands that might kill. "I also think he's done it before."

He wore an expression of pure shock. His shiny knuckles told a different tale.

"A woman in Bristol disappeared two years ago," I continued. "Her name was Gaynor Lassiter. She'd been stalked. Vile, isn't it?"

"Christ, Kim, you don't…"

"She had a raised birthmark on her cheek, quite visible. An odd similarity with me, don't you think?"

He took a drink by way of a reply.

"When I went to your place yesterday, it was in a terrible state."

"You know how it is, a guy on his own," he grunted. "Jen says I ought to get a cleaner."

"Don't apologise. It was quite telling, really."

Andy's eyebrows furrowed. "I don't understand."

"The thing about mess is that it makes it easy to pick out the bit that's tidy. You had a pretty neat patch near your computer."

Andy threw an indulgent smile my way. "That's because it's crucial to my work, duh!"

"And why I noticed two piles of newspapers."

The smile stretched wider, the teeth whiter than white. I should have been terrified. Instead, I felt triumph, vindication, justice all rolled into one.

"I didn't spot it at first," I continued. "My eyes focused on the headline in the *Gazette*. You know how it is when you see something from the corner of your eye?" I said, daring him. "I didn't know you read the *Cheltenham Standard*."

Initially, Andy's face was blank, then puzzled, then annoyed. "For God's sake, Kim, are you implying what I think?"

"You tell me. Before you get too cocky, it was open at the piece on me and Ellerslie Lodge."

"Because I know you, idiot-brain," he protested, flaring the fingers of one hand. "Fair enough, I'm guilty of ghoulish curiosity, and I'm not particularly proud of it, but how could you think that?"

"Think what?" Say it, you creep, you ghoul.

He shook his head in disbelief. "To be honest, I'm hurt," he blustered, snatching at his drink. "You're cracked."

"Isn't that the point?"

He gave me a slow, sideways look. "It's a good job we're mates otherwise I'd do you for slander, or defamation of character, or something. I pick up the local rag because I have clients in Cheltenham."

"What sort of clients?"

"Agricultural machinery specialists. I'm putting a digital programme together for them."

"You must have to visit," I said, cool and neutral.

"Nope. Like many budding industrialists, the main man has a holiday home here in Devon, which is how I managed to get the business in the first place. I'm cheaper than other outfits upcountry and, if you don't believe me, I can give you the name of the managing director. Now if you've finished grilling me, perhaps we could think about dinner. I'm quite peckish."

Andy appeared to have a convincing answer for everything. A hard pebble of doubt lodged in my throat. I did my best to gulp it down. Cunning and manipulative, he was playing me. I jumped to my feet and went back inside, giving him every impression that he was off the hook. Andy followed and watched as I took fresh lamb, red peppers, and tomatoes out of the fridge and laid them out on two chopping boards.

"Nice piece of furniture," Andy remarked, eyeing up a small cupboard I'd bought ages ago in the Suffolks.

"Yeah," I said, taking a chopping knife from the block, flexing the blade, poised. *He's almost part of the furniture,* Chris had said. Always there, *always had been*. He'd been Chris's friend long before mine. I straightened up, turned to face him, resting the small of my back against the work surface. "The day Chris was killed you were teaching."

Andy pulled up a chair, rolled his eyes, and helped himself to another can from the fridge. "So?" He pulled back the ring-pull. It gave a small hiss.

"How many kids in your class?"

"Thirty-three. Boys outnumber girls."

"Is that the way you like it?"

"It's the way it is," he said with cold delivery.

"So thirty-three alibis."

"Precisely."

"A damn sight better than poor me." I twitched a smile. "My only alibi's a passing motorist who failed to notice I was there." Andy laughed. I let him finish. "What time do lessons begin?"

"Surely you know," Andy said, straight-faced.

"My mind's gone blank."

He smiled without amusement. "Twenty after nine. Are you going to put down that knife, or are you going to keep waving it around?"

I looked at the blade in my hand, placed it near the meat, somewhere close, somewhere I could easily reach it.

"The call from Chris came through at seven fifty," I said. "If you were passing through the office, you could have overheard."

Andy's eyes were like chisels. "You must be joking. One: I never roll into school at that ungodly hour. Two: I don't go in the office. It's full of women."

"But you like women, Andy. You're secretly fascinated by them, isn't that right?" Especially if they have defects. "None of it matters, of course, because you might as easily have been lying in wait, stalking prey."

"Know what? You're starting to piss me off."

The air throbbed. The kitchen clock ticked then chimed. The sun, charged, gave off a deep umber glow. This was my home, my territory. Knives to the left. Meat cleaver to the right. The place teemed with domestic weaponry and, if provoked, I would have no hesitation in using it.

Andy let out a sudden sigh, his expression softening. The hard note in his voice melted away like snow in sunshine. "C'mon, Kim, this is all bollocks and you know it. We don't want to fight. We're both stressed out to the eyeballs. I know you have to examine all possibilities. I understand that, really I do. But, even if I knew about Chris's call, how long do you think it takes to get from school to Goodshelter and back again? Oh, and fit in a murder?" He hooted with derision.

"Too long."

"There you are then." He drained the can.

"Except that day wasn't normal. It was an intensive IT session that started first thing and didn't finish until the bell went for lunch." At least, that's what Jo Sharpe had told me.

"I still have to be there, you clown."

"That's the point, you don't," I said. "Today's kids have a high level of proficiency born out of endless hours on Game Boys, PlayStations, and computers. You can set reams of stuff for pupils to be getting on with in your absence. How long did it take, Andy? How long did it take for you to play the sympathetic friend, suggest a spin in Chris's new car to take his mind off his *personal* problems—an idea you'd already floated—and then, under the guise of 'blokes being blokes,' to coin your phrase, you ask to take a peek at his shiny new engine and stove his head in?" I was breathless. My chest hurt. So did my face and neck. I hadn't even got started on the forged letter, the anonymous messages, the porn. His stupefied reaction suggested that I'd confessed to a monstrous crime. The rap on the door made us both jump.

Andy cocked an eyebrow. "Are you expecting anyone?"

"No."

"We'll continue this later." He spoke in the way a teacher speaks to a recalcitrant teenager. He definitely didn't seem bothered. "You stay there. I'll go."

I snatched up my phone to call Fiona and was surprised to see I'd received a text from Josh Brodie. It read: CAMPER VAN LINKED TO TWO ABDUCTIONS. Startled, I looked towards the sitting room, taken aback by the sound of male voices—one Andy's, the other hauntingly familiar. Next footsteps, deliberate and slow, then a face appeared. In a split-second, two worlds crashed head-on and I was squashed in the middle.

EIGHTY-EIGHT

"What the fuck?" I choked.

His good side inclined towards me, Kyle Stannard arched a quizzical eyebrow. "I was going to ask you the same."

"Don't get clever."

He spread his hands out. "*You* wanted to talk."

I felt as if I had fog in my brain. Then it cleared as I remembered Brodie's message.

"Where do you park the camper van?"

"Are you one crazy bitch?" Stannard said. "Do I look like the kind of guy who drives one of those aberrations?"

"Watch your mouth," Andy snarled.

Stannard ignored him. "Your brother phoned me this morning, Kim. He said you wanted to straighten things out."

"What things?" Andy stood squat and belligerent, chest straining underneath his shirt.

"Who are you, her minder?" Stannard sneered.

I saw Andy's fist ball. Confusion gripped me. Stannard's bellicose stance remained. He glared at Andy. "He said Kim wanted a meeting here at the cottage. As we left on"—Stannard glanced at me—"dubious terms, I believed him."

"Luke wouldn't do something like that," I said.

"Luke? It wasn't Luke. It was Guy."

"Guy?" I felt as if all the air had been sucked out of my body.

"It was definitely Guy who called."

Had someone put a gun to my temple, I couldn't have been more shocked. "You fucking bastard, my God, you've done your homework." So this was it. Stannard *was* my stalker. I made a face at Andy in apology.

"You're dead, mate." Andy lunged. There was a loud crunch of bone as two bodies collided and crashed onto the tiled floor. Fists flew. Chairs overturned. Drawers wrenched out. Cutlery cascaded. A lamp smashed, shattering into jagged pieces, both men rolling in the broken shards, the air full of grunts and moans. Blood spattered a cupboard. Bigger and heavier, Andy had the advantage. Transfixed, my knuckles pressed to my mouth, I remembered my brothers' fight and my rotten decision. Got to get help, I thought, scrabbling for my mobile.

"Kim," Andy shouted breathlessly, "fetch a rope, or something we can tie him up with."

I ran into the small utility, grabbed a length of thick twine, a leftover from my father's sailing days, and handed it to Andy. He looked spent. His left eye ballooned. His lip was split and there was a nasty cut above his right eyebrow. Panting, he stood over Stannard, dripping sweat. Stannard, meanwhile, was barely conscious as Andy hauled him onto a chair. Blood gushed from his nose. His lip, too, was swollen. The two sides of his face seemed less distinguishable. A low moan burbled up from his stomach and tangled in his throat.

Andy roughly pulled Stannard's hands back and tied them together. "I need something to cut through the twine," he said. "There's a pen-knife in my jacket pocket."

I sprinted out to the sitting room. "We should phone the police," I called over to him. "Let them deal with it."

Andy's jacket was slung across a chair. There seemed to be hundreds of pockets. I patted them, tried to find the telltale shape. I yanked out a handkerchief, a cheque card, coins, matches, and a cheap lighter. My hands flew inside to a zipped up section that seemed promising. I wrenched it open, fingers sliding inside, connecting with something slippery and shiny. I snatched it out.

Hat pulled down. Sunshine lit my face. Sea in the distance, I looked beautiful that day…

Slipping the photograph into my back pocket, I returned to the kitchen with a frozen smile and buccaneering swagger. "Couldn't find it."

"Never mind." Andy let the twine trail onto the floor.

"You can't leave him like that."

"Why not?"

"He might choke or something with all that blood."

"After what he's done, I wouldn't worry."

Stannard let out another groan. "I've done nothing."

"I'll wipe away the mess," I said, swooping up a tea towel, plunging it under the cold tap, thinking and thinking what my next move should be.

"Leave it, Kim." Andy's voice was Siberian.

EIGHTY-NINE

I turned slowly. Every trace of geniality gone, his face a picture of hostility, a cruel light glittered in Andy's eyes. A glance at Stannard extinguished all possibility of help. He was too much out of it.

"This is all very nice and tidy," Andy grinned. He swiped the wet towel from me and dabbed at his wounds. "Quite a little party."

My mind flashed to the painting: two men, one woman. "You tricked Stannard."

"A willing dupe. Swallowed my tale like the proverbial hook, line, and sinker. There's definitely something of the stalker about him. He's clearly obsessed with you."

"And you're clearly obsessed with disfigurement."

"Broken beauties." He shivered, walking slowly towards me. "The ultimate turn-on." He reached out, traced the jagged line of scar tissue. I didn't flinch, didn't move.

"I know about the others, Andy. What did you do to them?"

"What do you think?"

His matter-of-factness left me speechless. I thought about Ivan Lassiter, his devastation.

"I'm ravenous," Andy said through fat lips, "but before you cook dinner, I think you should open your present."

I glowered at him.

"Don't be so ungrateful. Go on, it won't bite," he smirked.

I snatched up the box from the kitchen table, ripped off the paper, and attempted and failed to absorb the shock.

"Can't have a party without fireworks, can we?" Andy said. "I *love* rockets, don't you? I thought we'd have a display over the water. After that, we'll have a bonfire. You've got quite a bit of petrol in that old garage of yours. By the time the fire engines turn out and get here, the cottage should be well and truly ablaze. Tell you what," he said advancing, his alcoholic breath hot on my face. "Stannard can be our Guy Fawkes."

"You motherfucker."

The blow split my lip. "You need to learn some manners."

I put a hand to my face, tasted blood. "Is this how you treat Jen?"

"Stupid bitch," he sneered. "She's not even a decent shag."

"You doctored the letters, didn't you? You altered the dates to make it look as if Chris wrote them."

Andy shrugged. "I nicked his keys, got them cut, let myself in, and off I went. His signature was a doddle to forge. Chris really was right about the part-time nature of my job. I've got bags of time to pursue my own interests. It's all about being seen as busy."

I flared. "Why Chris? He was your friend."

"There you go," Andy mocked, "looking for some deep psychological motivation. The truth is I wasn't abused. My childhood was ordinary and painfully dull. I had a secure upbringing in a reasonably well-off family, no brothers and sisters to bug me or give me a complex, and my parents, poor suckers, offered pure, unconditional love."

Andy's moist red lips were almost on my face. I forced myself not to recoil. "Fucks up your psycho-babble, I'd say." His eyes contracted into two straight lines. "But you," he said, tipping my chin up with the crook of his index finger, "you were always special to me."

This time I winced.

"I know you better than you think," he goaded. "You smile for the camera, but it's an act. At heart, you're as false and as bitter and twisted as me."

My eyes swam with tears. Chill seeped into my bones. I wanted to scream.

"Did you know?" Andy said, entranced. "I saw you once, a long time ago, coming out of the local surgery. I asked my mum who you were. She told me you were the girl who got burnt. Fascinating."

"You sad fuck," I burst out. Was I the cradle of his obsession? Had I been the trigger, the start of it all? "And Chris, where did he fit?"

"You don't seriously think I give a shit?" Andy leant in close, pressed his lips onto my face. His fat tongue darted out and licked my ear. "I killed him because he was precious to you. I killed the others because …" His eyes glazed. Unexpectedly, he shot a hand out, groped my crotch. I felt cold, as if death crawled all over me.

Stannard groaned. Blood had congealed under his nose. His chin slumped onto his chest, breathing laboured. It looked as if the chair alone propped him up.

"Enough conversation," Andy said. "Let's eat."

"I'm not your servant."

Andy thrust me a look that would make a rattlesnake recoil. "Cook, or I'll kill him, right here, right now, in front of you."

NINETY

"I NEED THE KNIFE," I said, pushing away the boxes stacked on the work surface, clearing a space.

"'Course you do, but not that one," Andy said, sliding it out of my reach. "Way too small. This sharp enough for you?" He picked another out of the block. I trembled as he ran it down between my breasts before handing it to me. "I prefer a wider blade myself," he said, eyes panther black. "Try anything, I'll bash his head in." He jerked his chin in the direction of Stannard. "I'm sure the police will be happy to believe you killed him."

I cut the meat, sliced the peppers, minced a clove of garlic. I tossed olive oil into a frying pan, stir-frying the lot until the peppers were almost translucent and the meat cooked. I added wine and seasoning, brought it to the boil, reducing the liquid to a dark, glossy sauce. In another pan I boiled Basmati rice, adding a stick of cinnamon and a twist of nutmeg. I made a green salad and tossed it in vinaigrette. I'd prepared it all a hundred times before. I did it without thought, hands working automatically, independent of my mind. He'd be expecting scalding water, a knife, or boiling hot food. All it took was one act to inflict maximum damage.

With one chance to shock and annihilate, I flicked my eyes right and left and caught sight of a packing box next to the kettle, the top open. I wondered whether Andy had clocked it, whether it occurred to him that I had a kill-and-burn weapon right in front of me. I focused my entire concentration on finding the right moment, the exact time, and all the while Andy kept talking, prattling, liking what he said and saying what he liked, a monologue of self-congratulation.

"You got me started, Slade. Did you know that? 'Course I didn't realise it at the time, but then when Chrissie came into my life…"

"The girl in Holmes Chapel?"

"Yeah, it was all going so well. Had her wound up a treat, but then," he said, face darkening, "she went and fucked things up for me by topping herself. Never got the chance to make her mine, stupid bitch."

"And the others?" I didn't want to stop him, had to keep him engaged. Once the conversation ceased, the violence began.

His features dissolved into a warm, smug glow. "I'd perfected the art by then. Really got them dancing to my tune. By the time I closed in for the kill, they were glad. Did I ever tell you about my selection process, Slade?"

"No," I said, trying to prevent my teeth from chattering, my hands from shaking, desperate to keep him relaxed.

"See, every man and his dog is in the computer repairs business, but I offered exceptional rates, ads everywhere up and down the country." He took a slurp of lager. "Then when I had a female punter, I'd check them out on the Internet—easy and as quick as sending an email—all those social networking sites, all those self-aggrandising work portals."

"That's where you saw them," I said, tumbling to it.

"The amazing power of technology," he grinned. "Everyone leaves a communication footprint. Anita had her face pasted on Twitter—brave girl. Mel and Gaynor..."

"On work sites," I filled in, hardly able to form the words.

"Neat, huh?"

I laid the table under his precise instruction. Tablecloth, knife, fork, peppermill, saltcellar. Each arranged just so. I served the food on a large white plate, side salad separate. Andy drew up a chair. He seemed to have forgotten about Stannard altogether. When he demanded more lager I played servile, humiliated, under his thumb, and went to the fridge. I took out a can, set it on the table. Catching sight of Stannard, I caught the gleam in his good eye, the tightening of his jaw, the wriggling motion of one hand.

Andy pulled back the tab and drank straight from the can, wiping his mouth. "Sit down, bitch."

"I'll stand," I said, defiant, blocking his view.

"Suit yourself." He ate, gobbling quickly, a dribble of sauce running down his chin. His eyes never left mine, watching every flex of muscle, every expression.

"You won't get away with it. The police know I'm here. I'm expecting an officer at any moment. One sign of trouble and they'll be all over the place."

"We'll see, or rather I will. This is very good, by the way," Andy said, jabbing at the air with a fork. He looked down fractionally to shovel up another mouthful. I shifted stance, twisting towards Stannard, and caught the expression, the almost imperceptible nod. I'd no idea what he was planning, but I recognised that he was asking me to trust him. The man I'd never been able to trust.

"More?" I said to Andy.

"Yeah, that would be good." I went to turn. "Don't move. *I'll* get it," he said, shooting out of the chair. "Don't want you flinging any saucepans at me."

Stannard, freed, struck like a viper. The rope flew over and looped around Andy's neck. I grabbed a saucepan and clouted the side of Andy's head. It sounded like a hefty paperweight dropped onto a ceramic worktop. The impact reverberated up my arm. Blood trickling from his temple, Andy thrashed and bucked like a fish on a line. Stannard clung on. I grabbed the phone, hit speed-dial, got through to the police, and raised the alarm.

Incomprehensibly, in that short passage of time, Andy had seized the advantage, Stannard fast losing his grip against the bigger and stronger man. Dropping the phone, I leapt at Andy, but a vicious jab with an elbow spun me across the floor and into the wall. I gasped as pain shot through my side and nausea gripped my internal organs. Another jab into Stannard's already battered body turned the tables. As he collapsed, Andy followed up with a swift kick to Stannard's head and then his back, connecting with a kidney. The rope was now looped around Stannard's neck and Andy hauled it tight.

"Does it turn you on watching a man die?" he leered.

Stannard's face went very red, the eyes bulged, a rattling sound ejected from his throat.

I leapt up, grabbed the blowtorch, hit the ignition, and came at Andy. The oh-so-pale skin blistered, bubbled, and peeled away, melting before my eyes, his hands raw flesh. Andy's screams ricocheted off the kitchen walls; Stannard scrambled away from him, as though he, and not I, were the source of heat.

Coughing and retching, Stannard pushed himself to one knee and staggered to his feet. With one hand on his throat, the other reached out to me and dragged me away from what I'd done, from what I'd been forced to do.

NINETY-ONE

STUNNED AND HOLLOW, WE emerged from the cottage like fleeing refugees from a massacre, the pain I'd inflicted horrendous and beyond comprehension.

We kept moving up the steep, narrow road towards Holset, Stannard urging me on, hauling me forward until, exhausted, I felt my lungs would pack up. The sound of sirens wailed in the distance. Eventually, where the road bent and widened, he allowed me to stop. He took off his jacket and wrapped it around my shoulders.

There were two police cars and two ambulances. Darke and Hatchet got out and ran towards us.

"Andy Johnson's in the cottage," I panted, dazed. "He's burnt. I burnt him," I said quietly. "I did it."

"He tried to kill both of us," Stannard rasped, his voice a protest.

Darke instructed Hatchet to go to the cottage along with one of the ambulances. "You need medical attention," he told Stannard and immediately signalled for help.

"I'll be all right," Stannard croaked. He looked at me with desperate eyes. Andy was right in one sense. Stannard *was* obsessive.

"Go and get checked out, at least," I told him.

"Won't I have to make a statement?" Stannard muttered to Darke.

"We can take it later."

Stannard looked at me as if unwilling to let me out of his sight.

"Go on," I told him.

With reluctance, he consented. Two paramedics in green uniforms approached and helped Stannard into an ambulance.

Darke took a call from Hatchet. I watched his face stiffen. When he was done he said, "Kim Slade, I'm arresting you for attempted murder."

We went to the police station. Chadwick was summoned. I told my side of the story, repeated everything Josh Brodie had told me, pointing out Andy's fixation with disfigurement, and handed the photograph to Darke. "Chris took the picture that very last weekend, the day before I was due back at work. Andy must have taken the camera when he cleared the rest of Chris's things. Chris didn't have a lot of belongings. Andy may have destroyed them but I bet some of the items are at his house as trophies. You also need to check his camper van. According to Brodie, a camper van was sighted close to two of the abductions."

Darke took the photograph gingerly, holding the edge between thumb and forefinger. He looked but didn't say anything.

"When are you speaking to Andy Johnson?" Chadwick asked.

"As soon as he's fit enough to talk. The burns to his face and hands are pretty severe. He may lose the sight in one eye."

I lowered my head, mortified. "What if he doesn't confess? What if *he* presses charges against *me*?"

"Let's wait and see," Chadwick said.

"We're going to recheck his alibi," Darke said. "We're carrying out a search at his house. If your hunch is correct, it'll provide the evidence we need."

NINETY-TWO

The wait was interminable. Finally, Darke, Fiona North at his side, broke the news.

"We've got him," he announced, triumphant. "It didn't look good to start with but, once we'd found his secret hideaway in the attic, it proved plain sailing."

Fiona was totally animated as if it were the most exciting thing to happen to her in years. "An entire wall covered in photographs, a shrine to you and the other women, his fixation unmistakable."

"They're all dead, aren't they?" I said, suddenly bleak.

Fiona looked to Darke. "It doesn't bode well," he admitted.

I thought about Ivan Lassiter, how he'd no longer be able to cling to the hope that his wife was still out there, alive and wanting to come home. I felt unspeakably sad for him.

"There were pictures of where you worked, your flat in Cheltenham, people you visited," Fiona said. "And there were snaps of Kyle Stannard."

"The real clincher came when we found Chris's belongings, including a bloodstained jacket," Darke explained.

"What about the murder weapon?" I said.

"Not exactly the sort of thing we'd expect him to hang onto, but we'll keep looking."

"And Kyle? How's he doing?"

"Discharged himself, gave a statement to the Boss, and went back home."

"He's gone?" I said, perplexed.

Fiona rummaged in a large brown leather handbag and handed over an envelope. "He said to give you this."

I'd screened my post for so long my first reaction was *Don't open it.*

"Aren't you going to read it?" Fiona said, expectant.

"Later."

NINETY-THREE

SECRETS AND GUILT.

Kyle hadn't deserved his fate. He hadn't deserved to be plagued by flashbacks and nightmares and a face that repelled. I reread and folded up the letter again, slipping it into my jacket pocket.

Three days later, I was standing outside the Mathersons' home, a modern house that lay deep in the Welsh countryside. Set back from a winding road, it looked as if every brick, piece of gravel, and blade of grass was arranged for a purpose.

Frank Matherson opened the door. Instantly recognising me, his eyes turned to slits. "Why the hell are you here?"

"To talk," I said, calmly taking a step forward.

"You've got to be joking. Have you any idea of the damage you've done?"

"What about the damage *you* did?"

Frank Matherson blinked twice. He looked as if someone had fired at him with a stun gun. "I don't know what you're talking about."

"No, you don't, which is why you're going to let me in so I can tell you." Other men would have slammed the door in my face. Something in my determined manner got to him. He shrank back and stood aside. I marched in and turned left only because the door happened to be open. I found myself in a sterile-looking sitting room. Cushions plumped. No dust on the furniture. No marks on the carpet. No sign of homely clutter. The only sound was the low hum of anxiety and a mind on full load.

"Marie and Kirsten are out." His eyes darted. In spite of his earlier bravado, he looked pathetic and afraid.

I didn't tell him that I already knew, that I'd watched and waited, stalker-style. "May I sit down?"

"I suppose so."

Matherson sat down, too, or rather perched.

I eyeballed him. "I want *you* to talk about when Kirsten worked for Visage."

He rested his big hands on his thick thighs as if to anchor them. "Do you have children, Miss Slade?"

"No, I don't."

"Then you wouldn't understand."

"I understand a father's grief."

He met my eye and lowered his gaze. I think a part of him felt relief. His voice was husky when he spoke. "Kirsten was always special to me. She's my only daughter. My sons, Robert and Stephen, Kirsten's brothers, are fine young men, but it's a different type of relationship.

"I never wanted Kirsten to go into modelling. I hated the idea but Marie thought it too good an opportunity to miss. I suppose there was a bit of her that felt she'd liked to have been given the same opportunity." He glanced at the floor. "Kirsten was striking, a beautiful-looking girl. Still is, to me," he added, the fight gone from his voice. "It was all right in the beginning. I thought as long as Kirsten was enjoying it and it wasn't interfering with her school work it couldn't do any harm, might even give her some experience. I was right there," he said mournfully.

"Kyle Stannard," I said.

Frank Matherson's dark dolorous eyes fixed on me. "He raped my daughter."

"And you couldn't forgive him."

He gaped at me in disbelief. "Tell me a father who would."

"What if I was to tell you that he didn't rape her?"

"That's not true."

"But what if he didn't? What if it was a lie?"

"You've seen what's happened to Kirsten," Matherson said, unyielding. "The rape changed her. She became anorexic. Stannard did that to her. He almost killed her."

"If the rape was significant, why didn't you tell her GP when she first started to lose weight? Why didn't you inform Jim Copplestone? Why conceal it?"

Matherson stiffened. "Because we took care of it."

"*We?*"

"*I* took care of it."

"No, you didn't. You make a lot of noise, but at heart you're a coward. It's why you asked Robert and Stephen to administer the beating."

Matherson pitched forward, rubbed his face with his hands. When he looked at me his eyes told me that he knew the game was up.

"It wasn't hard, was it?" I said, biting back my anger. "They felt as aggrieved as you. All you had to do was encourage them, pump them up. You made it look like a mugging that had gone wrong. It was easy because you knew Stannard, being the arrogant sod he was, would fight back. Maybe you were there to make sure they didn't go too far in their punishment. You didn't want Stannard dead. You wanted him maimed. You wanted to crush his spirit. Afterwards you arranged for the boys to go to Australia."

He didn't answer. His hands kneaded the fabric of his trousers, coarse knuckles shining.

"Your daughter became sick because she buried a secret, a secret she and her mother have concealed for years."

He looked at me sharply. "I don't understand what you're saying."

"The rape was a story made up to discredit Stannard." I let the thought hang and hook into his mind.

"Made up by whom?" His jaw jacked open. Spittle crouched in the corner of his mouth.

"Your wife."

Matherson broke into an ugly smile. "That's a disgusting thing to say. Marie spent hours with Kirsten, slept in her room for months. She comforted her as only a mother can."

"Did you ever speak to Kirsten?"

"It wasn't my place."

"Why do you think Kirsten dropped the charges?"

"Because she couldn't face the ordeal of the witness box."

"Because she knew it was a lie. She fell in love, Mr. Matherson. Yes, Stannard treated her the same way he treated all his women but he didn't rape her," I said. "When he finished the relationship—a relationship your wife had encouraged from the start—Kirsten felt hurt and rejected and angry. It was easy for Marie to manipulate her.

But your daughter is a fine young woman. She has a conscience. She knew that what she was being asked to do by her mother was wrong."

Matherson put his hands to his face. "No," he said wretchedly. "Marie's a good woman. She wouldn't make up a story like that. She wouldn't lie to me. Not for all this time."

"She *had* to. You took the law into your own hands. You set your two sons on Stannard. If Marie told you the truth, you'd know that your sons had disfigured an innocent man."

His face caved in with dismay.

"And Kirsten's had to bear the guilt of that ever since," I finished quietly.

"Can't be," he said in a frail and frightened voice.

There was a movement by the door. Kirsten stood in the entrance, her face wan, her eyes blazing with conviction. "It's true, Dad. She's telling the truth."

NINETY-FOUR

We arranged to meet on neutral territory in a nearby park a week later. Stannard was waiting by the entrance. For the first time ever, I was not afraid to see him. "You fled pretty smartly."

"To convince you my interest is based purely on your professional expertise," he said with a sideways look, unexpected amusement in his eyes. I broke into a laugh and he laughed with me. It seemed to catch on the breeze and ripple through the trees. It made me think of Stannard's photograph, his head tipped back, no cares in the world. How I wished I could turn back the clock for both of us.

"Shall we walk?" he said.

We followed a tarmac path, past a wooden hut and a group of lads playing football on the grass.

"Your letter," I began.

"I wanted to put the record straight about Kirsten," Stannard said. "I wasn't kind to her. She was very young and I took advantage. Sure, I was a bastard, but I never raped her."

"I know."

"But all those things you said and believed..."

"I didn't know the truth then. I was hopelessly wrong and I'm sorry. Has your mother recovered from my visit? She was extremely upset."

"She wouldn't want to recover even if she could," Stannard said with dry humour.

We carried on walking.

"You wrote about being mugged and the resulting flashbacks."

"That's where I'd hope you'd come in." His voice quickened. "You see, I've started remembering. Not in detail, not yet at any rate. With your skill—"

"The point is," I interrupted him, "there are certain things you should know."

He turned, apprehensive, as if he feared I was going to give him the brush-off again. I quickly cast around. "Shall we find somewhere to sit down?"

We found a bench underneath a weeping willow that overlooked a pond. A family of water rats darted from the undergrowth and plopped belly-first into the water.

I told him about my visit to the Mathersons. Stannard listened, sat quite still, face bowed. When I finished he remained silent. I asked him what he was going to do.

"I don't know."

I viewed him with surprise.

"It doesn't change anything for me, does it?"

"I'm afraid not."

He gave a heavy sigh, weary, as if all his efforts had come to nothing. "Kirsten's brothers would need to be extradited."

"Shouldn't you at least attempt to bring them to justice?"

Stannard looked out across the surface of the pool. "Justice, or revenge, Kim? They're exiled. The family's split apart…"

"They have their freedom."

"Do they?" His half smile was serene yet bittersweet. He sat and stared into the middle distance. "I've wanted to get to the bottom of it for so long that I never thought beyond. I couldn't remember anything about the attack and that's the bit that was bugging me. I was desperate to unlock the key. I never considered how I might feel, all my energy consumed by the need to remember, to find out the truth. And now I do, it doesn't help." Wretched, he turned towards me. There was genuine pain in his eyes. "Perhaps by letting it go," he said, "by losing, it will make me a better human being."

I reached out and rested my hand on his. A better person than me, I thought. "I really think you should reconsider."

"You don't understand." He smiled sadly. "The life I had was taken away from me. I don't deny I mourn its loss. It's been," he said, his voice halting, "a life-changing and sobering experience. It made me realise exactly how much we're judged for the way we look. I still have days when I can barely face the world, when I feel eaten up with bitterness for my condition, when I want to spit in the face of fortune. But I'd be a liar if I didn't admit that I'd had a good run, better than most. I squandered and abused most of it. Sex, drugs, and rock and roll," he said, glib. "Once, I had it all."

Unexpectedly, my eyes filled with tears. He seemed so unbearably alone. I blinked them back.

"You didn't deserve what happened to you, Kyle."

"You don't believe in divine retribution?"

"No, I don't."

We sat, not talking, watching a water rat poke its head out from underneath a bush, scurry across the path, and join its brothers.

"When did you start remembering?" I said, breaking the silence.

"After I'd watched that TV programme you were on." He flashed a smile. "You became my Holy Grail."

"You thought I could put the pieces together."

"In a way, you did."

"Then you don't need me anymore." It seemed that everyone was leaving.

We got up and walked back across the park. "What will happen to Kirsten?" Stannard said.

"I have a sneaking feeling that she'll be all right. She's approaching nineteen now. Her parents can't put her in a clinic unless they invoke the Mental Health Act. I reckon she's stronger than all of them put together. Now that the secret's out, there's every chance she'll feel more in control of her life."

"She could make a full recovery?"

"I'd say so."

"And what about you?"

I looked at him with surprise. This was the man who appeared not to give a damn about anyone, who threatened and bullied to get what he wanted, and then I remembered the words of the women who'd known and loved him. Flick had described him as charming. Kirsten had said he was funny and wonderful. "I'll survive. I'll be fine." One day, I thought.

"I wanted to thank you for what you did," he said. "You saved my life."

"We saved each other."

We were back by the entrance.

"When do you move into the flat?" I said.

He laughed. "What a crap bit of coincidence *that* was. It's on hold at the moment. I've a large project on the Evesham Road that's swallowing up most of my time."

Good for you, Mrs. Foley, I thought with an inner smile.

"Are you going ahead with the sale of your cottage?"

What was I supposed to do? Chris was gone. Andy had tried to destroy me. I didn't know where I belonged anymore. "Why? Are you interested in buying?" I said with a laugh.

"Maybe we could meet up for a drink or something," he said uncertainly.

I flashed a warm smile. In my heart I thought it unlikely. Not knowing what to do next, I held out my hand, uncertain and strangely formal, part of me unwilling to simply say good-bye and walk away. Stannard stole the moment. He bent down, tipped my chin up, and kissed me once full on the lips.

"Good-bye, Kim."

"Bye." I shivered and turned to go.

"Kim?"

I turned back. "Yes?"

"Don't be sad."

NINETY-FIVE

I TRIED HARD NOT to be.

There was talk about Andy pressing charges for grievous bodily harm but in the end nothing came of it. Chadwick kept me informed of legal proceedings. Darke stayed in touch on the police side. So did Fiona North, who informed me that Andy's mother had undergone an operation to correct a cleft palate in childhood, the scar remaining. I took small comfort from the fact that, as Andy had led me to believe, I had not "got him started." Somewhere, deep down, his mother held the key to his Pandora's box of obsession. Specialist teams had been dispatched to Wales to search an old quarry, another to waste ground in the Midlands. Traces of Gaynor Lassiter's DNA had been found in Andy's camper van. Inexplicably, he refused to confess where he'd disposed of her body.

With Fiona's help, I organised Chris's funeral. He was buried at the same church as my father and brother. I invited everyone, including Alexa Gray, who looked in better shape than me, Ivan Lassiter, and Josh Brodie. My friends welcomed me back into the fold like a conquering hero. After that, and with my suspension lifted, I immersed myself in work. I gave Josh the interview he'd asked for. The cottage refused to sell and I spent no time there. I made few plans.

One cold late October day when the light was still and clear, I was walking through the Suffolks. A woman's voice called my name. I turned and saw Heather Foley on the other side of the road, frantically waving. She had a man with her, one arm linked through his. He was portly, grey-haired, and clean-shaven. I crossed over.

"What a treat to spot you! I had to let you know our little plan worked," Heather beamed. Her skin shimmered. There was an incredible radiance about her so that I wondered what kind of surgery she'd had. "Mr. Stannard phoned me back within twenty minutes of my make-your-mind-up call and apologised unreservedly. His lawyers were apparently at fault. Oh, forgive me, this is Des Overton," Heather said, introducing us. He had kind eyes, I thought, and an honest and open face. "We haven't seen each other in years and we're having a splendid time," Heather chattered, giving his arm a tender squeeze, utterly loved up, it seemed. Des returned the compliment with a look of undiluted adoration.

"I'm glad," I smiled.

Heather dropped her voice. "I didn't bother with the face-lift."

"You don't need it, darling," Des said.

You've got him instead, I thought. When you're loved and liberated, happiness makes us all beautiful. Heather Foley was living proof.

"Are things all right with you, dear?"

"Yes, they are."

"No more problems?"

"None."

"Well, lovely to see you," Heather said, giving Des's arm a tug. "Cheerio."

I stopped off at a café and watched the faces of passersby. I studied the young and the old, the couples and the singles, the beautiful and the not so beautiful, as if trying to unlock the secret of their success. Stannard talked of losing as if it were something positive, something he could learn from, something that held the potential to make him a better human being. I guessed it was the old maxim about a glass half full rather than half empty. He'd taken me by surprise. I thought him too bitter and twisted by what had happened to see any light in the darkness. It was humbling. Maybe I could learn from him. Perhaps, if I stopped looking backwards, if I carried on going through the motions—getting up in the morning, going to work, tidying the flat, cooking dinners, accepting invitations instead of turning them down, allowing my friends to help me, asking for support when I needed it and treasuring the friendship of others, male and female alike—if I stopped searching for love, then I'd find happiness. I didn't have to add loss upon loss. I was once beautiful to the man I loved. There was no reason why I couldn't be beautiful again.

ABOUT THE AUTHOR

Eve Seymour (England) has published articles in *Devon Today* magazine and had a number of her short stories broadcast on BBC Radio Devon. She has also written seven thrillers. *Beautiful Losers* is her Midnight Ink debut. You can visit her at eveseymour.co.uk and eveseymour.wordpress.com.